THE NIGHTMARE NOVELLAS

A PIECE OF THE RUHYSVET SAGA

J.N. KINDIG

NOTCHED BRIAR PRESS

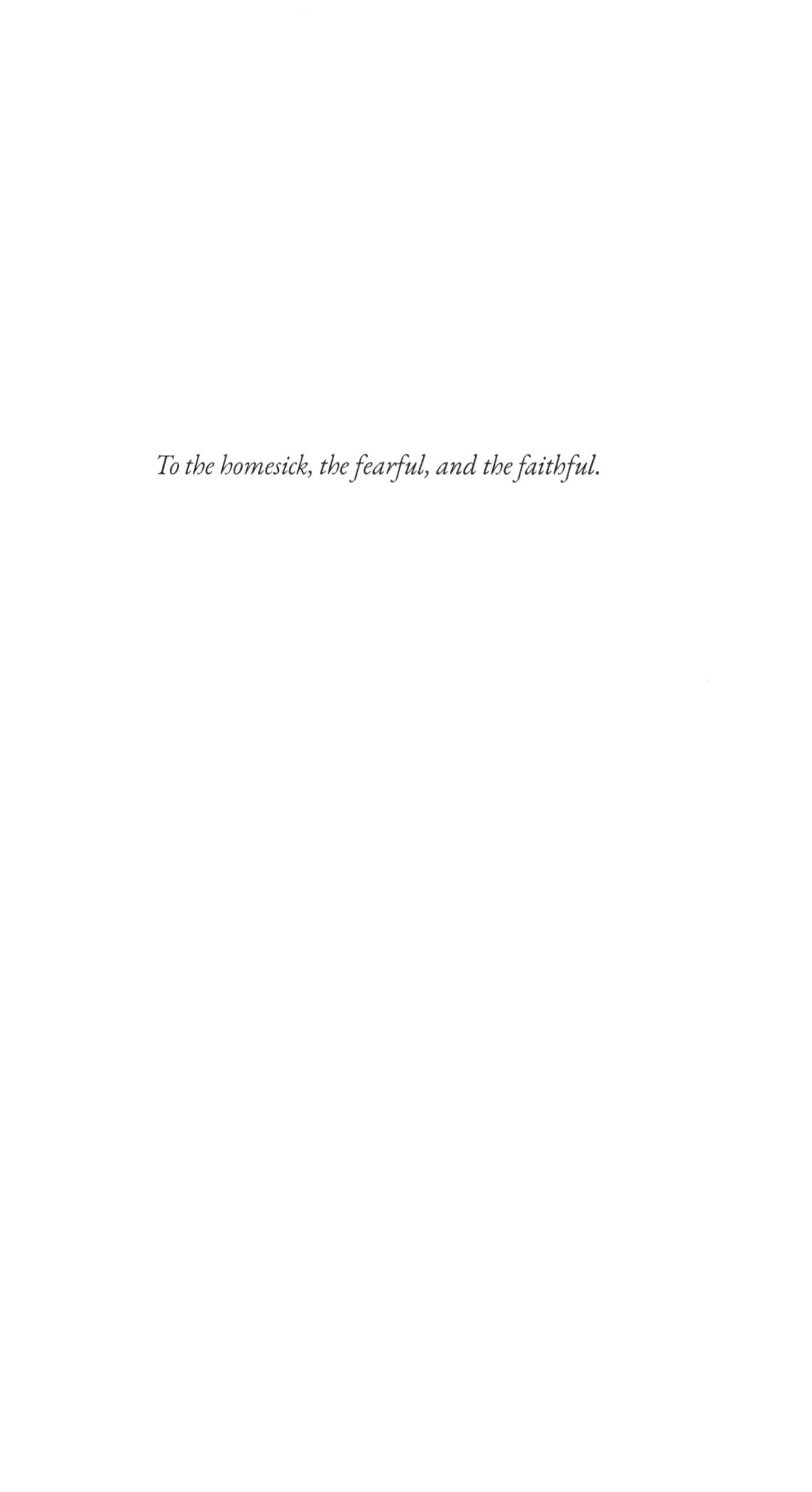

To the homesick, the fearful, and the faithful.

JASNIOSTVO
ZNOVIC
Echoing Forest
The Celesty
Karilan Atoll
Mezya Coas
Tmadrev Forest
Farriasty
Crater
Zijustvo

THE SILENT WASTE
PREZKA MOUNTAINS
VYEZHEIM
NOCOVOSTVO
WARRIND RANGE
ZELLENST
ASTLINOSTVO

FOREWORD

At the time of writing this preface, I, Lady Emera Rivasi, am the head of a research party chronicling the War of the Twin Suns at the request of His Royal Majesty King Vaimar Villari of Zijustvo and his wife, Her Royal Majesty Queen Carista Villari. If you're reading this, it means I've died and you've inherited my work, if not also my duties.

(Unless, of course, you're me, and are reviewing this information at a later date—in which case, I'd like to say I'm proud of you. This war hasn't bested us yet.)

Within this volume is all of the information I've collected on Ren Dearling and Sanne Esclarmonde, two hunters from the Order of Nightmares. History will remember them by different names, I'm sure, and perhaps by different merit. Regardless, I want to note that I'm proud to know them. They never thought this is who they'd become—but war changes everyone it touches. Let us remember that when we sit down to write our histories.

If you're reading this and are not future-Emera, I've laid out this information in two parts. The first is dedicated to Ren's story, and the second to Sanne's. In light of all they've told me, I feel this is the most effective arrangement.

However, Lady Eleya Greywarren, my fellow scholar and trav-

eling companion, disagrees. Because Ren and Sanne's lives are so intertwined, she thinks it best to read my notes chronologically. It matters little now, but I promised her I'd note her thoughts for posterity's sake.

I will list the orders for ease of reference.

To read in my preferred order is to read the notes as they're compiled:

1. The Town
2. The Castle
3. The Keep (or, Ren at Home)
4. The Lady Nightmare
5. The Eidolon
6. The Shining Heretic (or, Sanne Alone)

Lady Greywarren's preferred order, the chronological arrangement, is as follows:

1. The Town
2. The Lady Nightmare
3. The Castle
4. The Eidolon
5. The Keep (or, Ren at Home)
6. The Shining Heretic (or, Sanne Alone)

It has been my honor to learn who Ren and Sanne were before the war broke them. War is declared by kings and fought by soldiers, yet there are so many more who suffer. Their sacrifices are no less worthy of written immortality.

A table of contents will follow.

Lady Emera Rivasi
1.1.629

Table of Contents

Pronunciation Guide

<u>People</u>
Malaia Akari: muh-LIE-uh ah-KAR-ree
Baer Enorry: bare EN-or-ree
Cassander Esclarmonde: kuh-SAN-der ESS-kler-mond
Casimir Esclarmonde: KAZ-ih-meer ESS-kler-mond
Sanne Esclarmonde: SAH-nuh ESS-kler-mond
Morgaine Greywarren: mor-GAYN GRAY-war-in
Crannoc Mezd: KRAN-uck MEHZ-d
Tovar Moriya: TOH-var MOR-ee-yuh
Caullen Scara: KAW-lin SKAR-uh
Lara Sohli: LAR-ruh SOH-lee
Berrick Tmarrey: BARE-rihk tuh-MAR-ee
Adarilen Vestel: uh-DAHR-ih-lin VESS-tuhl

<u>Places</u>
(The) Celesty: seh-LEH-stee
Farriasty: fair-ree-AH-stee
Hrascara: hruh-SKAR-uh
Jasniostvo: YAH-znee-OHST-voh

Karilan Atoll: KAR-ih-lihn AH-tohl
Naisvet: NIGH-zvet
Nocovostvo: noh-koh-VOHST-voh
Rastlinostvo: RAHST-lihn-OHST-voh
Ruhysvet: ROO-ee-svet
Tmadrev (Forest): t-MAH-drihv
Zijustvo: zhee-YOOST-voh

<u>**Deities**</u>
Oddelen: OH-duh-lihn
Sumra: SUH-mruh
Svetlen: ss-VEHT-lihn
Zatva: ZAHT-vuh
Zdesen: zz-DEH-zihn
Zikat: zee-KAHT

<u>**Miscellaneous**</u>
Apprazit: ah-prah-ZEET
Divrech: DEEV-retch
Duokrist: DOO-woh-kreest
Lieren: LEER-rihn
Malinilka: MAH-lihn-nill-kuh
Prázeny: PRAH-zeh-nee
Saroszy: SAH-roh-zee

*An accompanying glossary can be found in the back of this
collection.*

Part One

Ren

The Town

7.9.626

In his eight years as a Nightmare hunter, Ren had been asked to do many strange things.

Could you trap the spirit in this jar for me?

Domesticate it, please. It would make a fine pet.

Is it possible to drive it into a—erm, physical body?

He did his best not to judge—everyone responded to the unholy in different ways—but even he had his limits. He was accustomed to strange requests. Even welcomed them, at times, as they kept his hunt from getting boring. But unreasonable ones?

"I'm sorry, Mayoress," he said. "Perhaps I misheard. How many cleansings?"

Mayoress Everinne Soma tilted her head, confusion in her amber eyes. Her small office, where they sat, was devoid of any personal touches; its wooden walls bore a coat of beige paint and nothing more. Ren figured she hadn't held her position long. "Four," she repeated. "Our lovely town hall, the Dusk and Dawn, a private residence, and our library."

"In three nights' time?"

"Yes," she said. The mayoress was one of the prismatic elves native to the kingdom of Zijustvo, where Tanglewood was located; her skin, hair, and eyes were all vibrant shades of yellow. The coloring of some prismatic elves dulled with age, but the mayoress—who looked to be in her early thirties, not much older than Ren—showed no signs of this diminishing. "The festival begins Hostden morning. Is that not plenty of time?"

Ren's jaw clenched. It was currently Klisden morning, which gave him three nights until the festival's start. "With respect, Mayoress, it isn't. One night per cleansing is considered the minimum." He stressed the last word, but she didn't take the hint.

"I have full faith in your abilities, Ren," she said, smiling brightly. Had it not been the only name he went by, he would've been offended by the familiarity its use suggested. "And your empty coin purse, yes?"

If his jaw tightened any further, he was going to crack a tooth. "That's correct, Mayoress."

"Don't worry," she said, opening her desk drawer and pulling out a contract with a flourish. "You will be handsomely compensated. Does the Order bargain?"

So she had never hired a Nightmare hunter. "At times."

"Tell me how this sounds, then: ten gold."

He arched an eyebrow. With only three nights, there would be no time for him to properly investigate; he'd be going into this hunt blind, and would need considerably more gold to make the risk worth it. "Twenty."

Her smile dimmed. "I'm afraid we can't spare twenty. Sisters' Harvest is our main source of revenue. My counteroffer is thirteen gold and free lodging at the Drowsy Dragon in one of its best rooms."

"Thirteen gold, lodging, and free food and drink."

"You drive a hard bargain, Ren."

His smile was a hollow echo of her own. "Empty coin purse, Mayoress."

She laughed, clapping her hands together. "Then I accept your terms." She scribbled his compensation into an empty line on the contract, signed it, and slid it to him. "If you'll sign— wonderful. What will you need to get this done?"

"If you have keys to the buildings, I'll need a copy."

She pushed a worn brass key across the desk. Its handwritten tag read *Library*. "I'll have the town hall left unlocked for you."

"And inform any residents of these buildings that they'll need to vacate the premises until I've finished my hunt," he said, taking the key and contract. "I can't work with mortals around."

"How ominous." Mayoress Soma winked. "Are your methods that secret?"

Ren met her gaze. "They're that dangerous."

"I see." Her eyes flicked from the twin sickles strapped to his chest to the ax at his back, and the teasing, playful glint in them dulled. Good—Nightmares hunted dangerous prey, and the sooner the mayoress understood the gravity of his hunt, the better.

Ren let her stare at his weapons a bit longer before clearing his throat. "If that's all?"

"Oh, yes. Of course." She stood, smoothing her cream dress. Mayoress Soma extended a graceful hand. "Welcome to Tanglewood, Ren. It's our pleasure to do business with you."

———

Ren stood in the threshold of his room for the next three nights and did his best to deny that, yes, it was quite nice. There was a mahogany desk, an overstuffed loveseat upholstered in a soft citrine fabric, a clothing chest, what looked to be a weapons rack, and even a partitioned off area with a porcelain sink and tub painted with tiny autumn leaves. And the bed—it was palatial, big enough for three and covered in a hand-stitched, brick red quilt.

Reia and Kyr, his Umbrals, leapt onto the bed. To laymen, Umbrals were beings of shadow and nothing more, but Nightmares knew better. Umbrals were specially made. Each one had been a flesh-and-blood creature before its death. If it was fortunate enough to have a Nightmare find its corpse and bring it to the Keep, the Order's headquarters, it would be laid on an altar of the death god Oddelen and prayed over. If Oddelen took pity, the creature was reanimated and reformed for divine service. Umbrals were ghostlike, but not true spirits; their bodies were shadowy and translucent, yet they were benevolent, and whenever Ren touched his Umbrals, he always felt a dim warmth.

Reia, his heeler, scratched at the quilt and settled down when it had been bunched up to her liking. Like most Umbrals, she could shift forms to a black mare. Kyr was a messenger raven, though only that—he wasn't able to shift forms, which was why Ren had been allowed two Umbrals to most Nightmares' one.

Kyr fluffed his wings and settled onto his favorite napping spot: Reia's back.

"Don't get comfortable," Ren muttered, walking to the room's lone window and crossing his arms. "We're leaving as soon as I'm paid."

The window looked onto what the locals called the town square—a name Ren found overly generous, as it was more of a misshapen, six-sided open area than a true square. Tanglewood was tucked deep into Tmadrev Forest, a dark wood so large it spilled over Zijustvo's borders into the lands of its northern neighbor Jasniostvo. It was the first month of autumn. Outside, children gathered up fallen leaves, laughing as they threw them at one another or shoved them down shirtfronts. Pairs of women bustled between shops, their package-laden husbands trailing behind them. The scent of thousands of crushed, decaying leaves drifted through the air.

Ren couldn't wait to leave.

———

He slid into the seat at the end of the bar and nodded to Azra.

"It's a little early to be drinking, even by our rustic standards," she said, walking over to him. Her skin, like her braids, was such a deep green it was nearly black. Her jade-colored eyes were bright. Though Ren's travels had taken him all over the realm of Ruhysvet, there was something he could always count on: small taverns that doubled as small inns. Azra Yorik was the proprietress of the Drowsy Dragon, which sat empty around them in the late morning light. She'd shown him to his room with little fuss, which he'd appreciated, and hadn't lingered as he unpacked, which he'd appreciated more. But then he'd gotten thirsty. "Bored already?"

"I'm not much good until dark, love."

She chuckled and flicked her mass of tiny braids over her shoulders. "Fair enough. How far'd you travel to take this job?"

she asked, eyeing the ridged horns curving from his head. There were few horned elves in Zijustvo. "You must owe someone a favor."

"No favors. Just traveling and low on funds."

She tapped her fingers on the worn wooden counter. "Did you come for the festival?"

Ren shook his head. Sisters' Harvest was celebrated across the realm. If he felt like celebrating, he could do so in the next town. "I'm leaving once I'm paid."

Azra stilled. "Soma didn't tell you, then?"

"What do you mean?"

He hadn't ordered a drink yet, but Azra poured one for him anyway. "You poor soul," she sighed. The tips of her pointed ears were flushed. "I want you to know this isn't how we normally do things here."

Ren eyed her.

"Brilde, Mayoress Soma's assistant, came in distraught the other night. I pitied her, so I let her stay past closing. When it was just us, she let slip that there's been some creative funding for the town since the mayoress took charge. That coin you were promised? It doesn't exist. It won't until after the festival." Azra set a tankard down in front of him, its contents frothing up and over the rim. She smiled at him, but it was full of pity. "So you'll be staying for Sisters' Harvest, Nightmare. You might want to start drinking."

———

Ren stayed in the tavern, nursing his drink and watching patrons filter in and out as the day passed. There was no bite of alcohol in the cider—it was either weak, as Ren suspected, or dangerous.

"There he is!" Azra crowed when a burly, ruddy-faced human man entered. "My favorite customer!"

He scowled, but came to the bar anyway. "Azra," he grumbled, nodding to her. "This the Nightmare?"

"It is." Ren straightened. His tattoo had been angled away from the man—if he'd seen it, he wouldn't have bothered asking. The black, sharp-edged curves of ink that marked him as a Nightmare crawled up the right side of his neck. The tattoo disappeared under his shirt collar and spread along his right shoulder.

Azra made the introduction. "Ren, this is Vess Pivar, owner of the Dusk and Dawn." She winked. "Consider his tavern your lowest priority."

Vess rolled his eyes. "Place is cleared out." He held a dull key out to Ren. "Sorry for the mess."

"Mess?"

Vess nodded. "The ghost likes to break things."

"I see. Thank you."

Ren pocketed the key, turning back to the tavern as Vess and Azra fell into teasing conversation. If the spirit was breaking things, it was likely a geist—not the most dangerous species, but definitely threatening enough to employ a Nightmare. At least he hadn't been hired for nothing.

The bell over the entrance jangled, the metallic sound cutting through the low chatter of the tavern's patrons. Mayoress Soma entered, trailed by a half-elf female who wore her dark hair in a braided crown. The tips of her ears, which stuck through the braid, were pointed, though not as much as Ren's or Azra's.

"Is that the long-suffering Brilde?"

Azra chuckled, wiping out a tankard. "No, that's Morgaine Greywarren, our librarian. She's nice, if you can get through to her."

Ren tracked Morgaine across the room, trying to settle the sudden stab of pain in his heart. Greywarren was too common of a surname for his liking. "I've found that few people are worth getting through to."

"Well, she'll be your client, won't she? You might not have a choice." Azra winked, disappearing down the bar to assist the next customer.

Ren settled back into his seat, watching Morgaine and the mayoress. It was some sort of business meeting—Morgaine had come with a leather folio of documents, but the mayoress had brought only a hollow, dazzling smile. When Ren concentrated, he caught a few words: vendors, profits, town traditions, festival. The furrow between Morgaine's dark brows deepened with each moment. Ren imagined he'd looked the same a few hours ago, yet Mayoress Soma seemed just as oblivious to Morgaine's irritation as she'd been to Ren's. The mayoress said something particularly damning and, before he could look away, Morgaine's stony gaze snapped to him.

"A moment," Ren heard her say. She rose and stalked across the tavern to him. She stopped an arm's length away, her hands clasped behind her back. "Excuse me. Are you the Nightmare hunter?"

Hardly anyone referred to them as "Nightmare hunters" anymore, not when "Nightmare" was quicker. Ren propped an arm on the bar. "I am."

She blew breath out of her nose like an annoyed horse. Up close, she was sharply pretty. Her dark eyes and pale skin looked as if someone had taken a book, torn out its pages, and formed her from the ink and parchment. "My name is Morgaine Greywarren. I'm Tanglewood's librarian. Our mayoress has decided I'll be one of your—" She clenched her jaw. "Clients. But I wanted to tell you that your assistance isn't necessary."

"Is that so?" He'd seen this before: clients in denial about the extent of their haunting or the limitations of their abilities or, as he suspected was true in this case, both. "Alright, love. State your offer."

She blinked. "What?"

"Your buyout offer. I signed a contract with the town of Tanglewood for the cleansing of four buildings in exchange for a fair sum. You want to change the terms? Buy me out of the old ones."

She scowled. "Is coin all you care about?"

"No, but I care about a roof over my head and food in my stomach. Coin provides those things."

The scowl deepened. "You're staying here for free."

"Yes. But the next town may not be so charitable." He smiled at her and spread his hands. "I'm sure you understand, love. I wouldn't ask you to stop reading the village children stories each morning."

"I am not that kind of librarian," she snapped, her back going rigid. Color rose in her cheeks and across her nose.

Ren's smile grew. She wasn't a hunter, either, and he was looking forward to proving that this town—that she—needed him. He took great satisfaction in making haughty clients eat their words. "Of course not. Your offer, then?"

She huffed and turned on her heel, her boots tapping on the floor as she retreated to the mayoress. Ren turned and caught Azra looking at him—she'd been listening. Ren just shrugged and drained his drink. He didn't need clients to like him, or even the townspeople, for that matter. He would be gone before most of them learned his name.

———

Ren returned to his room that night bloodier than he would have liked.

Reia and Kyr had beaten him there, traveling by shadow as their kind was wont to do. Reia lifted her head when he entered, but settled it back down when she realized he wasn't immediately getting into bed. They had done well tonight. The Dusk and Dawn, as suspected, had indeed been occupied by a geist. Reia had turned its penchant for throwing mugs into a game of fetch, and Kyr had flapped his wings around the geist's face while Ren recited the banishment spell. Each banishment spell was a prayer spoken in a dialect of Divrech, the gods' language. Casting these spells was one of Ren's favorite parts of the hunt—it meant he'd completed another job, and he took great satisfaction in bringing a spirit low with his ax before finishing it off with a prayer. A spirit could howl and slash and scratch, but none of them could stand against the invocation of Ren's gods.

Tonight, however, he'd had to speak the geist banishment spell twice—though this wasn't all that troubled Ren. During the second turn of the spell, the geist had thrown a table into him. It had fouled his mood so strongly that he'd grumbled curses under his breath the entire way to the town hall. The gods had been merciful, however; the town hall held only a shrinking mist, the lowliest of spirits. He'd exterminated it in less time than it had taken to unlock the door. The private residence, which belonged to a woman named Masha Winnith, had contained a shrinking mist and a bogle, another minor spirit. Though these latter two properties hadn't required much effort to cleanse, Ren was exhausted.

He set his ax and sickles into the room's weapon rack, the Nightmare steel glimmering faintly in the dim moonlight. Nightmare weapons were forged with an alloy of steel and copper, the blades cast in such a way that the warm-toned copper created a mottled, rippling pattern against the cold hue of the steel. Ren's ax was his pride and joy—he'd longed for it ever since he was thirteen, when he'd first arrived at the Keep and had seen it in the armory. Four years later, the ax had become his.

He walked to the bathing area, casting off clothing and armor as he went. One of the inn's staff had placed a bucket of water nearby; he emptied it into the tub. He signed the ward for heating, mumbling the spell under his breath, and settled into the bath when it had been set steaming. He ducked his head under, wetting his horns and dark auburn hair. The cuts on his face and arms stung, but it was a satisfying, antiseptic feeling—the cleanliness most deserved after a bout of hard work. His eyes slid shut. Ren stayed in the bath until his bronze skin blushed from the heat, collapsing into bed once he'd dried and dressed. Three buildings cleansed in one night. He'd outdone himself.

Reia curled against him, resting her chin on the flat of his stomach as she did most nights. Kyr nestled into the shadowy scruff at her neck and croaked contentedly. Ren sighed and closed his eyes, thankful he'd done his nightly prayers to Oddelen before hunting. All that remained was the library, and then he'd be paid and gone.

7.10.626

The next night, Ren stood in front of the Tanglewood library.

Sunset had been an hour ago, and the chill in the air had sharpened considerably since. Gone were the townspeople whose chatter and footsteps had filled the square; some had fled to the warmth of their beds, some to the warmth of the taverns. Leaves rustled as a cold wind blew them across the square. The sign denoting the library as such groaned on its hinges. The library stared at Ren with the indifferent gaze of a vacated building; in accordance with Ren's request, that smug little librarian would have evacuated by now.

Ren rolled his shoulders. His ax dragged against his leather armor, which he'd shoddily repaired that afternoon. It wasn't pretty, but it would hold well enough—especially if the worst Tanglewood had for him was a mid-level spirit like a geist.

Kyr, who he'd sent into the library with Reia to scout, squawked frantically. Ren surged up the steps, unlocked the library door, and shoved inside. Kyr didn't frighten easily.

Ren murmured the spell for nightsight, twitching his fingertips at his side to draw the ward. A familiar scarlet glow cast itself over the library's interior, revealing a small circulation desk. Shelves twisted along the walls, creating a labyrinthine path through the building. They overflowed with scrolls and books in every imaginable condition. Plants and artifacts labelled with small brass plaques broke up the visual monotony of spines and pages.

Ren, red eyes glowing, crept through the shelves until he found Kyr. The Umbral was pecking at a little stick-like spirit, one that shrieked and threw its spindly hands above its head—a bogle. "That's all?" Ren asked, straightening. "Just a b—"

Something collided with the back of his head. Stars crashed through his vision. His nightsight dulled, then disappeared. Ren grunted, drew his ax, and whirled.

A skeletal version of himself leered at him, its eyes glowing an acidic red. Not-Ren raised a bony finger, pointing at him. Rotting rags dripped from its limbs like liquid. The sound that came from its open mouth was a distorted laugh, a mockery of Ren's own. Ren's fingers tightened on the ax's handle. A ghoul—now that complicated things.

Behind him, the bogle screamed. Its long toenails skittered along the wood floor as it fled.

Ren spoke his word. The blade of his ax glowed with a holy aura, casting a warm white light over the shelves. He arced his ax over his head—curse the narrow aisles of this place—and aimed for the ghoul's skull. It split with a satisfying crack. Its essence slipped out of the hole like dark water.

The ghoul's form wavered—Ren was treated to the nauseating sight of his own skull leaking brain matter and blood—and vanished. Ren stalked the library's aisles, muttering the appropriate banishment spell under his breath. Ghouls were tricky, and a step above geists in the Order's spectral hierarchy. Both the spiritual and physical form had to be destroyed or the spirit would return. The banishment spell for such a powerful spirit was a dual prayer to the deities Zikat, the goddess of life, and her lover Oddelen, the god of death. To cast it, a Nightmare had to speak in two dialects of Divrech, Zikatic and Oddelenic, instead of only one. It had taken Ren weeks to commit it to memory.

He rounded one of the corners, the prayer-spell falling from his lips. The frightened bogle screeched, leaping in front of—gods above. There were *two* bogles.

Ren scowled, switching from the prayer to the lovers to the common-language bogle banishment spell without missing a beat.

With a strike from one of his daggers and its faint, word-induced aura, one of the bogles passed on.

Its companion shrieked, but Ren had already turned away. Kyr squawked and croaked, the bogle cried, his head throbbed where the ghoul had struck him—it all sent dread coursing through him. Three spirits in one place. He'd underestimated this damn town.

He saw it out of the corner of his eye when he passed the circulation desk.

Ren froze. Somewhere, the gods were laughing at him. They had to be, for there to be a fourth spirit haunting the library—and for it to be a gods-damned *wraith*.

The wraith, one of the most dangerous spirits in the Order's bestiary, hovered in the library's darkest corner. Vacuous slashes acted as its eyes. Its mouth was a yawning maw. It clicked and whirred and twitched, its atrophied body spasming below its dark cloak. Ren knew deep in his bones, knew in a gods-given way, that it was searching for him.

"*Hunter!*" Its voice was like a broken bone through skin—wet, repulsive, wrong. Had he been a greener Nightmare, Ren would have gone to his knees from fear.

From above came a metallic clang and a whistling screech. Both Ren and the wraith looked up; both of them moved, but Ren was faster. He barked the spell for will-o-wisps as he flew up the stairs. The wraith shrieked, but didn't dare follow past the growing orbs of light.

At the top of the stairs was a door. Ren shoved it open—the light would only discourage the wraith for so long, and if there were other spirits, he needed to—

Morgaine crouched on the floor, her hand halfway to a quieting kettle.

"Get out!" they shouted, her voice pitching high above his.

"Me? You're in my house," she snapped, straightening.

Ren glanced around. She knelt by a lit hearth, the kettle having fallen from its hook. To their left, the kitchen opened into a small living space with books stacked near an overstuffed armchair; a bed waited in the darkest corner, its quilts mussed. "You're not supposed to be here. Didn't anyone tell you?"

"No."

Damn this town. "Well, you're leaving now. Get your things."

She hung the kettle. "I am not."

"Do you know what's downstairs?"

"Yes. Spirits."

"Spirits I'm being paid to exterminate, which I can't do with mortals around."

"Spirits I don't need your help with." She crossed her arms and said, her voice full of puffed-up pride, "I got rid of one already."

"Of course you did, love." A traveling chest sat against the wall. Ren opened it and the armoire next to it; he began to throw in clothing. "Who can you stay with?"

"What are you doing? Those are mine!" Morgaine rushed to the chest, her hands outstretched. Ren shoved a heavy cloak into them—all she wore was a deep blue nightgown.

"You're leaving. Do you have family in town? Friends?"

"No," she snapped. "I'm a Greywarren, remember?"

Ren, having judged that he'd packed enough to get her through the night, shut the chest and heaved it onto his shoulder. "How could I forget," he muttered. There was a bucket of water near the hearth; he picked it up and doused the fire with one hand. He began walking to the stairs, Morgaine protesting behind him. "Once we're downstairs," he said, cutting her off mid-sentence, "go straight to the door. I don't care what you hear or see. Get outside."

She scowled at him, but slung the cloak over her shoulders and nodded.

Ren opened the door. It was quiet. The will-o-wisps had faded—no faint glow waited when they reached the bottom of the stairs. The door was mere feet away, yet he rested a hand on his ax.

"See? There's nothing," Morgaine hissed. "I told—"

A creaking hand seized her cloak and jerked.

"Move!" Ren bellowed over her scream, swinging his ax down onto the metal hand and cleaving the offending gauntlet from its arm. A suit of armor? Where in the three hells—

"What is that?" she cried. She'd frozen steps away from the door, her already pale skin gone ashen. She had seen the wraith.

"*Hunter!*" it wailed, its voice seeping into Ren's bones like the chill of the grave. It reached for them, one of its tenebrous fingers elongating and stretching out toward Morgaine—

Ren barreled toward the door, shoving himself and Morgaine through it. Mid-fall, he threw her chest out of the way; it cracked as it hit the ground. She landed on him, knocking the air from his lungs. He scrambled to his feet and hauled her up, shoving her behind him.

The wraith hovered in the open doorway. It had no eyes, but it watched nonetheless.

"What are you doing?" she asked, her voice rising to a frantic pitch. "Get—"

"It won't follow us." Sure enough, the wraith didn't cross the threshold. It was bound to the building. Spirits often were. "Now..." Ren knelt by the broken chest and crammed her spilled clothing back into it. He pointed across the square to the Drowsy Dragon. "You're getting a room."

———

"Azra." Morgaine placed her hands on the counter and leaned forward. "This isn't funny."

"Because it isn't a joke." Azra looked from Morgaine to Ren, at least having the decency to temper her amusement with an apologetic look. "We're full." Despite the lateness of the hour—or, perhaps, because of it—the tavern was packed with bodies. Among the humans and prismatic elves, which Ren had expected, there were also a considerable number of bronzed elves. Their metallic skin shone in the candlelight. It seemed word of Tanglewood's celebration had crossed kingdom lines.

Morgaine's fingers dug into the counter. "A closet, then," she said, her teeth clenched. "A large table in the tavern. Anything."

Azra shook her head. "You're not sleeping in my tavern."

Ren sighed. He balanced her chest on one broad shoulder. "You can have the bed, love."

"I want *my* bed."

"Your bed is in an infested building. Consider yourself lucky you haven't been gutted in your sleep."

Morgaine crossed her arms. "The spirits have never left the first floor," she grumbled, "and I don't go downstairs after dark. I was making do until you agitated them."

Azra's eyebrows raised, but she held her tongue. "If anyone leaves in the night," she said to Morgaine, "I'll give you first claim to the empty room."

A highly unlikely occurrence, Ren thought, but it seemed to pacify Morgaine. She grumbled her thanks to Azra and followed Ren up the stairs, stewing.

He closed the door behind them once they were in his room. "Off." Reia and Kyr lifted their heads and stared at him from the bed.

"I didn't realize you kept a menagerie," Morgaine said. She swiped a blanket from the bed and tossed it onto the loveseat. She bundled up her cloak and set the makeshift pillow at one end. Her fear had given way to a sharp-edged irritation, one that clashed against Ren's own like dueling swords.

"I said you could have the bed."

She flopped onto the loveseat, laughing dryly. "Oh? And deprive the great hunter of a warm bed?"

The wound at the back of his head throbbed. He needed to clean his ax, cast skinstitch to heal himself, and bathe—ghoul blood stained—but a dread obligation hung over his head. "Are you hurt?"

"No." She twisted around and regarded him for a moment,

taking in his bloody, disheveled appearance. "Is this your usual means of operation? Find a pretty girl with a haunted house in each town you pass through and drag her into your lodging?"

Gods above. "Who said I found you pretty?" he asked, even though he did—irritatingly, immensely so.

She narrowed her ink-black eyes at him and turned back over. "Good night, Nightmare hunter."

Her breathing soon softened; Ren thanked the gods that she'd fallen asleep. He went about his evening uninterrupted, smiling to himself as he bathed. He was clean, and she was quiet—it was a good night.

7.11.626

Ren stalked across the town square to the Drowsy Dragon, the back of his head pulsing with the start of another headache. Of course, the one morning he'd woken early enough to pray to Zikat at dawn, he'd found her temple abandoned. When he'd arrived in Tanglewood, he'd noticed how small her temple was—if it hadn't been the only building to have a statuette of the lithe goddess in front of it, he would have assumed it was just another house—but hadn't thought much of it. Tanglewood was a small town, not a city, and didn't need a grand temple with which to impress nobility or tourists. Ren hadn't expected magnificence, but he'd at least wanted to pray through the dawn before a dustless altar. He'd anticipated greeting a priestess, bright-eyed despite the hour, not being the only living thing in the temple. He hadn't thought most of the pews would be unusable, their green cushions threadbare and thin. He'd still sung his lauds, of course, as all Nightmares did each morning, but his prayer hadn't lifted his spirits. Nightmares were pledged in service of Zikat and Oddelen, and fought to preserve their clear domains of life and death. To see Zikat's temple so forgotten irked him.

The tavern was empty when he entered. He nodded to Azra before passing the bar and ascending the stairs to his room. When

Ren opened the door, Kyr cawed and hopped across the light-dappled floor to greet him.

Reia, the traitor, was next to Morgaine.

In his absence, she had risen and dressed. She now sat at the desk, braiding her dark hair in the mirror atop it. Ren liked her hair, liked that she took the time to weave it into an intricate style. With so much time spent in dank and dirty places with dank and dirty creatures, it was refreshing to see someone take pride in her appearance—though Ren couldn't help but think this time would be better spent working on her interpersonal skills.

As if to make his point, she greeted him with, "You're finally back. Did you know that you snore?"

He rolled his eyes. "I can't say anyone's ever complained."

"You sounded like a sawmill all night." She looked at him in the mirror. "Don't Nightmares train to need as little sleep as possible?"

"We do." It was far too early for him to be scowling—and how did she know a Nightmare's sleep habits? "That doesn't mean some of us don't enjoy it."

"I see." She tucked the end of her crown braid into itself, pinned it, and twisted around. "I need you to take me home."

"It isn't cleansed. You're not—"

"There are some things I need." She stood and patted Reia's head. The Umbral's tail wagged. "Sisters' Harvest starts tomorrow, and I'm the one in charge. It's the final day for preparations and all my lists are at home. That's our first stop."

Ren didn't like the sound of that. "First?"

Her smile was like one of his sickles, curving and wicked. "You insisted on inserting yourself into my business, so I thought the least you could do was help me today. Surely you didn't have other plans?"

———

Ren leaned against the office doorway, drumming his fingers on the frame, as Morgaine dug through a desk littered with notebooks and half-burned candles. He'd intended to check the building before letting her in, but in a show of bravery or stupidity—he couldn't decide which—she'd darted past him and unlocked it herself. The remaining bogle had screamed, the wraith had wailed, but neither had shown themselves. In the sunlight streaming in through the windows, they couldn't, but he kept a hand at his sickles anyway.

"How can you find anything in here?" Ren asked as she wrenched open another drawer.

"It's normally much cleaner," she muttered. "I'm being haunted, in case you forgot."

"Hm. And yet you actively resist my help." He wandered to the floor-to-ceiling bookshelves that covered one wall, his eyes sweeping over the little boxes on each shelf. He took one down; a cracked amulet rested inside, made of a light green stone set in a dark metal frame.

"I'm going to figure it out. I already banished one spirit—don't touch that. I haven't cataloged it yet."

This again. He set the box down. "Do tell."

The desk rattled as she shoved a drawer shut. "It was a persistent fog," she said, "one that followed me around and turned the air cold. I came across a spell in one of my books and banished it."

Ren tried to hold back a laugh. He half-succeeded—it came out as a snort. "Oh, love." He walked to the desk and placed his hands on it. He leaned forward. "That was a shrinking mist. *Children* can banish those. You don't need magic for it." And he suspected she had none—if the people of Tanglewood didn't care enough to maintain the gods' temples, he doubted their belief was strong. Magic came from the gods, and little faith meant little power.

She narrowed her eyes and mirrored his position. "It still worked."

"What's your plan? To work your way up in the ghostly

ranks?" He tilted his head. "Do you pray enough to use any magic? Have you forgotten how you screamed at the wraith last night?"

"I don't," she grumbled. Her eyes darkened. "And I haven't. But I'm sure you screamed your first time, too."

"No, love. I've never screamed." He flicked his eyes to the mess between them. A flash of text caught his attention; he dug through the papers and unearthed a worn copy of an entry-level textbook. It wasn't just any text, however—embossed across the cover in faded gold was *Blessed Brotherhood: An Introductory Guide to the Order of Nightmares*. Ren had used one of these his first year at the Keep. It contained a history of the Order and its mission, a brief overview of the spirits and beasts Nightmares most often fought, and a few low-level spells. Handwriting, traitorously feminine, cluttered the margins. He fixed her with a withering glare. "You can't be serious."

She snatched it from him. "That's mine."

"Where did you get it?"

"A traveling bookseller. We trade whenever he passes through."

"So you really have had no training. Just luck." Ren laughed, but it was humorless. "You understand that some spirits can kill you? Why do you think *you* have to banish them?"

"Because it's better than a stranger doing it." She clutched the book to her chest. Ren shook his head and stepped back. Though her determination was admirable, it was stupid and misplaced. She'd be better off directing her energy toward the festival preparations—just as he'd be better off fighting spirits instead of her.

Morgaine took a satchel from its hook and began filling it with books and notes. Ren saw *Blessed Brotherhood* go into it and rolled his eyes. Was he liable if she got herself hurt? How far did his obligation to this damned town go?

"I have what I need." Morgaine breezed past him, though she paused at the library door and waited for him to follow. Grumbling, half-wishing the suit of armor would come clanking at them again, he did.

———

Hours later, Ren squinted against the sunlight and held the end of a gilded leaf garland above his head. He stood on the highest rung of a ladder that precariously leaned against the tallest tree on the square; Vess held the other end on his own less-than-stable ladder ten feet away.

"Higher, please, Vess," Morgaine called, lifting a hand to block the sun. Her other hand held something Ren loved and hated—her to-do list. The wretched thing had sent them all over town, loaded him down with packages of donated supplies, and put him on decoration duty. He appreciated Morgaine's efficiency and thoroughness—even respected them, to an extent—but the list was exhaustive. When they'd stopped for a late breakfast at the Drowsy Dragon, Ren had taken a quick peek at it; by his estimate, they were only halfway done. Yet each crossed-off item got him closer to going back to his room and resting before returning to the library, so he'd grit his teeth and ascended the ladder when ordered.

"That looks even. You can tie it off."

Ren double-knotted his end around a protruding burl. Magic would have made the preparation simpler, but it was rare in faithless towns like Tanglewood. Magic was honed through devotion to the gods; holy cities like Farriasty, Zijustvo's capital, housed the greatest concentration of magic users, followed by universities and seminaries. Some remote towns housed incredibly faithful and powerful magic users, of course—Ren's hunt had taken him to a few of these exceptions—but small towns, especially one nestled in a forest as dense as Tmadrev, usually had little in the way of magic. Many priests and priestesses were accustomed to a particular level of comfort, and Ren suspected many holy ones were perfectly content to minister to city and suburban populations. A town couldn't worship gods they barely knew about. Judging by the grime Ren had found in Oddelen's chapel when he'd prayed there the evening before, Tanglewood knew of the gods' existence and little else. It was a shame.

"Thank you, Vess," Morgaine said, crossing that item off of her list. "We appreciate the help."

"Least I can do," Vess replied, nodding to Ren once they were back on the ground. "He's kept Azra from stealing all my business." With a good-natured pat on Ren's back, he was on his way.

"Lovely." Morgaine turned to her list. "Now—"

Someone shouted her name across the square and she was off. Ren trailed behind her like a stray dog, picking leaves from his hair and horns. They stopped at the fountain in the center of the square which, judging by the thick layer of decayed leaves at the bottom of the pool, hadn't worked in many autumns. Morgaine knelt by a group of human and elven women sitting on blankets. The women were of all ages; in the middle of their circle was a pile of autumnal flowers, buds, and foliage. Finished crowns and garlands sat in a pile to the side.

"Lean down, dear," one of the older women, a silver-haired elf, said. When Morgaine obeyed, the elf held an assortment of flowers up, testing the color against Morgaine's skin. "Pretty. Does your Nightmare want one as well?"

Morgaine stiffened. "Baba, he's not my—"

Ren did a poor job hiding his laughter. "Don't trouble yourself for me," he said when the elf looked at him curiously. "Really. I'm just passing through."

"Nonsense." The elf reached a thin hand up to pat his forearm. Her veins, deep purple in color, rose above her paper-thin skin. "Didn't you cleanse my daughter Masha's house? She is very happy to now sleep through the night undisturbed." Her fingers tightened for the briefest of seconds on Ren's arm, gauging the muscle there. "Hm. If you're not our Morgaine's—" She winked. "Masha is unmarried, you know."

"Baba!" Morgaine looked horrified. "The Nightmare hunter is here to work—"

Baba shrugged. "I'm only looking after my daughter. You cannot blame me for trying. Have I offended you, Nightmare?"

Despite himself, Ren smiled. Just as small taverns could be found across the realm, so could well-intentioned, meddling mothers. Perhaps his own mother would have been one. "You haven't."

"I will make you a crown just in case. Morgaine, I'll send it with yours." Baba waved her hand. "Now, off with both of you. You must be quite busy."

Morgaine grumbled her goodbyes, turning away to hide the flush on her face. Ren followed, not bothering to hide the smile on his.

———

He exterminated the second bogle that night, slinking back to the Drowsy Dragon with its screaming still ringing in his ears. The wounded ghoul and wraith had kept him from doing much else. The possessed suit of armor, puppeted by the wraith, had slashed his back and drawn blood; the wound wasn't serious, but there was a new tear in his armor that needed to be repaired. Ren slipped up the stairs to his room, mentally creating a supply list— the first thing he would buy with the Tanglewood gold was thicker leather armor.

The room was empty, barren of even the Umbrals. He racked his weapons and shrugged out of his armor and undergarments, tossing them on top of his chest. Between the day's sweat and the night's work, he needed a bath.

The moment after he'd spelled the water warm and submerged himself, the door creaked open. "I suggest averting your gaze unless you're feeling particularly untoward," he called.

Morgaine raised her folio to block her peripheral vision. "The warning is appreciated." She paused to let Kyr and Reia come in before shutting and locking the door. "Your creatures won't leave me alone."

He reached for a bar of soap. "For reasons lost to me, they must like you."

"Are you bathing again?"

He stilled. "Yes. Is something wrong with that?"

There was a soft clatter as she forced open her broken chest. "I've never met a male so obsessed with bathing. Do you even fit in that tub?"

"Yes." Barely. He had to lift his legs and prop them on the tub's rim, but, technically, he fit.

"Why must Nightmares be so large, anyway?" she asked. "Isn't most of your work done with spells?"

"A spell won't always stop something that's been possessed. Some spirits take a corporeal form, and they can be incredibly strong." He quickly scrubbed and got out—there would be no relaxing in the bath now that she was back. "Why, love? Are you looking to wrench a ghoul's head from its shoulders?"

"I'd rather be the one to do it than you." Her tone sharpened. "Don't come out. I'm changing."

For good measure, he turned to face the wall. The only sounds in the room were the rustling of fabric against her skin and the water dripping from his. He forced himself to think of something—anything—other than the moment between clothing when her skin would be bared. "A question for you."

"Yes?"

"You only refer to me as 'Nightmare hunter.' Do you know my name?"

A scoff. "Of course I know your name."

"Then what is it?"

A pause, and then, "I'm done changing, *Ren*." The loveseat creaked as she settled onto it. "Do you have a surname?"

"It's just Ren."

"Why?"

He tugged his pants on and stilled for a moment, lost in the memory of scarce meals and cruel whippings and young boys looking to him for answers because none of them had fathers. "It's the only name that matters."

"I see."

He finished dressing and stepped out of the screened-off area. Morgaine wore the same chemise he'd found her in two nights ago. "I have a name, too, you know. You don't have to call me 'love.'"

"I call everyone 'love.'" He tilted his head in mock pity. "Why? Do you want to be the only one?"

The tips of her ears reddened. "You are endlessly irritating," she muttered, grabbing her blanket.

"And you're being ridiculous. Take the bed, Morgaine."

She turned over and spoke no more.

7.12.626

Hostden morning was bright and crisp, perfect weather for the first day of Sisters' Harvest. Ren leaned against the Drowsy Dragon's exterior wall, his gaze roving across the town square. Again, Morgaine had risen first; he watched her nail a sign reading "Closed until further notice" to the library's front entrance. It bothered him that he hadn't yet been able to cleanse it—not just because he'd failed to prepare Tanglewood for the festival, but because he'd failed Morgaine. She likely would've loved to let festival-goers in, to show them her artifacts and books and give them the history of her town, and it was Ren's fault that she couldn't.

A flash of yellow caught his eye—Mayoress Soma was flouncing his way. No, it wasn't Ren's fault. This hunt had been doomed from the start.

Ren shoved off of the wall and crossed the square, keeping a wide berth around the mayoress. If he got trapped in conversation with her, he'd only say something he'd regret.

"Morgaine."

She looked up, her hammer hovering over the last nail in the sign. "Good morning, Night—" She paused, smiling tightly. "Ren."

"I—" Curse him. "I'm sorry the spirits persist. I imagine you wanted to have the library open for today."

With a single true strike, Morgaine drove the nail home. "You would be correct. But there's nothing to be done about it now." She faced him. She wore a simple dress of dusk blue, her hair braided away from her face as always, prettily practical and efficient. Propped in one arm was that infernal to-do list. "Perhaps it's for the best. There's much I have to oversee today."

He nodded toward the square. "It's an incredible crowd." Townspeople and visitors milled about, humans and elves mingling and chatting as they browsed vendor stalls. Toward the middle of the square was a cluster of tables surrounded by children. Chaperoned by a few adults, they carved gourds and strung together friendship bracelets from glass beads and acorns. A few boys batted a hoop and stick around the periphery of the square. "I think there are vastly more visitors than yesterday."

A smile flickered across her face. "I think so, too. It's wonderful. Our festival has grown to be the largest in the duchy." Her voice softened as she looked at the square. "Tanglewood was the origin site of a horrible plague thirty years ago. They had to close the gates and shut out the world so the infection wouldn't spread. It's lovely to see how things have changed. Healed, even."

Ren had never been one for crowds, but he couldn't deny that there was something beautiful before them: dozens of people, elves and humans, celebrating autumn together. The air smelled of crushed leaves and cider. The day had warmed since that morning, but a chill brushed Ren's neck with each breeze. Summer was dying, yet life persisted through autumn, stubborn until the first frost came.

"Morgaine." A female prismatic elf ran up to them, the light green of her skin warring with the pink flush of exertion on her cheeks. She shoved a paper into Morgaine's hands. "Everinne wanted me to tell you—"

Morgaine glanced at the paper. "Goddess' tits," she muttered. Ren's eyes widened. He hadn't thought she could be so crass. "Thank you, Brilde. You'd think that forcing us to add the diving competition would be enough for him."

Brilde pressed her lips together. "If only."

"Perhaps one day we'll know peace."

Brilde's smile was one of shared annoyance. "Perhaps. I'll see you at the pile."

Ren watched Brilde scurry off. "Is everything alright?"

"No. Lord Scara, the Duke of Tmadrev's son, has given us another 'request.' We already cleared a large patch of forest for the game he wanted, and he wants it leveled again. He inspected it last night and found it unsatisfactory." Morgaine sighed. "But we'll acquiesce, we'll have the games, and soon enough, he'll leave. His presence is a plague on the women."

"Is he cruel?"

"No. But he's persistent." She lowered her voice; Ren had to step closer to hear. "He's the type of man who doesn't understand why a poor, untitled, unmarried woman doesn't fawn all over him. Surely, he's everything I could want." Her words flew out quickly, and she noticed her lack of discretion too late. Her gaze slid to Ren.

He grinned. "It's you he wants?"

"He thinks I want him," she ground out, "and doesn't understand why I continue to deny it. We kissed on the feast day a few years ago—don't look at me like that. I was drunk. I had forgotten myself."

Ren tsked. "One kiss, and he seeks you out year after year? My, my, love. How skilled you must be."

The look she gave him could have sent an apparition crawling back into its grave. "It's not funny. He's an incredible hindrance."

"Of course." Ren lowered his mouth to her ear. "Would you like to tell him I'm your betrothed? We're growing quite intimate, after all. You've acknowledged I have a name."

"I'd rather not replace one pestilence with another." She

raised her naked left hand and wiggled her fingers. Her glare was cutting, but something playful twinkled in her eyes. "And I'd never accept a proposal without a ring."

"Pity. I'm a wonderful provider."

"Yet you're stranded here until you get your coin." She consulted her list. Her brow furrowed more with each turned page. "We have an odd number of competitors. Any chance you'd enter today's games?"

Ren snorted, crossing his arms. "No. I'm getting that damn ghoul out tonight, and I need—"

They had been facing the square, watching the crowd as they talked, but she whirled on him. "No, you are not!"

"We've been over this, love."

"Indeed we have—"

"This is the only way you can return home—"

"That's not true!" she hissed. "I've been—hells." She turned and hurried away, aiming for the thickest part of the crowd. Ren looked in the opposite direction. An ostentatiously dressed man strode after her, an easy smile on his face. Lord Scara had noticed her—lovely. She could bite his head off instead.

———

Ren stood at the back of the crowd that afternoon, grateful that his height allowed him to chat with Azra, sip cider, and watch the games from a distance. The festival's first day was dedicated to Zikat, the goddess of life; the games were intended to honor her. The day's victor would have a seat of honor at tomorrow's feast, which would honor Zikat's sister Zatva, the goddess of nature and the harvest. Though he owed much to both goddesses—Zikat was one of the patron gods of the Order, and Zatva had created the horned elves—he'd never attended a Sisters' Harvest festival. It was a flurry of activity.

Both males and females competed in the games, first facing off in a sword fighting contest and then a log throwing competition.

In between bouts, judges wandered between tables and took bites of competing pies and roasted meats, scribbling notes and conferring amongst themselves. Despite everything to draw Ren's eye, however, he kept searching the crowd for Morgaine.

He didn't find her until the townspeople began moving into the woods. "I've been thinking," he said, falling into step with her at the back of the crowd. "Since you want to be special, let's have something I only call you."

She groaned.

"Beloved?"

"No."

"Sweetheart?"

"No." She ducked under a low branch. "Isn't your plan to flee once you're paid and never look back?"

"It is."

"Then why are you bothering with this?"

He shrugged, picking his way over a tangle of tree roots. "I'm only so invested in who wins the games. I have to pass the time somehow."

Morgaine smiled at him. Something in it made him uneasy. "I'm so glad you said that."

———

As the elven male scrambled out of the leaf pile, brushing debris from his red skin, Ren hurried forward with his rake. He swept the scattered leaves into the massive pile and hurried back to the crowd so Lord Scara's mage could refresh his spell. "Darling?" he asked Morgaine. She shook her head, scratched a name from her list, and nodded to the mayoress to announce the next competitor.

"Little love?"

Morgaine's nose wrinkled. A pink flush crept up her cheeks. "That's the worst one yet."

They were nearly to the end of what she'd called the "diving competition," which he hadn't understood until they'd entered the clearing where the festival-goers were now. Fallen leaves had been swept into the biggest pile he'd ever seen. Boards had been driven into the wide trunk of a large tree to make a ladder. A particularly thick branch, which jut from the tree at a perpendicular angle, formed the diving board. The competitors jumped from it into the pile, which had been enchanted to provide a safe landing.

"If it's so bad," Ren murmured, "then why are you blushing?"

Morgaine rolled her eyes. "You're taking credit for the day's chill now?" She signaled the mayoress again. Her back went rigid when the last competitor's name was announced.

Lord Scara, a tall, blue-eyed human man with an aquiline nose, appeared at the top of the tree. The sun caught on his gold hair. He was handsome enough, Ren supposed, but entitlement oozed from him like fluid from a festering wound. As he looked down on the crowd, a few women to Ren's left giggled and whispered to one another—Ren estimated the lord was in his mid-twenties, and it seemed Scara was young enough for them to consider him a suitable husband. Scara heard the tittering and waved unctuously down at them, though his eyes swept the crowd until he found Morgaine. He smiled. The wolfish way he looked at her, as if she was there only for him, made Ren's fist clench.

The lord leapt.

From the way Morgaine groaned, Ren could tell it was a high-scoring attempt. Surely enough, the judges on the other side of the clearing held up eights and nines. A short human man, who Ren suspected harbored ulterior motives, gave the lord a ten.

Moments later, after the day's scores had been tallied, Mayoress Soma stepped forward. "Beloved citizens and esteemed visitors of Tanglewood," she said, beaming, "that concludes this year's festival games. I am pleased to announce that the winner of today's games, who will dine at my table at tomorrow's feast, is none other than the noble Lord Scara."

The clearing burst into applause. Morgaine fixed a smile onto her face, but its falsity was betrayed by the way her hands didn't quite collide to make sound. Ren didn't bother applauding at all.

"Are you regretting your choice not to compete?" Morgaine murmured. "That could have been you."

"It was all I could do to sit near her while she was hiring me," Ren said. "Why would I trap myself at her table for an entire feast?"

Morgaine chuckled. "To remind yourself why you're leaving, perhaps."

The words stung, and he looked at her in surprise. Did his plans sound that cruel coming out of his mouth?

Lord Scara raised a hand. The clearing quieted. "People of Tanglewood," he said, his voice carrying over the crowd, "this has been an insurmountably entertaining afternoon of sport. As your victor, I thank you not only for your willingness to compete and lose, but your hospitality as well." He spread his hands. "If anyone would like to celebrate tonight, find me in one of your little taverns. You will drink for free!"

———

Judging by the throng Ren had to push through when he left the Drowsy Dragon later that night, no one of drinking age had balked at Scara's offer.

He made it through the tavern with only a bit of ale spilled on him, and declined a surprising number of requests to join the revelry—clearly, his ax and sickles weren't enough to put anyone off. The air in the square was cool; the night was clear. If the few stragglers in the square heard the ghoul's quiet moaning float by on the soft breeze, Ren saw no indication of it.

Reia and Kyr were waiting at the library. Ren opened the door and followed them in. It was too quiet. He expected the sound of the door to prompt screams from the remaining spirits, but there was nothing.

The Umbrals dissolved, flowing on a draft into Morgaine's

office. Ren gripped his sickles and began pacing the library aisles. The building smelled of aged parchment and something sweet, something like death and flowers.

As he passed the office threshold, he stilled. The wraith floated before the shelf he'd stood in front of yesterday. Reia and Kyr watched the wraith from the shadows in the corners of the room, ready to alert Ren if it moved.

He crept on. It was odd that it hadn't noticed him—wraiths were incredibly intelligent—but he let himself be grateful for its momentary ignorance. He followed the ghoul's pained moaning to where it crouched in a corner, running half-there hands over the book spines. The wound he'd given it the other night was gone, but a chunk of spectral flesh was missing from its shoulder —courtesy of the wraith, perhaps, or the possessed armor. Ren hissed his word and raised his ax, ready to end its suffering.

As his ax sang through the air, the ghoul looked up and howled. Its form flashed to his the instant before the blade again rent its skull in two. Dark brown unblood splattered across Ren's face and ran down that of his reflection. He wrenched the ax free and drew it back again, starting the dual prayer-spell to Zikat and Oddelen. Between each swing of the ax, each separation of a limb, the ghoul changed forms: Azra, Mayoress Soma, Brilde, Vess. He knew the tricks of the ghouls and did not stop. At the last couplet of the spell, however, in the moment before the last cleave, Ren froze.

Morgaine, bloodied and in pieces, shrieked up at him from the floor.

He shook his head, struggling to grip the ax through the unblood coating his hands. It was a trick. It wasn't her—it couldn't be. He was killing this thing *for* her.

The ax slipped from his hands. Before it fell to the floor, he drew his sickles, plunged their curved tips into the ghoul's chest, and ripped. Its final scream melded with his cried prayer, their voices creating an unsettling harmony that made his pointed ears ache. The brown unblood began steaming. A gaseous essence, the same color but not as opaque, floated up from the pieces of the ghoul and the puddles of its unblood. Ren traced out the slowwind ward, his fingers aching from gripping weapon handles. He tagged his prayer with the ward's words and raised his hands to guide the created breeze. The spirit needed to be led outside, where it could drift to the heavens.

He stood in the threshold of the library, bloodied palms turned up. The ghoul's essence hissed past him, but hovered just beyond the porch awning. Ren frowned. He repeated the slowwind ward; another breeze blew, but the spirit didn't pass on until Ren repeated the banishment spell.

Ren groaned and rubbed a hand down his face, forgetting the unblood that marred it. Why weren't his spells working? Could—

Creaking metal hands dug into the neck of his cuirass and pulled him into the library; his back slammed against the wood floor. Ren jerked his head to the side, narrowly missing the suit of armor's fisted gauntlet. He rocked up and kicked the possessed armor in its chest, the clang of contact echoing unpleasantly through the library. He reached around his back—*idiot*. He'd dropped his ax among the aisles. His sickles would do little against the armor; so would the daggers he wore on his thighs.

Ren scrambled to his feet and ran for his ax. The wraith, oddly, had not moved from its spot in the office—with its ability to possess the suit of armor from afar, it had no need to, but wraiths were known for their malevolence. Why wasn't it attacking him too?

He wiped his hands on his pants, scooped up his ax, and spoke his word. He met the suit of armor halfway to the doorway. When the mottled blade met the pockmarked armor, the weapon's holy aura reflecting off of the armor in the moment before contact, the crash was terrific. The armor, brittle with age, collapsed into jagged pieces of metal. Ren threw open the door— he had to get the pieces outside before the wraith reformed them. For some reason, his spells were suffering; without properly banishing the wraith, it would be able to endlessly reform the armor and attack him. Without his spells, he wouldn't stand a chance.

As Ren gathered the misshapen shards of metal, weight dropped from his chest. He turned. A few steps behind him, his leather cuirass sat on the floor.

Though Ren was blessed by the gods and held shreds of their divinity within him, the string of curses that poured from him would've made any bystander think he'd never prayed a day in his life. There was no way he could fight a wraith with such a gaping vulnerability and survive.

"*Hunter!*"

Reia manifested in front of him and growled at the advancing wraith. Kyr flapped his wings in the spirit's face, evaporating and reforming on Ren's shoulder when the wraith swiped its taloned hand at him. Its eyeless face split open as it roared. Ren spat the beginning of a banishment spell at it as he retreated over the threshold, relishing in the way the wraith winced. He shouldn't provoke it, but he was angry and aching and exhausted. He'd lost his cuirass. He'd banished the ghoul, but it had unsettled him— disturbed him, even, by wearing those faces. Her face.

There was a reason Nightmares kept to themselves.

———

He arrived at the Drowsy Dragon covered in unblood, his ax balanced across his shoulders.

No one invited him over for a drink then.

"Absolutely not," Azra said when he took the full tankard from her and tried to sit on a barstool. "You're already drinking for free. You're not ruining my seats, too."

"Fair enough." He went up the creaking stairs to his room.

He nudged the unlocked door open with his foot, balancing the sloshing tankard and slippery ax between his hands. Morgaine sat at the desk, hunched over a book. She was dressed for bed, her hair damp and braided; its wetness caused spots of her chemise to stick lightly to her back. She turned, and whatever greeting she was going to snip out died in her throat. Her eyes widened. "Gods above, what have you done? Did you kill someone?"

"Something." He slung his ax onto the weapon rack, took a long pull from the tankard—the alcohol bit—and began removing his armor.

"Where were you?"

His fingers slipped on his unblood-slick pauldron buckles. He grunted in annoyance. "Where do you think?"

She stood. The book, unburdened by her fingers, flipped a few pages and lost her place. "I told you there was no need—"

"The ghoul is gone," he snapped, raising his voice over hers, "and I will be exterminating the wraith tomorrow night."

"No, you will not!"

"What are you going to do? Stop me?" His blasted head was aching again. Ren drank the rest of the ale in two swallows. "You should have tried tonight."

"I thought you were drinking with the others," she retorted, "or that you'd found someone's bed to warm. Sisters' Harvest is not for work, and—"

"Well, little love, as you constantly remind me, I'm in a great rush to leave."

"Then go now!" She crossed her arms over her chest, digging her nails into her skin. "Leave! You've done enough."

Ren scowled. The way she stood was strategic—she blocked what she'd been reading. He strode across the room. Morgaine backed against the desk. "You're going to get that thing's blood on me," she snapped, but he leaned forward and looked over her shoulder. It was just as he'd thought.

"I'm confiscating this," he said, reaching around her and grabbing *Blessed Brotherhood*.

"No!"

He maneuvered away from her reaching hands and skimmed the pages she'd been reading. It was the section on introductory spells. A dry, rasping laugh fell from his lips. "You're a madwoman," he said. "Truly. Do you see this?" He pulled down the collar of his shirt to expose his tattoo. "Do you know why it's here? Because this is where a spirit *cut me open* for the first time. It's a rite of passage. You aren't a true Nightmare until you've fought a spirit enough for it to wound you. Why would you subject yourself to grievous injury—maybe even death—instead of letting the hired Nightmare cleanse your library?"

Tears brightened her eyes. "Because I owe this town everything!" she cried. "I'm a Greywarren—a bastard at best, an orphan at worst. The Grey home I was raised in sent me away when I was fifteen. I had no one to turn to, nowhere to go, nothing to survive on. I wandered the woods for months until a hunting party from Tanglewood found me and brought me here. I stayed with a different family each month, fed and cared for only by their goodwill, but I knew those weren't really my homes. I was always on the periphery." Her throat thickened. Her cheeks glistened with tears. Ren lifted a hand to reach for her—children in Grey homes were supposed to live there until they were eighteen, yet she'd been turned out as a child—but she stepped away and continued.

"I never had a place to call my own. The townspeople—" She sobbed. "They knew how I ached. How alone I was. They convinced Mayor Soma to sign the library over to me. It's only because of them that I'm alive and that I have a home and work and—" She took a shuddering breath and wiped her cheeks. "I owe this town and these people everything. It is the least I can do to respect their dead and help them cross over when they're trapped. Their souls need to be cared for, and your kind has no regard for that. Nightmare hunters are cruel. I will not be."

Her dismissal stung. Ren dropped his hand. The Order's mission was merciful, holy—but of course someone untrained in their ways would only assume the worst. "If we're 'cruel,'" he spat, "it's because these spirits are dangerous—"

"I hardly expect you to understand," Morgaine hissed, jabbing a finger at him. "I've read enough to know that Nightmares pledge their service at a young age and live at the Keep until you leave to hunt. You have a place to go home to. You have people who care for you. You can't know the pain of what it is to have no one. To be a Greywarren like me."

He let her words echo and fade, waited for her ragged breathing to even out. He knew that pain. He'd borne it every day of his life. "What do you think Ren is short for?"

She recoiled. Her dark eyes widened to the whites. "I—"

"I came to the Order with no name," he said. "I'm called Ren because the others didn't want to say 'Greywarren' every time they needed me. No loving parents named me." Mean memories of his Grey home, crushing and heavy, added themselves to the weight of his exhaustion. He needed to bathe, to sleep. He had nothing left with which to soothe her. He could only say, "Take the bed. I've upset you."

"Ren—"

"Good night, Morgaine."

He wasn't sure what made her fall asleep so quickly, if it was her exhaustion from the day or their draining confessions or the quiet sounds of him preparing for bed, but he was grateful she had. He could ignore what was fluttering around in his chest then —could ignore that he, in all his travels, had finally found someone who understood. Not that it mattered, of course.

Nightmares always left.

7.13.626

After sleeping on the loveseat, Ren understood why Morgaine had woken early each morning. His joints creaked like an old door as he unfolded from the twisted position he'd slept in. Reia and Kyr had abandoned him, choosing instead to curl up at Morgaine's side in the bed. He dropped his chin into his hands and watched them sleep for a while, envious of the softness and true rest he knew was beneath the quilt. He, conversely, felt as if he'd shut his eyes and opened them only moments later.

Ren rolled from the loveseat to the floor, dropping to his knees to quietly sing his morning lauds. When his prayer was done, he stood, holding back a groan at the new stiffness in his back and legs. He'd managed to clean most of the unblood from his weapons and armor before falling asleep, and was able to dress and slip out of the room quickly.

The square was nearly empty in the early morning light, save a few men gathered near the leaf-filled fountain. Ren hurried by, intending to retrieve his cuirass from the library and assess the damage in the light, but a shout stopped him.

"Ren!" Vess waved him over. "Are you busy this morning?"

He bit back the urge to lie. "Not particularly."

"Heard you're good with an ax." Vess shoved one into his hands. "We've been tasked with chopping wood for this year's bonfire. It needs to burn from midday throughout the night—it's bad luck if it goes out. Morgaine's got the mayoress scared to death about it. Mind helping us make sure we've got enough?"

"You can't chop the wood as it's needed?"

Vess chuckled, a low rumble of a sound. "We'll be in no condition for that after the feast." One of the men behind him looked barely old enough to drink, but the other grinned and mimed tipping a tankard to his lips in case Ren hadn't understood.

"I see." It was still early, and the ax's weight felt good in his hand. He would have time to get his cuirass later. "Show me the logs, then."

———

As he had a habit of doing when it came to Tanglewood, Ren had underestimated the task at hand.

Hours later, the stack of split logs was nearly as tall as Ren. The two young men, who'd been introduced to him as Vess' sons Byrne and Oren, had volunteered to gather wood for them—Ren saw it for the excuse to do less work that it was, but Vess had only nodded and waved a permitting hand. Byrne and Oren had snickered, but kept up well enough; it had been a while since he'd seen them, though, and Ren was reaching the bottom of his pile.

"If I can ask," Vess said, speaking for the first time since they'd started, "the amount of spirits here is high for one place, yes? Higher than normal?"

Pulled from thoughts of Morgaine and her accusations, Ren drove his ax through his last log and nodded. "It is."

"What attracts them?"

Ren leaned on the ax's handle. "It isn't always an attraction," he said. "It can be, if there are graves or particular relics around, but it's mostly up to chance. The season can affect spirits too, though."

Vess wiped sweat from his brow. The day was chilly, but working in the direct sunlight had made them hot. They'd shucked off their shirts about ten logs ago. "Is autumn the worst?"

Ren shook his head. "Winter, actually." Winter was an in-between season, a time when the world was dormant. Because the Order's prey existed between life and death, defying Zikat and Oddelen's holy binary, they thrived in winter. "Autumn is when spirits grow agitated, though, so we're kept busy."

Vess nodded, relief easing the lines in his face. "That's helpful. I was afraid it was something we might have done."

A tendril of unease brushed Ren's back. "What do you mean?"

Vess' eyes darted back and forth. "If you say it's nothing—"

"But I didn't."

"The boys are coming with more wood—"

"Vess."

Vess pressed his lips together. "You may already know, but there was a plague here thirty years ago. The dead were buried in the clearing where the diving competition was. When we cleared the area, some bones and personal effects were accidentally dug up. We gave them to Morgaine so she could examine them and keep them safe, maybe even display them in the library. But when the hauntings started, I was afraid that our removal had caused them."

Ren stared at him. The removal might not have been the direct cause, but gods above, it very well might have made things worse. Wraiths were so dangerous because their grotesque forms shielded corrupted human spirits—human spirits that could have been aggravated by their physical remains being disturbed. It was why wraiths had to be exorcised by naming an emotion; the recognition forced the wraith to shed its spectral swaddling and cause the human spirit to submit. "How long—"

He was interrupted by Byrne and Oren dumping raw logs at his and Vess' feet. "Mama said she needs us," Byrne, the older, said.

Vess waved a hand. "Go on. Ren and I will finish."

They scampered off, laughing to each other. Ren doubted their mother needed them, but they'd disappeared into the growing crowd before he could have Vess call them back.

He set a log below his ax, opening his mouth to question Vess further, but Vess was already calling to someone else.

"Lord Scara!"

The nobleman stopped. "Hello, barkeep." His blue eyes roved over Ren. "Hunter."

Ren met the lord's eyes. A surprising sharpness lurked there. "I don't believe we've been introduced, my lord."

"You're correct. We haven't. But you are the only horned creature in town. Your reputation precedes you." Scara's eyes softened. He must not have judged Ren to be a threat. Pity.

"Would you like to help us prepare for tonight's bonfire?" Vess asked, holding the handle of a spare ax toward the lord.

Scara took the smallest step back, eyeing the handle with distaste. He looked over Ren and Vess, shirtless and sweating, and didn't bother to hide the way his lip curled. "I'm the guest of honor, my good man," he said. "I would hate to take my seat at the feast and be so disheveled."

Ren chuckled. "There is water here, my lord. Can't your squires manage drawing a bath?"

"I must decline."

"Of course, my lord." Ren smiled, and hoped the lord noted its falsity. "You must be exhausted after such exertion yesterday. I find I also get sore when I push beyond my limits."

Scara's eyes narrowed. "I don't appreciate the implication, hunter." His gaze flicked over Ren's shoulder. "Consider yourself fortunate that there are women present, or I would have to force you to take back your words."

Ren and Vess turned. Scara was right—a small group of women had clustered at the edge of the square. Morgaine, Brilde, and the mayoress stood beneath a tree, consulting their task lists and notes. From the way they averted their gazes when Ren looked at them, however, it was clear they had been secretly watching.

Vess chuckled, patting his generous stomach. A golden band glinted on his left hand. "It's not me they're looking at."

Ren met Morgaine's eyes, smiling at her as wickedly as he could before she blushed and ducked back to her papers. She could call the Order cruel all she wanted, but it seemed she liked the results of its rigorous training. "I'm fortunate indeed, my lord. It would be an ugly fight on what's meant to be a day of celebration."

Scara harrumphed and strode away, aiming for Morgaine, Brilde, and Mayoress Soma. Ren and Vess resumed their work, falling into an easy rhythm. It was Ren's turn to steal glances, however—he watched Scara charm the mayoress, watched her giggle and press her hand to her chest as Morgaine and Brilde rolled their eyes behind Scara's back. Scara turned his attention to Morgaine, bringing her hand to his lips and kissing it. Her expression softened and she played the part of being flattered well, but Ren noticed her stiffen.

He struck his next few logs harder and louder than necessary, flexing the strong muscles in his back each time he straightened.

He snuck a glance over his shoulder. Scara was talking to Morgaine, but she wasn't looking at him. Her cheeks weren't pink from whatever honeyed words he gave her. Ren winked at her just as Scara turned, scowling.

"I think that's enough," Vess said. "It's best not to taunt men with small egos."

"What can he do to me? I don't live in his territory."

"No," Vess said, wiping his brow. "But we do." Sure enough, Scara's face was stormy as he looked from Morgaine to the town square.

"It would take an act of the gods for Scara to frighten me," Ren said, but he reached for his shirt anyway. He didn't wish the people of Tanglewood ill, even if he planned to—

His brow furrowed. Yes. He *did* still plan to leave. "I'll see you tonight, Vess."

The older man took Ren's ax. "You're welcome to sit with us for the feast, if you'd like."

Ren nodded, tossed his shirt over his head, and headed for the library.

———

The good news was that his cuirass was salvageable.

The bad news was that he had nothing to salvage it with.

Ren turned the leather armor over in his hands. The wraith had gotten to it; jagged claw marks raked down its center. The straps had been cut entirely, but he owed that to the suit of armor shattering under his blow. He found his sickles, unharmed thanks to the enchantment that had been sealed in the Nightmare steel during forging. One was by the circulation desk, the other in the doorway of Morgaine's office.

He put his hands to the daggers at his thighs—was it a trap? Ren crept forward, conjuring and tossing a short lance of light into the office. Silence.

He entered, collecting his sickles. He knew he shouldn't

linger, but he found himself wandering to the shelf the wraith had paid such close attention to. The office was a wreck, but the cracked amulet still rested on the shelf, untouched. Ren picked it up. Its light green stone was nearly the size of his palm, and its setting was etched with simple markings he recognized as an old form of Divrech.

"I told you not to touch that."

Morgaine stood in the doorway, her face unreadable. She held out his cuirass. "I believe this is yours."

"It is." Ren set the amulet down and took his armor. "You shouldn't be here. It isn't safe."

"It's my home."

Their eyes met, the small office yawning like miles between them. Ren swallowed, remembering all too easily the tears that had fallen from her reddened eyes the night before. The library was all she had. "I know."

She exhaled, shifting her folio where she held it in the crook of her arm. "Last night—"

"You don't need to apologize."

She pressed her lips together. "I wasn't going to. Not for crying, anyway." Her smile was so quick he thought he'd imagined it. "I assumed much about you, and it was wrong of me. I'm sorry."

"You wouldn't be the first. But I accept your apology."

She walked to her desk and dug something out of her satchel. "For you. Baba gave it to me."

He took the flower crown from her, turning it over in his hands. Yellow alyssum and orange lantana had been woven through strands of dark greenery. "It's well-made."

"She was very proud that she was able to make one for you." Morgaine set her own crown on her desk, making room in her bag for more papers. "She and some of the women make one for each person in town every year. We all wear them for the feast."

Ren ran his callused fingers over the small blooms. He hadn't touched anything softer than steel or wood in a long time.

"Will you be coming?"

He tore his attention from the flowers. They needed to go. They shouldn't be lingering here, not with the wraith lurking somewhere. It wouldn't manifest in the light, but they stood in a room of fodder. "It wouldn't be—"

"Ren." She stepped in front of him. Her eyes searched his, looking for any way she could change his answer. The intensity of her gaze sent a flare of heat through him. "Tonight is a night for celebration. Promise me you won't slip away to face the wraith."

"It would mean staying with me for a night longer."

"It's a tight competition, but I suppose I'd rather stay with you." And then, to guard herself, "You finally let me have the bed, after all."

"'Let' you? I finally convinced you."

"Convinced me that you wouldn't come crawling into it in the middle of the night, perhaps."

Floorboards creaked overhead. He extended a hand, ushering her out. "Perhaps. But with the way you were staring at me, I don't think you'd mind."

"With the way you were showing off, I think you wanted me to." As they stepped into the square, she looked at him through her lashes and added brazenly, "There are only so many young men in Tanglewood. You can't blame me for looking when there's someone new."

Gods, she was quick—and he was enjoying this. "Be careful, little love," he said, lowering his voice so no passersby would hear. "Or I might start thinking you like me."

"It's a testament to your arrogance that you think tolerance is the same as affection."

"And how would I know the difference, when I get both from you so sparingly?"

She stopped walking and turned to him, her eyes half-squinted in annoyance. "Will you come to the feast or not? And —" She held up a finger, bringing it just shy of his lips. "Yes, I'm asking because I want you there. I don't have time for you to tease it out of me."

It occurred to him to take her hand and kiss it—he had a suspicion she wouldn't be so brusque with him then—but he just smiled down at her. "Because you were so honest, little love, then yes. I'll come."

"And you'll leave the wraith be?"

"For tonight, I'll leave it be—unless you're planning to sneak away to try and send it on yourself."

She caught the eye of someone across the square and held up a hand for them to wait. "I suppose you'll have to trust that I won't." Her eyes flicked down his torso and her cheeks colored, her flush from the cold deepening. "Or you can find me and ask me to dance, and keep an eye on me yourself." She turned on her heel and walked away, leaving him to stare after her. It seemed the ornery little thing had warmed to him.

Heat crept across Ren's cheeks. He hurried to the Drowsy Dragon, his fingers digging into the leather of his cuirass. Despite his best intentions, it seemed he had a feast to get ready for.

———

Ren went to the square at sunset. The bonfire he'd helped feed popped and crackled in the middle of the square, its flames leaping toward the sun-bleeding sky. A growing crowd milled about the square, nearly everyone wearing a flower crown: males, females, children, young, old. Some women had also braided flowers into their hair, leaving it loose and wild otherwise.

He hadn't wanted to admit this to Morgaine, but Ren loved the flower crown. His people, the horned elves, were native to Rastlinostvo, the kingdom dedicated to the nature goddess Zatva. For the first thirteen years of his life, before he'd escaped and joined the Order, his Rastlinostvan Grey home had been the only place he'd ever known. The mistresses running the Grey home had been cruel, their punishments easily given, but the verdant world outside the home's walls had been beautiful. Ren had endured many canings simply because he'd been made to take the punishment in front of a window—in his mind, he'd be running through wildflower fields and swatting at bees instead of feeling his skin pulse and welt. The natural world had always soothed him, and the flowers wreathing his head and horns felt as if they'd always been there.

The scent of roasting meat drifted to him on the breeze; his stomach growled. Ren wandered the perimeter a bit, returning the easy smiles of those who recognized him with hesitant ones of his own. Masha, a shy woman with red cheeks and redder hair, waved to him. He waved back. It was an odd thing, to be recognized. To be known, really. Would they miss him when he was gone? Would they notice?

"Ren!" Azra beckoned him over to one of the feast tables, which had been set up that afternoon. The crown atop her head was woven from cream-colored flowers and dark greenery. Vess, his boys, and his wife, Kerra, also sat at the table. Their crowns were matching arrangements of deep purple and pale yellow. Azra and Kerra's dresses were of a thick and soft-looking material; the mens' clothes looked new and relatively free of wear. Ren was glad he'd dressed in his finer clothes—black trousers, boots, and a dark grey shirt. He'd also strapped the cleaner of his two pauldrons to his shoulder.

"Happy harvest!" Kerra said. She was human like her husband, with the same ruddy complexion. The others echoed the greeting. "Sit with us. We owe much to you."

He did, but shook his head. "I'm only doing my job."

"Your job preserved our livelihood," Vess said. "It's hard to brush such a thing off."

Ren was unaccustomed to flattery. He was sure his tight smile indicated as much. "Then I'm glad I could help."

Azra leaned over and whispered to Kerra. The women

laughed, craning their heads at something behind them. Ren followed their gaze. Scara had appeared, and was notably the only male without one of Baba's flower crowns atop his head.

"Do you think he's noticed?" Kerra asked, poking her husband in the arm and nodding in the lord's direction.

"If he has, I doubt he cares," Vess snorted. "I'm sure he finds it too rustic."

Ren chuckled, wishing he had something to do with his hands as the others talked—a tankard to drink from, a knife to spin on its tip, anything. It would distract from the fact that he had little to add to their conversation.

The shadows in the square deepened as the sun sank lower. The tables around them began to fill, an understanding seeming to pass throughout the crowd. Ren twisted in his seat to take it all in. Torches burned around the edge of the square, and swags of dyed yellow and brown fabric had been draped between buildings. It was impossible to miss the bonfire, and—

A figure stood outside of the Drowsy Dragon, and Ren prayed his stare wasn't obvious. Morgaine had changed for the feast. A velvet dress the color of fresh green apples clung to her waist and hips. A cream-colored underskirt brushed against the toes of her boots as she walked. The neckline bared her shoulders to the cool air. And her dark hair—he wanted to run his fingers through it. He wanted it spread out on his pillows as she slept. It was long and loose, wavy from its constant braiding. She wore no adornment in it other than Baba's flower crown which, he dimly realized, matched his perfectly.

She paused and looked over the gathered crowd. The smile that tugged at her mouth didn't reach her eyes. She returned the greetings of those who passed her, but no one invited her to sit with them.

I knew those weren't really my homes. I was always on the periphery.

Ren was striding across the square to her before he realized it. "Morgaine." He was breathless. Why was he breathless?

"Hello, Ren." Her gaze swept over him. She'd put some kind of pigment on her lips, one that stained them a dark pink as if someone had bitten them. "I suppose I understand the weapons, to an extent," she said, gesturing to the daggers he always wore at his thighs, "but is the pauldron really necessary?"

"Here I thought it looked dashing."

She chuckled and ran a finger along its edge. "You're imposing enough without it."

"It's very telling that you find those things to be one and the same. Perhaps that's why you're not interested in Scara? I don't think he could frighten a flea."

"There are many reasons I'm not interested," she muttered. "Is he already here?"

"He is."

She sighed, lifting her skirts. "Then I suppose I should take my seat. He'll be waiting."

Ren took her by the arm before she could hurry off. It was so easy, talking with her, and he didn't want to sit through the feast alone. "Or," he said, his voice coming out quieter than he'd wanted, "you could sit with me. There's an extra seat."

She furrowed her brow. "The lord—"

"Will always be here." *I will not* hung, unsaid but not unknown, in the air between them.

She smiled at him, but it didn't chase away the sorrow in her eyes. "Indeed," she said, brushing away his touch. "Take me to your table, then."

———

Ren had never much enjoyed parties. He'd always skirted away from invitations to balls, making excuses or finding a hunt to keep him busy whenever the Order had been invited. It wasn't the dancing he loathed, or the clothes—he liked a reason to wear finer things, though he never strayed far from Nightmare black—but the small talk. The politicking. The false fronts put up to please those one most hated.

He found none of that falsity here. Conversation flowed easily, punctuated by happy shouts across the square whenever someone realized a friend had arrived. Dishes were passed around the tables and everyone helped themselves. Waitstaff replaced empty plates with a flourish and a smile, often chatting for a few moments with whomever was making the trade. Azra and Kerra leaned across the table to draw Morgaine into their conversation. An odd stab of gratitude struck Ren's heart. Perhaps she wasn't as alone as she thought.

Byrne and Oren kept him from paying close attention to the women, however; they begged him for stories of his worst hunts and biggest kills. As Ren talked, they ate honey-roasted fowl and gamey strips of breaded meat. Platters of baked cheeses and sugared stone fruits were passed around, accompanied by roasted root vegetables and rolls of marbled bread. And the drinks, gods above. Azra had been holding back on him. Ale, mead, cider, a wine made from fermented apples—all of it was delicious, and all of it was strong.

He wasn't sure when the bards began playing or the dancing started. He hadn't made the decision to get up and dance, but the alcohol and someone's callused hand tugged him into the moving crowd. The sun had fully set during the feast; the only light came from stars blanketing the sky and the bonfire's blaze. The warm haze of the fire smudged his sight, blurring the revelry into shades of orange and red and black. As he danced, concerned only with where he'd next put his feet, Ren let the music ease the burden of responsibility from his shoulders.

It was minutes or hours later when he collapsed back into his seat, drinking deeply of the cider he'd poured before Azra had dragged him to dance. Now that he was still, he knew it had been her—he also realized he'd danced with the mayoress, something he hoped wouldn't make collecting his pay awkward.

"Hello, Nightmare."

He looked up. Baba stood before him, a walking stick in her gnarled hand. "May I sit?"

"Of course." Ren turned one of the empty chairs around for her. "Are you enjoying the feast?"

"Oh, very much." She eased into the chair, resting her cane across her lap. Her dark-veined hands curled around it. "Of course, I can't dance all night like I used to."

"Have you always lived in Tanglewood?"

She nodded. "I was born here," she said, tucking her silver hair behind a pointed ear. "I've been here for many of its autumns. I have seen it grow and suffer and heal." A faraway look passed over her eyes like a veil. "The two years swallowed by the plague were some of the saddest of my long life. But the people here are special."

A whirl of green flashed before him—Morgaine, twirling by with Lord Scara. Her cheeks were pink with exertion. She noticed Ren and stumbled in her footing, their eyes meeting before Scara swept her along.

"Most of them may be too young to understand," Baba continued, "but this place, too, is special. We can all feel it. It's why we insist on thanking you, brave hunter. You help us protect it."

Ren chuckled. "You needn't call me brave, Baba. It's my job."

"That makes you no less brave. You don't see me chasing down spirits, do you?" She laughed, the sound a dry—but not unpleasant—rattle. "Brave souls should be celebrated and cared for. That's how we get more of them, and this world will always need brave souls." She glanced at him. "Is there anyone to care for you?"

The dance ended. Ren saw his chance and stood, staring into the crowd. "Please excuse me," he said. He knew he was being rude, but the answer to her question was "no." How could he confess that?

She followed his gaze to Morgaine. A knowing smile spread across her face. "Go on, Nightmare. Enjoy the night."

Ren hurried to Morgaine, the alcohol in his veins narrowing his vision to her. "Will you dance with me?" he said, tripping over the words as he held out a hand.

Morgaine hesitated, her eyes sliding to the edge of the crowd. "Lord Scara—"

"I don't care," Ren said. The bards strummed the opening chords of the next song. "He should have known you'd be in demand tonight, little love. Dare I say you'd like the excuse to be rid of him?"

She crossed her arms. "Do you know this dance?"

"I will if you teach it to me."

She smiled. He smiled back, because he knew she'd been trying not to. Morgaine took his hand and they began to dance.

———

They didn't part for countless songs after that—not when the music changed, not when one of them needed a drink, and definitely not when Scara crept closer and closer, hoping to steal Morgaine away for another turn around the square. The revelers didn't slow as the night wore on. The drinks flowed freely and the dances passed quickly, sending Ren and Morgaine stumbling to their seats, hand in hand and giggling, for a moment of respite before she dragged him back up. Ren was drunk, drunk on the apple wine and the cool air and the way the firelight danced in her dark eyes.

Their final dance was the most complicated, a routine that involved trading one's partner with other pairs of dancers. It was by no means the last dance of the night, but when Morgaine spun back into his arms, the firelight on her face wasn't the only heat burning there. "I don't want to dance anymore."

"Then we won't." He tightened his grip on her waist. Her velvet dress was soft against his palms.

The song ended. The crowd applauded. Morgaine employed her hands otherwise; she grabbed Ren's wrist and led him from the square. The firelight faded as they hurried from the feast, giggling again. Only the stars guided their path through residential streets and packed-dirt alleys, their silvery light disappearing as Ren and Morgaine entered the forest's edge.

"How can you see?" he asked.

"I can't," she confessed, slowing her pace. "I—" She shrieked as her foot caught an exposed root, causing them to stumble. Ren righted them both, but at a cost—Morgaine's back collided with a wide tree. "I thought Nightmares could see in the dark," she said, laughing and straightening her flower crown.

"We can," he said. "There's a spell for it. But I think you'd like this more."

He traced the ward for will-o-wisps and whispered the incantation. Small orbs of warm, cream-colored light flickered into being around them, drifting through the air like incandescent snowflakes. Morgaine gasped. She reached up to touch one. Her fingers shrank away from its heat, but that didn't stop her from staring at the wisps with wide eyes. "It's beautiful."

He couldn't help himself, not with how tempting she was in the soft light: her flushed cheeks, her loose hair, the wonder in her eyes, the knowledge that she understood his loneliness. He took the hand that had grazed the wisp and kissed her fingertips, murmuring, "Did it burn you?"

He hadn't thought it possible, but her eyes grew darker. "No."

Ren leaned over her. He twirled a strand of her hair around his finger, taking care to note the way her lips parted. "Do you want to kiss me, little love?"

She huffed. Morgaine tugged the strap of his pauldron and kissed him. He'd favored the wine and she the ale; he tasted both on her as the kiss deepened between them. She was irritating and stubborn and imperious, but she was intoxicating—the way she gasped when he kissed the curve of her neck at once sobered and inebriated him, coloring his vision with a wonderful golden haze. He wanted to chase that haze, needed to more than he needed air.

"Stay," she begged between kisses. She slipped her hands beneath his shirt. Her touch burned like fire. "Don't just go when the hunt is done."

He normally hated such a request, but gods above—if she kept touching him like that, he'd do whatever she wanted. She moaned into his mouth when he kissed her again. Though his eyes were closed, he nearly saw stars. Ren grabbed her leg and hooked it around his hip. She was lovely, so soft and lovely and willing, and he needed to be closer. He hadn't touched a woman in nearly a year. She was driving him mad—her nails dug into his back, and—

"Ren."

He stilled, their lips hardly an inch apart. "Yes, love?"

She put a hand to his chest and pushed. Her eyes darted to the edge of the forest. "I hear screaming."

He turned his head in the direction they'd come. Sure enough, screams drifted through the trees.

His blood chilled. The alcohol- and lust-fueled haze left him, and his sight cleared with startling immediacy. Ren stepped back and traced the ward for nightsight. The resulting red glow lit his eyes. He heard Morgaine's soft "oh" and thought she sounded frightened, but she didn't protest as he reached for her. The pink pigment had smudged around her mouth and he rubbed it away with his thumb, trying in vain not to think of how soft her lips had been. Morgaine took his hand. Their fingers twined together; Ren let himself enjoy it for only a moment before they started running.

———

The town square had devolved into chaos. The bonfire still burned, but instead of the dancing, it illuminated a great crowd surging away from the library. Women clutched crying children to their sides. Morgaine saw the white shreds floating through the air before he did; her cry nearly tore his heart in two. Book pages, ripped from their bindings, drifted through the square. From beneath the screams came a sepulchral howling. It twisted and warped, eventually taking the shape of *"Hunter!"*

The wraith had grown tired of waiting.

Morgaine started toward her library, but Ren held her back. "My ax," he said. She wasn't looking at him. He put his hand on her cheek and turned it, forcing her to look in his eyes. "Morgaine. My ax. Do you know where it is in our room?"

"Yes."

"Go get it."

"I don't know if I can carry—"

"Then have someone help you. Bring it to the library and call for me. Don't cross the threshold for any reason."

She shook her head. "You have no armor—"

"I'll be alright." They both knew he lied—Nightmares had fallen to lesser spirits than wraiths—but she nodded anyway. Ren squeezed her hand. "Go."

She disappeared into the crowd. Ren turned toward the library. The wraith screamed, the very building seeming to shake with the force of it. He wore only a pauldron, had only two Nightmare daggers strapped to his body. As he crossed the square, he plucked a log from the edge of the bonfire. A pauldron, two daggers, and a torch. It would have to do.

Reia and Kyr, alerted by the screams, met him at the entrance. The windows facing the square had shattered; the ground at his feet was littered with gutted books and bits of glass. "I need you to do all you can," he said to the Umbrals. "I'm not prepared."

Reia nuzzled his empty hand. Kyr chirped, settling on Ren's shoulder and tapping his beak against Ren's horns. Despite the dread mounting in him, Ren smiled to himself. They were good creatures. If he went down purging this wraith, they would be with him until the end.

Ren approached the door. It dangled from its frame by a hinge.

He took a deep breath, steeled himself, and surged inside.

The wraith fell on him immediately. Its nails clacked together as it swiped at him and missed. Ren buried his torch in its middle, rocking back a step as its body swallowed the fire. The wraith howled in pain. Foul breath washed over him, reeking of decay.

Ren dashed to the left, reaching for his daggers as Reia and Kyr attacked the wraith, distracting it as he planned. A wraith had to be separated from its body in order to be banished—which, if the library's previous spirits were any indication, was going to be more difficult than it should be—and then the physical form had to be dismembered to prevent the spirit from returning to it. It sounded simple, but wraiths were intelligent. Wicked. They had been mortal once, as Nightmares were, and over centuries had learned the Order's tricks. They demanded much, and Ren currently had so little.

He crouched by one of the shelves, shrouded by its shadow. He again cast nightsight, squinting through the red haze. Reia and Kyr had disappeared. The wraith hovered near the foyer, drifting back and forth. Its path was curious. It moved in a consistent arc, searching for him only by turning its head. Ren shifted on his feet. Kyr reformed and dove, screeching, at the wraith. It lunged but didn't turn, keeping its back to the little office.

The realization slithered into Ren's mind: it was guarding something.

Ren slowly rose. Whatever was in that office might be the key. He couldn't beat the wraith in a fight, so he'd have to rely on cleverness to subdue it—perhaps he could threaten whatever it wanted.

He drew his daggers and waited for his chance. As if the Umbrals had read his mind, it came. Reia and Kyr threw themselves, snapping and shrieking, at the wraith. It shrank under their onslaught, a death-rattle cry coming from its fleshless lips. Ren ran.

Steps away from the wraith, something hard and dense collided with his chest. Ren crashed against the shelves. He slid to the floor, groaning. A stone bust fell into his lap, its weight heavy on his thighs. He shoved it off and rocked onto his hands and knees. He couldn't breathe. The redness flickered from his vision as his nightsight faded in and out, his concentration broken by the pain radiating from his ribs. Up. He had to get up.

No sooner had he shifted onto his feet than he was crushed under a new weight. Ren was sent sprawling, knocked onto his stomach by an impossible force. One of his daggers slid across the floor. Something—no, some things—fell to the ground around him. Books. Gods above, they were books. The wraith had toppled a shelf onto him.

Ren twisted around and pushed against the shelf, shouting with the effort. He had to get it off—he was trapped from the hips down. There was no way he could defeat a wraith from the ground—

"Ren!"

He looked up. Morgaine stood on the threshold. The head of his ax rested at her feet, the handle gripped in her hand. She'd also found a sword and held it across her shoulders, although it would do them no good. "Stay there!" he shouted. "Don't cross—"

She craned her head and saw him. Her eyes widened. "Gods, Ren!" she cried, lifting the ax with great effort.

"Morgaine, no—"

But she was already inside. The head of the ax scraped against the floor. The wraith snapped its attention to her. Its resulting scream ended in a horrible gibbering that scraped at Ren's nerves. He roared in frustration. Morgaine screamed. Everything was chaos and noise and if he could only make this damned shelf lift just a bit more—

"I'm not afraid of you!" Morgaine shouted, her knuckles white around the hilt of the sword. She brought it down on the wraith, its blade flashing orange from the firelight outside.

The wraith snarled and caught the blade. The steel melted under its touch.

"Only Nightmare steel works!" Ren shouted. The shelf shifted, but not enough. He wiggled his hips free, but the weight only moved to his thighs. "Get out!"

Morgaine crouched and felt along the floor. His lost dagger shone in her hand when she stood. "I'm not leaving."

A scraping sound came from the wraith—laughter. Quick as a blink, it grabbed Morgaine by the wrist and squeezed. The dagger fell from her hand. The wraith lifted its other hand, extending its pointer finger and impossibly long fingernail. Slowly, knowing that neither she nor Ren could stop it, it reached for Morgaine's face.

"Don't touch her!" Ren bellowed, shoving against the shelf. Only his lower legs were trapped now. He'd read about what happened to those hurt by a wraith, of how it could strip them of everything but the emotion it felt or turn their bodies against them, bringing them into a sort of thrall. It couldn't happen to her. He couldn't let it happen—

She screamed as its nail tapped the space between her eyes, the sound ending in a sob that shook her body. The wraith was playing with her. Ren was going to rip it limb from limb.

It tilted its head from side to side like a dog considering a strange sound. It leaned closer. A bead of blood ran down Morgaine's nose.

"Why are you so angry?" she spat, turning her head away. It grabbed her chin and made her look into its eyeless expanse of a face. "So embittered?" She'd learned something from reading *Blessed Brotherhood*, then. But if the wraith wasn't tied to this plane by anger or bitterness or a need for vengeance—

Another drop of blood fell. "Why are you so afraid?"

It was as if time stopped. The wraith shrank back and released her.

Yet Morgaine didn't run as Ren hoped she would. She drew in a shuddering breath and repeated, "Why are you so afraid?"

With a movement like someone throwing off a cloak, the physical body of the wraith fell away. Its presiding spirit came only to Morgaine's waist. It was a child, a young boy no more than five or six. Its golden hair was thin, its clothes were in shredded tatters. It stared at her, blinking with wide transparent eyes as she knelt before it.

Ren pushed against the shelf again, straining. "Morgaine—"

She held up a hand to quiet him. "You're only a child," she said to the spirit. "What's your name?"

"I don't remember." Its voice was high with youth and hollow with death.

"Why are you afraid?"

It pointed a small finger at her. "Mama."

"You want your mother? She's—"

"Mama," it insisted. Its pointed finger raised to her dark hair.

Morgaine's brow furrowed. "I'm not—" She rose, realization clear on her face. She rushed into the office and returned before Ren could shout for her, a small box cradled in her hands. She knelt before the spirit and drew the cracked amulet from its box. The green of the stone was the same as her dress. The spirit shrieked when it saw it, its little hands reaching forward, but Morgaine held the amulet out of its reach. "Was this your mother's?"

The spirit nodded.

"And I have it now."

The spirit darted forward and tugged on her hair. "I want it," it said. "I want Mama."

"Your mother is dead," Morgaine said softly. "Do you know what that means?"

"Mama is gone. I can't find her. But you're like Mama."

"I look like your mother?"

The spirit nodded.

"Is that why you're still here?"

"I got woken up," the spirit said. Translucent tears gathered in its eyes. "I was with Mama but I got woken up. I can't find Mama."

Tears welled in Morgaine's eyes, too, but she held them back. "You have to look for Mama. She's in a different place. She's not here."

The spirit scowled. "But you're like Mama. I want to stay with you until I find her."

"I—" Morgaine swallowed. "You won't find Mama if you stay with me. I'm sure you're a wonderful boy, but you aren't mine. It wouldn't be very nice of us to keep you here. Mama might be looking for you, too."

The spirit's eyes lit up. "Do you think so?"

Morgaine nodded. "I think so. But you won't find her here. You have to let go of this place." Her hands trembled as she held the amulet in front of the spirit. "Can you do that? I'll give you this to hold onto while you look."

"Really?"

She nodded again. Morgaine touched the spirit's cheek, her fingertips pressing slightly through it. "But you have to promise not to come back," she said. "You've already looked here, and I have, too. I know Mama isn't here. There's only me."

The spirit pointed at Ren. "He's here."

Morgaine laughed, a few tears spilling from her eyes. "Yes, he is. But he's not Mama, either."

The spirit fell silent, staring at the amulet. "No," it said. "He's not." A few moments passed. Neither Ren nor Morgaine dared move. They watched the spirit, waiting.

Its little hands closed around the amulet. "I want to find Mama," it said, and disappeared. The amulet fell to the plank floor.

Morgaine burst into tears, bending over and sobbing into her hands. Ren, with a final push, wriggled free and scrambled across the floor to her, shoving ruined books and torn pages out of his way. "It's alright," he said, pulling her into his arms. Morgaine fell to pieces against him, wailing. "I know. I know, little love. It's gone. You did so well." He kissed the top of her head, cradling it in his hands. "You're safe. I've got you."

He held her as she trembled, as curious townspeople poked their heads in to investigate the sudden quiet. Ren paid them no mind. Reia and Kyr materialized over the inanimate lump of not-flesh that was the wraith's physical body. Reia prodded it with her nose to see if its spirit had really left. Her tail wagged.

"Morgaine," he said when her sobs slowed. It was time. "Little love, I need you to go outside."

She lifted her head. Her eyes were swollen and red. "Why?"

His ax rested on the floor, waiting. "You don't want to see what I have to do now."

———

Ren, having disposed of the body, returned to the Drowsy Dragon hours later. He'd also cleaned as much of the library as he could, but assessing the damage and making repairs would have to be done without him. It had taken three repetitions of the wraith banishment spell for Ren to be sure it was gone; each time he'd thought it had been successful, he'd heard a child laugh or cry, and he'd had to start again. When the banishment spell had finally brought silence, he'd recited the spell for cleansing a property until his throat felt raw. He left the library only when he was sure no shred of any spirit remained. The hunt was done. The only thing left was to collect his pay.

Endlessly weary, he stumbled up to their room. Morgaine sat at the desk, still in her dress and crown.

"You were right," she said. Try as he might, he couldn't ignore the touch of bitterness in her voice. "I couldn't do it."

Ren crossed the room and knelt in front of her. "Not all of it," he said, reaching for her hand. She let him take it. "But most."

They prepared for bed together, picking crushed flowers and debris from each other's hair before taking turns bathing. Morgaine didn't protest when Ren urged her to take the bed.

Once she'd fallen asleep, he quietly opened his chest and pulled out his bandages. Ren crept to the mirror by the bath and began cleaning and wrapping his wounds, wincing whenever he pressed a bit too hard. Every few minutes, he tried to cast skinstitch, but he was too drained for the spell to have any real effect. It felt as if hours had passed by the time he was done. Bandages wound around his aching ribs, the cuts on his chest, and the places on his legs where the bookshelf had broken skin. He was in pieces, but he'd live. Traveling to the next town would be uncomfortable, but he'd move on. And, no longer haunted, so would Tanglewood.

———

"*No!*"

Ren was at the bedside in an instant. Morgaine sat up, clutching the covers as if they were all that anchored her to the world. Tears streamed from her eyes; her breath came in shattered gasps.

"It was a dream," Ren said, cupping her face in his hands. Morgaine nodded. Her eyes were wild with fear. "A nightmare. You're safe."

"The wraith," she croaked, her voice hoarse from screaming. Her nails dug into his arms. "It had me—"

Ren crawled into bed and leaned against the headboard. "Come here, little love." Morgaine let him pull her close, resting her head in his lap and pulling the blankets up to her chin. "It's alright."

He felt her nod. Ren unraveled her long braid and ran his fingers through her hair. He never saw the aftermath of his hunts, never had to think about how the average person would recover from encountering a spirit, and it unsettled him. Part of him wished he'd left the moment the wraith vanished. Part of him knew he'd been right to stay the night. "It was just a dream," he repeated as softly as he could. "Only a dream."

Morgaine fell asleep minutes later, but Ren stayed awake,

listening for quiet cries or hitches in her breathing. He bowed his head and prayed, begging Zikat and Oddelen to watch over Morgaine and her dreams while she slept. While he was here, he'd do what he could to chase her nightmares away—but he was a Nightmare too, and like every bad dream should be, he'd be gone with the daylight.

7.14.626

"As agreed," Mayoress Soma said, sliding a burlap pouch across the tavern table. She'd approached Ren in the Drowsy Dragon, where he had just finished his breakfast, and sat at his table uninvited. "Thirteen gold." Her eyes were dull from a night of chaos and poor rest.

Ren took the pouch. "Thank you, Mayoress. I hope that you and the town fare well."

She smiled weakly. "I wish you the same. I suppose you're leaving today?"

"I am. Someone always needs a Nightmare more."

Mayoress Soma shook her head. "That's a shame, Ren. We'll miss you."

He didn't know how to respond to the mayoress' sullen demeanor, or her sentiment, for that matter. Nightmares weren't missed by their clients. "Thank you, Mayoress." Ren stood and walked to the bar, fishing gold from the pouch and sliding a coin across the bar to Azra. "For the expense incurred by my day drinking."

Azra chuckled and pocketed the coin. "Thank you, Ren. Safe travels."

He nodded to her one last time and left.

Reia and Kyr were waiting outside, Reia having shifted form from a heeler to a mare—he'd checked her tack and packed his bags before taking breakfast. Kyr perched between Reia's ears and fluffed his wings when he saw Ren approach.

"You're going."

Ren winced and turned. He'd hoped to leave before Morgaine woke. "I am."

Morgaine crossed her arms. Upon first glance, nothing looked amiss—she wore a cream-colored blouse beneath a blue sleeveless dress and had braided her hair—but he noticed the small scab on her forehead and the dark smudges below her eyes. They'd been woken twice more by her nightmares. The dreams had left her shaking, but he was relieved. She didn't tear her hair or throw herself from the window as he'd feared, and now that the wraith had been cast out, there was no chance of it enthralling her or driving her mad with fright. The prick had been shallow. The nightmares would fade. She would be fine without him.

"And without saying goodbye to me," she said. "That seems exceedingly cruel."

Ren cast his eyes to the ground. So he was 'cruel' again. He'd been called worse, but his heart ached to hear her say it. "Will you be able to make repairs?" he asked, nodding to the library. Townspeople milled in and out, carting the damaged shelves and books out and dumping them into a heap. Vess was among them.

"I will. But replacing the books that were lost…" She shook her head. "That will be the hardest."

Ren dug five gold coins from the pouch and held them out to her. "Let me help, then."

She stared at the gold. "It's not a matter of simply buying them," she snapped. "Some of those volumes were first editions. It's an emotional cost—something I suppose you wouldn't understand."

"Take the money, Morgaine."

She did, but scowled at him. "Why were you going to leave without saying goodbye?"

He pulled her into his arms. *Because looking at you makes me want to stay.* "It's often easier. But I'm glad you stopped me."

She dropped her head to his chest. "You could stay," she mumbled. "Even if it's just for a day."

"And when one day turns into another? When I've purged

every spirit that might haunt Tanglewood? Leaving would be more painful then." He placed a finger under her chin, tilting her face to his. "I'm sorry to go, but I have to. It's what a Nightmare does. Someone always needs us more." Though for the first time, he found himself wishing that wasn't true.

Morgaine was quiet. Her arms tightened around him. "Can you write to me?" she asked. "Your bird is a messenger raven, right?"

Ren smiled. "He is. I'm sure he'd like to visit."

"Alright." Morgaine lifted onto her toes and kissed him. Gone was the feverish urgency of the night before; she kissed him slowly, drawing out each quickly ending moment they had left. "Ren," she said, holding him close, "thank you."

"Of course, little love," he said, pressing a kiss to her forehead. "Take care of yourself. Don't get any ideas from reading that damn book." He didn't know when she'd taken *Blessed Brotherhood* back, only that he'd seen it among her things when he was quietly gathering his. He hadn't been able to bring himself to take it.

She laughed. "No promises. I'll be sure to give you my thoughts once I've finished it."

Ren shook his head, but he was smiling. He was going to miss her. "I'm sworn to secrecy about many of our practices," he said, swinging himself into the saddle, "so don't expect any esoteric tidbits from me."

"I wouldn't dream of it."

He looked down at her. She held her arms crossed and close, already guarding herself against his absence. "Morgaine?"

"Yes?"

Ren leaned down and kissed her one last time. "I'll write." He brushed his thumb against the spot where the wraith had pricked her. She'd be alright. She had to be—there'd be nothing he could do for her from afar. "As soon as I reach the next town, I'll write."

She stepped back and nodded, wiping her tears away. "I'll be waiting. Goodbye, Ren."

Two Months Later

Dear Morgaine,

I'm sorry it's been so long since I've written, and I'm sorry this letter will be brief. I'm trying to reach the nearest town before sundown. My supplies are running too low to spend another night in the forest. I've made it to the outer borders of the kingdom—I can throw a rock and have it land in Jasniostvo. I wouldn't dare, what with the war (there's a dispute over its throne, if you haven't heard), but it's an amusing thought.

I'm also sorry that your nightmares haven't stopped. Have you tried visiting Zikat's temple? I know a priestess doesn't maintain it, but a holy one's presence isn't necessary for a simple prayer. I can write some prayers for you that might help. Are you well otherwise?

The sun is setting faster than I anticipated. I'll get to the point.

I miss you. There are many things I want to tell you about, things that are too long for a letter (my hand is cramping as I write, and the cold doesn't help).

In the last village I passed through, I heard whispers of the Solstice festivals celebrated throughout Zijustvo. Tanglewood's name was mentioned. Is the town—or are you—planning a Solstice celebration?

Would there perhaps be a room in the Drowsy Dragon for me?

Ask Azra and let me know. I can pay her upon my arrival.

I miss you. I hope you're staying safe. Stop reading about nightmares.

Yours,
Ren
9.14.626

THE CASTLE

Dear Ren,

Your last letter came only a week ago—but I agree that it felt like a "long time." I've gotten used to hearing from you each morning. Kyr would wake me up by pecking my feet, and the first day he didn't come, I overslept and was late opening the library.

I've heard whispers of unrest in Jasniostvo, but nothing of war yet. How bad is it? Should I be worried? We don't get much news of the world outside Tmadrev, despite it crossing the border. Our news mostly comes from travelers, merchants, and those of us who keep a regular correspondence, which I suppose now includes me. Perhaps I should start a newsletter for the town.

No, I haven't visited the temple. I don't have much use for the gods. They've never had much use for me. I know you worship Zikat, but I can't help wondering why the goddess of life would have let me wander through Tmadrev and be so close to death for so long—maybe she thought Oddelen would like me more. Forgive me for not believing she'd spare some aid for a few nightmares. I'm getting used to them, anyway.

I'm well otherwise. Not much has changed since I last wrote. Theode, the traveling bookseller, is supposed to come today. He helps me keep a steady flow of new books coming into town. We make a day of it sometimes—we'll trade in the morning, he'll help me shelve the new books, and then we'll go to Azra's or Vess' for dinner. Actually, he's who I got the Order's textbook from. You wouldn't like him.

We should be planning a Solstice celebration, but as I'm writing, I'm realizing I would have met with Brilde to start discussing plans by now, so I suppose I'm not sure. Just to be safe, I asked Azra about a room for you. She said you're always welcome. Even if we don't have a town-wide celebration, maybe you could come anyway. I would like to celebrate with you.

I miss you, too. And I will not stop reading.

Morgaine
9.15.626

MORGAINE,

BOOKS AND DINNER WITH THEODE THE TRAVELING BOOKSELLER? IF I DIDN'T KNOW ANY BETTER, I'D THINK YOU WERE TRYING TO MAKE ME JEALOUS. HAVE YOU PULLED HIM INTO THE FOREST AS WELL?

I'M NOT SURE WHAT TO SAY ABOUT JASNIOSTVO. I CROSSED THE BORDER YESTERDAY AND IT'S BEEN QUIET. THE TOWN I STOPPED IN WAS CALM. I ASKED ABOUT THE WAR AT THE TAVERN I STAYED IN, AND FROM WHAT I WAS TOLD, IT'S CONSIDERED A CIVIL WAR AT THE MOMENT. THE KING CASSANDER ESCLAR-

MONDE, HAS A TWIN BROTHER WHO'S CLAIMING HE'S ACTUALLY THE OLDER OF THE TWO AND THAT THE THRONE IS HIS. THE PEOPLE DON'T LIKE TO SAY HIS NAME. WHEN I PRESSED FOR IT, THE BARKEEP LOOKED AROUND AS IF THE CHALLENGER WAS GOING TO STEP FROM THE SHADOWS AND RUN HIM THROUGH. IT MADE ME GLAD THE ORDER CARES LITTLE FOR POLITICS.

IF THINGS ESCALATE, THOUGH, I DOUBT ANYTHING WILL REACH YOU. I CAN'T IMAGINE AN ARMY WOULD VENTURE INTO TMADREV WITHOUT GOOD REASON, AND I HAVEN'T HEARD A WORD SPOKEN ABOUT ZIJUSTVO SINCE I ARRIVED. YOU'RE SAFE IN TANGLEWOOD, LITTLE LOVE.

TO OTHER MATTERS—WILL YOU AT LEAST TRY A PRAYER? FOR ME? ZIKAT'S DOMAIN INCLUDES DREAMS. ASKING HER FOR HELP MAY DO MORE THAN YOU THINK

ALL I WANT FOR SOLSTICE IS TO SEE YOU. I'LL DO ALL I CAN TO BE THERE.

I HATE TO, BUT I NEED TO END HERE. IT LOOKS LIKE I'LL BE TRAVELING AGAIN—I HAVE A LETTER FROM THE KEEP, SO I'M EITHER BEING SUMMONED OR HIRED. IT'S A PITY. I LIKED THIS LITTLE BORDER TOWN. IT REMINDED ME OF YOU.

YOURS,
REN
9.16.626

Dear Ren,

Write me a prayer and, for you, I'll try. Just don't expect to make a faithful woman out of me by Solstice. I hope that doesn't dim your excitement. I'd hate to disappoint you, knowing you came back just to see me.

I hope Jasniostvo remains quiet. I know you make a living from the hunt but, selfishly, I hope you don't find much to keep you busy. I'm looking forward to seeing you again.

And on the topic of Theode—you needn't be jealous. He and I don't maintain a flourishing correspondence like we do. I used to think I was in love with him, yes, but we kissed once and I realized I only liked him because he was different. You and I have kissed thrice, so I'll let you draw your own conclusions.

I'm actually not sure why I dragged you into the forest at Sisters' Harvest. I have many bad memories of wandering the forest after being kicked from my Grey home, and the thought of walking through it terrifies me. Perhaps Azra's ale was stronger than I thought. Perhaps wanting you made me brave.

Be safe.

Morgaine
9.17.626

Ren,

Are you alright? This is the third day Kyr hasn't come. I suppose you may not even get this letter, but it helps me to write it anyway.

Please write me as soon as you can. I know your hunt is dangerous, but I don't like thinking about the risks. I know you could stop responding to me at any time, but that knowledge doesn't soothe me—it's one thing to know it, but another to live it.

Please write. I'm worried.

Morgaine
9.20.626

Ren,

Tanglewood has made other plans for Solstice. We won't be celebrating in town, so there's no need to trouble yourself with making the journey.

I hope you're alright.

Morgaine
9.25.626

10.12.626

Tmadrev Forest rushed by in a blur. Ren pushed Reia faster.

This morning marked the fourth day he'd spent on horseback, the fourth day he'd spent fleeing south and trying to outpace the terror that clung to him. He was saddlesore and exhausted, and his body protested more with each passing minute, but he couldn't stop—not when phantom horrors lunged at him from between Tmadrev's skeletal trees. In his time away from the forest, winter had killed every bit of foliage and color he'd seen at Sisters' Harvest. All that remained were leafless branches and emaciated trunks. The shadows cast by the weak winter sun made the trees look like the bars of a dungeon cell. Claws swiped at him from behind the tree-bars, and though Ren shut his eyes against the imagined beings, he still knew their faces: his, warped by a ghoul; that of his old friend Sanne, her brown eyes blackened and full lips bloodied; and a featureless black smudge of a face, distinguishable only by its glowing lavender eyes.

Ren knew they were hallucinations, but the claws of fear wouldn't let him go. His body ached with the remnants of the injuries he'd sustained during his last hunt: the stabbing pain of a phantasmal spear in his side, the gut-wrenching agony of his ribs splintering like kindling, the harrowing emptiness he'd felt when the nameless entity he and Sanne had struggled against fed on him. Sanne Esclarmonde had been the reason Ren stayed in Jasniostvo; she was the contracted Nightmare of King Cassander Esclarmonde, and had written to the Keep for assistance. Ren had been the closest to the Stained Palace, where Sanne was located, so he'd been ordered to go. It had shocked him to see her again, and to know that *she* needed help—Sanne was one of the best in the Order. She'd been the first of their training cohort to receive the tattoo that marked them as full-fledged Nightmares. Ren hadn't gotten his until a year later.

Reia leapt over a downed tree and landed hard. The impact of her hooves on the frozen ground sent pain pulsing through the still-healing wound at his ribs. Ren slipped in the saddle and cursed; he bent forward and gripped Reia's mane with one hand while fumbling for the reins with the other. He hadn't taken a beating like this in years. The Stained Palace had been infested, and the lavender-eyed source had broken three of his ribs, punctured his left lung, and nearly sent him home to Oddelen as a godless husk. Ren refused to let himself remember what the source had truly been—the implications of its existence made his lungs seize with panic—but he couldn't forget the pain. He couldn't forget the terror that had seized him, or how the lavender-eyed entity had stripped his godhood, the small bits of holy essence bestowed upon all Nightmare hunters. He couldn't forget these things, but he could ignore them for as long as he was able. He had somewhere to be.

Ren had promised to join someone for Solstice.

He forced himself to look ahead—one of the faces leering at him from behind the dead trees was now hers. His correspondence with Morgaine had stopped when he'd arrived at the Stained Palace, and whenever he thought of the interruption, he felt ill. When he'd woken in his sickbed, only half-healed, he'd hoped for a stack of her letters to be delivered—Kyr had been kept in the palace's aviary, and Ren had hoped that the raven Umbral still made his rounds to the Keep and Tanglewood, that maybe the royal aviarist had held the letters for Ren to collect later. But there'd been nothing, not even a tear-stained note telling him Morgaine hated him and never wanted to see him again. Ren might have preferred that. He'd almost gone home to Oddelen, and in the fleeting moments he'd thought were his last, he'd only thought of her. The lack of letters made him worry she'd stopped thinking of him at all.

There had been one letter to reach him at the Stained Palace, though, and it was tucked safely into his bags. He'd been granted four months' leave because of his injuries—four months without a hunt, four months to stay in one place. If Morgaine was angry with him, or if he was late to the Solstice celebration, he had until the spring equinox to make up for it. He could give her what she'd wanted after Sisters' Harvest: for him to stay.

If, of course, she'd still have him.

Up ahead, the trees thinned. Ren spurred Reia again, his knuckles white as he gripped the reins. Reia galloped on, impossibly fast. She was crafted of shadow, not sinew and bone, and could move as fast as the wind if Ren pushed her. Kyr, similarly made, flew ahead to scout; his return was announced by an excited caw. Ren's heartbeat quickened. They were almost there.

They approached Tanglewood from the north. Reia skid to a full halt before the closed gate. Ren frowned. The gate had been fashioned from thick oakwood planks the height of three men; there was no way to scale it, and his still-healing body meant he wouldn't be able to simply shove it open. He'd never known the town gate to be closed—but the townspeople had expected visitors for Sisters' Harvest. Maybe they'd left the gate open for that reason. Maybe keeping the world out was their norm.

Stretching from each gatepost was a mass of branches and briars, the gnarled wood forming a wall around the town. Ren imagined how it looked in spring; leaves and flowers would cover the branches and hide the town entirely. Now, though, the cold death of winter had stripped the brambles bare. He saw white patches of snow-covered ground through the gaps.

Ren found an opening large enough for him to slip through and whispered a prayer of thanks—it was no small blessing, given the breadth of his shoulders. Reia became a heeler and followed, her ears pricking up as Ren hurried through residential streets. It was too quiet. All he heard was the suck of his boots in the slushy mud and his own labored breathing. No laughter, no chatter, no doors opening and closing as the townspeople visited one another.

He reached the center of town, the many-sided clearing the townspeople called their square, and stopped. The snow, which should have been churned by boots and the sweeping hems of cloaks, was mockingly pristine.

Kyr landed on his left horn, the one that had lost its tip in the Stained Palace, and chirruped. With no bodies to absorb it, the sound echoed through the square.

Tanglewood was empty.

"No." From door to door, porch to porch, house to house, Ren ran. He kicked aside small snowdrifts and half-rotted gourds left from Sisters' Harvest. He held his hands up to frost-covered windows and huffed against the panes, clearing the frost only to see nothing beyond the glass. They'd drawn the curtains before vanishing. What had happened? Had they gone? Ren thought of the turned-over pit in the woods, the mass grave that had produced the wraith pendant. Had something come out of it, something he could've stopped if he'd stayed? Had the townspeople been forced to flee?

He reached the Drowsy Dragon. The pain in his side was persistent and hot; when he pressed his hand to his side, it came away damp and red. Ren swore twice, once for the re-opened stitches and once for the note tacked to the tavern's door.

Closed for celebration of the Winter Solstice. Will return on 10.16.626.

He was too late.

Ren staggered from the Drowsy Dragon's porch across the square. Snow covered his feet and ankles. He fumbled in his pockets and pulled out one of the vials the palace nurses had sent him off with—a tincture for pain. Nightmares generally cast spells to heal themselves, but he was in no state to further drain himself by using magic. He wrenched the vial's cork free with his teeth, spat it into the snow, and drank. He hated every rancid sip, hated the way it made his throat thick and slimy and reminded him that he'd been made useless. The tincture dulled his pain, but couldn't slow the leaping of Ren's heart as he reached for the library door.

It was locked. Its curtains had also been drawn. Ren dropped his head against the door and fell to his knees before it, caring little for how the snow wet his clothes. He closed his eyes and screamed. Everything he'd been running from caught up with him: pain, exhaustion, terror, worry, unfulfilled hope. He'd dangled Morgaine in front of himself, soothed his aching body and tired soul with the thought of her, promised himself that he would be allowed to rest when he was back with her. But now he was too late. She was gone.

He lowered his hand into the snow. His fingers knocked against something hard beneath it.

Ren lifted his head. The corner of a box stuck out from the little snow pile he'd disturbed, dark brown beneath the bloodstained white. He used more snow to wash his hands and drew the box out. It was small enough to hold in his hands and decorated with blue-flowered vines at its edges. He opened the brass clasp and drew out a stack of letters. The top few were ruined—snow had seeped in—but on the third letter from the top, he found his name amidst the water-blurred ink. The letter was dated almost three weeks prior: 9.20.626.

The letter was unintelligible, so Ren dug further. The final letter was dated 10.10.626, only two days ago:

> Ren,
>
> ~~I don't know why I'm writing to you again.~~
> ~~I feel it necessary~~
> Hope is making me silly. Whatever feelings I have for you are making me foolish. I doubt you'll read this. I'm sure I'll come home to find this box of letters covered in snow and undisturbed.
>
> But if you do read this, the town has traveled to Hrascara for Solstice. We were invited by the duke. If I can trust what the others have told me, it's half a day's ride from Tanglewood.
>
> We leave tomorrow morning.
>
> Morgaine
> 10.10.626

The letter was brusque, even chilly. Ren imagined Morgaine bent over her desk, frowning and rewriting the letter. Bits of ink smudged the edges of the paper, and he wondered if it smudged her fingers, too—if her hands would bear the remnants of this letter when he held them again. Hope made her silly, but she still hoped, and knowing it made his heart lift.

Ren clutched the letters in his cold-stiff hand and sat back on his haunches. Half a day. He could survive the saddle for half a day.

His body protested as he rose, his sinews and tendons tightening and stretching like an out of tune instrument. He'd had the displeasure of meeting Lord Scara, the duke's son, at Sisters' Harvest; Morgaine's mention of his father meant that Hrascara must be the Scara family castle. If the entire town had been invited and, as the silence around him communicated, gone, the castle must be large. It would be quite noticeable amidst the snow and bare trees of Tmadrev.

Ren returned to the square. Tanglewood had three gates, the tops of which he could see rising above the low buildings: one to the north, one to the southeast, and one to the southwest. He was confident he'd know Hrascara when he came upon it, but that still left the question of which way to go. "Half a day's ride" meant nothing if he set off in the wrong direction. He could be in the saddle for days and miss Solstice entirely.

His stomach twisted. Missing Solstice was not an option.

Reia nuzzled his hand. "I know," he said, scratching absentmindedly at her ears. "Lie down and rest for a bit. We'll be leaving soon."

Reia whined, but went to the library porch. She used her nose to clear the snow away from the letter box and curled into a ball beside it. Kyr hopped over and settled in the middle of the curl.

Ren paced through the town square, letting the cold bite of snow shock him into action. This was no different from his hunts: he had a quarry to track and capture, though banishing her was out of the question. This time, they'd only part if she willed it.

He ran through his memorized spells, dismissing each one as it came to mind. He didn't need light or a breeze, so will-o-wisps, lightlance, and slowwind were out of the question, and the sun was bright on the snow, so nightsight wouldn't help. He inspected each porch, hoping someone had snagged a finger or other fleshy bit of themselves on a splinter or nail so he could use bloodtrace to track them, but had no luck.

Ren huffed into his palms and paced the square again, taking care to step in his old bootprints. How would they have gotten to Hrascara? Surely it was too much of a distance to walk. Morgaine had mentioned riding, but to his knowledge, there were no communal stables or horses.

He walked, squinting, toward the closed north gate. A sliver of something colorful jutted from the snow. Ren knelt, his descent slowed by another flare of pain, and grasped it. The sliver was smooth, flexible, and a vivid blue beneath his fingers. Ren bent it back and forth a few times before realizing what it was: a chip of paint.

He looked at the snow. There were no more chips, but this close, he noticed grooves in the snow he hadn't seen while standing. Between the grooves were horseshoe prints.

Carriages. Of course.

The tracks led to and through the north gate. Ren hurried to the wall of brambles and peered through the gaps; there were slim ruts in the snow outside. By the gods' will, the tracks had remained. He had a direction. Now he only had to go.

He whistled for Reia and Kyr. Snow began to drift down from heavy grey clouds. Ren's heart skipped—fresh snow would cover the tracks—and turned back to the library. Reia had transformed into a mare by the time Ren picked up the box of letters. She tossed her head and nickered.

"Good girl," Ren said, kissing her velvety snout. "Just a little further, and then we'll have a full night's rest."

He checked the straps of Reia's newly materialized tack. Like his weapons, Reia's tack and saddlebags were enchanted; they lingered in the same shadowy half-existence the Umbrals entered when they traveled by shadow, and appeared and disappeared as Reia changed forms. Satisfied, he stuck his left foot into the stirrup; before he could mount, however, a pealing cry reached his ears.

Ren turned. The square was still empty, but down the residential streets, two slim silhouettes darted between vacant homes. They wove in and out of sight, coming ever closer.

Slowly, without taking his eyes from the silhouettes, Ren reached for his ax. He was a Nightmare of the Apprazit distinction, meaning his training had focused on spirits and specters. His fleeting glimpses were enough to tell that the advancing silhouettes were no spirits, but he knew little beyond that. Ren was at a considerable disadvantage. He motioned for Reia to move closer.

With a call like the ringing of a rusted bell, two creatures darted into the square. Though one was a head taller than the other, they looked much the same: quadrupedal creatures that looked and moved like black branches lashed together in a vaguely equine shape, though without ears, a snout, or a tail. When Ren faced them head-on, they were no wider than his forearm; as they approached and slightly turned, however, the change in angle showed their true natures. Seen from the side, the creatures were at once muscular and hollow, their tendons and ligaments stretching around gaps where a living thing would have organs. Their three-jawed mouths hung open, showing off rows of serrated teeth as long as Ren's middle finger. The faintest suggestion of tongues dipped between each of the creatures' teeth, checking for any leftover morsels.

Ren reached for Reia's saddlebags. The creatures were lierens, if he wasn't mistaken—spectral beasts who were drawn to abandoned places. They fed on the echoes of life found in empty places: rubble in trash heaps, lovers' whispers absorbed by pillows, seasonings cooked into cast iron pans. The smaller of the lierens, which Ren assumed was the female, lifted its head and cried out. The male looked north, and Ren followed its gaze. His fingers closed around a length of enchanted rope.

The lierens wanted the carriage tracks.

"*Hey!*"

The creatures' heads swiveled to him, warping from oblong heads with bone-white eyes to black slivers. Like most of the

Order's prey, lierens usually hunted at night and were ill-suited to diurnal activity; as such, their eyesight was poor during the day. They hadn't seen Ren. In a town filled with the faint scents of dozens of living things, they hadn't smelled him, either, but he made sure they noticed him now. If the lierens consumed the carriage tracks, his only lead to Morgaine would disappear.

The female galloped toward him, her metallic call deafening. With a flick of his wrist, Ren snapped the rope like a whip. He shouted the ensnarement spell, one of the few in the common language, and ordered the rope to bind the female. It trussed her and she fell to the ground, braying. Ren charged toward her mate, drawing his ax as he ran. He'd never fought a lieren before, but after the wretched thing he'd faced in the Stained Palace, a spectral beast would be child's play. It didn't need to be banished—just killed.

The male cried out, a lower version of the female's clanging shriek, and reared back on its hind legs. One of its tendons broke loose from the suggestion of a lung and flew toward Ren. He drove his ax down, and the severed bit of tendon fell. If the lieren had been a living thing, the snow would've hissed from the flesh's heat, but the snow only crunched under the tendon's slight weight.

Something tapped Ren's ankle. He looked down to see a sinew from the female wrapping around his leg, taking advantage of the distraction her mate had provided. He didn't remember much of his classroom training on spectral beasts, but Ren knew a lieren had no use for a living thing. Unlike other beasts, they had no desire to drink blood or sink their teeth into warm flesh. Lierens killed so they could feast on the hollowness created by death, the emptiness left behind when a soul slipped free of its corpse. Ren had no intention of letting the lierens sate themselves on him.

Ren barked a subspell and the enchanted rope tightened around the female. Her cry turned into a rasp, and the sinew retreated. Ren continued speaking the subspell—as long as he did, the bonds would continue to tighten. If the gods were with him, the enchanted rope would kill the female lieren while he slaughtered the male.

The snow fell faster now. He was running out of time. Out of the corner of his eye, he saw the female lurch toward the carriage tracks.

Ren swung his ax at the male, his strength greater than his aim. The blade glanced off of the lieren's shoulder, the momentum of the bad swing pitching Ren forward. The blade buried itself in the snow. Ren snarled the subspell again, grunting in frustration as he wrenched his ax free.

The female lieren also voiced her frustration. Ren's head pulsed with the sound and he stumbled. He had to end this, and end it soon. He took a dagger from the holster at his thigh, dodged a tendon that shot out from the male, and flung the dagger at the female. It embedded itself in her eye just as the tightening ropes choked off her scream.

The male swung his head, distracted by his mate's death. Ren continued to repeat the subspell, his voice little more than a growl. His head throbbed. His ribs hurt. His hands ached from being curled around reins and weapon handles for four days straight. He wanted sleep. He wanted rest. He wanted a warm bed and a hot meal and an insufferable, beautiful woman to roll her eyes at him. He had no place to call this, but he knew what this feeling was: he wanted to go home.

"By the gods," he snarled, "just *die*."

This time, when his ax buried itself in his mark, it didn't stick. Ren drew it back with little resistance and brought it down again and again, chopping the lieren's front leg to pieces.

The male dropped to the ground and fell silent. Ren propped the bloodied blade of his ax in the snow and leaned on its handle. Most spirits' unblood was an oily black or brown liquid, but the lierens bled a dark forest green, the color of Tmadrev in the warm seasons. It looked odd against the snow, an out-of-season reminder of spring.

Ren brought a hand to his ribs and wheezed, red blood dripping from between his fingers onto the snow. The pain tincture had already worn off, likely due to the heart-pumping activity he'd just done—the heart-pumping activity he'd been ordered not to do for four months.

He turned to find Reia at his side, standing so that the saddlebags with the rest of his supplies were in easy reach. "Good girl," Ren panted, patting her rump. He fished through the bags until he found the other vials—he'd already drank the few tinctures he kept on his person. The elixir he downed smelled of rotten meat and tasted worse, but a welcome dullness radiated from his center once he'd finished. He leaned against Reia and let his eyes slip shut for a moment. The newly dark world smelled of horse and leather, of lieren blood and Nightmare sweat.

"Let's go," Ren murmured, resisting the exhaustion that crept upon him. He could sleep at Hrascara.

He opened his eyes and headed for the gap in the brambles. Reia and Kyr flit through shadows and appeared before him on the other side of the wall. Reia knelt in the snow and Ren's heart swelled—he wouldn't have to exert himself to mount this way. "Thank you," he whispered as he swung his leg over the saddle and held on. She rocked to her feet. Kyr settled on Ren's shoulder and tapped Ren's chipped horn.

Ren glanced down and reached for the reins. He was in a right state, covered in mud and two types of blood; smears of forest green were dappled with faint smudges of red.

Well. At least he'd arrive for Solstice festively dressed.

Ren was right. He knew Hrascara the moment he saw it.

He approached the castle at sunset, circumventing the town at the foot of the hill Hrascara looked down from. Ren squinted into the dying sunlight. A winding path had been cut through the snow, a brown ribbon against sparkling white satin. The castle itself sat at the highest point of the hill, with its barbican and lower bailey just beneath it. Atop the corbels, flags the same bright blue as the paint chip flapped in the cold wind.

"Almost there," he said to Reia. She was annoyed—he could see it in the way she flattened her ears—but she trotted forward when Ren nudged. The hill's slope was low; Ren grew impatient and ordered Reia to go faster. He held himself low to her neck to prevent the setting sun from burning into his eyes, which already smarted from the cold.

The castle rose in front of them, its spires seeming to prick the evening's clouds. The barbican and curtain wall were of dark brown stone, and—thank the gods—the tall wooden gate was open. Ren passed through the lower bailey and approached the gatehouse. Two guards were stationed outside, their blue coats trimmed with black fur.

"Who goes there?" one of the guards shouted.

Ren slowed Reia to a halt. A small crowd milled through the bailey behind the guards. "I'm here with the townspeople."

The interrogative guard scowled. "The townspeople arrived a day ago. You weren't with them. Be gone."

Ren made a show of sighing and turning Reia around. As part of his cold-weather clothing, he wore a black cloth over his nose and mouth; it kept the guards from seeing his grin as he faced Reia back toward the gate and dug his heels into her flanks. He'd come all this way. He wasn't going to be stopped now.

As he and Reia approached at a gallop, the guards shouted and crossed their spears. Ren scoffed and patted Reia's neck. "This is nothing for you."

She made the jump easily, though Ren fought to stay in the saddle when she landed. After a few strides, she slowed just enough for Ren to make a running dismount. Once his feet hit the ground, she shifted to a heeler and bound into the crowd.

To Ren's right was a stack of hay bales. He ducked behind it as the guards hurried into the bailey, their footsteps rushing past his hiding place. Ren dropped his head onto the nearest hay bale for a moment, catching his breath and grinning despite his pain—Reia's landing had jarred him, and a bit of fresh blood ran down his side. But he was here. He'd made it.

He stepped from behind the hay and swept his gaze over the bailey. Some kind of vendor market had been set up; small tents and tables formed a rectangle in the middle of the bailey, and townspeople—*Tanglewood* townspeople—drifted from vendor to vendor to inspect their wares. Ren had never been so happy to see them. Even the sight of Mayoress Soma, as exasperating as he'd found her, made his heart swell.

"Excuse me—"

A hand landed on his arm. Ren looked down to see Azra scowling at him, her box braids tucked beneath an apple-green hood. "I saw that little stunt with the guards," she murmured. "Is there a problem?"

He laughed, the sound ending in a wheeze. "Azra, it's me!" His face was still covered against the cold, so he lowered his hood and showed her his ridged horns.

Her sternness dissolved. "Ren! I didn't think you'd make it." She threw her arms around him. "How was your journey?"

"Long." He drew back and scanned the crowd. "Is Morgaine—"

"She's here." He heard rather than saw Azra's grin. "I'll let you find her."

"Thank you. We'll talk later."

Ren strode through the bailey, each step making his heart stutter in his chest. Vess, his sons, Baba—they smiled and waved, but their greetings only vexed him. None of them were why he'd come.

But then the crowd cleared enough for him to see the swirling edge of a blue cloak and dark hair braided into a crown. For a moment, he stopped aching.

"Morgaine!"

She'd been talking with Brilde, but turned at the sound of his voice. Her eyes widened; her mouth formed the familiar shape of his name, though he was too far to hear her say it.

"Morgaine," he said again, smiling like an idiot. He ran to her as quickly as the gathered crowd would allow, dodging townspeople and trying not to trip over cloaks. It was alright. His last hunt, the pain, the horrible strain of his ride here—coming back to her, seeing her, had been worth it all.

When he was steps away, his hand stretched out to touch her, his world tilted. Ren collided with the hard-packed ground. He swore and kicked at the man on top of him, but the two guards hauled him to his feet. "Thought you could sneak by?" one of them jeered. "You should have gone when ordered."

"I'm supposed to be here—"

"Really?" the other guard asked. "You're dressed like a criminal, all in black with your face covered. And I don't remember helping a horned elf off the carriages."

Ren contorted himself just enough to be able to pull the cloth covering his mouth and nose down. "I'm a Nightmare hunter," he snapped, resisting the urge to spit at the guards. She was *right there*. "The lord knows me. The townspeople know me."

"It's true," Morgaine said. "Let him go."

The guard to Ren's right scowled. "I don't think so, ma'am, and I suggest you keep your distance. He could be dangerous."

Ren tried to tear himself free, but the guards held fast. "Just because I don't listen to the orders of toothless—"

"Oh, hello, Ren!" Mayoress Soma appeared behind Morgaine. Ren's irritation grew. "I wasn't aware you were coming. What a lovely surprise!"

"Hello, Mayoress. I'd shake your hand, but as you can see—"

Someone pointedly cleared their throat behind Ren. The guards, rather ungracefully, turned him around so he could see who else had come to ruin his reunion. "Who have you apprehended that's causing so much fuss?" Lord Scara's aquiline nose wrinkled when he saw Ren. "Oh. It's you."

"See? The lord knows me," Ren said. "Now, if you'll let me go?"

The guards looked to Scara, who rolled his eyes and nodded.

"My lord—"

"Let him go," Scara sneered. "Just because he is mannerless in his late arrival doesn't mean we have to sink as low."

The moment the guards dropped his arms, Ren rushed to Morgaine. "Be angry with me later."

He threw his arms around her. She gasped—possibly because his hands were so cold and *gods*, she was so warm—but returned the embrace after a moment, sliding her arms around him beneath his cloak. He held her tightly, probably too tightly, but couldn't find it in himself to loosen his grip. He'd made it. She was here and whole and not just something he'd dreamed up on his deathbed. He buried his face in the curve of her shoulder. A few wisps of hair that had escaped her braid tickled his cheek. She smelled sharp and clean, of lavender soap and black ink. "I'm sorry, little love," he murmured, his lips brushing her skin. "Let me explain."

Her hands slid to his chest and pushed. "I don't—" Her words broke off into a cry, and she pulled her hands back. They were covered in green blood; when she stepped away, Ren saw that, in his excitement, he'd ruined her dress. The icicle-blue fabric was marred with the lieren's blood and spots of his.

"By the gods," the mayoress gasped, raising an umber-gloved hand to her mouth.

Ren reached for her. Their distance was already too much. "Morgaine—"

She stepped back, gaping at him. She held her hands aloft to keep the blood from staining her further. "I suggest you change and bathe, Ren," she said, her dark eyes boring into him. "I am going to my room. My lord, is there a place for me to take this dress? Do you employ a laundress?"

"Of course." Scara put a hand on the small of Morgaine's

back and directed her to the castle's entrance. "If you'd like a room, hunter, you'd better come along."

Ren followed, his face burning. There were many possible causes for the heat: humiliation, shame, confusion and worry from how Morgaine had received him, a fever from his wounds—but he settled on anger, anger at the way Scara didn't take his hand from Morgaine. He didn't think he'd lost her to the lord, not with how poorly she thought of Scara, but he wished Morgaine would swat at the lord's hand and stain his clothing, too.

"You there," Scara said, waving over a passing maidservant. "See to it that our late arrival is given a chamber. Regrettably, he's joining us for Solstice."

The maidservant, a freckled human woman with a long red plait, looked at Ren with wide eyes and nodded.

Scara's nose wrinkled. "And be sure he's brought a tub and water. He smells."

"And a healer," Morgaine added. There was no warmth in her voice, and she didn't look at Ren when she said it, but his heart lifted anyway. "Please."

The maidservant nodded. "Yes, my lord. Ma'am."

Scara and Morgaine disappeared down the hall. Ren stared after them, scowling. He knew Morgaine could do little to rebuke Scara here—it had been different at Sisters' Harvest, when the lord had come to Tanglewood—but it infuriated him to see Scara's hand remain on Morgaine as if he owned her.

"Sir?"

At the light voice and lighter touch on his arm, Ren looked down. He must have done a poor job tempering his gaze, for the maidservant shrank back. "If you'll follow me, please," she said. "The townspeople are staying in our guest wing." She rubbed her fingers together, frowning at the grime she'd picked up from touching him. "I'll send for a tub and water as soon as you're settled."

The maid showed him to a room and left him on its threshold, promising she would return soon with a healer. Ren stood just inside the doorway and waited—his boots were caked in mud, and the thick rugs on the chamber floor would be much harder to clean than the stone passageways the maid had taken him through. To Ren's right, a fire crackled in a hearth almost as tall as he was. Two cushioned chairs and a small table sat atop a lovat green rug in front of it. To his left was a four-poster bed large enough for three; it took all of Ren's willpower not to immediately collapse into it. The green of its quilt matched the hearth rug, and a pile of white Nocovostvan furs waited at the foot. A rack of antlers hung above the bed.

Three windows spanned the length of the far wall, stretching from the middle of it up to the ceiling. The room was on the third floor of the castle, so the windows looked onto snow-laden trees and a darkening sky. It was a lovely view, but he would care more for it after he'd slept. Right now, the most exciting thing about the windows was the black drapes that hung at each end, waiting to be pulled.

"Excuse us, sir."

Ren stepped to the side, making room for two men to haul a tub of water into the room and place it before the fireplace. The red-haired maidservant slipped into the room after them, a navy-skinned elven healer behind her.

"Undress, please, sir," the healer said once the men had left.

Ren had barely raised his hands when the maidservant reached out and unclasped his cloak. An unwelcome flush crept up his cheeks. "I've got it, love."

"You're moving too slowly, sir," she said, reaching for the buckle of his pauldron. "The water will cool."

Ren's flush deepened. She was right—the pain kept him from moving quickly—but he didn't want her to see the discoloration his body bore from the Stained Palace. "I can reheat it. I know a spell."

The healer joined the maid, and the two made quick work of removing Ren's armor. "You shouldn't strain yourself," the healer said, pulling his shirt over his head. She was shorter than he was, so he had to disentangle the blood-crusted fabric from his horns. When he could see the healer again, she was sweeping appraising eyes over him. Ren resisted the urge to shrink beneath her gaze. The draining he'd suffered had darkened the veins in his hands, arms, and torso, and he'd been so concerned with getting to Tanglewood that he hadn't stopped to examine the state of his ruined arteries. Ren glanced at his bare chest; though the deep purple discoloration had started to fade, the darkness was still far too noticeable. The healer, though, only said, "Come sit before the fire, Nightmare. Your wounds need much attention."

He sat before the fireplace, still and quiet, as the healer removed his soiled bandages and mumbled a few spells. He tried to cast skinstitch, hating to feel so useless, but Hrascara's healer hissed and echoed what he'd been told in Jasniostvo: that he was too weak to effectively wield magic. He closed his eyes and tried to feel grateful for the assistance instead of ashamed.

Everything was warm and soothing: the radiating sensation of the healing spells, the cheery blaze in the hearth, the water he sank into when the females turned their backs to let him finish undressing. He fell asleep for a few moments in the bath, and woke to the maidservant and healer's shrieks. Reia and Kyr had appeared, blinking into shape between one moment and the next. Reia began to lick Ren's hand, whereas Kyr flew along the ceiling and squawked.

"They're mine," Ren said, moving his hand out of Reia's reach. Kyr settled onto the lip of the tub and pecked at it. "They won't hurt you."

When he was dry and half-dressed in the softest pants he'd ever worn, the healer wrapped his wounds in fresh bandages. "Sleep, Nightmare," she said. "Linds will find me if you need further care."

Ren nodded, his eyes already drooping. The maidservant hustled him toward the bed and pulled back the quilt. Ren flopped onto the mattress.

"Would you like us to wake you for breakfast, sir?"

"Mm." Ren was already face-down in the pillows. "I'm not hungry, love."

"It isn't morn—I see. We'll let you sleep." A pause, and then, "And my name is Linds, sir."

"H'llo, Linds. 'M Ren."

"Hello, Ren. And good night. Sweet dreams."

He didn't hear her valediction. Ren was already fast asleep.

10.13.626

Ren woke to a series of soft thuds against his window.

He sat up and rubbed his eyes. Reia, who'd slept with her head on his stomach, sighed at the disturbance and settled her head onto the mattress.

His ribs pulsed with pain at the movement, but the ache was considerably duller than it had been the last four days—a full night's sleep had worked wonders, and the healer's spells had catalyzed his rapid healing. It was a blessing Zikat had given all Nightmares, one Ren had sorely missed in Jasniostvo. He glanced at the bandages wrapped around his ribs. They were stained with spots of blood, but less than he was accustomed to seeing, and none of it had run onto the quilt and furs he'd drawn up to his chin in the night. It wouldn't take four months for him to heal, especially at this rate, but he'd welcome the respite nonetheless.

Another low wave of pain rolled through him. Ren pressed a hand to the bandages and laid back down. The quilt was soft and heavy, the bedsheets warm from his and Reia's body heat. Any fire that had been in the hearth had long since died, and the world beyond his bed was cold. The drapes were still drawn; the room was dark. Would it hurt if he slept just a bit longer?

His eyes drooped. Reia stood, turned in a circle, and settled back down, resting her chin on Ren's stomach. He was nearly asleep when something—or multiple somethings, judging by the sound—hit his window.

Reia whined and hopped out of bed, walking to the windows and sticking her nose in the air. Kyr, who'd been sleeping on one of the unused pillows, raised his head. Ren grumbled and dragged himself from bed. The rugs were cold beneath his feet, chilled by the stone floor beneath. Ren fumbled for the cord and drew back the drapes, squinting against the bright mid-morning light.

Bits of snow stuck to the windows, the edges of which were littered with frost. Ren rubbed his face and looked out. His bedchamber overlooked a snowy field, the forest a hundred or so yards to the right. To the left, an iron gate and tombstones poked out from beneath the snow, grim reminders that winter wasn't only a cheery time of snow and holidays—it was ice and odd stasis, a season hovering halfway between life and death.

Blurs of motion and shreds of laughter drew him back to the field. Before the citizens of Tanglewood had come to the castle, perhaps the snowy field had been pristine, but Ren supposed he'd never know. The townspeople had taken it over for a snowball fight.

Cloaks, colorful against the bright snow, swirled as the townspeople launched and dodged attacks. Ren first found Azra among the fray. She shouted at someone he couldn't see—small blockades had been hastily constructed, and Azra's target had ducked behind one. Oren and Byrne, Vess' sons, were building a barricade while their father was taking the hits meant for them. A human man that Ren didn't recognize ran toward Mayoress Soma with an armful of snowballs, which the mayoress scooped into her arms and began to lob at her constituents.

A black blur flitted among the fight, a blur Ren realized was Kyr—when he turned back to the bed, the Umbral's pillow was empty. Ren chuckled, watching snowballs pass through Kyr. The raven croaked and dove toward the townspeople, beating his wings and hovering just above a woman in a cornflower blue cloak, one with her dark hair braided in a crown—Morgaine.

Ren stepped closer to the window and put his hand against the glass. She'd woven a red ribbon into her braid. When had she started wearing ribbons in her hair? She hadn't mentioned it in her letters. Had she thought he wouldn't care? Wouldn't notice?

Wouldn't be around to see it?

Kyr flew to Ren's window and tapped on the glass. Ren waved. "Tell your brother good morning," he said to Reia. She put her front paws on the window and barked at Kyr, her tail brushing Ren's calf as it wagged.

The raven cawed and flew away. Ren watched, his gaze following Kyr back down to the field.

Morgaine was looking at his window.

Their eyes met, and her gaze slipped to his chest. Her eyes widened. Ren became painfully aware of his half-nakedness, of the bloodstained bandages that cocooned his ribs. He had to speak to her. He had to explain.

A snowball collided with the back of Morgaine's head, the snow crashing against her braid. She whirled, looking for her attacker, and her laughter drifted up to Ren and through the frost-etched window. The sound warmed him just as well as his bed had.

"Go on," he said to Reia. She vanished, reappearing stories below in the midst of the fight. She began to chase the snowballs that Oren and Byrne lobbed at any moving target.

Ren turned from the window. He stood before the fire and peeled back the edge of the topmost bandage. Hrascara's healer—whose name he hadn't asked—had done good work. The puncture wound had scabbed at the edges, leaving only the middle of the hole raw and shining. Ren slipped his fingers beneath the bandages and muttered the spell for skinstitch. He wasn't sure if it would work, but the wound became taut and dull under his fingers as it scabbed. Thank the gods. He'd still have to be careful, but he wouldn't ruin more clothes.

Ren replaced the bandage and dressed. There were many things he needed to do, with notifying the Keep of his new location and conducting his missed prayers to Zikat and Oddelen high on his list, but those could wait. The memory of Morgaine's unblood-covered hands burned in his mind.

Ren drew his cloak over his shoulders and hurried from his chamber to find a way down to the field. The gods were with him—his room was steps away from the end of the hall, which led to a torch-lit stone staircase to the ground floor. As he descended, he had to pick his way around shards of marble on the second-floor landing; a sculpture had fallen from its pedestal and shattered in the night. Servants fluttered around it like moths near a flame, but they stepped out of Ren's way and greeted him with a "good morning, sir."

He waved and continued wordlessly on. The ground floor was cooler, and he followed the chill to a set of doors that had been thrown open to the snowy world beyond.

The field was empty, so still and quiet and rutted with footprints that Ren half-expected a lieren to come creeping from the forest.

Reia, who'd been rolling in the snow, bounded up to him and licked his hand. Her muzzle was cold.

"I'm the Nightmare," Ren mumbled, scratching her head. "They're the townspeople. Why am *I* having to seek out *them*?"

Kyr flew over and settled on Reia's head. A shred of something red dangled from his beak, a shred Ren realized was fabric and not viscera—it was a ribbon from Morgaine's hair, blood-bright against his black gloves.

"Good bird." He patted the raven's head and went inside. She'd have to speak to him now, even if just for a moment—but he could make do with a moment.

He paused beneath the arched entryway that led out to the bailey. Again, he found himself thinking as he did in his hunts: if he was cold and damp, where in a castle would he first want to go?

To find warmth. Where? In his chambers?

No—the townspeople had all been together. Surely they'd want to remain that way.

Ren smiled. He knew where they were.

———

Before he entered the castle's kitchen, he knew from the laughter and chatter spilling into the hall that he'd tracked them well. The townspeople clustered in small groups around the kitchen, some by the expansive wood stove and others around the massive prep table in the center of the room. The kitchen was large, but not enough to fit every townsperson and servant—something Ren quickly realized as he stood just inside the doorway and swept his gaze over the room. He didn't see Morgaine.

"You must be sweltering," Vess said, clapping Ren on the back and handing him a mug of something light brown and steaming.

"I thought I'd join you all outside, but it seems I was too late," Ren said, unclasping his cloak. He draped it over one arm and took the proffered drink, sipping. Warmth and spice washed over his tongue—the cocoa had been flavored with cinnamon.

Vess chuckled. "I'm sure that skirmish wasn't the last—not if my boys have anything to say about it. Hello, Baba."

The elven woman smiled at Ren as she approached. "You've come back to us, Nightmare," she said, resting a hand on Ren's arm for balance. The other wrapped around the top of her cane. "I hoped you would."

He'd noticed the darkness in Baba's veins at Sisters' Harvest, but the discoloration had meant nothing to him then—not like it did now, when his veins sported the same shadow. Fear coiled deep in his gut as memories rushed forward: pale purple eyes, a stabbing pain, gasping for air that wouldn't come. Ren fought to keep his expression steady. He was grateful he still wore his gloves. "I'm glad I could, Baba. How have you fared?"

"Well enough. These old bones can't weather the winter like they used to, so I was grateful for the duke's invitation." She looked up at him, though he couldn't stop looking at her veins. "I saw your unfortunate run-in with Morgaine yesterday."

He tore his gaze from Baba's hands before she could notice his distraction. Morgaine—he was here for Morgaine. That was all that mattered. "She dropped this," he said, showing Baba the ribbon. "Do you know where she's gone?"

Baba nodded. "She left through that door, if you intend on following her," she said, pointing toward the hearth with the tip of her cane. "But be careful with her, Nightmare. She hasn't been well."

Ren thanked her and hurried through the other kitchen door. He knew Morgaine had suffered from nightmares since their encounter with the wraith at Sisters' Harvest, but the heavy feeling in his chest told him Baba referred to something else. What had Morgaine written in the letters he never got—the letters he'd been too preoccupied with finding her to read?

He paused at the end of the hall. Voices drifted down the corridor to his left, so he turned and followed them. As he got closer, the voices sorted themselves into a man and woman's, the latter of which Ren knew. He'd found her.

He rounded the corner. Morgaine stood against the wall, her fists balled at her sides and lips drawn back in a sneer. Lord Scara stepped toward her, his head tilted to the side as if he was examining something curious.

"You're right," he was saying, "but you are no lady, Morgaine."

"As you are no man," she hissed. She drew her hand back, but Scara grabbed her wrist before she could slap him.

"Hold your tongue," he snarled. "You'll not speak to me this way in my own home. Should I call the guards on you, Morgaine? Or should I cast you out into the forest?"

Ren scowled. "I ask that you don't, my lord," he said, striding forward. "Or I would have come all this way for naught."

Morgaine and Scara's heads snapped to Ren. She shoved Scara away.

"This doesn't concern you, hunter."

"Doesn't it?"

Scara's upper lip curled. He turned to Morgaine. "Call your dog off."

Her eyes bore into Ren. "He's no dog," she said, and hope flared in him until she added, "He doesn't come when he's called."

Morgaine stepped around Scara and strode down the hall without looking back.

Scara looked at Ren, mischief in his blue eyes, and said, "Women are lovely when they're angry, aren't they? Even when they banish us to the kennels."

"By the gods," Ren muttered. He followed Morgaine, hastening his step when the swish of her blue skirts disappeared around the corner. He trailed her down the hall, through twisted corridors, and up two flights of stairs. Morgaine quickened her pace when they reached the guest wing, hurrying to one of the doors and fumbling with the knob. She turned to slam the door, but Ren shoved his foot in its way and stopped it with his hand.

"Morgaine, please," he said, trying to meet her eyes through the crack. "We need to talk."

She huffed, but stepped away from the door. Ren closed it behind him and stood in the middle of the room, his cloak still draped over one arm.

Morgaine crossed her arms. "I suppose you thought you'd have some fun with me?" Her voice dripped venom. "Toy with me? Tell me you're coming to Solstice and then ignore every one of my letters after so I understand you've thrown me aside?"

"Little—"

"*No.*" She'd been firm with him before, even harsh, but never this cold—never this angry. "Why didn't you write back?"

Ren took a deep breath. He had to watch his words, or the entire horror would come spilling out—he couldn't tell her everything. Telling her the whole story would force him to confront the memory, and he wasn't ready. "I was on a job."

"For who?"

"The king of Jasniostvo."

She sighed. "Ren—"

"It's true." Did she really think he'd lie? He might have

wanted to watch his words, but she had to know he wouldn't lie. "He keeps an old friend of mine, Sanne Esclarmonde, on retainer. The Keep sent out word that she needed help, and I'd just crossed the border into Jasniostvo. I was the closest, so I went. When I reported to the Stained Palace, I was forbidden from writing to you. The king only wanted me to communicate with the Keep, and even then, Sanne oversaw my correspondence."

The fury in her eyes would've been beautiful if it hadn't been aimed at him. "She couldn't have been convinced to let you send me any explanation?"

He frowned. He had. "I was permitted one letter before Kyr was taken to the aviary. Did you not get it?"

A twitch of movement caught his eye—her fists had clenched. "I did, but it was unreadable."

"What do you mean?"

She opened the chest at the foot of her bed and pulled out a letter. Morgaine held it between them, the folded parchment as accusing as the tip of a blade.

Ren opened it. His heart sank. His letter had been dismembered with black slashes. All that remained legible was that he was in Jasniostvo and was no longer able to write—not his explanation of why or by whose order, not his desire to return to her, not how he missed her. "Do you really think I intended for you to receive it like this?"

"No, but I—" Her voice shook. She tried again. "That is all I had: the words on this page, Ren, and those words rejected me. I wrote a reply, but Kyr never arrived to take it." Tears glittered in her eyes. "*That* hurt more than the letter itself, that you'd deny me even the opportunity to respond."

"But that wasn't what I wanted!" His voice came out louder and sharper than he meant, but he was just so tired: tired of being misunderstood, tired of waiting for her, tired of having to hold himself back when she was right in front of him. He stepped toward her. "Please, Morgaine. That wasn't what I wanted to happen."

She stepped back. "But that's what happened anyway."

"I know." Ren rubbed his hands down his face. "And I'm sorry. But I wanted nothing more than to finish the hunt so I could come back to you. I thought of you every night, and when I was healing I dreamed of you, and—"

"Healing from what?"

Ren dropped his cloak. He immediately wanted to pick it back up. "I'm not sure what to show you first." He wasn't sure he wanted to show her at all—he wanted her to know what he'd lived through to make it back, for her to see how much he'd wanted to be with her again, but it was going to scare her. He lowered his head, angling it so his broken horn was at her eye level. "This, I suppose."

"Oh." Her voice was soft and close, and he felt the pressure of her touch on the horn's chipped edge. "What did this?"

"A wraith threw me from a dais." Ren slipped off his gloves. Though the darkness was fading, his veins seemed to leap from his skin. He held out his palms. "There's also this."

She gasped. "Are you sick?"

"No." Before he lost his nerve, he shrugged out of his coat. It fell to the floor with his gloves. Ren met her eyes—if he stopped now, he didn't know when he'd find the strength to show her again. The memory of what had done this to him hovered too close to his consciousness. Its voice whispered too intimately in his mind. He needed to show her and he needed to be done with it. "Before I show you the rest, I want you to know that I'm healing, alright?"

Her brows furrowed, but she nodded. Ren raised his shirt.

Her jaw dropped. "Oh, Ren." Her fingers, gentle as a breath, traced the veins in his torso, the outlines of the ugly yellow-green bruises that splattered his left side, the edges of his bloodstained bandage. Her eyes flicked up to his before returning to his wounds. "I only saw the creature's blood. What did this to you?"

He'd gone so long without breaking down over his last hunt. He'd told himself he hadn't had the time, that this was the way it was for Nightmares: get hurt, rest only as much as you could, heal, and keep hunting. At the Keep, injuries were met with a sympathetic pat on the back—if your back wasn't damaged—and an "I'm sorry, brother." But here, with a woman whose eyes gathered with tears and who touched him like he was delicate, Ren felt the breaking come.

He took Morgaine by the waist and wrapped her in his arms. One hand went to the back of her head; he brushed his fingers against her ribbon-woven braid and let its softness soothe him. His tears dampened her hair. "There was something in that palace I've never seen before." Her head was pressed against his chest, probably too firmly, but he didn't want to let her go. He wanted her to hear his heartbeat. "Something ancient. It nearly killed me. It punctured my lung and broke three of my ribs. The healers told me I was getting no air, and that I could have bled out. And my veins—" He swallowed, unable to voice it. He'd only felt the emptiness of the thing's feeding a moment before losing consciousness—his godhood had been restored by the time he woke—but the hollowness haunted him. He hadn't known that feeling nothing could feel so sharp.

If Morgaine had questions, she didn't voice them. Her arms tightened around him, and her chest expanded against his as she breathed.

"I lost days while the healers tended to me," he continued. "I woke on the seventh and left the next day. Kyr wasn't with me until then. All I could think of was you, and how I'd made you a promise. I rode nonstop until I reached Tanglewood. I thought I could make it in time, but I didn't, so I tracked you here." He kissed the top of her head. "I'm sorry. I'm sorry for not making it in time, and not being able to write, and ruining your dress." His next kiss landed at her hairline. "But I'm here now, and I want to spend Solstice with you."

Morgaine didn't move, just kept her head buried in Ren's chest and her body pressed against his. "I don't...I don't know what to say."

Ren understood. Her life was still and quiet—the people of Tanglewood didn't live their lives only steps from Oddelen's threshold. She'd likely never known someone who'd almost met a violent death. "You don't have to say much," he murmured. "Just tell me you want me to stay."

He expected a smile, maybe a nod or a breathless *yes*, but Morgaine hesitated. "I do," she said, leaning back, "but won't you leave again?"

"Not for a while."

Her brow furrowed. "How—"

A knock sounded at her door. They startled apart moments before Brilde opened the door and poked her head into the room. "We're about to—oh." Her green cheeks grew plump as she smiled. "Am I interrupting?"

Morgaine flushed. She stammered for a moment before Ren reached into his pocket and pulled out her hair ribbon.

"Not at all," he said. "I came to return this."

"I see." Brilde turned to Morgaine. "Are you still coming to shop with us?"

"Yes." Morgaine snatched the ribbon from Ren's hand and turned to the mirror to weave it back through her hair. "Just give me a moment."

Azra's head appeared in the doorway. "How long is a moment? I'm afraid the mayoress will buy the bracelets I had my eye on before we get there. Oh, hello, Ren."

He'd knelt to retrieve his cloak from the floor, but raised a hand in greeting anyway.

At the mirror, Morgaine muttered and threw the ribbon down—Ren thought he'd heard a particularly nasty swear among the muttering, but he wasn't sure. "Let's go, then." She drew her cloak over her shoulders and headed into the hall without another look at him.

Azra motioned for Ren to come along, a smile spreading over her face.

Ren, as he always did when Morgaine was involved, followed.

———

When he wasn't running through it with the aim of avoiding guards, Ren found the bailey a soothing place to be. The air smelled of snow and stirred-up earth, of horses and roasting meat. A retinue of guards was changing shifts, their measured steps reminiscent of the way Ren and his fellow trainees would swap guard shifts at the Keep. About a dozen townspeople had reached the bailey before Ren, Morgaine, Brilde, and Azra, and though their steps were slower than those of the guards, they were no less purposeful. The townspeople drifted between the same canvas tents Ren had seen the day before, exchanging coin for trinkets and gifts.

Azra disappeared into the nearest tent, sighing with relief when she noticed a bracelet made of silver links. "Thank the gods."

"Miss Greywarren!"

Ren and Morgaine looked to a grey tent across the square, where an old male gloam elf with black skin and white hair beckoned her over. "Are you going to come take another look?" he called. "I'm sure we can make another good deal."

Morgaine shook her head. "I've spent my last bit of coin, sir!"

The vendor gave an exaggerated sigh, but didn't press further. The table before him glittered with knives.

"What did you buy?" Ren murmured.

Morgaine waved a hand. "Just something to protect myself with."

He frowned. He trailed after her, peppering her with questions as they went from vendor to vendor, but Morgaine refused to answer. "I'm hungry," she said, cutting him off mid-question, "and something smells wonderful. Would you mind finding us something to eat?"

Ren smelled it too, the heavenly fragrance of yeast and spice and sugar making his stomach growl. "Clever way to get rid of me," he muttered.

Morgaine smiled. "Thank you."

Ren turned on his heel. He couldn't bring himself to be truly annoyed with her—it felt too good to be needed. He left Morgaine in the bookseller's tent, scribbling titles down onto a scrap of paper, and followed the divine scent to a cart parked in the nearest corner. Strips of pastry rolled around wooden cylinders rotated over a small fire, the pastry baking golden brown in the heat.

"Have you ever had a chimney roll before?" an elven man asked, grinning. His bronze skin shimmered, though the sunlight didn't reach under the roof of his cart. Such was the way with bronzed elves—they were the creation of the goddess Svetlen and had been made for her light.

Ren hadn't, so he bought one, biting into the steaming pastry as he walked back to the marketplace. He had to stop his eyes from rolling back into his head. It was *delicious.*

"Gods above," he mumbled, his mouth full of cinnamon- and nutmeg-spiced dough. The baker had drizzled the chimney roll with honey before giving it to Ren, and he licked honey from his fingers as he searched the bailey for Morgaine.

He found her outside a dressmaker's tent, running her fingers over a bolt of red velvet. "I couldn't," she was saying to the seamstress, a tall woman whose deep purple dress hugged every curve. "Even with your enchantments. I don't have the coin for it."

The seamstress smiled. "But it would be such a lovely color on you."

Ren agreed. He stepped forward and asked, "For what she's wanting, how much would you charge?"

"For the cut and fabric she wants?" The seamstress' brow furrowed as her eyes swept Morgaine's figure. "Three gold. But for the style I would recommend—" Her eyes flicked to Ren and twinkled. She was about to make a sale, and they both knew it. "Six."

"When would it be done?"

"By the duke's Solstice feast tomorrow evening." The seamstress motioned to the table behind her, which held a filigreed sewing machine and small assortment of clear vials, all of which were filled with potions in varying shades of brown. "My equipment is enchanted. I'd only need to take her measurements, collect payment, and dictate the design for the work to begin."

"It's a fascinating process," Morgaine said, still stroking the velvet, "but truly, I don't—"

Ren held seven gold coins out to the seamstress. "She'll try to make herself happy with the cheapest option you have. Don't let her."

Morgaine started to protest, but Ren and the seamstress ignored her as the coin changed hands. "I have dresses," she said, tugging Ren's arm. Her eyes widened when she saw the fat coin pouch in his hand. "You don't need to buy me a new one—"

"I ruined one of yours. Consider this a replacement."

The seamstress arched a brow. "Ruined it?"

Ren could imagine what the seamstress was thinking—a ripped dress on the floor by a bed. He didn't hate the thought. "What else do you need to get started? Her measurements?"

"Indeed." The seamstress motioned Morgaine forward. "Take your cloak off, Miss—?"

"Greywarren," Morgaine said, doing as the seamstress asked. Ren stood at the edge of the tent's entrance as the seamstress waved her hands around Morgaine's body, directing the enchanted measuring tape to take the circumference of Morgaine's hips and waist.

"I haven't met many Greywarrens," the seamstress said. She nodded to Ren. "Let alone ones with such generous benefactors."

Ren fought the urge to roll his eyes. *Benefactors*, as if a Greywarren couldn't make a living for themselves. "Our relationship isn't like that, madam," he said. "It's just a gift."

"Then what is it like?" the seamstress asked, returning Morgaine's cloak. Her eyes swept over Ren, as if assessing the value of his clothing and weapons. "You're not just a friend, not at my rates. Are you her husband? Lover?" The seamstress tilted her head and smiled. "I should have enough fabric left to make you a matching coat or vest, if you'd like."

"The dress is enough." Morgaine snatched her cloak and swept it over her shoulders.

The seamstress laughed. "Very well. You can expect it tomorrow, Miss Greywarren."

"Thank you." Morgaine left the tent, letting the worst of her scowl slip when her back was to the seamstress.

Ren followed. "It's an awkward way to drum up business, isn't it?" He tore off a bit of the chimney roll and offered it to her.

She took it and chewed, her brow wrinkled in thought. "Where did you get that much gold?"

Ren thought of the pack Sanne had shoved into his hands as he'd fled the Stained Palace, of the four rare books and the impressive pouch of coin it had contained. "The same place I got your Solstice gifts."

She stopped. "You got me Solstice gifts?"

He stilled, too, his cloak sweeping snow onto his feet. "Of course."

Morgaine's jaw ticked. "Then go cancel the dress order."

"I will do no such thing."

"I see. Is spoiling me a way to assuage your guilt, then?"

If only it was that easy. Ren knew no amount of gold would buy back her faith in him. "It's a way to make up for the things of yours I've ruined." And the list was longer than he'd like it to be: her library, her dress, her security. "Unless you can think of a better way?"

Ren wanted her to snap at him, but it wasn't so; seeing her shoulders drop and her eyes deaden in surrender was worse than the fight he wanted. "I don't want this to be about you buying me things," she said. "I want this, whatever this is, to be about *us*, but we both know you can't—" Morgaine stepped back. Her eyes welled with tears. "I need to be alone."

He reached for her—he could tell her about his leave now. "Little love, please—"

"I need to be alone," she repeated. "I'll see you at dinner. Thank you for the dress."

Ren watched her go. He understood why most Nightmares kept to the road, why many of his brothers didn't like putting down roots anywhere other than the Keep: it was to avoid this, to avoid the pain of seeing what their absence had done to those they'd left behind. To avoid facing the knowledge that, one day, they'd leave again.

But for Ren, that day was months away, so he stood in the center of the bailey and watched Morgaine hurry back into the castle. She needed time, and for once, he had that to give.

———

Hrascara's great hall was located on the ground floor of the castle. Ren and the townspeople had been forbidden from going in.

Linds, one of the maidservants standing guard outside the hall's double doors, had shaken her head and crossed her arms when Ren had tried to enter. "We're still preparing," she'd said. "The duke has requested that no guests enter until dinner. Your friends have scattered among the parlors and receiving rooms." She pointed to Ren's left, where three open doors led to rooms bustling with activity and laughter. "We'll fetch you when it's time."

Ren smiled at her. "Thank you, Linds."

She nodded again, but this time with a small smile on her lips. "You're welcome, sir."

Ren entered the first room he reached. The stuffed heads of bucks, bears, and other game hung around the top of the room, looking down on the townspeople who slouched in brown leather chairs and slung legs over the arms of couches. The seating was concentrated around small tables, whose dark wood shone beneath carved game boards and stone coasters. A fire roared in the hearth, though the crackling of its logs was drowned out by competitive chatter.

Ren drifted to a stone-topped sideboard and poured himself a cup of tea while he watched the games. Byrne and Oren faced off over a deck of cards at one table, their friends cheering on their favored brother. Azra was playing Zijustvan chess with Kerra, Vess' wife, and another card game was starting at the table nearest the hearth.

"You're cheating!" Oren shouted, scowling at his brother.

"I'm not!"

"Then where are my face cards?"

They didn't realize that many cards were scattered beneath their table. Ren finished his drink and set down the teacup, intending to walk over and tell them, but stopped short when he saw the cards lift as if swept up by a breeze. They danced and leapt over each other before settling atop Oren's boots.

Ren frowned. Oren and Byrne were too focused on their card game to have cast any low-level spell on the cards, and the boys around them showed no signs of doing so—no hands were hastily shoved into pockets to conceal a ward, no boy nudged another to show off his prestidigitation. Something else had moved the cards.

A pocket door sat open to Ren's left, and he slipped through it to the adjoining room. The room was marginally quieter—he could actually hear the crackling of the fire—but still full of talk. A low table was laden with cheeses, fruits, and crackers; townspeople had crammed themselves onto the couches and were talking around the food in their mouths and hands. Baba, seated in an armchair at the head of the table, smiled and waved to Ren.

Ren waved back, but his attention was on the candelabra against the wall behind Baba. No one was around to blow on it, yet the small flames guttered and went out before reigniting on their own. As Ren watched, his apprehension spreading through him like a weed, the flames shaped themselves into five-pronged arrows.

A woman on the couch nearest Ren shrieked, running a hand over her red hair and glaring at the man beside her. "Stop pulling my hair," she hissed, cutting her eyes at him.

He raised his hands. "Tamsin, love, it wasn't me—"

"Bull—"

Ren watched as another lock of Tamsin's hair lifted of its own accord. "Gods above," he muttered. This was geist activity. It seemed no one had told the spirits he was on leave.

He started forward, reaching for the precautionary dagger he always wore at his thigh, but halted when a servant strode into the room. "Dinner will be served immediately in the great hall," he said. "Please find your seats by locating your place cards."

The townspeople began to leave. Ren wrapped his fingers around the hilt of his dagger and stepped deeper into the room. He intended to inspect the candelabra, but stopped when the servant cleared his throat. "Hunter?"

Though a head shorter than Ren, the servant managed to look down his nose at him—the perfect fit for the Scara household. The servant motioned to the door. His eyes never left Ren, and Ren knew this man wasn't going to leave him alone. "His Grace looks forward to serving you."

———

Ren had been seated at the end of the great hall's massive table, his place marked by a card that read *"Hunter"* in looping calligraphy. Any other time, he would have been insulted by the dismissal of his position—he wasn't just a hunter, he was a Nightmare hunter, and by the gods, there was a great difference—but he was too busy searching the hall for signs of the spirit to care. How long had the geist activity been going on? For how long had he failed to notice?

He didn't notice when Duke Scara entered the hall. Azra, who was seated to his left, nudged him with her elbow. Ren hastily stood—everyone else already had—but darted his eyes around the room, taking in the vaulted ceiling and exposed rafters that had been draped with fragrant pine boughs. The massive chandelier above the table rocked gently from side to side, but its dozens of candles burned steadily. The candles that studded the greenery-laden tablescape of the feasting table also did, though Ren half-expected one of them to lift and set one of the red bows on the backs of their chairs on fire.

"Welcome, everyone," Duke Scara said, his sonorous voice carrying from the head of the table to where Ren stood at the foot. He was the perfect prediction of what Lord Scara would look like in twenty years; his hair was light grey, and his blue eyes sat deeply in his wrinkled face. Age had given him a belly, though Ren could see remnants of strength in the shoulders beneath the duke's coat. "My son and I are pleased that you all accepted our invitation to celebrate Solstice with us. Please consider this Solstice Eve feast your formal welcome to Hrascara."

The greeting continued, but was drowned out by Azra leaning over to Ren and whispering, "You missed this conversation on our carriage ride here, but we think we were only invited because Lord Scara feels guilty for the role he played in what happened at Sisters' Harvest."

Ren's eyebrows raised. "Guilty?" he murmured, taking his seat when everyone else did. "I didn't realize he could feel such a thing."

Waitstaff entered the hall and began to serve wine and mead, filling the duke's cups with both when he couldn't choose.

"So we're to get the dregs," Oren, who was across the table, muttered.

"Don't be rude," his mother chided. "You're not to get any alcohol at all."

Oren rolled his eyes as Byrne laughed. "Just be glad we're not responsible for cleaning up." He turned his attention to Ren. "Do you have any new stories for us, Ren?"

Ren had to be asked a second time—he'd been looking for Morgaine, and was dismayed to find her only a seat away from Lord Scara. "I'm afraid I don't," he said. Was it a lie? Absolutely, but the only story he could think of was what had happened in Jasniostvo. A celebration like this didn't need that darkness.

He chose the mead when the waitstaff asked, but took small

sips. Another set of staff had already started serving the soup course to the head of the table. The rafters were still quiet. The chandelier still gently swayed. Duke Scara talked and laughed with the mayoress, and Lord Scara spoke with Brilde while stealing glances at Morgaine. Nothing seemed amiss, but the bit of dread in Ren's stomach had grown to the size of a stone. Another stronghold, another spirit. What secrets slunk about in Hrascara's halls? What horror was this geist going to reveal to him?

"Would everyone like soup?"

Ren and those around him nodded, awkwardly shifting from side to side to allow the waiter to ladle pumpkin soup into their bowls with little obstruction. None of the soup meant for Ren, however, made it into his bowl—the terrine was knocked from its cart and spilled its contents onto him, the hot liquid burning through his pants and the bottom edge of his black tunic.

"By the gods," he hissed, leaping from his chair.

"I'm so sorry, sir!" The waiter reached for the extra cloth napkins on his cart. His face was pale. "I didn't mean—"

"It's not your fault," Ren said through grit teeth. At least the soup had missed his bandages. "You can't—get down!"

He tackled the waiter to the floor as the soup terrine across the table flew toward them. It crashed into the wall behind them, clanging horribly against the stone.

Screams reached Ren's ears before he could stand. "Get out," he grunted to the waiter, fumbling along his soaked legs for his dagger. He stood and swept the room for the geist, but what he saw wasn't a geist at all.

The half-translucent image of a dark-haired human woman hovered before the fireplace, her once rich dress now dark brown tatters hanging from her gaunt figure. Ren swore. He'd been wrong. It was an apparition—the spirit left behind by someone who'd died without closure. Nightmares rarely dealt with this type of haunting. Like wraiths, apparitions were mortal souls that had gotten stuck between life and death; apparitions, however, had managed to resist the corruption of the orderless realm between, and were reportedly few in number. They were a degree closer to their humanity than wraiths, but that made no difference to Ren. They still defied the order of life and death established by Zikat and Oddelen—the order that Nightmare hunters were tasked with preserving. The apparition had once breathed and ached and lived like Ren did now, but that would matter little under Nightmare steel.

The apparition raised a shriveled hand and pointed at Ren. "*You!*" she wailed, her mouth gaping wide, her jaw swinging against her torso. She disappeared from the hearth and manifested behind Ren, her too-long nails tearing at him before she again vanished and reappeared behind a screaming Kerra. Ren's shirt opened at the shoulder, revealing his full Nightmare tattoo.

"Get out!" Ren barked at the townspeople. The apparition howled and rose to the ceiling. Silverware and metal goblets lifted into the air around her. The tips of the knives and forks pointed at Ren. The townspeople and staff had run to the edges of the room, the crowd of them flowing from the walls to the door. The Scaras had leapt to their feet, the Duke drawing a sword that would do him no good. Lord Scara only stood and stared. And Morgaine—Ren shouted at her to move. She was *standing* and not *running*, fumbling with something beneath her skirt.

"*Nightmare!*" the apparition shrieked, her voice two-toned, half of the grave and half alive. "*You dare return to this castle? You would mock me in this way?*"

"You have me confused!" Ren shouted, stepping onto his chair and then the table, crushing tree branches beneath his boots. "I've never been to this castle. I'd remember a face like yours."

"*Lies!*" Some of the knives shot toward him. The apparition cackled as Ren danced to avoid them. "*You did not banish the wraith! See how it ruined me!*" She swept down until she was at eye level with Ren. The smell of her was stomach-turning, the stench of offal and grave dirt drifting on a stagnant breeze. She lifted her hands and reached for Ren's temples. "*Share in my madness, hunter.*"

Just before her touch connected, a dagger embedded itself in her translucent neck. The apparition hissed and turned her head to find the source of the attack, but Ren didn't make the same mistake. He sank his dagger into the other side of the spirit's neck, driving it in until only the hilt protruded. He kept his grip tight and began speaking the geist banishment spell—apparitions were so rare they had no banishment spell of their own, and it was left to a Nightmare's discretion which technique to use. The apparition behaved like a geist, so Ren would destroy it like one.

Before he could complete the spell, however, the spirit disappeared. Echoes of its departing shriek dissipated in the air, leaving a stunned silence to settle over the hall.

Ren dropped his hands to his knees, shutting his eyes and breathing deeply—his ribs ached again. He opened his eyes only when the scents of pine, firewood, and spilt pumpkin soup cleared the spirit's stench from his nose and his pain had recessed. He squatted and retrieved his dagger, which had fallen to the table when the apparition disappeared. Odd—there was another Nightmare dagger on the table, its blade the same steel-and-copper swirl as Ren's, though its hilt was wrapped with brown leather instead of black.

A pale, slim hand reached out and snatched it.

"You're hurt." Morgaine stood before him, reaching for his torn shirt. She clutched the dagger in her other hand.

"You know these bandages aren't new." He hopped to the floor. First the Order's introductory textbook, now this—where in the three hells was she getting Nightmare supplies? "Where did you get that dagger? It's not yours."

"I paid for it, so yes, it is."

Just something to protect myself with. "Gods above," Ren muttered, reaching for it. He was going to have some words with that elven vendor. "You're going to get yourself hurt—"

"I'm not the one bleeding," Morgaine snapped, jerking the dagger out of his reach. "The geist cut you."

"She wasn't a geist," Ren said just as sharply. How did

Morgaine expect to banish a spirit if she couldn't even identify it? "She was an apparition. She was human once."

"Indeed," Duke Scara said as he approached, slightly out of breath and fumbling with his sword—it wouldn't slide back into its ceremonial scabbard. "If I recall correctly, that was my great-great-aunt Silia." He shuddered. "A horrible woman. I used to have nightmares from the stories my father told me."

"What happened to her?"

Lord Scara, who stood behind his father, rolled his eyes. "Didn't you hear? Clearly, one of your ilk failed to protect her from some spirit. Dare I say that your presence is what brought her back?" He crossed his arms. "Hrascara was quite peaceful before you arrived."

Ren wanted to drive his fist into the lord's smug face, but the younger Scara had a point. "It's possible," he grumbled. "If one of my brothers played a role in her death, then yes, my presence may have caused an awakening."

"Then I'm glad you're here to fix it, Nightmare." Duke Scara patted Ren on his shoulder and went to attend to the townspeople and staff who'd gathered in the corners of the room.

"You heard my father," Lord Scara snipped. Though his tone was short, his eyes glittered, and Ren knew he enjoyed this. "Fix this. How can we properly celebrate with an ongoing haunting?"

The cut at Ren's shoulder was beginning to sting, and beneath the bandages, his ribs throbbed. He could say no. He could tell Lord Scara that, actually, he'd been so badly hurt that he was forbidden from hunting, and enjoy seeing the lord scramble for a solution.

The words were about to spill from his lips when motion caught his eye—Morgaine had taken a cloth napkin from the table and was wiping the apparition's unblood from her Nightmare dagger. If Ren said no, would she hunt in his stead?

Ren looked at the crowd of townspeople. Though the hall was dim—many of the candles had gone out during the apparition's attack—he saw shaking shoulders and tearstained faces.

They were afraid. They hadn't thought this would happen again.

The townspeople needed him.

Ren turned to Lord Scara. If the Triumvirate found out, he could be punished for disobeying their order. He needed to go about this quickly and without getting hurt—and be well compensated for the additional risk. "Alright. I'll hunt. But first, my lord, let us discuss my payment."

———

Solstice Eve should have been a night for revelry, but Hrascara was quiet and still in the darkness.

Ren suspected he was the only living creature up and about. From the height of the moon, which he made sure to note each time he passed a window, he estimated it was an hour after midnight. Hrascara's halls bore a chill that hadn't been noticeable before, but the apparition had been absent since her dinner debut. No other spirits had manifested. Ren had half a mind to return to his chamber, tend to his wounds, and fall into bed, but two things kept him moving through the castle: first, the realization that he didn't know his way around Hrascara without a companion or a servant's directions, which was essential for a successful hunt, and second, that a massive stag's head hung over his bed. The apparition was manifesting geist abilities, and the last thing he needed was to wake up impaled.

Ren ascended a staircase to the second floor, following the hallway to a mezzanine that looked onto the great hall. Arched doorways were dotted around the mezzanine; when Ren ducked into the first one, he entered a room colored with shards of prismatic moonlight. Three rows of short birchwood pews with cream velvet cushions faced a white stone altar, atop which sat a bronze statuette of Svetlen, the goddess of light. Unlit candles sat in gold candlesticks.

Ren walked to the altar. He didn't often pray to Svetlen—if

he were to choose a third deity to worship, it would be Zatva, the spiteful goddess of nature—but Sanne did, and he'd left her in Jasniostvo to recover from their hunt alone. He struck a match and lit one of the candles for her, murmuring a prayer for healing under his breath. His Svetlenic dialect was rusty, but he believed it was the intent behind a prayer that mattered most, and he was sure Svetlen would understand.

The next chapel was dark and gloomy, dedicated either to the death god Oddelen or his sister Sumra, the goddess of night. Ren didn't stay long enough to differentiate—he'd prayed to Oddelen in his chambers before beginning his hunt, and the chapel was empty. Knowing where it was located was enough to satisfy him.

He stepped into a third chapel. It was as tiny as the others, housing no more than three rows of pews and an altar. The six statuettes atop it were in the image of Zikat, her pointed ears and lean body lovingly sculpted from white granite. Candles of varying thicknesses, heights, and hues of green burned around the room—some in candelabras, some in wall sconces, some in molten wax heaps upon the altar. Two floor-to-ceiling windows behind the altar showed Tmadrev Forest, the snow-laden trees twinkling silver in the moonlight.

A woman sat in the front pew, her head bowed. Ren recognized her pale blue nightgown and her soft weeping—it broke his heart that he knew the sound of it so well. He sat in the pew behind Morgaine. "You should be in bed."

She didn't speak. Though dim, the colored light was enough for him to piece together how she'd braided her hair; he imagined her in her chambers, weaving her hair into one long braid and coiling it around itself until it was flat against the nape of her neck and comfortable for sleeping. He imagined her slender fingers weaving this new ribbon, which matched her nightgown, through the braid until it was secure. If he took one end of the ribbon and tugged, would she let him? Would she let him run his fingers through her hair until it fell loose around her shoulders? Would she relax then? Would she forgive him?

"Are you having nightmares again?"

"I am having nightmares *still*."

A few curls, too short for her braid, brushed the nape of her neck. Ren wanted to touch them, but stopped himself. "What about?"

"The forest." Her voice was barely a whisper. "Before the hunters found me."

"Do you want to tell me—"

"No."

Outside, snow began to fall. Ren tracked a flake from the top of the window to the bottom, watching it take its meandering path to the ground below. Just before it disappeared from sight, another snowflake brushed against it. The two joined together and vanished.

"Do you think the gods make mistakes?"

His answer was easy, thoughtless. "No."

She laughed, but it was hollow. "Of course not," she muttered. "One of their faithful would never think so."

Ren left his pew. The cold of the flagstones seeped into his skin when he knelt before Morgaine. "Talk to me, little love."

She didn't look at him. Candlelight reflected in her dark eyes, small sparks in a flat void. "I thought I would always be in Tanglewood," she said. "Over the last eleven years, I accepted that I'd likely live out my days and die there. It was a nice idea at first. I had a place to call mine. I had food. I had work. I had good people around me—you know this story. But what I haven't told you is that as the years wore on, it began to bore me. I told myself that it was good to be bored, because boredom meant I was safe. My life didn't feel quite mine, as you know, so what did it matter if I was bored? I had no real potential being wasted. I was alive only because of Tanglewood, so back to Tanglewood my life would go. I resigned myself to reading about the rest of the world and knowing I'd only ever see it that way.

"But then I met you." Her voice thickened with tears. "And the things I read about became real."

He wanted to ask which things. Instead, he rested a hand on her knee and said, "But then I left."

"Yes. You left." A tear fled down her cheek, disappearing under her jaw before she could swipe it away. "And for everyone else, it was like you were never there. But I remembered. We wrote, and with each of your letters, I hated Tanglewood a little more. I wanted to leave, but what could I do? I'm terrified of the forest. I know no one outside of Tmadrev. I was stuck. I *am* stuck —even coming to Hrascara, I'm here with the town—and you were on the verge of death a kingdom away and I had no way of knowing it." Her voice trembled, but she forced out, "I don't understand how the gods can create a world that is so big and beautiful and horrible and allow me to see so little of it."

Tears streamed down her face, but she kept staring at the statuettes of Zikat. Ren sat beside her. Silence spread between them like mold. The gods, the realm, the Order, Sanne—they all needed him, all in such different ways and degrees that Ren knew he could never be everything to everyone. He could try, and he did, but he'd accepted that he would never be enough to do it all. The acceptance had brought him a guilty, yet stubbornly held, peace; all he could give was the best parts of himself for as long as he could.

"I just want something that's mine," Morgaine said, and her words were almost a whimper.

Someone always needed him more. But no one had ever needed him like Morgaine did, and he wanted to give her everything. "You have me."

He didn't know what broke him open more: the hope in her eyes or the doubt in her next words. "Do I?"

Ren took her hand and tugged her to the floor before the altar. "Kneel with me."

Morgaine lowered to her knees beside him, bowing her head when he did.

Ren closed his eyes and began to pray. He knew Morgaine didn't understand the Zikatic dialect, but he hoped she'd be comforted nonetheless, and perhaps even understand that he was praying for her. He laid himself bare before Zikat, confessing everything he'd repressed for the sake of his hunt: the fear that reared its head whenever he remembered what happened in Jasniostvo, the nagging knowledge that he'd soon have to face that memory, the anxiety that one day his protection wouldn't be enough, the opposite pulls he felt whenever he thought of what Morgaine and the Order each wanted from him. He told Zikat that what he felt for Morgaine frightened him. He told Zikat that he was the reason the woman beside him couldn't sleep, that he was the reason she was hurting, and that he knew he was ultimately powerless to stop it. He told Zikat that Morgaine needed her help. He begged for it, because he knew Morgaine wouldn't.

When he opened his eyes, his vision was blurry with tears. Morgaine was weeping, too; a teardrop winked in the candlelight as it dropped from her cheek to the flagstones. She reached for him and he pulled her to his chest, burying his neck in the crook of her shoulder.

"You have me," he murmured, rocking her. "For as long as you want me, you have me."

She sobbed against him. Ren didn't know how long he held her on the chapel floor, only that when she pulled away, his arms and legs had gone stiff from the position he'd been in, and that his ribs ached again. He'd been saving his final tincture. Perhaps it was time to use it.

Morgaine took one of his hands and turned it up. She ghosted her fingers over his palm. The darkness had mostly faded, but for a moment, Ren saw his veins blackened like soot. "When you showed me the darkness, it looked like the plague," she whispered. She looked up at him, her lashes damp and glistening, her eyes red. "Were you sick, Ren?"

Her words provoked an acidic feeling in his stomach, and a connection between Jasniostvo and Tanglewood that he didn't want to follow. There would be time to pull that thread later. "No, little love. This was—" Ren swallowed and, for a moment, thought purple eyes flashed at him from the corner. He raised his hand to her cheek, and she leaned into his palm. "Now isn't the time. I want to enjoy Solstice."

She sighed, and Ren thanked the gods that she didn't push. "I have no Solstice gift for you."

"That's alright. It's enough just to be here." Ren brushed his thumb across her cheekbone, then her bottom lip. "Although, if you want to grant me a kiss tomorrow, I'll gladly accept."

She let out an amused exhale, but didn't smile. "I can do better than a mere kiss," she said, pushing herself to her feet. Morgaine brushed dust from her skirt. "Give me the night. I'll figure something out."

From the floor, Ren frowned up at her. "You should sleep."

"So should you, yet here we are."

He couldn't argue with that. He took one of her hands and pressed a kiss to it. "When can I see you tomorrow?"

Morgaine thought for a moment, brushing her thumb against the back of his hand. Gods, he'd missed her touch. "I'll come to your chamber in the morning. And I better find you in bed."

Ren grinned, rising. "'Better than a mere kiss,' indeed," he murmured, wrapping a hand around her waist and kissing her forehead.

Morgaine gave that same joyless breath of a laugh, but he thought he saw the ghost of a smile cross her lips. "Because you better have gotten some rest," she said, pushing him away. "I don't care what Scara says. You're still healing."

"Anything you say, little love. Let me walk you to your chamber."

She rolled her eyes, but took his arm when he offered it. "No, take me to the library. Scara gave me the room closest to it. It's the kindest thing he's done in a while."

"It may not be safe—"

"The apparition doesn't want me, remember?"

Ren sighed. He kept his free hand on a sickle as they walked to the library, but they reached the entrance without incident. "Scream if you need me, alright?"

"It's a library. I would never."

Ren glared at her. "Should I come inside, then?"

"No," Morgaine insisted. She placed a hand on the library's door and turned to Ren. She smiled, truly smiled, and he desperately wanted it to be morning. "I don't know how the Order does it, but in Tanglewood, Solstice gifts are meant to be a surprise."

10.14.626

Morgaine didn't get her wish to see him in bed. Ren was already awake when she knocked on his door late the next morning.

"I judged rightly," she said triumphantly, striding into his chamber when he opened the door. "I knew you'd sleep in and miss breakfast."

She carried a covered silver tray in her hands and set it down on the little table in front of the fire. Linds had already been in that morning to feed it.

"I recall someone ordering me to get some rest." Ren grabbed the pack with Morgaine's gift in it and sat in the wingback chair she hadn't taken. Swaths of purple hung under her eyes—she hadn't slept, then—and flour was smudged in her hair and by her knee, but the smile on her face was warm and lovely and real. "Merry Solstice, Morgaine."

"Merry Solstice." She clasped her hands together in her lap and beamed. He couldn't help but smile back. More and more with each letter they'd sent, this had been what he'd wanted: the two of them, safe and alone and together. "Would you like to open yours first?"

He held up the pack. "Would you like to go at the same time?"

She nodded and reached for the bag. Ren closed his hand over the handle of the tray's cover and counted to three; he lifted the cover at the same time she opened the bag's flap.

A misshapen pastry sat on the tray, deep red icing oozing down its sides. She'd garnished the platter with pomegranate seeds and little sprigs of greenery, the way it was traditionally served, but Ren knew the sweet roll by its scent alone: malinilka, a vanilla sponge layered with winterberry and pomegranate filling. If Morgaine had done it right, there'd be a red swirl inside when the pastry was cut. Malinilka was a holiday staple in Rastlinostvo; the horned elves, Ren's people, had developed the recipe. Ren hadn't had it since he was a boy in the Grey home—the mistresses' willingness to make it for special occasions had been one of the few bright spots of his childhood.

"How did you know?"

Morgaine didn't register his question. She stared at the four books in her lap. "Ren, where did you—how did you get these?" She traced the letters on the spines delicately, almost reverentially. She turned to the front matter of the book on top, her eyes widening. "These are *first editions*."

"They're from the Stained Palace. Sanne chose them for you." He'd snuck a look at the books during one of his hour-long rests in Tmadrev. The title page of each book was stamped with the Jasniostvan royal seal, and an adapted version of it indicating that it belonged to the royal library.

"Gods. I don't know what to say." She settled back into the chair, tucking her feet under herself and reading the spines again. "One of these is a history of Tanglewood! I have a newer edition in my library." She looked at him, frowning a little. "And you said Sanne chose these?"

Ren nodded. "I told her you were a librarian. She gave those to me as I was leaving."

"I'll have to write her. These...I can't believe this." Morgaine opened the topmost book and pressed a hand to her mouth. "I'll have to build a special display case."

Atop the silver tray was a pot of coffee, cups of sugar and cream, and two delicate porcelain coffee cups. Ren filled them both. "I could help, if you'd like me to."

"Maybe." She disappeared into the book from the nose down, her dark eyes ticking back and forth as she read.

He cleared his throat, smiling at her when she looked up. "Tell me what you made me, little love."

She blushed. "It's hardly as good as your gift for me," she said, setting her books down. "But I know you're from Rastlinostvo, and I wondered if you ever miss it. I thought baking you something from there would—" Her words faltered. She drew a ribbon from her hair and fiddled with it. "I know it isn't your home," she said quietly, "not really. So I gambled. I'm sorry if it brings up bad memories, but it seemed like a good idea in the morning's third hour, and I didn't have time to second-guess myself and still have something for you."

Ren smiled at her. "It's perfect."

He cut slices for them both, and Morgaine watched him take a bite. For all its odd little lumps and saggy places, the malinilka tasted heavenly. "I much prefer this over what I gave you," Ren said, his mouth too full for the words to come out clearly.

Morgaine rolled her eyes, but smiled as she ate. "It's better than I thought," she said, reaching for one of the steaming cups of coffee. "The kitchen staff looked at me like I was mad when I told them I wanted to bake."

"You'll have to make it for me again."

Their eyes met over their coffee. Morgaine set her cup down. "I don't entertain men who simply pass through."

"I find you plenty entertaining."

She set her empty plate on the table. "You're insufferable," she muttered, turning herself sideways and wedging herself into the chair with one of her books.

Ren knew better than to be insulted. "I think you're wonderful, too."

Morgaine huffed and lifted the book so it obstructed her face. Ren helped himself to another serving of malinilka. He ate it before the windows, watching snow drift lazily down and fill in the footprints left by yesterday's snowball fight. Reia and Kyr, who he hadn't seen since the day before, flickered into form by the bed.

"Where have you been?" he murmured scratching under Kyr's beak when he landed on Ren's shoulder. Kyr pecked at the crumbs on Ren's plate.

There was murmuring behind him, too, and Ren turned to see Morgaine scratching between Reia's ears without pausing her reading. A fullness swelled in Ren's entire being, a happiness he hadn't felt—well. Since the second night of Sisters' Harvest. This was what he could have. This was what he could call home.

He sat on the edge of the bed, taking care not to make much sound, and let himself just look: the snow outside, the fire in the hearth, the warm light the flames cast over the room, his Umbrals relaxed and comfortable, and Morgaine, safe and content and finally nearby. Jasniostvo and its terrors felt worlds away, his shattered ribs and ruined lung like distant memories. Was life always like this outside of the Order, this peaceful and soft?

Ren slid his eyes shut and whispered his morning lauds to Zikat. They ended in whispered thanks this morning, thanks for the rest and the quiet and the reminder of why he hunted: to protect those who always lived like this.

When he opened his eyes, the book had dropped to Morgaine's chest. She'd fallen asleep.

It was easy to admit it to himself, tucked in a warm room with snow falling outside and the horrors of the realm cast away. There was nothing to hide behind here. There was only Ren and his Umbrals and the woman he loved.

He blew out a breath and let himself admit it again.

He loved her.

By the gods, he loved her.

Ren wanted to wake Morgaine and tell her everything: how he felt, how he'd been given respite, how he could stay in Tanglewood and court her and that maybe, somehow, they could make this work. He wanted to tell her what had happened to him, the entire terrible story, and know that he would no longer have to face it alone.

But she was still, and Ren knew he would wait. He pressed a kiss to her forehead, taking the book and setting it down so it wouldn't fall and wake her. The gods knew she'd suffered enough. He couldn't bring her waking nightmares, too, not when he himself couldn't face the entire truth. For just a little longer, he would fight the memories back. He would bear them alone, and he would let Morgaine rest.

Ren picked up *Tanglewood: A History* and settled into the chair across from her. He would let her rest, and he would be here when she woke. They would have time.

He only read a few pages before he fell asleep, too.

———

When Ren came to the great hall for the Solstice feast, Linds was again blocking the entrance.

"It's not time yet, sir," she said, crossing her arms.

Ren crossed his arms, too. "If I'm not to call you 'love'," he said, "I'd prefer it if you didn't call me 'sir'."

Linds scowled. Good—he didn't want her to place him on the same level as the Scaras. "Very well, Ren."

"Thank you, Linds." Ren lowered his voice. "Have you seen anything odd while preparing?"

"Not a thing."

"And you were able to conceal my ax?"

Linds nodded. "It's behind the column nearest your seat."

Ren relaxed the slightest bit. He'd be able to get to his weapon without anyone in his path—there was considerably less risk of collateral damage that way. He just hoped that when the apparition came for him, it wouldn't attack anyone else out of spite. "Will you and the staff be celebrating with us tonight?"

She shook her head. "We don't eat with the Scaras," she said. "It isn't the way things are done with our masters."

"What if we asked you to?"

"You'd likely be laughed at."

"But it's a holiday," Ren said. "You and the staff should at least join us for the dancing."

"Our masters wouldn't like that."

"You'll find we're not like your masters."

"And thank the gods for that."

Ren's heart skipped at the new voice. Morgaine stood behind him, her hands clasped in front of her. The seamstress had kept her word—not only had the velvet dress been finished in time for the feast, but it fit Morgaine perfectly. Like her dress at Sisters' Harvest, this one was full length and long sleeved, but the neckline of this one plunged far lower than the apple-green dress from the festival, exposing her pale sternum. Morgaine wore a thin gold chain around her neck, but no other jewelry; half of her hair fell around her shoulders, while the other half had been braided into a crown and woven with cream ribbons. "Well?" she asked, turning so Ren could see the back of the dress, which dipped as low as the front. The little heels on her boots clicked with each step. "Are you happy with your purchase?"

"Incredibly." Ren couldn't take his eyes off of her. "Are you happy with it?"

"Incredibly." A blush rose to the top of her cheeks. She stepped close and ran her fingers along the dagger holster strapped to his thigh. "I see you're still confusing weaponry with formal wear."

"I seem to remember you liked it." Ren kissed the back of her hand. It was completely devoid of rings, but jewelry wasn't the metal good he was concerned with her having. "We never finished discussing *your* weaponry, little love. You know I can't let you keep that dagger."

Morgaine jerked her hand back, pressing it to the boned bodice of her dress. "I paid for it. It's mine."

"It's a Nightmare's."

"I didn't buy it from a Nightmare," she said. "Think of it this way—I purchased it with gold you gave me. It's as if Nightmare gold paid for it."

He swept his gaze over her figure, searching for any giveaway bumps—that was what he told himself, though it was only partially true. "Do you have it with you?"

"Of course. You're still hunting."

Ren scowled, remembering how she'd lifted her dress the night before. "It's under your skirt, isn't it?"

Morgaine stepped back. "It is."

Ren held out his hand and waited.

She laughed. "I'm not going to give it to you! You'd have to take it off me yourself."

Her gaze snagged on his. The air between them grew taut. The gathered crowd of townspeople shifted, and the jostling shoved him closer to her. Heat flared in the pit of Ren's stomach. "Is that an invitation?" he murmured, lowering his voice so only she would hear. "Because I'm not above it."

He remembered how soft she'd been beneath his touch when they'd kissed at Sisters' Harvest, how she'd greedily initiated. Judging by the hazy look in her eyes, Morgaine was remembering, too. "No," she said, "but you're a decent male. A good one, even. You wouldn't dare touch me like that here."

How had he gone this long without kissing her? "You're right, little love. You'd have to get me alone first."

The doors to the great hall swung open, and the resulting rush of air broke the spell between them. Ren and Morgaine were swept up in the crowd, though he still reached for her hand; they echoed the crowd's awed exclamations and gasps of excitement when they stepped into the great hall.

The servants had outdone themselves. At the Solstice Eve feast, only the rafters and railings of the second-floor mezzanine had been wrapped in greenery; for tonight, however, pine boughs had been arranged on the walls and grand fireplace in massive swags. Snow-laden twigs hung from the chandelier. Two hired mages stood in the corner, signing wards to conjure and direct a gentle snowfall. A bright fire glowed in the hearth. Clusters of candles burned in each corner and along the walls of the room. Candelabras had been grouped along the center of the feast table, the snow on them spelled to remain frozen as if the candelabras had been formed from the snow itself.

"It's beautiful," Morgaine said, craning her neck back to take in every inch of the room. The enchanted snow fell into her hair but didn't melt. "Isn't it?"

Ren had heard stories, probably no more than tales told to caution children from playing in the snow too long, about beautiful women of ice and snow who were said to lure those who wandered through the winter woods to their deaths. *Come with us*, they were said to whisper, *and get warm*. Ren didn't think the stories were true—he'd have learned about these snow-women at the Keep if they were real—but on the off chance they were, he'd always thought he would be able to resist. But if these snow-women of legend looked anything like Morgaine did, the snow bright against her dark hair, he was as good as dead. "It is."

All five dinner courses, to Ren's surprise, passed with little issue. The fare more than made up for last night's interrupted dinner: a fresh batch of sage and pumpkin soup, a salad of winter greens, roast chicken and lamb with sautéed mushrooms. Though it all smelled and tasted incredible, Ren ate small amounts; though the magicked snowfall and cozy lighting did everything it could to tempt him into relaxing, the apparition could appear at any moment. He didn't like that she had been so quiet—a silent spirit, especially one as intelligent as this, meant a plotting spirit. It took a great amount of energy to move material objects like the apparition had, and Ren believed she was lying in wait until she was at her full strength again.

His apprehension made him a terrible dinner guest. Azra tried to engage him in conversation multiple times, only to roll her eyes and give up when he was too distracted to hear her question a third time. During the dessert course, he couldn't take the anticipation any longer. Ren unsheathed his dagger and set it on the table as a waiter placed a small plate of bird's milk cake before him. The Nightmare steel clinked against his plate. Lord Scara, having noticed from the head of the table, met Ren's gaze and shook his head.

Morgaine noticed, too. She lifted her skirt, ignoring how Scara gaped at her bare leg, and set her own dagger on the table. She looked to see if Ren had noticed.

He had. She was going to get herself hurt—at the very least, they were never going to be invited back to Hrascara—but Ren was touched by her solidarity, and even a little proud. She'd had no training, but Morgaine had the heart of a fighter.

Dessert passed without incident. Ren and the townspeople were ushered to an adjoining ballroom, which had been decorated in the same fashion as the hall. A string quintet, nestled into a candlelit corner, played the opening strains of a waltz as the townspeople spread throughout the room.

A hand fell onto Ren's arm before he could find Morgaine. "Would you spare your first dance for me, Nightmare?" Baba asked. She wore a simple green dress, and had woven her silver hair into a braid. "I'd hoped to steal you away at Sisters' Harvest, but you were quite busy."

Ren chuckled, covering the old elven woman's hand with his so he wouldn't have to see her veins. "Of course, Baba. I'd be happy to." He had, in truth, intended to sweep Morgaine into a dance before Scara could claim her, but it was hard for him to say no to Baba. Nightmares died young and jaded, and he found her persevering optimism endearing.

He led Baba to the edge of the dance floor. She leaned her cane against a column and shuffled along, leaning on Ren. Other couples filled the floor around them, moving through the waltz as the music swelled. Ren and Baba, however, were content to rock side to side.

"How is Masha?" Ren asked. The woman in question swirled by with Byrne. She smiled at Ren, but the expression turned to one of gaping shock when she saw her mother in Ren's arms.

Baba met her daughter's eyes, pointed to Ren, and winked. Masha shook her head, turning her attention to Byrne as the waltz swept them away. Baba shrugged. "She is alright. Still unmarried." She sighed. "But there are so few options in our little town. You know that."

Ren smiled. "I recall."

He continued their slow sway as Baba looked him over, her gaze tracing his Nightmare tattoo down the line of his neck and shoulder until it fell on his hands. "There was a darkness here," she said, taking his left hand and inspecting it. The deep purple veins in her hands seemed to draw out the slight discoloration that remained in his. Ren fought not to tear his hand away when his veins seemed to flash black. Baba's bright eyes were sad when she looked at him. "Does the plague still hold this realm in its clutches?"

"Not quite." His ribs ached. For a moment, he was overcome by the sharp horror of not being able to breathe. "This was an isolated incident."

She nodded, seemingly satisfied with his answer. "I hope it wasn't difficult to get the prayers you needed to overcome it. That's how I survived." She chuckled, the sound low and grating. "Twice, if you can believe it. This old heart beat through it all, though I still bear the stains." Baba patted his arm. "We are marked, but we are survivors. I hope these shadows remind you that you've lived."

The waltz ended. Ren kept his hold on Baba as she looped her arm through his, supporting herself so she could applaud with the others. Morgaine stood halfway across the ballroom, the dark red of her dress easy for Ren to find in the crowd. Scara, of course, was at her side, the cobalt blue of his jerkin garish against Morgaine's dress. He leaned down to whisper something to Morgaine, but she wasn't looking; when her eyes met Ren's, she excused herself and left the lord behind.

Baba watched Morgaine weave through the crowd. "I'd hoped

for another dance with you, Nightmare, but I know when I've been beat. Take me back to my cane, please."

Ren complied. He did feel a bit guilty—this had happened at Sisters' Harvest, too, and he didn't want the older elf to grow resentful. "I apologize, Baba—"

She waved away the sentiment and reached for her cane. Once it was firmly in hand and she stood on her own, Baba looked at Ren and smiled. He was starting to grow fond of that knowing look in her eyes. "Think nothing of it. I only ask that you invite me to the wedding."

"May I cut in?"

Baba took Ren's hand and placed it in Morgaine's. *Wedding* echoed in his mind like the chiming of bells. "He's yours."

Morgaine led him to the middle of the floor before he could speak. If Morgaine had heard, though, she said nothing about it.

"Stealing me away from a sweet old lady?" he asked, shaking his head. "For shame, little love. For shame. How's the lord?"

"Two left feet as always. How's your hunt?"

"You know as well as I do." Ren spun her, pulling her close when she came back to him—much closer than he had dared to hold Baba. "We'll all know when she appears again."

Morgaine rose on her toes, looking over Ren's shoulder at the crowd. "I'm surprised you're dancing," she said, "what with the apparition hiding somewhere. Do you think she's watching you?"

"It's possible. But why are you surprised? Do you wish I'd left you to skulk through the halls until sunrise?" He grinned. "Do you want Scara all to yourself?"

Morgaine glared at him. "I'd rather take a turn about the floor with a wraith."

"I danced with you at Sisters' Harvest when said wraith was shrieking for me," he said, rubbing his thumb back and forth on her waist. "You were in danger then as you are now. Does that risk mean I shouldn't enjoy a pretty woman's company?"

She blushed. "This is just like Sisters' Harvest, isn't it?" She looked down at herself and laughed dryly. "I'm even in a velvet dress. You must think my taste is incredibly boring."

"Not at all." Ren skirted his hands lower down her back. By the gods, this had been a worthy use of his gold. "You feel wonderful in it."

Her eyes widened. "There are people here who watched me grow up," she whispered, reaching for his hands and raising them to a chaster place.

Ren laughed; as they moved through the dance, he saw Scara eyeing them. He leaned close. "And there's another man here who wants you." If this was just like Sisters' Harvest, that meant they had time to slip away. His lips brushed the shell of her ear. "Let your dog mark his territory. We had so little time together at Sisters' Harvest."

Her eyes burned a cold fire in the pit of his stomach. "Get me out of here, then," she whispered, lifting her chin as if in a dare. "Get me alone."

Ren slid his hand into hers, fully intending to, but a scream sounded from the other side of the room.

"Gods above," he snapped, Morgaine hissing "goddess' tits" at the same time. The gods were laughing at them. They had to be, for this to be happening *again*.

The apparition hovered by the ballroom's chandelier, rattling the multicolored crystals and howling. "*You will pay*," she screamed, pointing a ragged hand at Ren.

"Go, little love." He pushed Morgaine toward the door. The townspeople had started to flee, Mayoress Soma at the front of the crowd. Duke Scara took up the rear, barking at his son to see to it that Ren finished the spirit off this time.

Morgaine instead reached under her skirt for her Nightmare dagger. "No. Not this time." She gripped the hilt so fiercely that her knuckles whitened. "I'm not running."

The apparition screamed again, the sound shriller than the first. "*Nightmare! Do you not hear me? Do you not fear me?*" She swooped down until she was parallel with the shoe-scuffed floor and shot toward Ren and Morgaine. "*I am your fault!*"

Ren barked the spell and signed the ward for lightlance, summoning a bolt of radiance in each hand. He hurled the glowing javelins at the apparition. She howled as they pierced her from head to foot, her form splitting into halves before rushing up to the ceiling and reforming. The lightlance bolts slid across the floor and collided with a low-hanging tapestry. It burst into flames.

"Are you *mad*?"

Ren and Morgaine turned to Lord Scara, jaws agape. "Why are you still here?" Ren shouted.

"This is my castle, you fool!" Scara strode across the ballroom. "And my father charged me with making sure you do your infernal job!"

The apparition cackled, her laugh spreading along the vaulted ceiling. "*Yes, little nephew. Make him do his job.*"

Scara recoiled. "'Little'?"

Morgaine reared back, but Ren seized her wrist before she could throw the dagger. "It's a bad angle. If you want to help, go get my ax. It's in the great hall."

She huffed, but gave Ren her dagger and ran.

He walked to the middle of the room, spreading his arms wide. His ax was too heavy for Morgaine to easily carry; she'd have to drag it, and that would slow her down. If this went his way, the apparition would be gone before she returned. "Silia, is it? Here I am."

"*Yes.*" The apparition lowered herself to his level, hissing like a serpent. "*The one who failed me was like you. We never should have let him into our halls.*"

Ren forced himself to stay still. The apparition was drifting closer, and he held a dagger in each hand—two daggers for two spectral eyes.

"*I died in a hysteric fugue,*" she continued, "*but in this state, I remembered. I vowed to get my revenge.*"

They attacked at the same time. Ren lunged forward, burying the daggers in the apparition's eyes as the chandelier crashed to the floor where he'd stood moments before. The outermost arms of the chandelier raked down Ren's back. The crystals tore at his clothes and skin. He howled and fell to his knees—but dragged the apparition down with him.

"Ren!"

"Bring it to me!" He shouted his word. The apparition thrashed beneath him, spitting and screaming, and he twisted the daggers, roaring back.

Morgaine dragged the ax to him, its glowing blade sparking as it scraped against the ballroom floor. Scara ordered her to stop. They ignored him.

Ren took the ax in one hand, angling it just so and dropping it. The glowing blade plunged through the spirit's neck, going deep enough for its tip to ring against the floor. Dark brown unblood spurted from the wound.

Morgaine and Scara let out twin shouts of disgust and turned away. Ren got halfway through the geist banishment spell before the apparition's gargling sounds became a clear-throated laugh. His ax, puppeted by invisible hands, rose from the spirit's neck.

"*Try harder*," the apparition hissed. She vanished.

The ax and daggers fell, the metallic sound of the collision— of failure—ringing in Ren's ears. He rose from the puddle of unblood, shattered crystals tinkling against the floor as they fell from the folds of his clothing. Damnable thing—was he not owed an easy exorcism after Jasniostvo? Was he not owed more than a moment of celebration?

"Scara."

The lord, hearing the growl beneath Ren's voice, knew well enough to only ask, "Yes?"

"She's your ancestor."

"Yes."

Ren fixed his gaze on Scara, half-hoping the lord would talk back—he wanted an excuse to snap. Damn this castle. Damn this family. "Take me to her grave."

———

Scara led Ren and Morgaine—who'd followed despite Ren's protests—to the cemetery behind Hrascara. Their feet crunching in the snow, the creak of the iron gate as Scara drew it open, Ren's quiet casting of nightsight—these were the only sounds the little party made as they walked among the graves. Moonlight silvered the graveyard, but nightsight washed it red and pink like viscera. The cuts on Ren's back stung. The bruise over his ribs hurt. He couldn't feel his toes in the snow. Reia and Kyr, who he'd summoned as they left Hrascara's warmth, did little to improve his mood.

"Here she is." Scara pointed to a worn headstone that read *Duchess Silvia Scara, 531-566*. The only grave ornamentation was a silver vase half-filled with snow.

"You haven't had a Nightmare here in sixty years?"

"We haven't needed one," Scara snipped, though with less irreverence than usual.

"Not even to put Silia to rest?" Ren knelt and started clearing snow from the grave. "No wonder she's so angry. Help me dig."

No hands joined him. Ren lifted his head and saw Scara and Morgaine looking at each other, though with none of the usual lust on his part or veiled disgust on hers—no, they looked afraid. Unsure.

Morgaine drew her arms around herself. "Ren, is this really the best way?"

"It is." Even though he didn't like it. Digging through a grave felt deeply profane, but the banishment spells hadn't worked. Ren had to escalate. Having cleared the snow, he drew a dagger and began to pry up frozen ground. "Of course, you've only read the Order's introductory textbook. Apparitions aren't mentioned until volume two."

"Don't be an ass," she muttered, but knelt anyway. "You're buying me a new dress if this one is unsalvageable."

Silence fell as they dug. Scara stood at the edge of the grave, weakly protesting until Ren snarled for him to "shut up or dig." Scara chose the former, deciding to pace back and forth in the path.

Ren didn't look at Morgaine as they dug—he couldn't. Shame crept into his heart. This was what being a Nightmare really was: lowering oneself into death-ridden earth, getting one's clothes stained with unblood and getting grave dirt caked under one's fingernails. The Order's work was messy. It was ugly, and she'd no doubt admired it—admired him. Would she still see him as a Nightmare after this, or as no more than a starving dog digging for bones?

Scara cleared his throat. He stood over them, holding a shovel out to Ren. He held another in his hands. Ren hadn't realized the lord had wandered away. "She shouldn't be doing this," Scara said. "And you shouldn't be dulling your blade for it."

Ren grudgingly accepted the offering. With the shovels, Silia's coffin was unearthed in half an hour—it hadn't been buried as deeply as Ren expected. The males stepped into the shallow grave and, with matching grunts of effort, threw the lid open.

"Ren." Morgaine sounded frightened.

"Are you going to be ill?" Scara asked, turning. "She's only bone. If you favor a Nightmare, you—gods." The lord fumbled for a shovel. "She's back."

The apparition of Silia Scara drifted toward them, an amused smile on her too-gaunt face.

Ren drew his ax and stepped from the grave. It was time to end this. Over his shoulder, he ordered, "Start breaking bones."

"Are you mad?"

"What did you think I was going to do, polish her remains? No. Break her bones. It will make this easier."

The apparition increased speed. *"What are you doing, Nightmare?"*

"She is my *ancestor*, hunter, and Morgaine will hardly—" A crunch sounded behind Ren. "By the gods, Morgaine! That's her skull!"

It worked—the left side of the apparition's skull sunk in. "Good, little love. Do it again."

Another crunch, and the apparition's head disappeared entirely.

"*By the gods!*"

Ren ignored Scara. He spoke his word and charged the headless spirit. His ax cleaved the body nearly in two, and would have if the spirit hadn't raised her arms and gripped the handle. Spirits often got an animalistic rush of strength when they were cornered; though the apparition was human in origin, she got the bestial rush of power all the same. "*Kill me if you can*," it screamed despite its missing head, "*but how will you save her?*"

Ren tore his ax from the spirit's body and swung the blade horizontally. It made contact with the sound of a butcher knife through flesh.

The spirit cried out. Its right arm snapped just below the elbow. "*I see its mark on her*," it bellowed, trying to raise a hand to point at Morgaine. Ren hacked the hand off. He began to cast the banishment spell, alternating between the Zikatic and Oddelenic dialects. Nearly every line was punctuated with a new cry from the spirit or another bone cracking.

Ren reached the penultimate line of the spell and drew a deep breath, preparing to repeat it, but the spirit fell in a heap to the snow-laden ground. Steam rose from its form. Rivulets of unblood melted tunnels in the snow. Its right leg bent to the side, snapped at mid-thigh. Ren raised his ax over his head and drove it into the apparition's chest, wedging the blade in with his foot. As the last line of the geist banishment spell left him, so did the spirit's essence lift from it. Ren cast slowwind. A cold draft sent Silia's spirit onward.

Morgaine stood with one foot in the coffin. She held two

halves of a human femur in her hands. Shards of it were scattered on and around the headstone. "Is it gone?"

Ren nodded, his heart swelling with pride. The spirit knew nothing of her.

"For good?" Scara asked.

"Yes. Be sure to tell the duke of your assistance, my lord." Ren gathered up the bones Morgaine had destroyed and cast aside. He poured them into the open coffin. "I no longer need your help. You can go back inside, both of you. Tell the townspeople the festivities can continue."

Scara didn't need to be told again. He turned on his heel without another word.

"You aren't coming?" Morgaine asked, stepping from the grave when Ren motioned for her to move.

"I need to bless the grave. It can take some time."

"It isn't that late." Morgaine picked up their daggers and knelt in the path between graves. She spread snow over the blades, washing most of the unblood from them. "I can wait for you."

Ren looked beyond the cemetery's iron fence to the forest, which loomed a few hundred feet away. The trees were a mass of darkness. "Are you sure?"

Morgaine followed his gaze to the forest. She stared at it for a moment; in the red glow of his nightsight, Ren saw her throat bob as she swallowed. She didn't give voice to whatever memories or relived nightmares undoubtedly rushed to meet her, didn't change her mind and run into the castle. Her eyes flicked to his, unreadable pools of black meeting his glowing red irises.

She nodded. Morgaine held her hand out for his bloody ax. "I'd rather stay out here with you."

———

Inside Hrascara, the Solstice ball was underway once more. Laughter and music echoed down the halls, as did a resounding cheer when waitstaff appeared with another round of fine Zijustvan wine.

Ren and Morgaine weren't around to hear it. They hadn't made it anywhere near the ballroom. He'd pulled her into the first open door he'd seen, shucked off his weapons, and kissed her until they were breathless.

"Do you think anyone—"

He silenced her with another kiss. "No one saw us come in." He didn't know where they were, but in the darkness of the room, he could make out a desk shoved against the far wall. He lifted Morgaine and settled her on it, cupping her calves and wrapping her legs around his hips. "Even if they did, I don't care. I've waited too long for this." He ran his lips along the spot on her neck that he knew she liked—he'd thought about kissing her there for months. The sound she made didn't disappoint.

"I missed you," she whispered, tightening her legs around him. She ran her fingers through his hair and gripped some of his curls to hold him still. She nipped at his bottom lip and he groaned. "I've thought so much about what we did in the forest."

Ren ran his hands along her waist, reveling in the feeling of the velvet and her warmth beneath it—she was here. She was his. "I hated to leave you," he confessed, sliding his hand to her leg, soft and bared to his touch and the room's cool air. He brushed his fingers further up her thigh, tracing a gentle pattern as he moved. "There are things I didn't say in my letters, little love, things I knew I wanted—"

Her hand shot out and grabbed his wrist. "Stop."

But Ren had already felt them. He stilled, his fingers moving over the raised, puckered skin at the top of her thigh. "What—"

She pushed him away and pulled her skirt over her thighs. Morgaine looked away. "I suppose it was stupid to think you wouldn't find them eventually. Not with what I want from you."

"Scars?"

She nodded.

"How many?"

Morgaine took his hand. She guided his fingers over her scars; he couldn't count them all, but could tell they were arranged in the unmistakable shape of a bite. "When I was thrown from the Grey home," she said, her voice quiet in the darkness, "I don't know how long I wandered in the forest before being found. I was starving and weak, so I slept long hours. One day—" She took a deep, shaking breath. "I opened my eyes and saw a scavenger beast sink its teeth into me."

Ren pulled her into his arms. Scavenger beasts were merciless creatures. They fed on whatever carcasses they could find, but if food was in short supply, they weren't above slaughter. Their jagged teeth made them efficient killers.

"I think it thought I was already dead. My screams are how the hunters found me."

Ren ran his fingers over her scars. They didn't bother him—a Nightmare without scars was no Nightmare at all. She wasn't sworn to the Order, but she was no less of a fighter than he was. "Did you think some scars would scare me away?" he asked, taking her hands and sliding them under his shirt. He placed one on the bandages over his ribs, the other over the scar below his tattoo. "*Me?*"

Morgaine dropped her head into the crook of his neck.

"We've survived," Ren murmured, kissing her forehead. He glanced at his hand on her thigh, imagining how his dark veins would have looked against her skin—his reminders against hers. "And we will keep surviving."

Morgaine kissed him. It didn't take long for her hands to begin roaming beneath his shirt, tracing the contours of his shoulders and chest. "Take me to your room," she said, kissing down his neck. "We've danced around this long enough."

Ren stilled. He wanted her—by the gods, there was no doubting that—but he wanted her slowly, indulgently. He wanted her in a place that was theirs. "Morgaine—"

"What?" She pulled back, propping herself up on the desk. "I want you, Ren. I want you, and you're *here*, and—"

He rested his hand on her flushed cheek and leaned his forehead against hers. "You don't need to rush just because I'm here. We don't need to rush. I don't want to."

He felt her frown, felt her lips move as she hissed, "Aren't you leaving now that Solstice is over?"

Ren laughed. "I have another Solstice gift for you, little love." He kissed Morgaine before her anger spilled out in words she'd regret, and said, "If you'll have me, I can stay."

She stiffened. "What?"

He wrapped his arms around her and told her about his leave: four months with no hunt, no responsibilities to the Order, no need to travel. "I want to come back to Tanglewood, if it's alright with you."

"Why do you need my permission? You're free to go wherever you want."

"Because I'd be coming back for you," Ren said, running his fingers through the loose sections of her hair. He swallowed—how was it that, with all the terrors he'd faced in his life, proposing this was what made him nervous? "To court you properly, if you would like that."

"Oh."

"I've never courted anyone before." He'd kissed his share of women, of course, and knew he could be a terrible flirt, but Ren was a stranger to romantic commitment. Most Nightmares were. But she made him want to try.

"That's alright. No one's ever courted me." Morgaine drew back. Her fingers traced his hairline, his cheekbones, the skin just under his lips, his jaw. "I might be terrible at being courted."

"I might be terrible at courting."

She giggled and kissed him. "Figure it out with me, then?"

"Happily."

Their kiss was slow and languid, unhurried and exploring. Ren lost himself in the taste of her, in the wordless promises they were making, sweeter and headier than any wine they missed out on by hiding themselves away. They didn't do everything he'd dreamed of on the nights he'd written her letters, but that was alright. They had plenty of time for that.

Morgaine ended the kiss and wrapped her arms around him. "Ren," she said, her smile evident in her voice. She smelled of lavender soap and black ink and grave dirt and him. "Come home with me."

10.15.626

Reia was unhappy to be a mare again. She tossed her head and snorted whenever Ren so much as lifted the reins.

Morgaine laughed, settling her forearms on the sill of the carriage's window and resting her chin atop them. "Poor thing," she cooed to the Umbral. "At least you're walking this time."

"That's what I told her." Ren patted Reia's neck. "But she'll be happiest once we've stopped."

Ren and the townspeople had been riding back to Tanglewood for the better part of the day. The carriages had been full on the trip to Hrascara, so Ren wasn't able to ride with Morgaine, but they made do—he rode beside the carriage instead of in it. Kyr had busied himself by periodically flying ahead of the caravan, then returning to settle atop Reia's head. He'd tried to fly inside the carriage as well, but Brilde had screamed and Kyr had quickly retreated. He was currently perched on Ren's shoulder, his head tucked beneath a wing.

"I'm sure she isn't the only one." Snow began to drift down between them. Morgaine drew the hood of her cloak over her head before asking, "What do you think you'll do when your leave expires?"

"Already eager to get rid of me, little love?"

She blushed. "No. I just…" Her voice trailed off. She stared at the reins wrapped around Ren's hands. "I want to know what to expect."

She expected him to leave again—she hadn't said it, but she didn't need to. Ren didn't want to consider that she might be right. He didn't want to go back to letters. "I don't know what I'll do," he said. "It depends on what you and I are."

Morgaine pressed her lips together. "I suppose that's fair." And then, to stop the tense silence that had settled between them from descending any further, she laughed to herself and said, "I recall you mentioning marriage at Sisters' Harvest. Something about being 'a wonderful provider'?"

Her hand rested on her blue cloak, pale against it. The emptiness of her ring finger seemed to glare at Ren. He knew it had been a joke, but unease settled in his stomach. Few Nightmares married. "That I did."

Silence fell over them completely. Ren kept his gaze pinned to the vanishing point between Reia's ears, the eternally moving place up ahead where the snow-covered ground met the sky. One of the posts of Tanglewood's town gate appeared in the distance.

"Forgive me. I'm being foolish," Morgaine muttered, staring at the carriage wheels as they turned. "You probably aren't allowed to get married."

The town gate had grown much closer by the time Ren said, "We are, actually. It's just—"

He was interrupted by the caravan jilting to a halt. He pulled Reia's reins to stop her, too. "Go ahead," he ordered, and Kyr took off to scout.

Morgaine leaned from the carriage window, holding herself so far out that Ren lifted a hand in case she started to fall. "What's going on?"

"I'm not—" Shouts came from up ahead, then frightened screams. Ren scowled. "Stay here."

The carriage at the very front of the caravan, the one containing Mayoress Soma, had stopped just before the town gates. The mayoress stood on the side of the road, her yellow face pale. A large brass key dented the snow at her feet.

"What is it?" Ren asked, dismounting. Reia became a heeler.

Mayoress Soma raised a shaking hand. "What is that creature?"

Stalking through the town square was a four-legged, stick-like thing. Green blood crusted in places along its skinless, gap-filled body. When it saw Ren, it opened its three-jawed mouth and let out a sound like a broken bell.

The damn lieren had survived.

"Get into your carriage, Mayoress," Ren said. He drew his ax. "I'll tell you when it's safe."

The lieren fell quickly in the end—it had feasted while the townspeople were gone, and its engorgement made it slow. The townspeople trickled through the gates to find Ren standing over the lieren, his chest heaving as he watched the creature die.

He greeted Morgaine as he had three days ago: covered in unblood, standing in a snowy courtyard surrounded by the people of Tanglewood. But this time, no guards threw him to the ground, no haughty nobles interrupted their reunion. This time, he kissed her.

This time, he was home.

The Keep (or, Ren at Home)

LOVE,

VESS WAS JUST BY. HE THINKS WE'LL GET SNOWED IN. CAN I COME OVER?

I'LL BORROW A PILLOW AND BLANKETS FROM AZRA. I'LL SLEEP IN YOUR ARMCHAIR, OR ON THE FLOOR IF I NEED TO. I'LL BEHAVE FOR AS LONG AS YOU WANT.

LET ME KNOW—THE SNOW IS FALLING FAST.

REN

11.14.626

Ren,

Scheming to get snowed in with me? How conniving.

Please come over, though I can't promise I'll be the most entertaining company. Theode gave me a good deal this morning, and if we get snowed in, the town will close. It's the perfect time to reorganize the library and shelve my new books.

I'm not going to make you sleep on the floor. There's my armchair, and also the loveseat—but if you're good, maybe I'll let you sleep at the foot of my bed. ~~If you're bad~~

I'll see you soon. Bring some food if you can. I'm not sure I have enough for the two of us.

Morgaine

(I'm not writing the date, as my reply is immediate.)

"Reia. Off."

The Umbral lifted her head from Morgaine's lap and stared at Ren from their place on the loveseat.

"Go," Morgaine laughed, pushing against Reia's rump. Reia huffed, but went to the fire and turned about thrice before curling into a ball before it.

Morgaine lifted the blanket and Ren settled onto the worn leather loveseat. He held two cups of spiced tea aloft as Morgaine readjusted, leaning back so that she rested between Ren's bent legs with her head on his chest. She rested her open book on her legs and reached back for her tea.

"What are you reading to me tonight?" Ren asked, making sure the cup was well in her grasp before he let go.

"Another adventurer story," Morgaine said, flipping through *Intrepid Escapades: An Anthology of Ruhysvet's Explorers*, one of the books he'd given her for Solstice. It was the only one she hadn't already finished. "It looks short, though, so I can read two if you'd like."

Ren kissed the top of her head. He used his free hand to tug at the ribbon in her hair until her braid came undone. He wasn't sure he'd make it to the end of the first story; Morgaine's apartment was dark except for the fire he'd built in the hearth, and the dinner of meat stew he'd brought from the Drowsy Dragon sat heavy in his stomach. The blanket Morgaine settled over them was thick and soft, and the weight of her against his chest anchored him. He wasn't exhausted, wasn't tired—he was drowsy, relaxed and warm and content. "Start with one." He took a sip of tea. "And then we can decide if we'd like another before bed."

She nodded and began to read, the firelight just enough for her to see by. The story recounted one of Sir Lissan Rivasi's last exploits before his disappearance fifteen years ago. Ren nursed his tea and ran his fingers through Morgaine's hair as she read. He was glad she hadn't chosen *Stories of Naisvet*; it was her favorite, but each time she reached for it, he remembered he and Sanne's hunt. Shame tugged at him each time, whispering that he hadn't tried enough to reach out to Sanne and see how she fared. He didn't want their friendship to die again—but writing to Sanne meant remembering. Being back in the Drowsy Dragon and staying in the same room he'd used during Sisters' Harvest made him unwilling to dredge up past horrors. Every time he reached for it, Ren ultimately stopped himself from taking out his quill and paper. He was allowed some peace.

Yet the memories increased in their persistence, and it was getting harder to ignore the fact that he hadn't told Morgaine everything. It was harder to deny that not telling her felt more and more like keeping a secret she needed to know. She didn't revere the gods as he did, but she knew how Ren held them at the core of his being. He wanted to hold her in his heart, too; she would have to know his secrets one day.

Morgaine paused to laugh at a joke on the page. The sound loosened one of the anxious knots around Ren's heart, silenced the loudest whispers of shame. The Stained Palace's entity had been destroyed. The Keep had ordered him to heal. That was what he needed to focus on. He would reckon with the realm's horrors when he returned to the hunt.

Ren kissed Morgaine's head again and relaxed against the corner of the loveseat. A month had passed since Solstice, and he and Morgaine had spent many nights like this. He saw her every day now. In the mornings, he'd come to the library and do whatever she needed him to—at first, this had been sourcing materials for and building a glass-topped display case for the books he'd given her—before breaking for lunch and spending his afternoon hunting game or doing odd jobs for Azra. He'd proposed a deal to her, chores in exchange for reduced rent so he wouldn't run through all of his coin, and she'd happily agreed. He'd meet Morgaine just after sunset for dinner, where they'd talk over the afternoon's work. Since Sisters' Harvest, she'd been cataloging the rest of the artifacts the townspeople had uncovered in the forest; her little office was overrun with notes, boxed-up artifacts of differing sizes, and stacks of books splayed open with paper-weights. She'd tell him about the artifacts she'd examined that day, and he'd tell her whether he'd wielded a blade or hammer that afternoon. Depending on the answer, she'd either invite him home or he'd ask her up to his room—an afternoon of hunting meant Morgaine made them tea and kissed him while the water boiled, and odd jobs meant he had the energy to kiss her for much longer. He'd walk her home, return to the Drowsy Dragon, sleep, wake, and do it all again the next day. He'd once thought a routine would mean tedium, but he didn't miss the harshness of the hunt as much as he thought he would. There was a peace in softness.

Morgaine turned the page of the book and hissed. A red drop of blood beaded at the tip of her finger.

Ren reached around her and turned the page, which had fallen back into place. He wiped the blood away with the pad of his thumb and kissed the little cut. "Careful, little love." He drained his tea and set the empty cup on the ground, now free to wrap both arms around her. "I've killed too many spirits for a book to be what takes you from me."

She rolled her eyes, but pressed her lips to his before turning around to continue reading. Ren watched the snow fall outside. They'd spent their nights apart since he'd started his leave, but if Vess was right, Ren would stay with Morgaine tonight. He would see her as soon as they woke. He could kiss her good morning, and it would be as if he'd slept next to her.

Morgaine turned the page, and the snow tumbled down. After a few more pages, her soothing voice and the pleasant fullness of his stomach and the warmth of the room and the weight of her in his arms proved to be too much. Ren's eyes drooped.

He woke to a chill—Morgaine had disentangled herself from him. "You fell asleep. Let's get ready for bed."

Ren fumbled for the blanket and drew it up to his chin. The fire was dying, and without Morgaine's warmth to counteract it, the room was cold. "This is where I'm sleeping, isn't it? Unless I've been good enough to be allowed at the foot of your bed."

She laughed. "Not quite. You fell asleep at the best part of the story."

"Very well. At least I'll have Reia to keep me warm."

"No, you won't." Morgaine nodded to her bed.

Ren sat up and looked over the back of the loveseat; Reia had settled herself amongst the blankets on Morgaine's bed. "By the gods."

"Poor thing. Perhaps Kyr will take pity on you." Morgaine kissed his forehead, smiling as she did. "Good night, Ren."

11.15.626

Ren crawled into Morgaine's bed shortly after sunrise. "Little love," he murmured, slipping under the blankets and tugging her against him. "Wake up. I want to kiss you."

"Mm." She rolled into him without opening her eyes. "That can't be the only reason you woke up."

"It very well can be. I have no hunt to otherwise occupy my thoughts. Do you not like having my full attention?"

She slung her arms over him. Their legs tangled beneath the blankets. "You don't have to be this charming. You've already got me in bed."

"So that's a no?"

Morgaine's eyes flew open. "I never said that."

He kissed her, morning breath and all. "How'd you sleep?" She still had nightmares as a result of the wraith's attack at Sisters' Harvest, but since Solstice, Morgaine had reported sleepless nights less and less. Ren had an idea why; since praying for her at Hrascara, he'd been sure to mention her in his daily prayers to Zikat and Oddelen. In addition to life and death, they overlooked dreams and sleep. It seemed the gods had listened.

She smiled. "Very well."

"No nightmares?"

"Not even a dream." Her smile dimmed. "If I had a nightmare, you would have known."

And it would have been his fault. Ren kissed the place on her forehead where the wraith had pricked her. He ran a hand along the scars at her thigh, the reminders of the attack she relived every time the nightmares came. His hunt protected the sanctity of life and death, but his leave had given him something just as precious to watch over. "If it happens tonight, I'll be here."

"Tonight?"

He nodded. "Look outside."

Morgaine got out of bed, cloaking herself in a blanket as she padded to the window. Her long plait, braided with a periwinkle ribbon, brushed her back. Ren knew what she'd see, for he'd seen it as soon as he'd woken: the town square swathed in white, windblown snowdrifts piled against some doors—including the library's. No one would be able to go in or out until the snow melted, and more snow already fell.

Morgaine's breath fogged against the frost-covered glass. "Vess was right!"

Ren smiled. "You'll get to reorganize your shelves all you want."

"I will." Morgaine stood at the window for a little longer. When she turned, her eyes had darkened, and she reached for him as she crawled back into bed. There was a wicked little grin on her face. "But there's something else I want to do first."

———

It snowed for two days straight, a mess of flakes floating through the air and heightening the already tall drifts.

Ren had never thought he'd enjoy being trapped in any building, let alone a library, a place dedicated to silence and quiet knowledge. He'd always favored a hands-on approach to learning, having honed his fighting abilities through controlled, practiced application of the techniques instead of reading about them. The blunt collision of a wooden sword against his arm or shoulder had been a far better teacher than Cazret, his old sparring instructor, telling him he'd misremembered the proper execution of a pirouette. Libraries had bored him. The written word seldom excited him.

Now, though, he didn't want the snow to stop.

They spent the entirety of the first day reorganizing the library. The last few times Morgaine had traded with Theode, she'd shoved her new books onto the shelf in the library's entryway; the new acquisitions numbered less than a dozen each time, but their months of trading resulted in almost fifty books that needed to be fit into the library's shelves.

"And some of the shelves are already full, so we'll need to move some books onto the shelves below," Morgaine explained, walking Ren around the library. "Which means we need to first move these, and so on."

The world outside was still and quiet, and this seemed like the most important task in the realm—after all, what else could they do? Ren held out his arms and waited for her to start loading books into them.

The reorganization efforts continued into the next day. After a slow start to their morning, which involved Morgaine having to heat three kettles' worth of water because the first two went cold each time Ren kissed her, they finished rearranging the library in the early afternoon. Ren sat on the stairs to the apartment and watched Morgaine flit between shelves for one last check before she declared the task complete. She twisted a hair ribbon around her fingers as she looked.

"Do you approve?" he asked when the ribbon stilled.

"For now." She stopped in front of the glass display case housing the first editions he'd given her, lightly running her fingers over the top. "I think this is my favorite part."

"Really?" Ren rose and walked to her, wrapping his arms around her waist and resting his chin on her head. "Not the cabinet of curiosities you've kept locked away?"

She twisted to look at him. "Do you want to see?"

He did—she'd forbidden him from going into her office. "I thought you were afraid I'd disturb your curated chaos."

Her shoulder bumped against his chest as she shrugged. "We finished this faster than I thought we would. We don't have much else to do."

"We could go upstairs."

She giggled and leaned away from the teeth he grazed against her neck. "Well, I'd like to show you, if you're still curious."

"What's changed?"

She took his hand and pulled him to her office. "You've proven yourself to be a very good library page," she said. "I'd say you've earned a peek behind the curtain."

Ren paused on the threshold. Morgaine picked a meandering path through the room. "If you follow my steps, it should be fine."

He hesitated. He'd seen her office in passing glances and hadn't realized how many incredibly breakable things were on the floor: pieces of pottery, shards of etched glass, bits of jewelry and fragments of old blades, the metals of which had gone brittle and thin with time. The longer he looked, though, the easier it was to find suitable places for his feet, and he wound his way across the floor to her. "What's your plan for all of this when you're done with it?"

"Well," she said, rummaging around on her desk, "I figured I'd display some of it here, and that the mayoress would like some of it for the town hall. I'm not sure about the rest." She found what she was looking for and held the little box aloft. "This is one of my favorite things from the pit."

She'd nestled it into scrap paper, something small and golden that winked when it caught the light—a button. Ren picked it up and ran his thumb over it, a coil of dread causing the old wound at his ribs to pulse. The button was emblazoned with a sigil, a goddess in profile constituting the left half of the circle and a shining sun filling the right.

"I tried to figure out what house the crest belongs to, because it's obviously a royal symbol," Morgaine said, "but the only books I have on the subject pertain to Zijustvan nobility, and none of the illustrations matched."

"Because it's not a Zijustvan crest." Ren set the button back into its box, his breath shortening. For a moment, the veins in his hands went dark. "This is the Esclarmonde sigil, the Jasniostvan royal family's. Sanne had it on her armor." But why was it here? Why had an Esclarmonde been in Tanglewood during the plague?

Morgaine took the button and ran her fingers over the half-sun. "Fascinating." She said it with the distant tone of voice Ren had come to associate with her thinking. "I suppose that makes sense, with how close we are to the border. Actually—" She darted from the room, hopping around and over artifacts waiting for her attention. By the time Ren caught up with her, she'd pulled a worn edition of *Tanglewood: A History* from its new place and was flipping through it.

"You're not using the first edition?"

"Gods, no. I only read those because I'd brought no other books to Solstice, and I was too excited to stop myself. They're *first editions*, Ren. People don't actually read them."

"You're reading *Intrepid Explorers* to me."

She waved a hand. "That's different. I'm a librarian." She found what she was looking for and grinned, the excitement of discovery making her eyes glitter. It made him feel sick. "I thought so. When the plague hit, the Esclarmondes—"

"Morgaine." He didn't want to hear that name. From the

moment he'd seen the Esclarmonde seal, a persistent disquiet had wound through him, spreading out from his ribs like ants tunneling into soil. He'd have to face it soon. He'd have to name it soon, and the peace he'd found with her would end. The hunt would consume him again. "Is it alright if we don't talk about it right now?"

Her brow furrowed. "Of course." She closed the book and set it back in its place. "Is it because—"

Her words were cut off by Ren pulling her into his chest. He buried his face in her neck, breathing in ink and soap and the sharp tang of the slight sweat she'd worked up as they'd reorganized. "Later," he breathed, spreading his hands across her back. "We can talk about it later. Just let me be with you now."

11.18.626

On the fourth day, they woke to the sounds of a sleepy town stirring: doors opening and closing, children laughing as they played outside for the first time in days, men calling to one another as they shoveled snow from their porches and front steps. Morgaine all but leapt out of bed, hurrying around the apartment and dressing while Ren watched from the loveseat, snuggled beneath blankets. He reached out and snagged the edge of her skirt as she passed by.

"I've got to open," she protested, swatting at his hand.

Ren held fast—he wasn't ready for their slow mornings to end. "Must you?"

"Yes, I must." She kissed him, but danced away before his hands could wrap around her waist and pull her onto him. "Come downstairs, if you want to be around me so badly."

If. Of course he did.

Having dressed and prayed, he trotted down the stairs minutes later. Morgaine stood on her tiptoes in front of a shelf, her fingers just brushing against the book she was after. She waved him over. "Ren, sweetheart, could you—"

"'Sweetheart'?"

She stilled. "Ren—"

He grinned. She'd resisted 'little love' at first, but look at her now, all flustered over letting her own pet name slip. He liked it. He wanted her to say it again. "Don't correct yourself on my account."

Morgaine put her hands on her hips. Her neck and chest were turning red. "Will you please get this book down?"

He kept his eyes on her as he walked to the shelf. That was one of the endearing little surprises he'd discovered by staying in one place: when she blushed, the color rose from her heart to her cheeks. "Of course, little love." He plucked the book from the shelf, but dangled it above her. "You think I'm a sweetheart?"

She reached for the book and huffed when he lifted it higher. "It would seem so." But she was smiling, and so was he, and when he set the book down and pushed her against the shelves, she let him kiss her for a moment. "Alright, let me get back to work. It's almost time to open."

"Not yet." Ren wasn't done. He trailed kisses down her neck, nipping at the place where her neck curved into her shoulder. He dragged the collar of her dress down and bit harder. His laugh rumbled against her skin when she shuddered. "Keep telling me how sweet I am."

She draped her arms over his shoulders and sighed. "I should have watched my words. I knew you'd never let it go."

"How long have I been your sweetheart?"

"Since Solstice."

He wrapped his arms around her and kissed her again. She giggled, the sound turning into a moan when Ren bit her bottom lip.

"Ren, the curtains are open—"

"I know."

She kissed him, the tension between them heavy with need. Ren could have done this forever, could have pushed against her and slid his hands under her dress and relished in her little sighs until the moment he died. It would have been a life well lived.

He couldn't remember the last time he'd been this happy.

I love you. If "sweetheart" was her confessed secret, this was his. He opened his mouth to whisper it into her hair, but a throat cleared behind them. Morgaine gasped.

"Mayoress," she said, breathless. Her flush had made it to her cheeks. She pulled her dress back over her shoulder. "I'm so sorry. How can I help you?"

Mayoress Soma smiled brightly at her. Ren bit back curses. A brass key dangled from the mayoress' hands; the library door was ajar behind her. Curious bits of snow spilled onto the floor, coming to see what was behind the door they'd blocked. "Good morning, Morgaine. I've come to see if my book from Farriasty has arrived, now that the snow has melted a great deal."

Morgaine's brow furrowed, then relaxed. "Oh. Yes. Theode brought it by before the snow came. Let me get it." She hurried into her office, a muttered "goddess' tits" catching Ren's ears before she disappeared.

Mayoress Soma's eyes flicked up and down his body. "Good morning, Ren."

He crossed his hands in front of himself. "Mayoress."

"You're not keeping my librarian from too much of her work, are you?"

"Of course not."

"Good."

Silence stretched between them, broken only by the rummaging sounds that came from Morgaine's office. He'd been able to kiss her so freely these days that he'd forgotten how infuriating it was to be interrupted. His hands felt cold.

"Do you have a shovel, Ren?"

He looked at the mayoress. Her expression, cheery as usual, gave nothing away. "No, but I'm sure I can find one. Why do you ask?"

"Some of the men have started shoveling snow and clearing the streets. It seems like the type of helpful thing you'd like to do."

Morgaine reappeared with the book, her cheeks decidedly less pink. "Here you are, Mayoress."

"Thank you, Morgaine." Mayoress Soma tucked the book into the satchel beneath her cloak. "Though I must ask for one more thing. Can you spare your Nightmare for the morning?"

———

Shoveling snow was deceptively sweaty work.

Ren's cloak was made of thick wool, which meant it attracted every bit of the weak winter sunlight and held the heat close. After every few streets, he'd open his cloak for a few minutes to let the cold air dry his sweat. He'd hoped it would prevent him from smelling, but his hard work was clear each time. If his snowy seclusion with Morgaine was truly at its end, he'd return to the Drowsy Dragon tonight and would properly wash himself and his clothes. He hadn't wanted to fully undress in front of her, not yet. There were still ten weeks left in his leave, and the gods only knew what he and Morgaine would be to each other then. Oh, he would flirt with her and kiss her and daydream about bedding her —but the realization of those daydreams couldn't come until, at the very least, he'd told her he loved her. It wouldn't be right otherwise.

Ren stabbed his shovel into the ground and lowered his cloth half-mask, sucking in the cold midday air when his nose and mouth were uncovered. If he'd been in any other profession, he would wed her first, but marriage was a high demand for a Nightmare. Anyone who wed a Nightmare spent most of their time alone, either waiting for their husband to return or waiting for the day when he wouldn't. Nightmares died young. Ren couldn't imagine asking Morgaine to take him as a husband only for him to die before her hair had silvered. He knew there was a chance that his skill and ferocity as a Nightmare would only increase after marrying her—he'd fight through each of the three hells if it meant coming home to Morgaine—but he knew better than to think love would make him invincible. If Morgaine married him, she would bury him, too. He would leave her as lonely as he'd found her.

His shoveling had taken him to the edge of the residential area, and he turned back toward the center of town. Reia manifested from the shadows and bound toward him, her dark tongue lolling from the side of her mouth. Ren used the shovel to flick some snow at her; she snapped at it, but the flurries fell through her mouth. She slowed and picked her way to Ren, lifting her paws out of the snow with each step.

"If you don't like muddy snow, you didn't need to come outside," Ren said, squatting down and scratching her ears. She'd played in the field at Hrascara, but that snow had been white and clean. This snow had become a rutted, muddy slush.

Reia whined. She bit the corner of Ren's cloak and tugged him toward the town square.

"Are you hungry?" Umbrals didn't need to eat to survive, but Reia had gotten a taste for Azra's roast turkey.

She grumbled and shook her head.

"Then what is it?"

Reia just kept tugging him forward.

He raised his half-mask and hoisted his shovel over his shoulder. He could do with a break. "Alright, girl. Take me to Azra."

When they reached the town square, Reia dropped Ren's cloak and ran to a flock of black birds perched on the lip of the frozen-over fountain. Ren went into the Drowsy Dragon to see if Azra had saved any scraps.

Unless the mayoress or Brilde was taking a late lunch, the Drowsy Dragon was typically empty at midday. Ren was therefore startled to see nearly three dozen males in the tavern. As far as he knew, there were no holidays or festivals coming soon, no reason for outsiders to flock to Tanglewood. He slipped through the small crowd, aiming for his favorite spot at the bar.

He met Azra's eyes as he settled onto the corner stool. Azra, who was in the middle of pouring drinks for two men waiting at the bar, held up a hand for him to wait.

Ren lowered his half-mask and hood. Thick curtains hung over each of the Drowsy Dragon's windows, all of which except for those on the windows facing the square were closed; as a result, the bright midday sun reflecting off the snow only went so far. Candles lit the rest of the room. It was partially why Ren favored Azra's tavern over Vess', the Dusk and Dawn—Nightmares thrived in the dark, and Ren knew he could find shadow in the Drowsy Dragon at any hour.

A black-clad man reached up to clap another on the back. A black tattoo, identical to the one on Ren's shoulder, swirled across the man's hand.

"Sorry about that," Azra said, slinging her bar towel over her shoulder. "I've gotten wonderfully busy. You thirsty? Hungry?"

Ren tore his attention from the tattoo. "Neither. Reia is."

Azra grinned. "I'm all out of roast, I'm afraid—and that's roast *anything*." She nodded at the crowd. "You can thank them. It seems like they're your—"

"Ren?" One of the males down the bar stared at him incredulously. "Is that you?"

Ren looked into a face he somewhat recognized: brown eyes, black skin, tipped ears pointing through cream-colored locs. A jagged scar interrupted the elf's light eyebrow and dipped past his eye. The scar was new—he didn't remember this Nightmare having it, but the last time Ren had seen him, they'd only been kids. "Khai?"

Khai grinned and nodded. Ren hopped from his stool and briefly embraced his fellow Nightmare, slapping him on the back as he did the same to Ren.

"You finally got some muscle on you." Ren nodded at Khai's wide chest. "How long did that take?" Khai had been small at the Keep, half a foot shorter than Ren and half as wide.

"You've changed a bit yourself." Khai motioned to Ren's chipped horn. "How'd that happen? Lover's quarrel?"

"I wish."

"This is Faust," Khai said, nodding his head at the Nightmare behind him. Faust raised a hand in greeting, too busy downing his ale to say hello.

Ren swept his gaze over the crowd. Now that he knew to look for them, he saw Nightmare tattoos everywhere: wrapping around fingers, curling around temples and cheekbones, sticking out of shirt collars like his. His heart swelled. The last time he'd been around this many of his brothers, they'd all had their heads bent in wet-eyed prayer. He recognized some of them as he looked: Sers Mezd and Tmarrey, two of the three members of the Triumvirate, the Order's governing body, and Housemaster Graeme, who had overseen the trainees' living arrangements. "Has the Keep moved?"

Khai nodded. "We arrived in the forest this morning. I'd ask why you're here, but, uh—" He and Faust exchanged a shit-eating look. "We heard you tend to hang around the library. Any reason why?"

Ren arched a brow. "How do you know that?"

"Azra told us." Faust's voice was so deep Ren nearly felt his own chest rumble with it. "Baer asked after you."

Ren stilled. He and Baer Enorry had once been best friends, but Ren had let their correspondence die. Shame for what he'd done had stilled his pen. "Baer's here?"

"He went to the library. Said he was looking for you."

Ren had seen Baer the last time he'd seen Sanne—three years ago, before he'd left in the middle of the night without saying goodbye. They hadn't written to each other since; Ren had felt too guilty, and he'd figured Baer had been too angry. "Did he say why?"

Khai shook his head. "Not exactly. It seemed urgent, though." He took a long pull of ale. "Baer's temper has shortened lately. You better go see what he wants."

Ren left the Drowsy Dragon and headed across the town square. Baer and Morgaine—he wasn't sure what to expect from that pairing, but the growing dread in his stomach sat heavy like an omen. He shoved the library door open. Morgaine looked up from behind the circulation desk, but the excited look on her face wasn't what bothered Ren—it was the two Umbral ravens, not just Kyr, sitting on the desk and watching her.

"Ren!" Morgaine hurried around the counter. "You aren't the only one with a raven. This is—"

"Fanning."

The owner of the voice stood at the mouth of an aisle, leaning on a cane. Ren struggled to reconcile the Baer before him with the Baer he'd last seen: that Baer had been hale and strong, his hazel eyes slightly dulled by the exhaustion of the hunt. He'd stood on two legs in Oddelen's chapel at the Keep, the moonlight glinting off of sandy blond curls as he sang and wept and mourned his best friend's death. This Baer's eyes were ringed in shadow, half from his scowl and half from the purple smears beneath his eyes. His hair was the same color and texture, but long enough to brush against his shoulders now, and he leaned on a carved cherrywood cane. His left leg ended at mid-thigh. The prosthetic limb strapped to his hips was made of Nightmare steel, whorls of which had been welded together to make a lightweight replacement for his leg.

"Her name is Fanning." Baer stepped closer, his cane thumping hollowly against the plank floor. "But he remembers that. Don't you, Ren?"

By the gods. Ren needed to stop staring, but he couldn't. Other than Sanne, Baer had been the cockiest of the four of them, sure he was going to earn a place on the Triumvirate one day. Ren couldn't believe Baer had been wounded like this. This was a hunt-ending injury. "What happened to you?"

"The same thing that always happens to us. I was hunting."

Morgaine, her eyes darting between the two of them, cleared

her throat. "Baer came by looking for you." She drew her arms around herself. "He said you're all here."

Baer nodded. "I need to deliver a message. Morgaine, would you mind giving us a moment?"

"She can hear it," Ren said, prickling. Short temper or not, Baer had no right to order her about in her own home.

Baer arched a brow. It was such a different expression than the heartbroken one Ren had last seen, so much more detached, that Ren almost couldn't look at him. "It's from the Triumvirate."

Ren felt cold. Did they know he'd broken the terms of his leave at Hrascara? Would they revoke his leave if he was found to have disobeyed their order? Or was this about the Stained Palace? Had the time to face it come? "You can say it in front of her."

Baer looked from Ren to Morgaine, noting the way she'd come to his side and brushed her hand against his. "I see," he said quietly. "You're being asked to meet with the Triumvirate to discuss your hunts in the Stained Palace and here in Tanglewood. I noticed some similarities between your reports and brought them to the Triumvirate's attention. Kyr was supposed to bring you a notice this morning, but we never received your response. Was it not delivered?"

Kyr had indeed delivered a letter that morning. Ren had been too busy making Morgaine blush to read it—but something else Baer had said caught his attention. "You read my reports? Have you become the Keep's curator?"

Baer smiled tightly. "I can't hunt, can I?"

An awkward silence settled over the room. The question had been delivered with the cadence of a joke but the flat intonation of someone dying to leave. Ren sighed. "Baer—"

"It's how I can serve the Order while I learn to fight with my prosthesis," Baer continued, "so yes, it's me for now. What answer can I take back to the Triumvirate?"

Take back to the Triumvirate, as if they weren't across the square draining Azra's casks of ale. Ren had forgotten the frustrating way Baer weaponized formality. "I'll attend."

"Good. You'll be expected at the Keep by the morning's ninth hour."

"How far is it from Tanglewood?"

"About an hour's walk, but shorter on horseback."

Ren nodded. No more slow mornings with Morgaine, indeed.

Her hand ghosted against his again, but this time she lightly twined their fingers together. "Can I come?" she asked. "If it's serious—"

"He isn't facing disciplinary action," Baer said, though his tone was softer. "He's in no trouble."

Morgaine leveled her gaze at him. "I'd still like to come, if I can. As you've realized, Baer, Ren means very much to me. I'm appreciative of the Order and its mission—he opened my eyes to the true dangers of it. It would be an honor to see the Keep."

Ren met Baer's eyes. If Ren recalled the bylaws correctly, day visitors were allowed on the Keep's premises. As long as Morgaine wasn't left to wander the halls alone, there should be no issue. "She'll need to be accompanied during my meeting."

"She can wait in the library with me." Baer gave Morgaine the faintest hint of a smile. "We were having an interesting conversation before you arrived."

"Is that alright with you?"

Morgaine nodded.

"It's settled. I'll inform the guards you'll be arriving with a guest." Baer offered Ren his hand, and they shook. "Morgaine. It was a pleasure to meet you."

"Likewise," she said, though Ren noted hesitance in her voice. "We'll see you tomorrow." She waited until the library door closed behind Baer before saying, "He told me he was an old friend of yours."

A memory flashed behind Ren's eyes—Baer, Sanne, their friend Tovar, and himself sitting on the floor of their suite at the Keep, teaching themselves darkdrape in the middle of the night. "He was."

"You don't act like it."

Ren reached for her. "Things change, little love."

She looped her arms around him. Ren rested his chin on her head. This was his favorite way to hold her, arms around her and his head lowered as if he could tuck her into him completely. He'd held her like this at Sisters' Harvest after the wraith had vanished, had shielded her body with his even though the danger was gone —but it was never really gone for Nightmares, not truly. If he tried, really tried, he could hear Umbrals calling in the square and Nightmares carousing in the tavern. His two worlds were colliding and, sooner than he'd wanted to, he had to consider that one of them might not survive. The time for secrets, for hiding, was ending.

How things changed, indeed.

11.19.626

"Are you alright?"

Morgaine smiled down at him. She sat in Reia's saddle as Ren led the mare through the forest. There were no walking trails in Tmadrev, but the visiting Nightmares had worn desire paths into the forest floor. Sunlight wavered through the skeletal trees, casting watery shadows onto the snow around them. "I'm fine."

Ren ran his thumb along the leather reins. "Tell me if you feel a panic coming on."

"I will. But I feel fine, Ren, really." She patted Reia's neck. "I'm not alone."

He'd gotten to the library early that morning, expecting that he'd have to wake her—she usually woke earlier than he liked to, but during their snow-in, she'd risen later and later each morning. The door, however, had been unlocked. She'd been waiting on him, already dressed for the cold.

"You're up early," he'd grumbled, still shaking off the last bits of sleep. Azra had brewed a pot of coffee by the time he'd gotten downstairs, and he'd convinced her to lend him one of the Drowsy Dragon's mugs for the road.

"I'm excited," she'd said, and reached for the mug to steal a sip of coffee. "I didn't actually think you'd let me come."

"Which reminds me." Ren had wandered the shelves, searching for a familiar brown and gold spine. "You've got something of ours to return."

Blessed Brotherhood now sat in one of Reia's saddlebags.

"I wish you'd let me keep the textbook," Morgaine said, looking at the saddlebag and frowning.

Ren shook his head. He didn't fully believe Baer's statement that he wasn't in trouble; if he was going to be questioned by the Triumvirate, he wanted there to be as little against him as possible. The textbook had to be returned. "Be glad I let you keep the dagger."

"Hm. That's right." Morgaine leaned against Reia's neck, trying to be more level with him. "Why did you?"

"Because a book isn't going to protect you if something were to happen," Ren said, "and I've seen your kitchen knives. They can barely cut bread." And, in her hands, the Nightmare dagger she'd bought at Solstice would be just that—a dagger. The word needed to activate it would only be known by its original owner, who Ren suspected was long gone. "Take this victory, little love."

She straightened and scoffed.

"Why do you need a Nightmare book and dagger, anyway?" Ren asked, crooking his finger in request. "You have a Nightmare."

Morgaine rolled her eyes, but when she leaned down and kissed him, she was smiling. "Maybe I'm trying to be worthy of him."

He rested a hand on her knee. His heart, which galloped in his chest, slowed just a bit. "You already are."

They rounded a bend in the desire path and Morgaine gasped, standing up in the saddle. "Gods," she breathed. "Is that it?"

Ren grinned. "It is."

The Keep was in ruin, but its deteriorated state took little away from the awe of seeing it for the first time. Ren still remembered the way he'd felt when he'd stumbled upon the Keep as a boy, thirteen years old and half-starved. All he'd known was the cruelness of the Grey home and its poor conditions: four children to a bed, rodents skittering around at night, holes in the roof patched with thin slabs of wood that leaked when it rained. The Keep, a warm, dry castle of solid grey stone whose spires rose into the sky, had taken his breath away. He thought he'd been hallucinating, that places like this only existed in storybooks.

"It's beautiful."

Ren led Reia forward, but slowed their pace so Morgaine could take it in. The Keep's left side cascaded into rubble, the remnant of some destruction wrought on it during the Cataclysm. From the inside, the holes had been patched, but the debris and half-standing walls had been left as a reminder. The Order was to fight against such destruction, and it would survive the consequences of the Cataclysm as its stronghold had weathered the end of the world.

"What are these?" Morgaine asked. They walked through small ruins, their path strewn with rubble and shards of petrified wood.

"They were the ancillary buildings," Ren said. "The Keep dates back to Naisvet. It was a castle for an ancient ruler. When the Cataclysm struck, the keep itself was the only thing that survived, hence the name." He curled a hand around her calf, and her warmth soothed him. "Did you skip that section in *Blessed Brotherhood*?"

"I must have. You should let me keep it."

Ren helped her dismount when they reached the gates. Reia shifted to a heeler and disappeared to the right. Kyr, who'd been following from the sky, swooped after her—the Umbrals were housed in that direction.

"Welcome home, brother," one of the guards said, a boy Ren didn't recognize. No Nightmare tattoo was visible, and Ren suspected it was unearned rather than unseen—the Keep required trainees to take guard shifts as part of their training. "Is the woman—"

"She's with me."

The guard nodded and waved them in. "Welcome to the Keep, ma'am."

Their path to the Keep's entrance was enclosed by two worn stone walls, one of the holes in which led to the sparring yard. This close, they could see the particolored veining that ran through the Keep's dark stone. A morning training session had already begun—Ren heard the clatter of wooden swords colliding and grunts of effort and pain.

"You train outdoors even in the snow?"

"Spirits don't care about the weather," he said, tugging open one of the grand wooden doors. "We learn to fight in all conditions."

Morgaine hung back, staring through the gap in the wall. "There are girls in that ring."

Ren dropped the door's handle. Aside from Sanne, the Order had only ever trained boys—what had changed? He walked down the steps and stood by Morgaine, peering into the sparring ring. Two elven girls faced off, a girl with a shortsword dodging the advances of another with daggers. Though one's hair was white and the other's was dark blue, both of them wore their long hair in braids.

Ren wondered if Sanne knew.

The instructor barked out commands. The white-haired girl raised her wooden practice sword higher. Morgaine watched, entranced, as the white-haired girl swung her sword upon the blue-haired girl, who had stumbled and fallen to the frozen ground. Their breath puffed in the air.

"Let's get you inside," Ren murmured, ushering her back to the door. She looked as if she'd wanted to join, but followed without protest.

The Keep's grand foyer rose before them, the vaulted ceiling stretching two stories high. Morgaine craned her neck to stare at the large filigree lantern that swung gently from side to side. "Is that fire changing colors?"

"It's blessed by Zikat," Ren said. "It burns at all hours." He watched the changing color of the flame reflect on her face, red and blue and green. It shifted the colors of the tile below their feet and the shadows in the corners, shadows which Umbrals melted from and ran or flew across the room. Morgaine watched each one, the smile on her face growing by the second. "Come on, little love." Ren took her hand. "We've got some time before my meeting. I want to show you something."

He knew the place that had made her who she was, and he wanted to show her his. Ren led her up and to the left, toward the place where the Keep crumbled away: the dormitory wing. They ascended the winding stone staircase of the wing's tower, Ren's heart rising with each step.

They stopped outside an arched wooden door, one that didn't close quite right in the summer—Ren and his friends had needed to kick it shut, as the summer heat made it swell. He ran his fingers over four deep cuts in one of the door's panels. From left to right, the cuts had been made by Baer's, Tovar's, his, and Sanne's blades. They'd wanted to mark the place as theirs. "This used to be my room."

"Can I see it?"

Ren shook his head. "It's probably in use, but I can describe it to you. The whole room used to be a guest suite. I slept in the sitting room. Sanne slept in the office, and Baer and Tovar shared the actual bedroom." A lump formed in his throat. Though he'd lived in this room for six years, all Ren could think of was the last time he'd left. "They were my best friends."

Morgaine rested her head against him. "What happened?"

Ren took a deep breath. He still remembered how it felt to read the Keep's notification of Tovar's death—for a moment, all the air had left his lungs. "Tovar died."

"Oh."

Ren told her of the last time he'd seen his friends: Tovar in a closed casket, Baer and Sanne weeping next to him in Oddelen's chapel and then with him in their suite, the three of them huddled together in a space that had only ever felt full with four. "We went to sleep," Ren whispered, his eyes stinging with tears, "and I left in the middle of the night. I couldn't bear to tell them goodbye, too."

Morgaine reached up and brushed his tears away. "It wouldn't have been forever, sweetheart."

He grabbed her hand and held it in place. "I know that now. But then, a goodbye hurt too much."

"I know the feeling." She brushed her thumb along his cheekbone. "But you came back to me. You went back to Sanne, and now you're back here with Baer. And one day—" Her voice thickened. She hugged him before he could see the tears start to fall. "And one day, you'll go back to Tovar. A goodbye isn't always forever."

Ren wound his arms around her. Goodbyes weren't always forever, but one day, his would be. How many more of them could she take?

A two-tone bell sounded, the first pitch higher than the second.

"That's the quarter until the hour." Ren wiped his tears. "Come on, little love. Let's get you to Baer."

———

Morgaine looked around the Keep's library with the same awestruck expression she'd had when she first saw the castle. Ren thought he knew why—it was two stories high, the second floor a mezzanine that wrapped around the room and whose shelves required rolling ladders to reach the top. The bottom floor could have fit four of her libraries.

"And you maintain all of it?" she asked Baer. "This is a massive collection."

"I have for the last year and a half." Baer shot a glance at Ren.

A year and a half—so that was when he'd lost his leg. "Would you like a tour?"

"Please."

Ren kissed her forehead and tried to ignore how Baer stared. "I'll come get you when I'm done." To Baer, he said, "I'd keep an eye on her hands, if I were you. She's always trying to get new acquisitions for Tanglewood."

Morgaine started to protest, but quickly stopped—they both knew it was true.

Ren went to the Triumvirate.

The meeting hall was on the second floor at the back of the castle. It was one of the few rooms at the Keep that was excessively grand, chosen and decorated with the intent of impressing visitors: a circular oakwood table dominated the center of the room, and the chairs around it had thick velvet cushions. The windows overlooked the first floor's chapel wing, the view stretching beyond it to the snow-covered ground and skeletal trees of Tmadrev Forest. Ivory taper candles burned in an iron-and-antler chandelier.

Three males sat at the far side of the table. They rose when he entered. "Ren, we're glad you were able to meet with us," Ser Berrick Tmarrey, the longest-serving Nightmare and head of the Triumvirate, said. His remaining amber eye crinkled as he smiled and motioned for Ren to sit. "It's good to see you home."

Ser Crannoc Mezd, a grey-skinned male shaded elf, and Ser Reddin Cazret, a pale human male—the other two members of the Triumvirate—also smiled at Ren, but theirs were considerably more strained. Mezd and Cazret had been two of Ren's instructors before ascending to the Triumvirate, and Ren couldn't recall ever seeing them look so apprehensive. At least he wasn't the only one. "Please sit," Mezd said. "How have you been healing, Ren?"

A tray with pots of coffee and tea sat in the center of the table. Though his hands shook, Ren reached for a pot. He poured himself more coffee as he answered—he'd left his mug from Azra in the library. "Well. I'm grateful for the rest."

"I can imagine," Tmarrey said. He produced and opened a folder, and Mezd and Cazret did the same. "After what happened to you in the Stained Palace, we'd say you've earned it tenfold."

Ren swallowed. His throat felt thick. "Is that why you've called this meeting?"

"For the most part, yes," Mezd said. "It was pointed out to us that your hunt prior to that in the Stained Palace, the one in Tanglewood, had some similar characteristics of what you described in your report." He laid his copy of the reports on the table. Someone—Baer, Ren supposed—had circled certain passages and drawn arrows to others. "We also have Sanne's letter regarding your injuries, but not much more."

"And you both left out crucial details," Cazret said. "For instance, what actually hurt you and how." His dark eyes settled on Ren's hands. The darkness in his veins had faded, but Ren felt the urge to hide them anyway. "We'll start there. What was this entity?"

Ren was quiet for a moment. "What did Sanne tell you happened to me?"

Tmarrey consulted his copy of her letter. "Three broken ribs, a punctured lung, and a great deal of blood loss."

She hadn't mentioned his draining. Ren took a deep breath. Sanne had wanted them to keep quiet about what they'd found, but she had her king to think of. Ren didn't. If he was going to relive this, he was going to confess it all. "You've heard of the Prázeny Era?"

Tmarrey frowned. "Of course." Any educated individual had. When the Cataclysm destroyed Naisvet, the old world, the realm had entered the Prázeny Era. It was named for its divine emptiness; the gods, whose recklessness had caused the destruction of Naisvet, were banished from the mortal realm entirely. The universe had created a wretched Stone and used it to subdue the gods; whatever deity came into contact with it had their godhood siphoned into it. Only the disappearance of the Stone had allowed the gods to return to the realm. Cowed, their lessons learned, they'd crafted Ruhysvet from the ruins, and it had stood for over six hundred years.

Ren's cup rattled as he set it against its saucer. "And the Prázeny Stone?"

The members of the Triumvirate exchanged looks. Ren's heart leapt in his throat. Opinion on the legend of the Stone was mixed—most believed it was gone, though there were, of course, outliers. Some believed that the Stone still existed. Others believed that suggesting this was the highest form of blasphemy. Ren realized he had no idea where the Triumvirate fell.

"Yes," Mezd said. "But it's gone."

"We didn't think so." Ren let the memories surge forward. He told the Triumvirate everything he'd seen in the Stained Palace: the spirits' resistances to exorcisms, the wraith that had shifted forms like a ghoul and spoken like an apparition, and the horrible lavender eyes that he sometimes imagined peeking at him from dark corners. He told them about the entity that had come from the Stone, how it had thrown him around like a straw doll and eaten from him like one sucked marrow from a bone, and how he faintly remembered being prayed over by priests and priestesses. "The legends we found said nothing about the Stone's appearance, but given what it did to us, I believe that's what it was." He kept his words hypothetical, erring on the side of caution in case, by some miracle, he and Sanne had been wrong. "I think that's why our spells didn't work within the walls of the palace. The Stone, if that's indeed what it was, blocked the power of the gods."

The Triumvirate stared at him. They didn't gasp, and no jaws hung agape—they were far too battle-worn for that—but Ren saw shock register in their eyes. He didn't blame them. If he hadn't seen it for himself, he wouldn't believe a word he said.

"What happened to it?" Tmarrey asked, his voice so hushed it barely made it across the table to Ren.

"Sanne did."

Tmarrey's shoulders lowered, and Mezd leaned back in his

chair. "Thank the gods," Mezd sighed. "If it, or its effects on you, remained—"

"I know." Without his bits of godhood, Ren wouldn't be a Nightmare. He'd just be an elf with an ax and a grudge.

"Are you sure it's gone?" Cazret asked, frowning and drumming his fingers along the table. Ren wasn't surprised. The old man had never liked Sanne. "You didn't confirm it? You didn't stay to verify the kill?"

"With respect, Ser," Ren said, "my leave started immediately. Sanne verbally released me from the hunt, and I was paid for my services. Per your instruction, I was not to stay."

"How was Sanne when you left?" Tmarrey asked.

"Shaken, as I was, but she seemed fine. She healed faster than I did."

"Have you heard from her since?"

Ren shook his head.

Tmarrey pressed his lips together. "We tried to write to her, but our letter was returned."

Dread crept along the back of Ren's mind, but he pushed it away and said, "When I was at the Stained Palace, I was forbidden from most correspondence. The letter I managed to send was heavily censored."

"Her kingdom is at war with itself," Mezd said, but the words had the hollow, meaningless ring of repetition. Before Ren could push the matter further, Mezd looked at him and continued on. "The spirits in Tanglewood, did they bear any resemblance to what you fought in the Stained Palace?"

Ren shook his head. The only commonality the Tanglewood spirits had with those in the Stained Palace was their difficulty to banish, and he told the Triumvirate as much. "I suspect something external caused the Tanglewood infestation, though," he said. "There was a mass grave in the forest that had been recently overturned. Grave goods were disturbed, and some were brought into the town proper. The wraith I banished was directly connected to one of them."

"Yes, your report mentioned the grave," Tmarrey said, "and the plague. What's odd to us is that we've never had a Nightmare report the same difficulty banishing spirits in two separate places, let alone two separate kingdoms. That greatly concerns us." Tmarrey settled his elbows on the table and leaned forward. "If it was indeed the Stone that you fought, Ren, could it have been connected to Tanglewood? Or are we potentially facing a mutation of our prey?"

In the darkest hours of the nights since he'd left Jasniostvo, when Reia's warmth or Morgaine's breathing hadn't been enough to soothe him to sleep, Ren had wondered the same thing—he'd forced it from his mind each time, wanting to enjoy his mandated rest, but he'd wondered nonetheless. A connection between Tanglewood and the Stone would explain the similarities in he and Baba's veins, but the spirits at Sisters' Harvest hadn't resembled those in the Stained Palace. They hadn't been as vicious. "I don't know."

"That's where you've been for the duration of your leave, hasn't it?" Cazret asked.

"With the exception of a trip to Hrascara, the local duke's castle, for Solstice, yes." And he didn't want to say a word about that.

"Is Tanglewood where you'll remain until your leave expires?"

"Yes."

Tmarrey reached for the platter in the center of the table and poured himself coffee. The motion broke the tension; Ren got the sense the Triumvirate had asked all they'd intended. He wasn't sure what they'd do with his information, but had no doubt it was only one part of a greater matter they were considering. That was what the Triumvirate did; not only did they govern the Nightmares, but they worked to stay aware of any threat to the Order. If spirits were mutating, they'd want to know. Classroom lessons would need to change, banishment techniques would need to be reviewed. The Stone might have been gone, but Ren didn't think he'd relived its torment for the last time.

"And when your leave ends," Tmarrey asked, "what are your plans?"

Ren sighed. A banner displaying the image of a Nightmare's tattoo against a field of white hung on the wall behind the Triumvirate. He couldn't walk away from the Order, yet he couldn't walk away from Morgaine. "If I may speak freely?"

"Of course."

"I don't know."

Cazret's response was gruff. "Why not?"

Ren had grown up with no real family. He'd been something like a big brother to the younger boys in the Grey home, shielding them from the worst of the mistresses' abuse, but he'd of course lost touch with them when he'd escaped the home. His fellow Nightmares at the Keep had become his big brothers, the instructors and Triumvirate his surrogate fathers. The Order was a brotherhood. It was an unorthodox family. Ren had to believe they would be happy for him, even though he was frightened to admit, "There's a woman."

Their faces remained still.

"Baer told us you brought someone with you," Mezd said. "Is that her? The librarian?"

Ren nodded.

"Does she care for you?" Tmarrey asked.

"Yes."

"And you for her?"

"I love her." And, because he hadn't said it out loud yet— because he didn't want to think about Stones or spirits anymore —Ren blurted, "I'm thinking about marrying her."

The Triumvirate was quiet, so quiet that Ren could hear Umbrals calling through the window's thick glass. Ren wished they would say something. Even though he was twenty-seven and a head taller than Mezd, the largest of the Triumvirate, he felt like an impulsive child waiting to receive his punishment. Most children grew up with one father; when he'd come to the Keep, Ren had gone from none to three.

Cazret tented his fingers together. "Does she know what marriage to a Nightmare entails?" he asked, though the shortness in his tone was gone. "You wouldn't be exempt from the hunt just because you'd have a wife waiting for you."

"I know." Ren cleared his throat. "She knows."

"We're Nightmares, Ren. We die before our time."

"I know."

"Someone always needs us more."

"Maybe," Ren said. He was someone, too. "But I need her."

The ghost of a smile passed over Tmarrey's face. "If you propose, Ren, please notify us of the outcome. The two of you would be welcome to a suite here if she accepts."

"And if she declines?"

Cazret rolled his eyes. "Then you work through your sorrow by finding something to kill."

"Thank you for meeting with us, Ren," Mezd said. He stood, and the others followed suit. "I'm sure we'll see you in town."

The dismissal was abrupt, but Ren expected nothing less. The Triumvirate operated on efficiency, and they'd gotten what they needed. He shook each of the males' hands. "Of course."

"Rest well, Ren. We're grateful for your service and dedication to the Order."

Ren's mind whirled with possible connections and the implications of all he'd seen, but he did his best to quiet it. He wanted Morgaine. He wanted to go home. "Thank you," he said, nodding his head in deference and bidding the Triumvirate farewell with the traditional Nightmare valediction. "Rest well."

———

"You're being very quiet."

Ren rubbed his thumb along the back of Morgaine's hand. She'd wanted to walk back instead of riding, and he was grateful to have her at his side. So was Reia—she ran through the forest around them, chasing squirrels around the bare trees. "I have a lot on my mind," he said. "And much of it, I don't want to think about."

"Is it because of your meeting?"

"Yes."

"Because of my artifacts?"

"Some of them." Like that damned Esclarmonde button. The Stained Palace would always follow him—his conversation with the Triumvirate had proven that. He'd suffered so much to have this little bit of peace. Couldn't the matters of kings wait?

No. After speaking with the Triumvirate, Ren knew they couldn't. They weren't just the matters of kings anymore. If the Triumvirate was right and Nightmare prey was truly mutating, it was a matter of the Order, of Ren's livelihood.

Morgaine's fingers tightened around his. She reached up with her other hand and smoothed the wrinkles between his brows. He hadn't realized he was scowling. "Are you ever going to tell me what happened to you?" she asked, her voice soft. "What really happened?"

He stopped walking and threw his arms around her. Ren thought of the scars on her thighs, how she'd gotten them in the same forest they stood in now, and how she'd walked into Tmadrev to accompany him anyway. She was braving a deep fear for him, and he had only ever hid his from her. "Nightmares have godhood in them."

"Yes," she said cautiously. "I know."

"Mine was taken from me." His psychological scars had been reopened, and he forced himself to keep them bleeding. He brushed his thumb across the nape of Morgaine's neck as he told her everything he'd said to the Triumvirate. The motion calmed him, kept him steady, but also kept her close—what if she didn't understand why he'd kept this to himself? What if she no longer wanted him?

When he found the courage to look at her, Morgaine had gone pale. He waited for her to tell him he was crazy, or that he was blaspheming, but she didn't question his encounter with the

Stone. He should have known she'd believe the books, and therefore believe him—the legends said the Stone was gone, and Morgaine traded in stories. "I knew it was bigger than a few powerful spirits." Her voice was barely a whisper. "The darkness in your veins looked like Baba's."

"I wasn't sick—"

She shook her head and stepped back. "I think you were," she said. "I've been researching it and reading whatever I can find, but you haven't wanted to talk about it. I know why that button has the Esclarmonde sigil on it. Baer confirmed it for me. And if you had the plague, and this *thing* was in Jasniostvo—why did you keep this from me?"

He stared at the ground. The boot-treads of dozens of Nightmares had churned the snow into a muddy slush. Shame burned low in his gut. "I was going to tell you."

"When?" Dismay was evident in her voice. It shaped her question into a dull blade, one Ren wished was sharp enough to cut him clean through. "I knew something was wrong. I would have listened."

Panic spread through his chest, stretching up to his throat and cutting off his air like grasping fingers. This was exactly what he'd wanted to avoid. "I didn't want to think about it," he said, reaching for her. "I just wanted to be with you, and be happy. I didn't want to think about the hunt—"

"But you'll go back to it after the equinox."

He would, but— "We don't have to think about that. I'm here now, and we have time. We don't have to think about Stones or spirits or marriage or—"

"Marriage?"

Ren hadn't watched his words. He'd said it too soon. He hadn't even told her he loved her yet—but he couldn't, not like this. "Morgaine—"

She narrowed her eyes. "What have you been thinking about marriage, Ren, that you haven't told me? Or is this another one of your cruel jokes?"

"Cruel?" He got his wish. Her words stung like a sharp blade. "You think I'm *cruel*?"

"Maybe not cruel. But I think you're being cowardly." Her eyes glittered with tears. "Tanglewood, and *I*, aren't just something to distract yourself with. I know you must heal. I know you need rest. But you have to face what's happened, and I don't want you to marry me as a way to avoid doing so. Answer my question, Ren, and by the gods, be honest with me." Her voice trembled. "What have you thought about marriage?"

He sucked in a breath. The cold air pierced his lungs. "I like the idea of marriage," he said, choosing his words carefully. "I like the idea of marrying you. I like the idea of not leaving you in ten weeks. But I—" He drew in another breath. This one shook. "I'm not going to live a long time, Morgaine. No Nightmare does. Everything that happened to me in the Stained Palace proves that. I would marry you knowing I'm going to make you a widow. That, to me, is what's cruel."

Tears burned in her eyes, but she didn't shed them for sorrow —they were too bright for that. Morgaine wept out of anger. "So you would deny yourself any happiness at all? Because of what *might* happen to me? Because of how I might be forced to grieve you?"

He started to protest, to tell her there was no "might" about it, but she raised a hand to stop him.

"Don't speak as if you're Oddelen himself," she spat. "The truth is, Ren, you don't know when you'll die. You don't know how. You can tell yourself how it is to spare yourself your own fear, but you. Don't. Know." She jabbed a finger at him with each word. "You could die tomorrow. You could die after living a long life with me—"

"I almost died in Jasniostvo—"

"Yet we're having this conversation." She wiped her tears from her face, but fresh ones immediately replaced them. "You *almost* died. But you didn't. It's more to my point than yours. If you love me, and I think you do, then tell me. If you want to marry me, ask me. If you don't, then tell me you don't. But don't you dare punish yourself and call it protecting me."

She stared at him for a moment. Ren stared back. Anything he could have said slipped into nothingness. Her words had flayed him, laid him bare and steaming and bleeding on the snow.

She was right.

He was afraid.

I love you, he wanted to say. *I love you more than I've ever loved anyone, and I want you to be mine, but I know the pain I'll put you through. I'm afraid I won't be worth that. I'm afraid my love won't be enough.*

But he said none of it.

Morgaine turned on her heel and walked away before he could.

11.21.626

Ren stood in front of the library at first light and knocked again. "I know you're awake, little love." He could hear her booted feet shuffling around behind the door. Ren pressed his hand against the worn wood slab. "Please let me in. Please."

She'd refused to see him the day before—the letter he'd sent over with Kyr had gone unanswered. Ren had laid on his bed in the Drowsy Dragon and stared at the ceiling as the day passed, listening to the Nightmares carouse in the tavern below when night came. He'd never hurt quite like this, and the thought of spending the rest of his life alone had never scared him so much.

Her voice was muffled. "Why are you here, Ren?"

"I want to borrow a book."

She opened the door just enough for him to see her. She wore her nightdress and a heavy house coat of grey wool. Her hair was unbound. Ren held his breath, waiting for her to say the library wasn't open, but instead she asked, "Which one?"

"*Tanglewood: A History.*"

She let him in. There was an odd quirk to her mouth, one that didn't match the sadness in her eyes. "I was hoping you'd come for it."

He stood by the circulation desk as she vanished into the aisles. He half-expected to see Fanning swoop from behind a shelf, but the library was achingly still.

She reappeared with the book in hand. They didn't speak as she wrote his name on a checkout card and slipped it into the envelope in the back of *Tanglewood: A History*. "Here."

"When is it due?"

Morgaine took another library card and worried with it, tearing small rips in its edges. "In ten weeks."

Ren couldn't do this. He couldn't bear becoming a stranger to her. "Morgaine, I—"

"The library hasn't opened yet. I need to get dressed."

"Just a moment. Please." He came around the desk. She didn't flinch when he placed his hand on her cheek. "I'm sorry. I want this. I want you. I love you. That's why—" He swallowed. "That's why I've been so hesitant. You're right. I'm a coward. I love you, and I'm afraid because that means that one day, some-how, I'm going to lose you. You're going to lose me. And I don't know if I'm worth that."

She took his hand and lowered it. "How worthy I find your love isn't for you to decide."

"I know. I'm trying to understand—"

"Then let me put it this way." Morgaine twined her fingers through his, but Ren took no joy in it. Shadows creased under her eyes. She looked so tired. "You don't need to protect me from you. I know what happens to Nightmares. I know that one day I'll be left alone. And I'm not afraid of that." She drew her house coat around her, and it was as if shadows swallowed her whole. "But I'm afraid of you deciding I am and walking away from me because of it. I don't know how else to say this. I love you, and if you asked me to marry you, I'd say yes."

He reached for her, but she stepped back. "Morgaine—"

"I'm not done." Their eyes met. She dropped his hand. "I love you, but there's nothing here for you until you know what you want. I'll gladly face this with you, but you have to face it first." Her voice wavered. "And until you have, you should go."

Her words hung in the air, lingering like the weighty silence that came after an exorcism, when there was only Ren and the unblood on his hands and the death he'd just caused. Her words, in a way, were the same as his ax; they sliced and stung, but they brought order. Rightness. He couldn't expect her to fix him. He had to do this on his own.

So he left.

———

Though the sun had risen only minutes ago, Zikat's chapel was empty.

Ren knew better than to be surprised. Those who'd left the tavern sober last night had walked to the Keep and would pray in Zikat's chapel there. Those too drunk to make the trip had fallen into spare beds in the Drowsy Dragon and were likely still sleeping. Even if the Nightmares hadn't been present, Ren didn't think the chapel would have been full; any townspeople rising this early likely did so in order to do chores, or they simply didn't care to make the little trip. Perhaps they didn't feel they needed a chapel to pray—Ren didn't.

Yet he was awake, and he was here, so he knelt before the altar and bowed his head.

The Zikatic dialect rasped from his throat. "Lively one," he said, and that was all it took. Tears fogged his vision. He barely made it through the ritual laud before they fell to the plank floor. He bared himself to Zikat, confessing his wants and fears and the tangled mess the two had become. "I know you don't often speak to your faithful," he said, slipping into the common tongue, "but please give me a sign. I want her. I love her. Am I allowed her?"

Because that was the thrust of it—Ren didn't know if

someone like him, who traded in bloodshed and exorcisms, was allowed such a constant peace.

Ren wanted to say more, but held his tongue and opened his eyes. He waited for a sign—a touch at his back, a creaking of floorboards—but nothing came. All he could think of was the shadows beneath Morgaine's eyes and the book he'd borrowed and the vine-wrapped town around him. *Tanglewood: A History.* Tanglewood: a relic. A remnant.

Tanglewood: A History sat at his side. The sunlight cast across the book seemed to shift in hue, glowing green for a moment before turning the pale yellow of morning again.

His heart skipped a beat. "Zikat," he murmured, "was that you?"

The chapel around him was still and silent.

Ren ended his prayer with a short word of thanks and snatched the book up. He settled onto a velvet-cushioned pew to read.

The plague had been thirty years ago, so Ren flipped to the section of the book pertaining to the 590s and skimmed for any mention of it. He found the first mention midway through the section: in the autumn of 596, the priestess of Zdesen, the goddess of fear, had reported strange symptoms to the town healer. She'd suffered from dizziness and shortness of breath for a few days before her veins had turned a blackish-purple.

Ren pushed away the memory of his own hands bearing that discoloration.

The priestess had also reported feeling Zdesen's absence: *her prayers felt as if she was shouting into a void*, the book said, *and her goddess did not answer her.* The priestess died a few days later.

Ren skimmed faster now, his heart beating just as quickly. Zikat's priestess took ill in the same manner and died, and so did Oddelen's priest. The most faithful among Tanglewood's townspeople also sickened and died, the disease in their veins taking them swiftly regardless of how much they prayed for healing. The sickest among them spoke of terrible visions, of seeing black spirits with lavender eyes hovering at their bedside—seeing these spirits was a sign that the end was near, an omen that Ren knew all too well. As Tanglewood's citizens died, so did its reputation and its faith. Svetlen's, Zatva's, and Sumra's priestesses fled Tanglewood's temples, leaving the townspeople to fend for themselves.

The mayor at the time, Henric Soma—Ren supposed this was the mayoress' father—wrote to the king of Zijustvo, His Majesty Vaimar Villari, and requested aid. The king declined.

Ren rolled his eyes. On principle, he cared little for kings, and he'd heard nothing about the Zijustvan king that impressed him. Whether a kingdom was blessed with a good ruler or saddled with a poor one was almost entirely up to chance, and it seemed that King Vaimar had been just as inept then as Ren felt he was now.

Yet the mention of another king chilled Ren to the bone:

Though the Villaris declined to send aid, afraid that the contact between their staff and the townspeople would cause the plague to spread to the capital, they appointed Duke Malon Scara to oversee the relief efforts. A royal messenger was also sent across the border to King Oran Esclarmonde, as the Celesty, the capital of Jasniostvo, was significantly closer to Tanglewood than the Zijustvan capital. To Mayor Soma's surprise, Duke Scara traveled to the town's outskirts and established a camp there in a matter of days; to the shock of the mayor and the duke, King Oran appeared at this camp within the week.

Oran—the late father of Cassander, in whose palace Ren had nearly died.

Ren's lung seized. He closed his eyes and took measured breaths until the memory passed.

He kept reading. Oran had traveled to Tanglewood twice a month, bringing a fresh supply of food, water, and healers with him each time. He and Scara spoke with the townspeople and consulted with Mayor Soma in attempts to root out the cause of the plague. They had little success; the sickness haunted Tanglewood for another seven months before infection rates began to slow, though this was theorized to be because the population had been so affected. There were simply less bodies for the plague to inhabit.

A mass grave had been dug in Tmadrev in the thirteenth month of 597. A chill swept over Ren—he knew exactly where that grave was. A fresh outbreak rattled Tanglewood, as the men who dug the grave immediately fell sick and died days later. Scara and Esclarmonde forbade everyone from using the new grave until they'd deemed it safe. Mages and holy ones and more healers were summoned, though they spoke to no one in the town.

To the townspeople's surprise, the plague's spread continued to slow. Those who had already fallen ill healed quickly. The mass grave was cleared for use in the first month of 598, and King Oran left Tanglewood for good a month later. A footnote mentioned that one of his mages had been spotted carrying something in a glowing reliquary from the grave in the middle of the night, but the woman who'd witnessed this had been too frightened and too sick to question it.

After Oran's departure, the plague died out almost completely. It was ruled to be officially over in the fourth month of 598, when Tanglewood again opened its gates to Tmadrev.

The cause of the plague, the book said, *was never officially determined.*

Ren felt sick. He knew. He'd borne the remnants of it in his veins.

The Stone in the Stained Palace—it had come from Tanglewood. He'd survived Tanglewood's plague.

He tossed the book onto the pew and pressed his hands to his eyes. Everything he'd been through in the last few months—the difficulty of his hunts, his draining and brush with death, the agony he'd suffered—it all led back to Tanglewood. It had all started here.

He was on his feet and walking to the library before he

could think twice, his mind a maelstrom. In the center of the storm, however, calm and steady amidst the tumult, was one thing.

The Stone had brought emptiness and sickness and death to mortals and gods alike, but it had brought something else, too: fear. Ren had felt it in the Stained Palace, had felt the shreds of divinity in him shy away from it before he and Sanne had known what it was. He saw the fright that persisted on the townspeople's faces when they spoke of the plague. He'd looked fear in its glowing eyes and had felt it leach his life from him, yet he had survived. His gods had returned. The plague had cleared. Tanglewood had opened its gates, and the townspeople still smiled and laughed and loved each other despite it. The townspeople had saved Morgaine, an outsider, despite it.

Fear was constant, but so were divinity and joy and hope and love. He couldn't succumb to fear when there was so much else to be had.

Everything came back to Tanglewood, yet Ren came back to her.

When he entered the library, Baer looked up from behind the counter. "She's in her office."

Morgaine and Baer had gotten a considerable amount of work done on the artifacts—Ren didn't have to watch where he stepped, and he was glad for it. Morgaine rose when he came through the threshold and rushed to her. Ren dropped the book on her desk and pulled her into his arms.

"I had your plague."

He felt her swallow. "You did." Her arms snaked around him, slow with caution. "What does that mean?"

"I don't know. I just know that it's gone. But that isn't why I've come." Ren kissed the top of her head. The realm would be worried over in its own time. He needed to tell her this now. "You can expect my proposal soon, little love."

She raised her head, her eyes searching his. "Ren—"

"I mean it." He wound his fingers through hers. "I love you. I don't want marriage to be something we only tease each other about. I want it to be ours."

A smile slipped across her face before she could hide it. "I want that, too. I want *you*."

And he'd give her all of him, even the parts he'd tried to hide. "Just give me some time. I want to ask you the right way."

"Well, that's simple. Get on your knees and ask."

Ren laughed. "Remember what you said to me at Sisters' Harvest?" he asked, holding her bare left hand up before her. "There's something you must have before you accept, little love, and I want you to say yes—so I'll need to get you a ring."

———

Though the Nightmares had been coming to Tanglewood for three days, Ren hadn't gotten used to seeing the Drowsy Dragon full. He squeezed between two trainees, whip-thin boys he severely doubted were old enough to drink, and raised a hand to signal Azra.

She darted over. "Your usual?"

He nodded. "Morgaine's, too. Take your time, though. I'm waiting on her."

Azra laughed. "I'll pour it now, while I still can. Your people are drinking me dry." She returned moments later and settled two mugs, foam spilling over the rims, in front of him. "Anything else?"

"Just a question." Ren leaned forward—the Nightmares around them produced a small din, and he didn't want to shout to be heard. "Merchants still stop in Tanglewood every now and then, right?"

Azra nodded.

"Is a jeweler ever among them?"

A sly smile spread over Azra's face. "Yes. Why?"

"Do you know the next time they're due to arrive?"

Azra leaned down, her grin becoming smug. Gods above—

was the entire town about to find out he'd asked this? "Tell me why, and I'll tell you when."

"I've decided to get my ears pierced."

Azra tutted. She tucked her braids behind her pointed ears, which were studded with gold and silver piercings from lobe to tip. "It's a shame you're lying. I think you'd—"

The tavern door slammed open. "Excuse me!"

Ren whirled. It was Morgaine's voice, but he couldn't see her—the only movement in the crowd was from Nightmares shifting to allow the Triumvirate through. They strode to the bar, Tmarrey in the lead. As the crowd moved to let them pass, Ren saw Morgaine. She trailed behind Cazret, scowling. Baer followed, expressionless.

"You can't just take it," Morgaine snapped. "I paid for it."

Cazret barked a laugh and said, not bothering to turn around, "Whoever sold it to you, I promise it wasn't their rightful property to begin with."

Baer walked over to Ren, the tapping of his cane barely audible beneath the murmuring crowd and Morgaine and Cazret's argument.

"What's going on?"

Baer sighed. "The Triumvirate asked to see Morgaine and I's work, so I took them to the library. She had what looked like a Nightmare dagger on her desk. I tried to ask her about it discreetly, but Tmarrey overheard and confiscated it." He looked at Ren from the corner of his eye. "Did you know she had one?"

It was Ren's turn to sigh. He should have known this would come back to bite him. "Yes."

"And you didn't take it?"

"No."

"Why not?"

In front of them, Cazret raised his voice to be heard over Morgaine's protests. "Do you even know what you had, Miss Greywarren?"

Her fists clenched. "It's a dagger of Nightmare steel, which is

an alloy of steel and copper. During the forging process, it under-
goes a series of enchantments—"

"Morgaine," Ren warned. No, he didn't like how Cazret
spoke to her, but he'd told her from the moment he knew about
the dagger that she wasn't allowed to have it. He should have
pushed the matter harder. He should have confiscated it before
she'd a chance to wield it at Solstice. The least he could do was
diffuse the situation now.

As one, Morgaine and the Triumvirate turned to him. Each
one bore some degree of a scowl. "Ren," Mezd said, "did you
know about this?"

He straightened and braced for their questions. "I did, Ser."

The Triumvirate regarded him. Ren hoped they remembered
what he'd told them about Morgaine, and hoped they understood
he'd let her keep it out of love. He'd wanted her to feel safe.

But Mezd's face gave nothing away. "I see."

Tmarrey took the dagger from the sheaths at his thigh. "In
that case—Enorry, it's yours now."

Baer took it without a word, though Ren saw the smallest bit
of guilt flash across his face. Their business done, the Triumvirate
walked to an empty place at the bar and flagged down Azra.

"I've got your drink, little love," Ren murmured, touching
Morgaine's hand—she was glaring across the tavern at the
Triumvirate. Khai, who was walking to the bar, accidentally inter-
cepted her piercing look; he shrank back into the crowd and
rerouted.

"I want my dagger," she muttered, but let Ren twine their
fingers together and pull her to his barstool.

"I'll get you a new, non-Nightmare blade."

"It isn't—" She sighed. "Fine. I suppose it'll serve the same
purpose."

"Any dagger would."

"That isn't what I mean." She hopped onto the barstool and
took a drag of ale. "I bought the Nightmare dagger because I
missed you."

"How sentimental." Ren reached across her to get his drink, but ghosted his other hand over her waist in the process. It was quite touching, why she'd bought it—and maybe he could distract her from what she'd lost by touching her in return. "And here I thought you'd bought it out of spite."

She narrowed her eyes at him. "It was sentiment-fueled spite. I wanted to irritate you just as much as see you again."

Ren chuckled and kissed her temple. "Well, you've accomplished both." She scoffed, but he saw a smile flicker across her face. He lowered his lips to her ear and murmured, "Finish your drink. Maybe you can irritate me further upstairs."

Her chest flushed scarlet. By the time she'd finished her ale, the color had crept to her cheeks.

When Azra came back to their spot, summoned by the sound of two empty mugs hitting the bar, Ren and Morgaine were already gone.

11.22.626

Ren spent the next four days trying to weasel information about the traveling jeweler out of Azra. He suspected she knew why, of course, but couldn't begrudge her for wanting the satisfaction of hearing him say it.

"If it's for the reason I'm thinking," she said as she slid his ale across the counter, "it's happening because of me and my incredibly popular tavern, you know. Remember that when you're planning your wedding feast."

Ren shook his head and took the ale, but winked at her before walking away.

Morgaine started joining the Nightmares for their revelrous dinners, hovering at Ren's side and slipping away as she grew more comfortable with each passing night. Her iciness toward the Triumvirate thawed, and she quickly learned not to spend too much time around Cazret unless she wanted to be goaded into an argument. "I think Mezd is my favorite," she confessed to Ren as he walked her home one night. "He told me tonight that he's impressed with how I've helped Baer."

Ren smiled. He was, too. "Mezd used to terrify me, you know. He was one of my instructors."

Her jaw dropped. "Him? No."

"Oh, yes." As they walked across the square and into her apartment, Ren told her how even the sight of Mezd struck fear into the hearts of every trainee at the Keep. His recall stopped only when she pulled him onto her bed and kissed him until he forgot what he'd been saying.

When he rolled from the bed, either minutes or hours later, Morgaine tried to pull him back down. "I've got to go, little love," he laughed, drawing her hand to his lips and kissing it. "My bed is across the square."

Morgaine dropped her hand. "Very well. But I miss when we were snowed in and you slept right over there."

"I do, too." Ren perched on the edge of the bed, half-hoping she would drag him back down. "But soon I'll sleep right here, if you want."

She pressed a light kiss to his lips. "Where else?"

"You could come to the Keep."

She leaned back. "Really?"

Ren nodded. "A Nightmare's wife has the same options as a Nightmare: travel the realm and stay in taverns or a town, or have quarters at the Keep. If you accept my proposal, when it comes—"

Morgaine scoffed. "'If'."

He smiled. "—you could stay in Tanglewood and I'd come back between hunts, or we could move into a suite at the Keep."

"Oh." Her eyes widened. "Really?"

He nodded.

"Doesn't the Keep move around?"

"It does." As the Keep was from Naisvet, so was the magic that enchanted it. Portal magic, one of the most ancient types of magic, had been woven into each of the Keep's flagstones and the mortar between them. Portal magic was famously difficult to harness, and practitioners of it were rare—yet not so rare that the Order didn't always employ at least one portal mage. "We would move with it."

"Oh," she said again. Morgaine drew a ribbon from her hair and wound it around her fingers. "That's a lot to think about. If I came to the Keep, what would I do?"

His heart sank a bit—he had hoped she'd be more excited by the thought, given her complicated feelings about Tanglewood, but he understood. This had been her home for eleven years. She'd put down roots. She had a purpose here. "I know, and I'm not sure," he confessed, kissing her temple. "I wanted you to know it was an option. But wherever you want our home to be, little love, that's where it'll be. I only need it to have you."

Ren got his wish. Morgaine tugged him back onto her bed.

He walked to the Drowsy Dragon with swollen lips and a lightness in his heart. He could see himself coming back to Tanglewood between hunts, settling down until the Keep sent word that he was needed somewhere else. He could just as easily imagine coming home to the Keep, running up the castle's winding stairs until he reached the chamber where Morgaine waited for him. He didn't care which option she chose, only that she picked whichever would make her happiest. He'd be happy either way.

After all, he'd have her.

11.27.626

When Ren woke the next morning, it was to Kyr hopping on his knee and cawing wildly. He clutched a letter in his beak.

"By the gods, where have you been?" Ren muttered, sitting up. He hadn't seen his Umbrals in days—they'd likely been at the Keep, playing with the unbounded Umbrals while they could.

Kyr dropped the letter and flew to Ren's chipped horn, pecking at the exposed white center. Ren opened and read it.

The color drained from his face. He read it again, and then again to make sure he wasn't mistaken. "Gods."

He shot out of bed, threw on some clothes, and drew his cloak around his shoulders. Snow was falling, and he arrived at the library with snow in his hair and the letter crumpled in his fist. He'd seen fewer Nightmares in town that morning, less Umbrals than usual in the square. It seemed some of his brothers had already heeded the letter's command. "Morgaine?"

Her head popped out of her office. "Good morning. You're up early." She took him in, his heaving chest and stricken expression, and frowned. "What's wrong?"

Ren held out the letter. He didn't have the words to tell her.

Morgaine set her teacup down, unfolded the letter, and began to read. She gasped.

The library's front windows faced the town square. Ren watched the snow fall, watched it fill in the footsteps of every Nightmare who'd walked through Tanglewood.

NIGHTMARES,

THIS IS A MESSAGE OF THE UTMOST IMPORTANCE, AN ORDER OF THE HIGHEST PRIORITY: RETURN TO THE KEEP IMMEDIATELY. LEAVING A HUNT UNFINISHED IS PERMISSIBLE THIS ONCE, THOUGH YOU WILL NEED TO RETURN ANY UNEARNED FUNDS.

YOUR SAFETY IS MORE IMPORTANT TO US.

CONTINUE TO REPORT YOUR LOCATION TO THE KEEP WHEN YOU CROSS BORDERS. AVOID THE CAPITAL OF JASNIOSTVO—IT'S THE AREA KNOWN AS THE CELESTY, IF YOU'RE UNFAMILIAR WITH THAT KINGDOM. IF YOU BECOME SIGNIFICANTLY DELAYED, TELL US. WE ARE LOCATED WITHIN TMADREV FOREST ON THE ZIJUSTVAN SIDE. LET YOUR UMBRALS GUIDE YOU. WE WILL GO TO GROUND AND GIVE THE REASON FOR THIS RECALL ONCE

THE ENTIRE ORDER HAS RETURNED AND IS
ACCOUNTED FOR.
   DESTROY THIS LETTER.

SIGNED,
SER BERRICK TMARREY
SER CRANNOC MEZD
SER REDDIN CARRET
THE TRIUMVIRATE OF THE ORDER OF NIGHTMARES
11.27.626

"Ren, what is this?"

"I don't know."

The letter shook in her hands. Her face crumpled. "I thought we had more time."

He closed his eyes against the tears that threatened to spill. He'd thought so, too.

"What does this have to do with you? Why do you have to go? You're on leave."

"I don't know, little love," he said, though he did. He was a Nightmare. When the Triumvirate ordered something, he did it—and if they were giving such an extreme command, it meant that matters were grave. Ren had heard of individual Nightmares being called home, but never the entire Order. A goodbye didn't mean forever, but it didn't mean this wasn't going to hurt. "I don't know."

She set the letter on the circulation desk and went to him. "Ask me now."

"What?"

"Ask me to marry you now. Don't wait on a ring. I don't need one."

"Morgaine—"

She curled her fingers around his shirt as if the Triumvirate was coming to drag him away themselves. "*Ask me.*"

A knock sounded at the door just before Baer shoved it open.

"You're here," he panted, leaning on his cane and letting the door fall shut behind him. "Thank the gods."

"What's going on?" Morgaine demanded before Ren could. "Why is Ren being called back?"

Baer pressed his lips together. "The Triumvirate finally heard from Sanne," he said. "She's abandoned her hunt. From what the Triumvirate said she told them—" He adjusted his grip on his cane with shaking hands. "She wasn't truthful. The Stone wasn't destroyed. Between Tanglewood's plague and your and Sanne's accounts, Ren, the Triumvirate has seen what it's capable of. They fear for the Order should the Stone—" His voice pitched higher. Baer took a deep breath and closed his eyes. After a moment, having collected himself, he opened his eyes and quietly said, "The Stone is still out there. We are in danger. That's all that matters right now."

A cold hand buried itself in Ren's gut, fumbling around his intestines until it reached up and found his lung. It squeezed, digging its claws into the organ until he couldn't breathe. Piercing pain shot through his side. Ren gasped, pressing a hand to the place where his ribs had shattered—there was nothing there. The pain was only a ghost. It was only a memory, but its source had survived. Would the Order meet the same fate he had beneath the Stained Palace? Would there even be an Order if that happened?

By the gods. Sanne had lied to him.

Multifaceted emotion flared in Ren, shifting and heating like a fire: anger, sorrow, disappointment. Fear. "Is Sanne—"

"She's alive. That's all I know." Baer's stiff formality had vanished. Before Ren stood the unmoored young man he'd abandoned the night of Tovar's funeral. There had been something between Baer and Sanne in those days; Ren and Tovar had felt their relationship shift, but the four of them had never addressed it out loud. If Baer was afraid of losing her, he didn't voice it. "And she's coming home."

"Well, she has to, doesn't she?" Morgaine snapped. "When are you leaving? Immediately?"

Baer shook his head. He raised a hand as if to touch her. "No. We'll be in Tmadrev until the entire Order is accounted for. It could take weeks, or even months. We have Nightmares all over the realm. And we might not even move when they've all returned —the Triumvirate has said nothing about that."

Morgaine jerked away. Ren could see in her eyes that she didn't want to be soothed. "But why would you stay? The letter said you were going to 'go to ground'." She held it in front of Baer, though they all knew what it said. "If the Stone is still a threat, and if it's in a palace that's only a few days' ride away, why would the Keep stay here?"

Baer narrowed his eyes at Ren. "She read the letter?"

"She deserved to see it."

Morgaine turned away. The library fell silent.

Her shoulders began to shake.

Ren's heart broke. "Morgaine—"

"No." Her voice wavered. "I need to be alone."

"Morgaine—"

"*No*," she snapped, cutting Baer off as she had Ren. "Both of you, just go."

"Very well." Baer turned and walked to the door, his cane thudding against the floorboards. The library door creaked when he pushed it open. "Ren?"

Ren brushed his fingers across Morgaine's back, but she didn't turn. The air between them felt too much like Sisters' Harvest. He was leaving again. The moment she'd dreaded had come, and there was nothing he could do. He kissed the back of Morgaine's head. "I'm sorry," he whispered.

She didn't reply.

Ren left the library.

———

Ren walked without direction or thought, winding through the streets of Tanglewood until the dirt and gravel thoroughfares gave way to the unmarked snow of the forest. The air was colder here than it was in town, the mass of trees thick enough to block the sunlight even without their leaves. The world around him was frigid and lifeless and still. He wanted to sit against one of the winter-dead trunks and dissolve into the ice, to be as blank as the snow. He would be free of duty then, of obligation. His only responsibility would be to sit and melt, and his death would water the trees and bring life to Tmadrev. The simplicity of it made his heart ache.

Baer followed him, but neither spoke. A wordless understanding passed between them, that of boys who'd grown into adulthood together. Though they'd parted on poor terms, there was a loyalty to one another that lacked definition. Baer would wait, and Baer would listen.

Ren stopped at the edge of a clearing. The tree to his left still had boards driven into it, arranged horizontally to form a ladder to the thick branch that stuck out over the clearing. Baer caught up and stood beside him, silent as stone, as they looked at the plague pit. Unmarred snow blanketed the ground, but Ren knew what was beneath it—turned earth and skeletons emptied of their grave goods.

"This is the site, isn't it?"

Ren nodded. "They held games here, in autumn," he said, his voice hushed. He'd stood at Morgaine's side here only months ago. "That was why the grave was disturbed."

"I see."

The Nightmares, partially mortal and partially divine, looked over the clearing. It was an amalgamation like them, a place where life and death tangled together.

"I was going to ask her to marry me, Baer."

"You still can."

Ren exhaled a laugh, but it was mirthless. "She won't want to stay here while the Keep takes us gods know where."

"She doesn't want to come to the Keep?"

"She isn't sure." A gentle snow began to fall. Ren tipped his face to the sky, feeling the snowflakes melt on his face. "Other than her time in the Grey home, Tanglewood is all she's known. She'd be leaving everything for me." *If I came to the Keep, what would I do?* she'd asked, and Ren had no answer. He couldn't give her a life of sitting and waiting. But hadn't she told him she wanted more than Tanglewood? Hadn't she confessed to wanting to see the realm?

Baer ran his thumb over his cane. The tip of it had been carved into a raven's head. "I could use her at the Keep, you know," he said. "Someone will need to mind the library and archives once I'm able to hunt again."

Ren let himself picture it: Morgaine in a new dress, black like a Nightmare's armor, swirling around the Keep's library and keeping the candles burning for any trainees studying late into the night. Coming to her after a hunt, getting any books she needed but was too short to reach, holding them from her until she called him sweetheart or paid for the favor with a kiss. "Do you think the Triumvirate would permit it?"

"If I present it, yes." Baer took a deep breath. "And they're afraid. If I found a replacement, it would allow me to practice more. If the threat presented by the Stone is as bad as they think, they'll want as many Nightmares in fighting form as possible. She'd be doing the Order a service."

This was dangerous. Ren was starting to hope again. "But Tanglewood—"

"By the gods." Baer glared at him. "You haven't changed. Stop being self-sacrificial, Ren. Yes, Morgaine cares deeply for Tanglewood, whether she likes that she does or not—but she also cares for you. Don't decide for her. Don't feel you have to protect her from missing Tanglewood."

Overhead, ravens called. Fanning settled onto the branch over the clearing, Kyr perching at her side a moment later.

"If you want her, Ren," Baer said, his voice low, "don't wait for the Triumvirate's approval. Don't wait for me to offer her the job. Wed her." His hazel eyes unfocused for a moment. "Don't assume you'll always have enough time to ask."

Ren's hands shook, but from excitement this time—the pieces were falling into place. He could offer her a future. He could offer her the realm. He could offer her *him*, forever. He just wanted to do it right. She deserved that much. "I don't have a ring, Baer."

Baer's eyes refocused. "Gods, Ren. We have a forge at the Keep." He unsheathed one of the daggers he wore at his thighs and handed it to Ren—it was the blade the Triumvirate had taken from Morgaine. "And I've come into some extra steel."

12.1.626

Baer heard from the Triumvirate two days later. If Morgaine accepted, Baer's position at the Keep would be hers.

"The gods are smiling on you," Baer said when he gave Ren the news. A small smile crept over his face, the first Ren had seen in years. "You've done something to earn this kindness, Ren. Don't waste it."

Ren grinned and held the door open for Baer—it was sunset, and the Nightmares were crowding into Oddelen's small chapel for evening vespers. "I don't plan to."

As the gathered Nightmares prayed, led by Oddelen's priest from the Keep, Ren fingered the rings in his pocket. He'd fetched them from the Keep that afternoon, a coordinating pair formed from Nightmare steel. His was a thick band, marbled as a Nightmare blade was, but Morgaine's was slim and delicate. He'd asked Ailas, the forger, to separate the copper from the steel and form them into two separate strands that twined together like a rope. Ailas had been thrilled to present them to Ren, beaming as he said, "And don't worry about it not fitting her—I rewrote one of the enchantments. It will size itself."

Prayer ended sooner than Ren expected, but he'd been lost in thought for the majority of the service. He and Baer followed the crowd out. The Nightmares spilled from Oddelen's temple into the snowy square, their black cloaks fluttering like Umbral wings.

"We're eating at the Dusk and Dawn tonight," Baer said, holding his fur-trimmed cloak shut with one hand. "Azra threatened to ban us from the Drowsy Dragon if we drank her dry again. Are you coming?"

Ren looked across the square. Candlelight fell through the library's windows and pooled on the snow. Each time he'd tried to see Morgaine, she'd quietly asked him to leave. He'd given her the space she wanted, but now, with their rings jingling in his pocket, he couldn't pull away any further. He couldn't let her think she faced their end. "I'm going to see if Morgaine wants to join us."

Baer stopped in his tracks. "You have the rings. Is it happening now?"

Ren fished out the rings. Since the Stained Palace, Ren had avoided looking at his hands—he only ever saw the shadows in his veins, though they'd now faded. He liked, though, seeing his hand when the rings were in it. They were warm from his body heat; if the gods willed it, they would never be cold again. They'd be separated, one on her finger and one on his, but never for long. He would hear them clink together every time he took Morgaine's hand. "It could."

Happiness struck him like a blow. It could happen now. He'd wanted to decorate his room in the Drowsy Dragon and ask her there—it had, after all, once been theirs—but why wait? Why make her worry over their future any longer? Hadn't he learned in the Stained Palace that things could change in a matter of seconds? Didn't he feel the reminder of that lesson every time he took a breath?

Hadn't he learned that she was who he always came back to?

"I want to go home," he whispered, staring at the glowing library window. Her silhouette flitted past it. He gripped Baer's arm so he wouldn't run to her. "I'm going to ask her, Baer. Gods." Ren turned to his friend, his eyes wide and wild. "I'm about to be engaged."

"You're *what*?!" Khai shouted from behind them. "To who?"

"How dense are you?" Baer asked. He pointed at the library. "To her."

Khai and some of the Nightmares around him whooped. Their hands clapped Ren's back, jostling him as they bounced around in their excitement. He hadn't expected this outpouring of support, but didn't it make sense? Wouldn't males who spent so much time alone want to revel in the joy of their brothers whenever they could?

Perhaps Ren had never been as alone as he'd thought.

He started to sweat, both from the body heat of the Nightmares around him and a sudden wave of doubt. Morgaine had said she'd accept, but what if she'd changed her mind since then? Talking about it was one thing. Asking was another. "You talk to her first," he said to Baer, nudging him forward. "Offer her the job."

"What?"

"Please, Baer."

Baer scowled. "You're being a coward, Ren," he said, but he walked across the square. Heart in his throat, rings back in his pocket, Ren and the swarm of Nightmares followed.

Morgaine looked up as they approached; though the glass of the windows was dirty and warped, Ren saw her brow furrow. She opened the door for Baer, candlelight and warmth spilling onto the frosty porch. "What's going on?" she asked. "Does the Order want a bedtime story?"

Baer clasped his hands on the top of his cane. "Can I come in?"

"Just you?"

"Yes."

Morgaine let him in, but her eyes were on Ren as she closed the door.

Ren turned his back to the library and faced the gathered Nightmares, dropping his hands to his knees. He couldn't breathe. He'd faced ghouls. He'd killed wraiths. He'd dug his hands into graves and bone piles and viscera without a second thought. He'd been drained of all godhood and breath and he'd lived. Why was this terrifying him so?

"Breathe, Ren." It was Tmarrey. Gods. Of course the Triumvirate had trailed along. "Breathe."

"I'm going to ask her," he gasped.

Mezd chuckled. "We figured."

He loved her. She loved him. Why was he afraid?

"Talk to me, Ren," Tmarrey said, resting a hand on his shoulder. "What's going on?"

"I don't—I don't—" He raised his head and confessed, "I'm scared."

"We'd be worried if you weren't." Behind Ren, the library door creaked, and Tmarrey smiled. "We train to bring death. That doesn't mean we shouldn't also live."

"Ren?" Baer's steps sounded across the porch, the thumps of his cane matching the thuds of Ren's heart. "She accepted."

"Gods." He drew in a shuddering breath. One more obstacle removed. "Alright. Thank you, Baer."

"Ren?"

At the sound of her voice, Ren turned. Morgaine stood in the open doorway, limned golden by the light. "I know Baer didn't bring a cadre just to make me a job offer. What's going on?"

"I've come to return your dagger."

Her gaze flicked to the Triumvirate behind Ren. "I'm sure that's not the case."

Ren took a deep breath. "Can I come inside?"

She ushered him in. The gathered Nightmares watched through the windows. "Gods. I should have bought you curtains," he grumbled, placing his hand on the small of her back and pushing her into her office—damned if he was going to let this moment be for anyone but them.

"I'm sure Baer's told you," she said, "but I'm going to be—"

"I know." For good measure, Ren closed the office door. The floor was almost completely clear, the majority of the artifacts sitting on shelves or neatly in boxes with small labels. He wouldn't have to be careful where he knelt. "Close your eyes."

"What? Why—"

"Gods, Morgaine, *please.*" His voice cracked. If he had to wait one more moment to ask, he was going to lose his nerve. "Please, little love. I want to ask you something."

He wasn't sure what tipped her off—the gathered crowd, the anxious air about him, the way he kept one hand in his pocket— but her eyes sparked when she figured it out. Morgaine pressed a hand to her mouth. A hysterical giggle still slipped out. "Ren."

"Close your eyes."

She did.

Ren lowered to both knees, as was the Zijustvan tradition. The floorboards creaked as he shifted his weight to one side and then the other, pulling her ring from his pocket and quickly shining it with the edge of his cloak. He held the ring between them. "Morgaine?"

She opened her eyes. At the sight of the ring, she burst into tears.

Ren swallowed, forcing his own tears back so he could finally, *finally*, ask. "I was going to wait," he said. "I was going to decorate my room in the Drowsy Dragon with the flowers we wore at Sisters' Harvest. I wanted to do this the right way. I wanted to create the perfect moment, wait for the perfect time, before I asked you. But waiting for perfection meant waiting even longer, and then the Keep's letter came, and—" His throat grew thick. The ring trembled in his hand. "This moment is perfect because it's with you."

Morgaine knelt. She held his wrist to still the shaking.

"And I don't want to wait for you any longer," Ren continued. His vision blurred. "I don't have a last name to give you. I don't even have a damn box for the ring. But if you want it, Morgaine, the rest of my life will be yours. Everything I have will be yours." *Zikat*, he prayed silently, *let me come home*. "Morgaine Greywarren, will you marry me?"

The office was quiet for one fleeting, heart-stopping moment.

"Gods above, Ren." She laughed, wiping her tears away. "*Yes.*"

When they walked onto the porch of the library, tear-stained and smiling and holding hands, the Nightmares surged forward to meet them. Baer threw his arms around Morgaine and the Triumvirate clapped Ren on the back, but no one pulled them far enough apart for their hands to drop. Ren tugged Morgaine close and kissed her, smiling against her lips as the Nightmares cheered around them.

When Morgaine shoved open the door to the Drowsy Dragon, Ren and the Nightmares in tow, Azra scowled. "Absolutely not," she said, flicking her towel over her shoulder. "I told them what would happen if they drained my supply again."

Morgaine raised her hand, the one tangled in Ren's and bearing her new ring. "Azra, we're engaged!"

The elf's jaw dropped. "Really?"

Ren grinned and nodded.

"By the gods." A smile spread over Azra's face. She opened her arms wide. "I take it back!"

Drinks began to flow, and word that there was a celebration going on spread through the town like a fire. The revelry lasted far into the night, and Ren thought he saw every townsperson pass through the crowd of Nightmares to find them. Mayoress Soma, Brilde, Vess and his wife and boys—they all smiled and hugged and congratulated Ren and Morgaine, some of them with tears in their eyes.

"When's the wedding?" Brilde asked, shouting to be heard over the crowd.

Ren kissed Morgaine's temple. "Whenever she wants!"

She laughed. "So as soon as we can plan it!"

Ren, warm from the cider and the crowd and Morgaine perched on his lap, drew her close and kissed her. When they separated, Baba had taken Brilde's place at their table.

"Oh," Morgaine said, pressing a hand to her mouth. "I'm sorry, Baba."

The old woman smiled. "No need to be. I only wanted to offer my congratulations." Her eyes glittered. "And to say I knew this was coming." She pointed a gnarled finger at Ren. "You've looked at her like a lovestruck puppy ever since Sisters' Harvest."

Morgaine giggled. "He has, hasn't he?"

Baba patted Ren's hand and winked when he rolled his eyes. "Have you discussed what name you're going to take?"

Ren opened his mouth, about to tell Baba he had no name, but Morgaine leaned forward. "Is that tradition still followed?"

"I'm not sure. It was better known in my day, but perhaps it's fallen out of fashion." Baba shrugged and rose, fumbling for her cane and placing it upright on the ground. "It is only something to consider from an old elf. I'm so happy for the two of you."

Ren turned to Morgaine, wanting to ask what Baba meant, but Azra settled another round of drinks onto their table. "Courtesy of the Triumvirate," she said over the din. "Drink up."

Ren's opportunity to ask came an hour later when he walked Morgaine home. She'd fallen deep into her cups, and stopped in her tracks every so often to look up at him and giggle. "We're gonna get married," she slurred, stumbling against him.

Ren laughed and righted her. "We are."

"I like my ring. 'S pretty."

When they reached the library, he dug the key out of her pockets—she found it hysterical that he wasn't "waiting for our wedding night to stick your hand up my skirt"—and helped her to her apartment. "Go change. I'll make you some tea, and then bed."

Her fire had died to embers, so Ren built it higher before setting the kettle over it. By the time Morgaine plopped onto the loveseat, wearing a nightdress and thick socks, some of the alcoholic haze had faded from her eyes. "I'm coming to the Keep with you."

Ren nodded. "How do you feel about it?"

She let her head fall onto his shoulder. "I'll miss Tanglewood," she said quietly, "and the people here. They were good to me, even when I wasn't the kindest to them. I think I'm ready for something new, though. I'm frightened, but I'm excited to be frightened." Morgaine looked at him and frowned. "Does that make sense?"

The kettle screamed. Ren let it for a moment and kissed her. "Absolutely." The kettle's shriek died as he lifted it from the flame. As he poured the tea, he turned over his shoulder and asked, "What was Baba talking about?"

"It's an old Zijustvan tradition," Morgaine said, tucking her feet under herself. "When a couple wed, they could choose a new surname to use. It was mostly meant for Greywarrens, so any child that came from the marriage wouldn't be born with that name. Like Baba said, though, it isn't done much these days. I don't think two Greywarrens often marry."

Ren handed her a cup of tea. The idea made something stir in his chest, something warm and light. "What do you think of the custom?"

"I think it's sweet." She eyed him over the rim of her cup. "Why? Do you want to do it?"

He nodded. He would have a family name, undeniable proof that he belonged not just somewhere, but to someone. He wanted it, badly, and he wanted it with her.

A smile slipped across her face. "It would make that sweet little line in your proposal a lie."

"I don't think so. I said I had no name to give you, not that we couldn't choose our own." He took her hand and kissed her ring, meeting her eyes. "And you liked that line."

"I loved it. I almost interrupted you to say 'yes' right then." Morgaine drained her tea and set the cup on the floor. Her eyes were bright, the last shreds of her intoxication burned away by the excitement of a task. "Do you have any ideas?"

"No, but you've got a wealth of ideas downstairs. We could go look."

"Now?"

"Why not? I'm sure no one's expecting me back in my room

tonight." He leaned forward and nipped at her neck, smiling against her skin when she laughed. "Unless you're too tired?"

Morgaine crawled into his lap and kissed him. As soon as he thought they wouldn't make it down to the library, she drew back and said, happy and breathless, "Not at all."

They read by candlelight, plucking books at random from the shelves, flipping to any given page, and shouting possibilities across the aisles to each other.

"Serren?"

"No."

"Meza?"

"No."

Ren laughed, then shouted, "How about Scara?"

She appeared at the end of his aisle, her hands on her hips. "Are you serious?"

"What do you think?" Ren wrapped an arm around her waist and kissed her, holding the book aloft. "Though," he murmured, "I think we should at least invite them to the wedding. Let the lord know he bet on the wrong dog."

When the soft tendrils of first light crept through the library windows, Morgaine approached him with an open book in her arms. "I think I found it." He'd settled onto the floor by the back corner and had, in truth, been fighting sleep. She sat, arranged the book so it spread over both of their laps, and pointed to an eight-letter word. "What do you think?"

Ren tested it out, tacking it onto her name, his, and then both together. He smiled. Their name was sweet as honey. "I think it's perfect."

12.3.626

Two mornings later, after Ren and Morgaine had rested and planned—and after the Nightmares had fully recovered from their engagement-induced hangovers—a two-ringed crowd stood around the plague pit. The townspeople, dressed in their darkest clothing, made up the inner ring. Nightmares constituted the outer ring, laden with weapons and Umbrals in case something happened. At the head of the crowd, Mayoress Everinne Soma stood with six priests and priestesses from the Keep, one for each god. Ren, Morgaine, and Baer stood to the left of the holy ones, the Triumvirate to the right.

"I'm proud of you, little love," Ren said. He kissed the top of her head, though it was covered by her cornflower blue cloak. "You're doing a good thing."

"I know." She leaned against him. "It didn't feel right to just leave."

A box of artifacts, already blessed by the holy ones, rested at her feet. Morgaine had determined these to be the most personal of the grave goods found in the pit: jewelry, buttons or scraps of clothing, shreds of letters with only an errant loop or full stop still legible. The rest, things like weaponry and pottery shards, were going to be split between the town hall and the Keep.

These, however, were going back to their owners.

Mayoress Soma nodded to Svetlen's priestess. The priestess, a bronzed elf with brass-colored hair, raised her hands and shot golden flame across the clearing. The snow melted.

"People of Tanglewood," Mayoress Soma called. "You all know our history. Some of you remember firsthand when the plague decimated our town. Some of you remember those lost." A tear glimmered as it spilled down her cheek. Ren bowed his head —a week ago, Morgaine had shown him a clasp she'd found, one that matched the clasp on the cloak the mayoress wore now. Her mother had been claimed by the plague. "Let us honor them, and let us finally ensure they are laid to a peaceful rest."

Morgaine stepped forward and set the box in the center of the plague pit. She took an amulet with a cracked green stone from the box. She knelt, dug a small hole in the moistened ground, and buried the amulet. When she came back to Ren's side, he took her hand and held it tightly, not caring that her gloves were smudged with cold grave dirt.

One by one, the townspeople followed suit until the box was empty. One by one, the holy ones stepped forward and spoke a blessing over the mass grave.

When the final one, Oddelen's priest, finished his prayer and stepped back, the Triumvirate cleared their throats. Tmarrey, Mezd, and Cazret began to sing, using the Oddelenic dialect as the priest had. Ren's heart twisted—the last time he'd sung this prayer, it had been at Tovar's funeral.

The vesper caught and spread around the circle as, one by one, the Nightmares also began to sing. Ren glanced over at Baer. Tears spilled freely from his eyes.

Ren was the last Nightmare to join in. As he did, the song scraping low in his throat, he laid a hand on Baer's shoulder. Ren had run from their shared grief, and in doing so, he'd hurt his friends beyond words. He wasn't going to do it again.

The vesper ended with every Nightmare exhaling until their lungs emptied. A death rattle hovered over the clearing and dissipated into the trees.

Morgaine let out a shuddering breath. It fogged in the cold. Ren stayed at her side as she thanked the Triumvirate and the holy ones. He stayed at her side as the townspeople and Nightmares and even Baer left, starting the cold trek through Tmadrev back to Tanglewood. He stayed at her side when they were the only two left by the pit, when she finally allowed herself to cry.

"Do you think I've done enough?" She brushed a tear away as it slid down her cheek. Dirt smeared in its place. "To repay the town?"

He wiped the dirt from her cheek. Not only had she coordinated this service, she had helped Mayoress Soma and the Triumvirate arrange for the Keep's holy ones to spend their afternoons in Tanglewood's temples. Until the Keep moved, its holy ones would work to bring the gods back. "I don't know what else you could do."

She sighed, a short huff. "Tanglewood gave me my life," she said, "and in return, I've brought it—"

"Peace," Ren said, pulling her against his chest. "You've brought them peace, little love. Nothing is meant to exist after death. It's agony to do so." He stared at the empty box. "They'll rest now. For good."

Tmadrev Forest was still around them. Snow began to fall. In a few hours, it would be as if they hadn't been there at all.

———

He married her that night.

Townspeople and Nightmares poured into Zikat's temple, cramming into pews and standing along the edges of the room when there was nowhere else to sit. Ren stood by the altar with Zikat's priestess. He looked over the guests—gods above, his wedding guests—and smiled like a fool. Nightmares sat amongst the townspeople, dots of black in a sea of wintery blues and greens. Hushed chatter filled the room. Every so often, someone would look up at him and smile—Baba, Azra, one of his brethren. He felt as if his heart would burst a little more each time.

"Breathe, Ren," Baer said from the front row. "You look terrified. She already said yes. This is the easy part."

Ren cut his eyes at his friend, but drew in a breath anyway. "You overestimate me." He put his hand in his pocket again. His ring was still there—he would give it to Morgaine during the ceremony, and she would return it to him as they exchanged vows. He counted his weapons—they were all accounted for, ax and sickles and daggers. Given how uncommon it was for a Nightmare to marry, they had few wedding customs of their own, but the Triumvirate had insisted he wed Morgaine in his best armor and be arrayed as if he was going to hunt. It honored Zikat and Oddelen, they'd said, and it honored the Nightmares' profession. Ren liked to think it honored Morgaine as well. She would take him as he was, sharp edges and all, and he would use those sharp edges to protect her if the time to do so ever came.

With the threat of the Stone, it very well might.

Before Ren's thoughts could spiral into ones of spirits and Stones, someone pointedly cleared their throat. The temple doors opened.

It was all Ren could do not to run down the aisle and kiss her.

Morgaine was in the red dress she'd worn at Solstice. Her hair fell, unbound, around her shoulders. It was too cold for fresh flowers, but Baba had found some of the alyssum and lantana she'd used at Sisters' Harvest preserved in her cottage. Morgaine held a small bouquet of them. She had no veil, and wore no jewelry other than her steel-and-copper ring and a thin gold chain, but Ren didn't care. He didn't need ornamentation. He just needed her.

The liturgy was blessedly short. Ren stumbled through the vows and had to be prompted multiple times—he couldn't stop staring, disbelieving and lovestruck, at Morgaine. Every time the priestess gave him the line, Morgaine would smile or touch his hand, and Ren would forget. "I mean them, I swear," Ren said, and those gathered laughed. "I've just wanted this for so long."

Morgaine, of course, said her vows perfectly, and slid Ren's ring onto his finger as she did. "Forever, Ren," she said, barely having to be prompted. He suspected she'd memorized them. "By the passing of this ring, from you to me and now back to you, let us mark the never-ending circle of our love. Our commitment. I am yours, Ren. Forever."

The world was happiness and joy and warmth, and when the priestess had them kiss to seal their vows, Ren barely heard. Morgaine tugged on his cuirass and kissed him, and the room exploded into cheers around them. She laughed against his mouth and he kissed her again, dipping her low. His cheeks ached. He couldn't stop smiling. He'd finally gotten home.

Outside of the confines of Tmadrev Forest, a threat to the Order loomed. When the Nightmares returned to the Keep, there was no telling where they would go or what they would do. Fear swirled in the night sky, dancing above the winter-bare trees of Tmadrev and seeking to plunge down to those within.

Ren knew this. Fear skittered across the nape of his neck like an insect. He sat with it for a moment, allowed its familiar claws to prick and prod inside him. His heart beat faster, his lung seized, the scar at his ribs throbbed. But there was a new heaviness on his left hand, and he smiled as he looked at his wedding band in the candlelight. Fear would no longer be all that drove him. There was too much to celebrate.

He sat in his favorite spot in the Drowsy Dragon and watched his wife laugh and smile and dance her way across the room to him. They'd go back to her apartment tonight and he would give himself to her. In the morning, they'd begin moving their things to the Keep. From there, Ren knew it was fruitless to plan. The Order would convene. The true extent of the threat would be assessed, and action would be taken. The Keep would likely move.

Morgaine stumbled into his lap and kissed him, her cheeks red from the cider and the tavern's warmth. "I want to go home."

He cupped her face in his hands. Her cheeks burned. "Are you sure?"

She flicked her eyes down his body and nodded.

They said their goodbyes and left the tavern, the cold night air sharp against the heat of their skin. Ren swept Morgaine into his arms and laughed as her surprised shriek echoed to the stars above.

He didn't need certainty. He could do without a plan. He had his wife and their vows, and no matter what came, that would be enough.

No matter what came, Ren and Morgaine Dearling would face it together.

PART TWO

SANNE

THE LADY NIGHTMARE

9.13.626

Sanne took a step and plunged into darkness.

The red glow of her nightsight disappeared as the spell died. She pressed herself against the stone wall of the Stained Palace, whispering the spell and hurriedly signing the ward. Nothing.

Panic seized her chest. Anger rushed to cloak it. Spells didn't fail, not for her. She squeezed her eyes shut, took a shuddering breath, and opened her eyes. The darkness washed her vision black.

A quiet rattle sounded to her left. She tightened her grip on Peacebringer, spoke her word, and swung. The wraith screamed as her glowing hand-and-a-half sword made contact, slicing through half-there flesh. Unblood slicked Peacebringer's hilt.

The wraith roared as she ripped Peacebringer from its torso. The sound dug claws into the farthest reaches of her mind and the lowest parts of her belly, reaching for a vulnerable place to rip and tear and wound, to plant a parasite's fear in her and make her stumble. The roar wanted to ruin her, and that was how she knew what drove the wraith.

"Vengeance," she hissed. Her eyes adjusted. In the cold light of the clear, moonlit night, she saw the wraith hovering an arm's reach from her. "You want *revenge*."

It should have shed its skin. It should have revealed the broken spirit within. She should have been able to cast it out.

But none of those things happened. Sanne was knocked to the floor, the wraith's claws raking across her temple and forehead. A scream escaped before she could bite it back. She rose, holding Peacebringer in her left hand and fumbling for a dagger with her tattooed right. Her vision swam from pain. Blood dripped into her eyes, making them sting and water.

She couldn't see the wraith. She wiped away the blood. "Come on!" she snarled, bracing for another blow, but none came. She cast bloodtrace, waiting for the familiar tug in her chest to tell her where the wraith was, but there was nothing. The spell had failed.

The wraith had escaped.

Alone on the mezzanine, Sanne swore. Spirits did not *escape* from her. Her spells did not *fail*. She was too devout, too skilled of a fighter, for her hunts to go unfinished. And yet, in the light from the arched window behind her, she bled with nothing to show for it.

Thunder rumbled.

She glanced at the window. The night was clear—no rain fell, no clouds drifted before the moon. There shouldn't have been thunder.

She lifted her head and stilled. A figure stood at the edge of the mezzanine, paused in a half-step as if it had ascended the stairs and been surprised by her presence. Its shape was that of her own body, her short height and muscled limbs wrought in darkest shadow. When it stepped forward, the silvery moonlight disappeared into it. A void-like aura writhed around it.

The light in Sanne's veins, her family's divine blessing, stretched out toward it. She readied her blades.

"Hello," the figure said. A pair of eyes slid open. They glowed a pale purple; in the faint light they cast, Sanne saw an upturned nose and full mouth like hers. *"Shall we play?"*

She came to on the floor of the receiving hall. The early light of dawn drifted down to her from the mezzanine above. She'd landed in the middle of the golden sunburst mosaic in the floor. The force of her fall had cracked some of the glimmering tiles. Sanne wiggled her eight fingers and ten toes, then bent each limb —nothing was broken.

She rose, swaying as blood rushed through her. The wound at her temple pulsed; she lifted her hand to it and murmured the incantation for skinstitch. She had to repeat it thrice before the spell knit her skin back together.

This was the third night that had ended with her blood being spilled, the third night without any banishments or exorcisms. The third night without results.

The understanding settled on her heart like a stone.

She needed help.

9.14.626

"No, Sanne."

She turned away from the map of Nocovostvo she'd been examining. "'No'?"

"No," Cassander repeated. He picked up a carved figurine from the battle table, turning it this way and that before putting it down in the same place. She'd found him in the hidden war room, where he spent most of his time these days. Svetlen had smiled on her—he was alone. "Is there anything else?"

Sanne splayed her hands on the table. The realm of Ruhysvet stretched between them. "I'm going to ask again, *my king*," she said, her voice low. "Will you permit me to write to the Keep for assistance?"

He met her eyes. In the torchlight, his thin golden diadem glimmered against his honey-colored curls. "No. You're enough. I don't need another Nightmare."

"But I do. This is an infestation, Cassander, one I cannot handle on my own."

"I'd think that would dull your shining reputation."

She crossed her arms. The new skin of a healed-over wound on her shoulder tightened. The Order knew her strength. It knew how capable she truly was. Though she was a bit embarrassed to ask, it would take more than one request for assistance to tarnish her reputation. "The Order doesn't consider it shameful to ask for help."

"Your reputation stretches beyond your Order."

Sanne had served Cassander for almost a year, but had known him her whole life. She'd learned to discern the true meaning of his words. "You're ashamed of my failure, then?"

"Are you not?" The torches in the room blazed brighter, their flame turning from orange to gold. "You don't think word of my Lady's failure will spread through the city? Through the realm?"

Sanne waited for the fires to die down before speaking again. Cassander was two years her senior, yet acted as if the gap between them were ten times that. The events of the last two years had placed a considerable burden on his shoulders. Cassander had become king on the tails of his father's death and his twin brother's exile, and they both knew Sanne would never bear the weight of Jasniostvo's throne. She couldn't blame him for being short. "It isn't a failure. Not yet."

"It's a damning weakness. One you know we cannot afford."

She shook her head. "The Order is politically neutral. Whatever my help sees here, he'll have no reason to spread it to someone else. Nightmares don't answer to kings."

He cocked an eyebrow. "You do."

"Because I signed a contract with your father and you inherited me. I'm an outlier, not the standard." She swallowed—reminding him of this was always dangerous. She held the peace between them like fragile crystals in her hands. "I'm sworn to the Order before I'm sworn to you, but I belong to you both. I wouldn't ask for help if I didn't trust their discretion."

Cassander removed his diadem and placed it on the table. He ran a gloved hand through his hair. "Sanne—"

"Look at me."

He raised his head. Her myriad cuts and bruises, all in various stages of healing, prickled under his gaze. The freshest were from the night before. She let him look without interruption, let him take in the stubborn smears of blood in her blonde braid, the tattoo winding around the remaining fingers of her right hand, the dark brown eyes that were just like his. The smudged-purple circles under her eyes were like his, too. Sleepless nights ran in the family.

"I'm doing this to protect you," she whispered. "Not just as the crown, not just as the rightful king, but as my cousin. My blood. Do you trust me?"

"Yes."

"Then trust the Order. I do."

Cassander sighed. His shoulders slumped and, just for a moment, the veil dropped. She saw how exhausted he was. "Sanne..."

She made herself say, the words like spikes on her tongue, "The Order has no ties to the Black Sun."

It was as if she'd blasphemed. Cassander stiffened—a brother ready to fight, a king ready to execute. A fire sparked in his eyes at the mention of the would-be usurper. "You do not speak of him."

The reprimand was a familiar one, but Sanne kept trying. She pushed because the Black Sun had broken her heart, too. "We give him so much power by refusing to say his name. He wants to scare us. Casi—"

"*No.* There is only the Black Sun now."

The chasm between them, the one that opened every time they had this conversation, yawned a little wider. Sanne balanced on its edge. "Fine. But no one from the Order will speak to him. No one will spread intelligence to him."

Cassander rubbed the bridge of his nose, then turned away and dragged his hands down his face. "It woke us again last night," he said. His voice trembled. "Malaia first. I woke to her screams. I cannot keep doing this, Sanne, I cannot fight a war in and out of the palace—"

"Then grant me this aid. Let me fight this for you."

He sank into the closest chair. "You're as stubborn as he was."

Sanne's nose wrinkled. "Don't insult me."

"Can you truly promise discretion from your Order?"

The lip of the chasm crumbled beneath her feet. Cassander was on one side, the Order on the other; in the darkness between, there was nothing. Both sides of the chasm demanded her footing, her loyalty, yet she'd never known how to bridge the divide. She didn't know how to give the Order its desired neutrality and

Cassander his expected fealty. His father Oran had understood her competing devotions, but Oran was dead. "I can promise you my discretion," she said, "and what the Order doesn't know, they can't act on."

Silence descended, the only sound in the room the torches crackling in their sconces. The flames calmed from golden to a mundane yellow—the worst of Cassander's panic had passed. He raised his head. "I want to question him when he arrives. I'll decide if I trust him then."

The floor beneath her feet was solid again. "Thank you."

Cassander rose and placed the diadem back on his head. "I want results from this, Lady."

She recognized the dismissal. "Yes, my king."

9.17.626

Even though it was midday, Svetlen's chapel was empty.

Though smaller than a temple sanctuary—the Stained Palace's chapels were meant for personal or small group reflection, not large services—Svetlen's chapel was the largest of its kind in the palace. Six rows of oakwood pews faced an altar and the arched stained-glass window behind it. Red, orange, and yellow shards formed a blazing sun, and the azure and cream glass surrounding it depicted a cloud-filled sky.

Sanne knelt in her usual spot at the altar and removed her weapons. Peacebringer's marbled steel-and-copper blade glowed gold and blue beneath the chapel's fragmented light. The sword had been a birthday gift from her parents, but all that remained of the original was its opal-studded hilt. When Sanne was seventeen, Peacebringer's blade had been replaced with one of Nightmare steel, one that better suited her strength and new position in the Order. It was one of the few things in her life that allowed her to be an Esclarmonde and a Nightmare at once.

The sword chimed as she set it on the stone floor next to her daggers. During her training, it had been driven into her that

Nightmares were not to conduct ritual prayers while armed. Some would have kept their weapons on had they been in her position —she was far from the eyes of the Keep here—but Sanne had no interest in flouting the holy.

She prayed thrice a day, once to each of her gods: morning lauds to Zikat and nighttime vespers to Oddelen, the gods Nightmares worshipped, and midday prayers to Svetlen, the goddess of light. The kingdom of Jasniostvo was devoted to Svetlen; the goddess had blessed the Esclarmondes from the beginning of their line, and Sanne's family had ruled Jasniostvo for over two centuries. At the Keep, Sanne had been allowed to leave her midday lessons early to pray to Svetlen. When she'd begun her tenure as the Lady Nightmare, though, there'd been no need for accommodations. The royal family prayed to Svetlen each day, and Sanne always joined.

But that was then.

Sanne set the last of her blades down and looked over her shoulder. It was nearing the end of the prayer hour, but no one approached. It seemed she'd be praying alone again.

She bowed her head. The gods accepted prayers in the common tongue, but preferred receiving prayers in Divrech, the divine language. The supplicant would enjoy an even greater favor if they spoke the god's unique dialect, which, of course, Sanne did.

The Svetlenic dialect was bright and breezy, spoken with one's upper register and plenty of aeration. Sanne slipped into it easily, leaning into her natural accent. She'd been born in Jasniostvo, raised in a country estate not far from the Celesty, the holy capital city. Because of Svetlen's blessing, the Esclarmondes, the only entirely human royal family in the realm, enjoyed the fighting prowess of humans as well as the magical inclination of elves. They were well-equipped to defend a throne—or to challenge it.

Sanne stumbled in her prayer and tried to rein her thoughts in. Six generations of Esclarmondes had peacefully held the Jasniostvan throne, and it was her generation, the seventh, that threatened that peace. Darkness smudged the edges of her vision, the way it always did when she thought of the Black Sun. As Cassander was her cousin, so was he; the twins had sworn paladin's oaths to Svetlen as adolescents. The Black Sun, however, had strayed. He'd broken his oath to Svetlen and sworn a new one to Zdesen, the parasitical goddess of fear and horror who perched at the back of Svetlen's golden head. Under Zdesen's influence, the Black Sun had disputed Cassander's place on the throne. Sanne still remembered the sound of her shocked laugh when she'd heard, the way it had echoed through the throne room—it hadn't even been two years ago. When King Oran had told her the alleged justification for the Black Sun's challenge, however, she'd stopped laughing. Zdesen had sullied her cousin's mind, spoiled it as her created horrors ruined Svetlen's gift, and this challenge only proved it.

A hollow rattle sounded behind her. She stiffened, curling her fingers into her palms and fighting the urge to turn. Cassander was right. Nothing good came from thinking of the Black Sun—his goddess liked to toy with Sanne. Zdesen wanted to corrupt her, too.

"Leave me, Zdesen," Sanne hissed. "This is a holy place."

It was a weak protest—unfortunately, there was nothing unholy about Zdesen—but an amused laugh scraped at the back of Sanne's mind, and her vision cleared. Sanne sighed, relieved. She knew the Zdesenic dialect, too, but hated to speak it; it always left a filminess in her mouth as if she'd vomited.

She tucked a fallen bit of hair behind her ear and bowed her head.

Someone cleared their throat.

She groaned at the interruption. The parasite had left her dirty. Sanne needed her goddess to burn her clean. "Can it wait?"

"It cannot, Lady."

How easy it was to forget that she was the only one who used this quiet hour for its intended use—prayer. She rose. Vallen, the captain of Cassander's palace guard, stood two pews behind her, still as a stone in the aisle. His guard's helm dangled from gauntlet-covered fingers. His hair, the silver that came only with age, clashed with the shimmering bronze of his skin and tipped ears. "His Majesty is requesting your presence in the throne room. Your Nightmare has arrived."

"Already?" She gathered her weapons. Peacebringer gave a satisfying ring as she slipped it into its scabbard at her back. "I wrote for help only days ago."

"He was already in the kingdom." Vallen held an arm out to lead her to the door. Their armor—hers gold, his white—clattered as they hurried to the throne room. Sanne knew little about Vallen personally, but professionally, she regarded him highly. The old elf had been the captain of Oran's guard during the late king's reign, and Vallen had done all he could to ease Cassander's ascension to the throne after Oran's death. The two males met twice a week to discuss security concerns, but it wasn't unusual for Sanne to see them walking the palace's hallways lost in other conversations.

"Have you spoken to him?" Sanne asked.

"His Majesty already questioned him. He arrived hours ago."

"Then I suppose the king approves?"

The guards stationed outside the throne room snapped to attention as they approached.

"His Majesty does." Vallen clasped her forearm. She took his and they shook. "Best of luck, Lady. I hope he provides the help you need."

"Thank you, Captain." Sanne faced the throne room doors and murmured a quick prayer to Zikat: let her cleanse this infestation with this Nightmare's help. Let him prove to Cassander that she'd been right to seek aid.

She shoved the doors open and strode in.

Whenever Sanne had visited the Stained Palace as a child, she'd squinted every time she'd entered the throne room; now, though, she knew to brace for its brightness. The entire eastern wall was a single-paned window of clear glass, and midday light bounced off of the throne room's white tile floors, white walls, and thick columns of gold-veined marble. Black and gold tiles in the center of the floor formed an eclipse with a sliver of metallic sun at its left. Carved into the western wall was the Sohli Prophecy, whose couplets confirmed Cassander as the rightful king. A slim black scorch mark slashed across it, connecting the first and final lines of the prophecy. Above it all was a kaleidoscopic ceiling of thick stained glass.

Directly in front of Sanne was a black-cloaked figure and a dais with two bone-white thrones, Cassander on his and Malaia Akari, the queen, on hers. She smiled and nodded to Sanne in greeting. A golden diadem, the dainty twin of Cassander's, glimmered atop her black hair. Sanne returned the warm expression, hoping Malaia didn't notice her nervousness. She and Cassander had wed two years ago, and their union had solidified the alliance between Jasniostvo and the Karilan Atoll, an island nation off the kingdom's eastern coast. Malaia deferred to Cassander in most matters and had a gentle reputation, but every now and then, Sanne caught a flash of sharp perceptiveness in the queen's dark eyes.

"Lady," Cassander said, "you've joined us."

"I was in the chapel, my king," she said, stopping before the dais and bending the knee.

"Rise. What in the chapel kept your attention so?"

She tried not to show her annoyance as she stood—she hadn't seen Cassander in the chapel in months. Of course he wouldn't know. "It is midday, my king. I was praying."

The cloaked Nightmare chuckled. "If I recognize that voice," he said, lowering his hood, "it seems that nothing has changed." Ridged brown horns emerged from the hood. Below them was a windblown mess of auburn curls.

Sanne's heart dropped.

"Lady," Cassander said, "the Keep has answered your request. This is Ren."

She clenched her jaw, fighting to keep her composure. Thank

the gods it was him and not some greenhorn—but the last time she'd seen Ren, he hadn't deigned to tell her goodbye, and the slight still smarted years later. He was just as she remembered him: red-brown skin, pointed ears, broad shoulders and strong arms, and deep red eyes that shone when he laughed. His Nightmare tattoo crept along his neck.

"Ren," Cassander continued, "this is Sanne Esclarmonde, the Lady Nightmare."

Ren's brow furrowed. "Esc—"

"We're familiar, my king." Ren had known her by another name, and she didn't want to explain it to Cassander. Sanne smiled, glossing over her interruption, and continued, "We trained together at the Keep. How long has it been since we've seen each other, Ren?"

A shadow crossed his face. She knew exactly how long it had been, and he knew it. He'd gone only months before she took her position as the Lady Nightmare. "Approximately three years."

In truth, the gap between them was wider—they'd lost touch long before what happened three years ago—but the answer seemed to satisfy Cassander, and that was what Sanne needed. If he was satisfied, he was trusting, and if he was trusting, he would let them work in peace.

"Good," Cassander said. "I expect that the two of you will work together to efficiently rid us of this torment." He addressed them both, but his eyes bore into Sanne's. He reached between the thrones and placed his hand on Malaia's. "The queen and I trust you to get this done. Lady, you will make any necessary introductions, yes?"

"Yes, my king."

"Good." Cassander rose. "Then you are dismissed."

———

Sanne,

Consider this a formal notification that Ren's presence and assistance here is conditionally accepted. I understand he has two Umbrals instead of your one. I've ordered his bird to be housed in the aviary and his other creature, be it a dog or a mare, to be kept in the kennels or stables depending on its shape. For the security of the Stained Palace, his communication will go through you. Please discourage him from any correspondence unless it is strictly necessary. He is forbidden from the war room and Malaia and I's chambers. I prefer he be kept from the grand library, the armory, and the guards' quarters, but if he must enter those places to assist you, I ask that you accompany him at all times. Please notify him of these terms. They are non-negotiable.

Please keep the rest of this between us: I expect you to report any word or action of his that you deem suspicious. I cannot stress enough, Sanne, that I do not want him to know you're watching him. In my conversation with him, he did not show any outright loyalty to anyone other than your Keep, but ~~my~~ the Black Sun is clever. Zdesen is clever. He might not realize he's been influenced until it is too late. Anyone outside of the Stained Palace must be kept at a distance until we are certain they can be trusted.

I am depending on you. The safety of my throne and my wife and my people depends on you.

Cassander

Sanne finished summarizing Cassander's conditions for Ren and lowered the letter. "Do you accept?"

He leaned back in his chair and crossed his arms. "Do I have a choice?"

Sanne wanted to roll her eyes. She grit her teeth instead. "Technically. But I'd prefer it if you accepted."

Ren had been taken from the throne room by servants and shown to a guest chamber to bathe and rest after his journey. Sanne's instructions had been to wait for word from Cassander before proceeding; she'd gotten his letter two hours later and summoned Ren to her chambers after reading it. The little sitting area outside her bedroom was where they sat now, staring at each other over a brass-wrought breakfast table with a vase of oleander flowers and an untouched pot of tea.

"Do you have any questions?" Sanne continued.

"Plenty." Though there was much in the room to look at, particularly the tapestry on the wall that illustrated Svetlen's birth and the creation of light, Ren's eyes bored into Sanne. "I can't even have Kyr? My raven?"

"You can visit him in the aviary," Sanne said. "You shouldn't need your Umbrals for the hunt." She didn't. Her gyrfalcon Marra was currently in said aviary, likely sleeping after feasting on a fat rat. She sometimes used Marra to scout for spirits—the Stained Palace was a big place, and Sanne was only one woman—but Marra never made the killing blow. "They're tools, not weapons."

"I need to write to someone."

"Have you not reported your location to the Keep yet?" It was the first thing Nightmares were taught to do when they accepted a hunt.

Ren's eyes flicked to the ceiling in a half-roll before he stopped them. Sanne's jaw clenched. He was being so childish. She was the one who had the right to be angry.

"I maintain a correspondence with someone," he said. "I can't suddenly stop writing her back."

Sanne crossed her arms in a mirror of Ren's pose. Cassander had put it quite plainly, and while Ren was here, he had to abide by Cassander's rules. No meant no. "What other questions do you have?"

Something flared in Ren's eyes. "Who is Sanne Esclarmonde? I know a Sanne Bastillen, but no Sanne Esclarmonde. Have you married?" He nodded at her bare left hand, sneering.

So that was where they were starting. "My name has always been Esclarmonde."

"I would've remembered training with a royal."

"I used my mother's name at the Keep," she said. "I didn't want preferential treatment."

Ren had never been one to obviously show anger—irritation, yes, but he didn't shout and strike things like other men did. Sanne saw a hardness creep into his eyes nonetheless. He thought she was making excuses. "I see. What are you, then? The king's sister?"

"His cousin. My father and the late King Oran were brothers."

Ren rose and turned his back to her. He sighed. "By the gods. You lied to us."

She prickled. Of course not. Nightmares didn't lie to one another. "No. You always knew I was a noblewoman and, technically, I am a Bastillen."

He scoffed. When he lowered his arms, his fists were clenched. "So if enough of your family dies in this war of yours, will you abandon the Order to sit on the throne?"

She recoiled. The war was a civil conflict—how had word of it spread enough for Ren to hear? How long had he been in the kingdom? "What do you know of our war?"

"Don't deflect. Answer the question."

She huffed. "I'll never sit on Jasniostvo's throne."

"Why not?"

"I gave it up."

"Why?"

She'd had enough of his questions. *He* had been the one to leave. *He* had been the one to vanish without bothering to reach out. So what if she'd protected who she was? "For this," she snapped, lifting her tattooed hand. "To join the Order. To be like you. Is that what you wanted me to confess at the Keep all those years ago?"

"Yes!" Ren whirled and slammed his palms onto the table. The teapot and cups rattled on their tray. "We were best friends, Sanne. You knew where I came from, and where Baer and Tovar did, too. How could you have kept this from us?"

The mention of their old friends and roommates, one now dead, gripped her heart and twisted it. She had clawed her way to becoming the Nightmare she was, and she'd done it, for the most part, alone—why did it matter who her family was when she'd rejected her filial duty? She rose and spat, "'Friends,' Ren? That's what we were? Would a 'friend' have left the way you did?"

She got what she wanted. Ren recoiled as if she'd struck him. "When I—"

But she kept at it. She hadn't become the Lady Nightmare by relenting when her prey was down. "Did you even see Tovar's stone in the daylight?"

She knew he hadn't. When their friend Tovar Moriya had been killed three years ago, struck down in his hunt when they'd been twenty-four, she, Ren, and Baer Enorry had returned to the Keep for the funeral. The service had been in the evening, as was the custom—the souls of the dead crossed to Oddelen more easily at night, guided by Sumra's stars. Baer, who always returned to the Keep between hunts, still slept in their old suite. After the funeral, Ren and Sanne had, too. She'd cried herself to sleep feet away from where Tovar once slept. When she'd woken, she'd left her room to find Baer staring, mute, at an empty bed. Ren had left in the night.

"I was called to hunt," he said, but he wouldn't meet her eyes. "One job turned into another. By the time I returned to the Keep, you'd gone, too, and Baer wouldn't even say your name." She watched the anger in his eyes melt into sorrow. The sitting room fell quiet between them, the air turning heavy with their shared grief. Ren's eyes flicked to hers. "What happened between the two of you?"

It wasn't something she was willing to share. "If you'd stuck around, maybe you would've found out," she said, but the venom was gone from her voice. Away from Cassander and the compulsion to play the part of his Lady, she didn't have to watch her emotions for the first time in a while. Fighting with Ren had satisfied a twisted part of her, the part that relished in holding a grudge, but she was exhausted now.

Ren frowned. "That's not fair—"

"Neither is the way you left." Sanne sat and again crossed her arms. The metallic rustling of her plate armor soothed her a bit. "What happened with Baer and I has no bearing on why you're here, anyway."

Ren looked at her for a long time. She imagined it was difficult for him to reconcile, how the four of them had once been so close and were now splintered. Sometimes, when Sanne couldn't keep the memories at bay, it hurt her, too. When she'd arrived at the Keep at age fifteen to start her training, she'd been assigned to room with Ren, Baer, and Tovar. Baer had been one of the housemasters' most trusted pupils, and he, Tovar, and Ren were inseparable. The three boys ate together, studied together, sparred and bled and laughed together. They were best friends, and Sanne had become their friend, too.

But then they'd grown up.

Ren lowered himself into his chair, and there was grief in the way his shoulders sagged—during her tenure as the Lady Nightmare, Sanne had become very familiar with sorrow's signs. "You still wear your hair the way he showed you."

Sanne's hand went to her braid. She and Tovar had both kept their hair long, and when she'd joined the boys for sparring lessons, her hair had been an easy target. After a week of Sanne returning to their suite with a bloody scalp, Tovar had shown her his favorite braids. She'd spent many nights sitting on the floor with Tovar perched on the edge of his bed, his fingers winding through her hair as they talked and laughed with Ren and Baer. The braid Ren referred to was one she called her huntress braid; Tovar, and eventually she, divided her hair into four quadrants and braided each one before combining the tails into one long braid down her back. Sanne kept her hair long after leaving the Keep—it was one of the vanities she refused to surrender to the hunt—and wore her hair in a huntress braid nearly every day. She didn't always think of Tovar when she braided her hair, but it was always a reminder of who she was: the Lady Nightmare, the first of her kind. "It's the best way for me to wear it." And then, as an apology, she poured them tea and said, "He was a good kid."

Ren took the offering, but didn't drink. Steam curled into the space between his eyes before he said, "He was. He would have been a good man, too."

Sanne let herself imagine it: Tovar, grown and strong, his black skin and white hair stained with unblood as he hunted spectral creatures across the realm. Had things been different, perhaps he would've been sent to assist her instead. "We begin our hunt at sundown," she said. "I suggest resting until then. Eat beforehand."

She'd chosen the short words to stave off the sadness welling in her, the bitter longing for who she and Ren had once been. The air between them had somewhat cleared, but a haze of caution still lingered. Sanne didn't want to push.

It worked. "As you wish." Ren's teacup clattered against its saucer as he set it down. He left Sanne's chamber without a word.

Both servings of tea went cold.

———

Their hunt was off to a poor start.

They'd been wandering the halls of the Stained Palace for two hours, most of which had passed in stony silence. Ren muttered every now and then, just in case Sanne had forgotten his annoyance with Cassander's terms.

"I need Kyr," he said again as they reached the bottom of a marble staircase. "I need to write to Zijustvo."

"Have you reported to the Keep?"

"Yes. Don't smother me."

She frowned. "What part of Zijustvo?"

"Tmadrev Forest. It's essentially within your borders."

It was. Tmadrev crossed the kingdom line, spilling from its center in Zijustvo into Jasniostvo's lands. "I see."

"Kyr would barely have to leave the palace," Ren said. Sanne knew that wasn't quite true, but kept quiet as he continued. "Can I at least write her to say she won't hear from me until this hunt is done?"

Sanne wondered if this *her* was a friend. No, if he was willing to beg, she was something more than that—his lover? Wife? "Fine. Give it to me and I'll post it for you." She'd send it to the palace censors first, but he didn't need to know that. It was as much privacy as any palace guest would've been given.

Relief was audible in his exhale. "Thank you."

Silence enveloped them. Sanne had started them on a path through the halls at the outer edges of the palace, thinking it best to work their way inward. Most of the spirits she'd encountered had been closer to the heart of the palace; she'd considered starting there, but that afternoon's conversation had convinced her to delay the inevitable. For them to be successful, they needed to hunt as extensions of the same body, to act as one mind. Their conversation had placed a layer of gauze over their shared wound, but this particular gash needed stitches. The relative peacefulness along the Stained Palace's perimeter would give them time to heal.

Outside, the moon was full, and it was easy to see down the hall. She watched Ren as they walked, noting how he craned his neck to follow the height of the windows. The Stained Palace had been designed to let in as much natural light as possible, and many of the outward-facing walls were studded with floor-to-ceiling glass windows. Some were tinted yellow and blue, others were clear and intricately etched. In terms of aesthetic choices, it was an eternally lovely one—whether golden sunlight or silver moonbeams shone through the panes, the effect was breathtaking. Sanne couldn't help but wonder, though, how quickly these windows would become a weakness if the Black Sun chose to invade.

"You asked me if I was married," she said, tapping the daggers strapped to her thigh. "Are you? Is that who's in Tmadrev?"

"Gods, no. If I had a wife, I'd be where she is, not riding through the realm in search of jobs."

Sanne didn't believe him. Nightmares weren't known for their ability to stay in one place. Even she got restless at times. "What does she think of our profession?"

"Why would—" Ren stopped and held an arm out. His voice dropped to a whisper; his hands went to his sickles. "What is that?"

She looked ahead, to where the hallway turned to the right. Something white hovered there, half obstructed by the corner. It fluttered like a banner in the breeze, but there were no drafts in the hallway, no open doors or windows. It seemed to be the edge of a cloak. "I'm not sure."

"Do your servants work this late?"

The last bells had tolled thrice. "No. There are guards on watch, but they only leave their posts if summoned." She cast darkdrape, the Sumric dialect of the spell hissing from her mouth, and signed the ward. Shadows cloaked her before her fingers had stopped moving. Beside her, Ren did the same. They pressed themselves against the wall, moving as far away from the windows as possible so their cocoons of shadow wouldn't seem suspicious. Nightmares could see through the summoned shadows, but only just—when she motioned to have Ren follow her, she had to exaggerate the motion. "Shall we?"

As they crept down the hall, the bit of white wavered and vanished. Sanne quickened her pace, her footfalls muffled by the shadows around her. Adrenaline flooded her veins, and despite the defeat and beatings she'd endured lately, a smile crept over her face. The initiation of pursuit was always her favorite part.

Ren followed at her heels. They rounded the corner and stopped at the end of an interior hallway, one lit by sconces burning with yellow flame. The moonlight from the windows behind them cast long shadows down the hall. Their silhouettes stretched into the darkness waiting at the heart of the palace. Heavy tapestries hung against the walls. In threads of cream, gold, and shades of blue, they depicted the origin of the five major gods and the parasite.

The white-cloaked figure was nowhere in sight.

Sanne whispered the counterspell. The darkdrape haze dissolved, but her vision barely improved.

"Not our best decision," Ren muttered. When Sanne looked over, his eyes already glowed red with nightsight.

"Agreed." Sanne cast nightsight. The world around her went red-scale, the tapestries washed in shades of pink and oxblood.

Midway down the hall, a torch lifted itself from its cradle. A high-pitched cackle echoed down the hall just before the torch hurtled toward them. Ren dove to one side of the hallway and Sanne to the other, the small fire scalding her cheek as the torch sailed by. Before she could draw Peacebringer, a tapestry flung from the wall and enveloped her, restraining her from head to toe.

Ren swore, and then metal chimed against metal. All Sanne could see was Svetlen and Zdesen in their unified, two-faced form—her goddess and the parasite rendered in loving, hand-woven opposition. She tried to lift her arms. The tapestry wove tighter. "Can you see it?"

"Yes!"

"A geist?"

Metal collided with metal again, and what she presumed was a sconce clattered to the ground near her feet. The edge of the tapestry caught fire.

Gods above.

"Yes!"

The air around her smelled of sweat and smoke and too-hot leather. She couldn't reach Peacebringer or a dagger. A lesser Nightmare might have panicked; Sanne, however, took a deep breath, welcomed the burn of smoke in her lungs, and flattened her palms against the tapestry. Svetlen hadn't only placed devotion in Sanne's blood—the goddess had set her alight, too.

Tendrils of holy golden flame snaked from Sanne's fingertips into the weave of the tapestry. She sent the flames slicing upward, expecting the woven hanging to fall away in pieces, but the fire died halfway up. Sanne growled in frustration and fumbled for a strip of tapestry. She tore at the smoldering fabric until she was free. Peacebringer sang as she unsheathed it—the geist wasn't the figure they'd tracked, but it was still something to kill.

Ren advanced on the spirit with his ax drawn. Its blade glowed from within. The geist, rail-thin and visibly decaying, wasn't cackling now. Its maw opened and it screeched—a sound Sanne thought was a cry for mercy—before Ren cleaved it in two with one fell swoop.

"Well," he said, walking down the hall. He took a tapestry scrap and wiped the unblood from his ax. Its blade dulled. The holy aura faded. "That was easy, all things considered. Why do you need me?"

Sanne jerked her chin, indicating the corpse behind him. She didn't sheathe Peacebringer. She didn't revoke nightsight. "Turn around."

He did. As she'd known it would, the geist rose from the floor, its severed half sliding back into place.

Ren's hold on his ax slipped. "Are you ser—"

The geist's roar tore down the hallway. Sanne shoved past a stunned Ren and met the spirit halfway, thrusting Peacebringer forward. The geist, unable to stop, ran itself onto the blade. Sanne spoke her word and Peacebringer glowed, the shifting-opal light of Zikat burning through the haze of her nightsight. The geist howled in pain.

Ren recovered. He drew his sickles, barked his word, and plunged the curved blades into the geist's back. It writhed and swiped spectral claws at them. One of them caught Sanne just below her hairline. Her vision ran a slick red, one darker than nightsight.

No matter. She didn't need to see to kill.

Her hands were covered with black unblood. She adjusted her fingers around Peacebringer's hilt and waited for the oily essence to become tacky.

The geist thrashed. One of its claws swept across Ren's cuirass. He flicked his wrists to bury his sickles deeper. "Do it!"

Sanne dragged Peacebringer upward, stumbling back from the momentum that came when Peacebringer broke free. The two halves of the geist hung from Ren's sickles. He spread his arms apart to keep it from stitching itself back together. Nightsight burned in his eyes.

He began to speak the banishment spell, the alternating Zikatic and Oddelenic dialects so soft they were nearly lost to the crackling of flames in the sconces around them. The halves of the geist wept unblood, but did not come together. Sanne wondered, not for the first time, what horrors had stalked through Naisvet if things like the geist were what had survived the Cataclysm—if, here in the new world, half-mortal and half-divine things like she and Ren were what was needed to defeat them.

The spell ended, but the essence of the geist didn't disappear —it hadn't worked, as Sanne had known it wouldn't. "Say it again."

He did. Nothing happened. His eyes dimmed as he broke nightsight. "What—"

"Again."

The effect was the same—none at all.

"Banish it." Her voice was ragged. A laugh sweeter than that of the geist's snaked through her mind. "If you think I don't need you."

Ren looked at her with wild eyes. "Sanne, *help*." His arms sagged with the growing weight of the corpse.

For a moment, just a moment, Sanne watched him struggle. Worry and fear flooded her, but below them was a thin riptide of relief. She wouldn't have to convince Ren of her difficulties as she had Cassander. It wasn't just *her* spells that had failed—it seemed that any Nightmare would struggle here.

The laugh echoed through her mind again. A two-tone voice hissed, *It was never just you. This is bigger than just you.*

Sanne gasped, whirling, but there was no one behind her. Bile rose in her throat. She recognized Zdesen's voice all too easily.

"*Sanne!*" Ren's arms spasmed. The geist's halves were trying to reunite. One of its feet, which came to a toeless point, dragged through the tapestry shreds on the ground. When Sanne glanced down, the scene of Svetlen bringing light to Ruhysvet was flat on the ground before her.

Svetlen. Light. Warmth. Peace.

The corpse halves were almost together. "Sanne, *help me*—"

The two of you are right to be afraid.

Sanne snapped her head up and blocked out the parasite's voice. She began to recite the banishment spell, her voice falling against Ren's like weft against warp. She took one of the laden sickles in apology.

They stayed in the hallway and whispered the spell until the geist's shimmering essence passed from its body.

"Outside."

Ren didn't protest. He followed Sanne into a secluded corner of the bailey. She held out a hand and he gave her his half of the corpse. Sanne dropped them and knelt over the halves, holding her hands flat above them and calling forth fire. The corpse caught flame, and she and Ren stood side by side as it burned.

"It's happening to you, too."

She looked up at him, squinting against the full moon. "What do you mean?"

When the corpse was reduced to ash, he answered. "Let's go inside. I should tell you about my last hunt."

9.21.626

The next three nights passed in the same manner: she and Ren hunting their prey, engaging it, then struggling to kill and banish it. They'd part ways in the early hours of the morning, slipping into their chambers without a word. Sanne would clean her armor and weapons until sun-up, go to Zikat's chapel to pray through the dawn, then nap until a servant notified her that Ren had woken. They would take breakfast together, spend the day sparring or resting, then meet at sundown to repeat it all again. With each night, the conversation between them came a little easier— every so often, Ren would smile or laugh in a way that reminded Sanne of who he'd been at the Keep—but something unsaid still lingered between them. Sanne felt it, but didn't know how to address it. She didn't want another fight.

The morning after the third night, Ren followed her to her chambers. "I've been thinking," he said. A tray with a pot of coffee and cups sat on her desk—the servants knew she liked it after a hunt—and Ren helped himself. "Our spells, our *prayers*, are failing. As I said, it's like what happened in Tanglewood. Their temples hadn't been touched in nearly thirty years, and it was harder for me to banish the spirits than it should have been. Have you contacted your temples to see if anything's wrong?"

A note rested on the tray, the thick white paper pristine despite the coffee accompanying it. Sanne broke the gold wax seal and read it—Cassander wanted a report.

"The temples are detached from the palace. They're in the city." She poured coffee and warmed her hands with the cup. She had nothing to report, other than the fact that she and Ren sported new bruises and needed to sharpen their weapons again. "I think you mean our palace chapels, and the answer is no. No one staffs them. They're maintained by a holy one from their corresponding temples once a week."

Ren arched a brow. "I know that."

"You do? You aren't in the chapels during morning or evening prayers."

He scowled. "I pray, Sanne."

"I haven't seen you."

"I don't rise as early as you do."

"Zikat is meant to be praised with the dawn."

He chuckled. "You don't have to adhere to the Keep's schedule anymore, you know," he said. "The gods are forgiving. Besides, I'm not meant for early mornings. I think Zikat would prefer I pray to her when my mind isn't focused on returning to bed."

Sanne let silence fall between them. Zikat with the dawn—which was coming soon, based on the deep blue shade of the sky outside—Svetlen at midday, Oddelen at dusk. It was her schedule. It kept her devout, kept her holy.

Yet their spells, her spells, were failing. Perhaps Ren was right. Perhaps going to the temples would give her something to tell Cassander.

"Alright. We'll go into the city when the sun has risen."

"Today?"

"Unless you're too tired." She met his eyes over the rim of her cup, hoping he caught the taunt beneath her teasing. Shadows pooled beneath his red eyes, shadows that matched the ones smudged under hers.

"Me?" He pressed a hand to his chest. "Never."

"Good." She waved toward the door. "Go clean yourself up. Come back and I'll walk you to the stables."

"Not the chapel?"

"No." She'd follow Ren's lead. Her prayers to Zikat could come later than the dawn just this once. "We'll pray in the Celesty."

————

Sanne stepped from Svetlen's temple into the circle of the Celesty and wiped the sweat from her brow—the holy fire in Svetlen's temple kept it hot year-round. It had been an hour since Ren had slipped between the bone-colored columns of Oddelen's temple and agreed to meet her in an hour's time, but as she looked around the circle, he was nowhere to be seen.

Like many things in the Celesty, the temple district was organized in the shape of a sun. Instead of a square, the cobbled roads meandered away from a circular forum, at the center of which was a large fountain. A brass sculpture of Svetlen served as its centerpiece. Water spilled from her hands in wide sheets. Covering the center was a stained-glass dome, which cast reds and greens and purples onto the cobblestones below. Children often played in the fountain during the warm seasons, drying their feet on the stones before slipping their shoes back on. It was autumn now, though, and the chill in the air made Sanne grateful she and Ren wore cloaks.

He'd washed himself of blood and kept on the clothing and armor he'd hunted in, adding only his dark cloak before they'd come to the Celesty. Sanne, however, had changed. She'd hunted in her black leather Nightmare armor, which was identical to Ren's except for its gold stitching instead of black. Leaving the palace on royal business, however, had necessitated she wear her Esclarmonde plate. Only the royal family wore the golden armor, which had their sigil, a circular crest with half of a sun and Svetlen's face in profile, emblazoned on the breastplate. Beneath the armor, Sanne's gambeson and leggings were Nightmare black. Her cloak was sky blue, its lining the color of midnight.

Upon arriving in the Celesty, they'd prayed in Zikat's temple before speaking with High Priestess Rada, a prismatic half-elf. They'd discovered nothing and then split up; Sanne questioned High Priestesses Cardaril and Sohli—Sumra and Svetlen's high priestesses, respectively—while Ren spoke with Oddelen and

Zatva's. He'd agreed to meet her by the fountain, but Sanne saw no one dressed in black.

Hope flared in her chest. Her interviews hadn't given her any leads, but maybe, just maybe, Ren was late because he'd discovered something. Sanne walked toward Oddelen's temple—it made perfect sense. Many of the Order's banishing spells were prayers to Oddelen. Something interfering with them would surely be felt in his temple if not Zikat's.

Sanne was nearly inside, her hand outstretched to pull the skull-shaped door handle, when she heard a familiar laugh. Ren stood outside of Zatva's temple. Dark greenery had been woven into his hair, through his armor, and around his horns. High Priestess Lirwood, clothed in a flowing pink dress and similarly adorned with greenery, trailed behind him. Slim black horns twisted up and away from her scalp, curving on an axis like Ren's.

Ren saw Sanne approaching and raised a hand in acknowledgment. "I've got to go," he said, drawing Lirwood into a hug. "But it was wonderful to meet you, High Priestess. Thank you."

She smiled. "Any time you need a bit of home, Ren, come see us." She returned to the temple. Ren fell into step beside Sanne.

"Do you know her?" Sanne asked. *Home*, the high priestess had said—but Ren was a Greywarren, an orphan. As far as Sanne knew, the Keep had been his home.

Ren chuckled. "No," he said, plucking some of the fronds from his hair. "Just another of my kind." His hand dropped— he'd left the greenery around his horns and armor intact. "I haven't seen another horned elf in almost ten years. There aren't many of us in the west."

Lirwood had referred to their ancestral home, then. "I see," Sanne said, though she didn't understand. Her ancestral home was all around them. She hadn't lost her family or been taken from it—the only time she'd left, she had begged to.

"No one I spoke to reported any kind of disturbance," Ren said. "Oddelen's temple has actually had a boost in attendance."

Sanne sighed. "High Priestesses Cardaril and Sohli haven't

noticed anything, either." She looked back at Svetlen's temple. The front of the building was bright and welcoming, its white doors open wide between two slender stained-glass windows. A beautiful day bloomed around them. Most of the temples and businesses had propped their doors open, trusting Svetlen's light to burn away the morning's chill and keep their establishments warm. Shreds of night still clung to the bottom of the city, however, and it was to the world below the shadowed ground that Sanne's mind went. The last temple waited there, reserved for a goddess who was patient and dark. A goddess who all would meet, whether they wanted to or not. A goddess who wasn't content with one Esclarmonde, who had taken her cousin and set her sights on Sanne, too.

The memory of slick laughter echoed through her head.

"Sanne?" Ren's voice was gentle—he must have repeated himself.

She dropped her arms. She hadn't realized she'd wrapped them around herself. "Follow me."

They set off across the square. Sanne took deep, slow breaths to calm her racing heart. Esclarmondes were guided by the light. Esclarmondes had no reason to be afraid. She clutched one of her daggers to still her trembling fingers. "Do you have a way to cover your face?"

"Yes."

Sanne sidestepped into an alley. "Then do it." She turned her cloak inside out, pressing the sky blue comfort of her family close. She drew her hood over her head and a half-mask over her mouth and nose.

"Why the secrecy?" Ren's voice was muffled. In the slit left exposed by his mouth covering and cloak hood, only his red eyes were visible.

"I don't want us to be seen," Sanne said, and led Ren down the alley to an adjoining one. Cassander had enough to worry over —he didn't need reports of his Lady Nightmare slinking into

Zdesen's temple. Sanne was confident no one in the Celesty knew what was happening inside the palace, and she intended to keep it that way.

A plain black door waited before them. Sanne turned to Ren. "Are you ready?"

Ren flicked his eyes down her person, and when his eyes met hers, she hated the understanding she saw there. He stepped in front of her and pushed the door open without a word.

They entered onto a small landing. When the door swung shut behind them, white candles burning with a silver-tinged flame were all that lit their way. A black stone staircase led down to the temple. The walls and the ceiling, also of dark stone, were too close.

"Lots of black," Ren remarked. The tips of his horns scraped the ceiling as he looked around. "We should feel very at home here."

Sanne stiffened. *Nothing* about Zdesen belonged in her home. The goddess was a parasite, a menace souring Svetlen's blessings— she had taken advantage of the gift of light to make sure no bit of horror went unseen—and yet they were inseparable. Even their temples were a testament to their entanglement; Zdesen's was built behind and below Svetlen's, the same way Zdesen existed as Svetlen's second face. Her temple relied on Svetlen's like Zdesen used Svetlen's body.

"Let's go," Sanne muttered. Ren followed without another word.

The staircase deposited them at the opening of an underground cavern. The flagstones shone beneath their feet, free of footprints and grime. Four thick obsidian columns supported the ceiling; though they'd been smoothed and polished, the rock of the walls and ceiling had been left sharp and jagged. A red stone altar was in the center of the room, the length of a man but half as high. Like the floors, it had been polished to a shine.

Priestesses in flowing white dresses and bone masks milled

around the edges of the cavern, slipping in and out of cave openings that Sanne knew led to a maze of halls and smaller rooms. The Black Sun had undergone his trial here—that meant there was a dungeon somewhere close by, and an armory. Sanne stilled, her heart in her throat, and turned to make sure the door they'd come through was still there. She wouldn't put it past the parasite to have enchanted her temple with some ancient, fear-inciting magic.

"Hello, visitors."

At the sound of the voice, the priestesses froze. As one, they faced Ren and Sanne.

Sanne snapped her head forward. A woman robed in swaths of black fabric stood before her and Ren, flanked by two priestesses in grey. Like them, she was masked; her face was obscured by a slim eyeless skull that had been painted black. Seven eyes had been carved into the mask, the paint stripped away to reveal dull white bone. Though her eyes, forehead, and cheeks were covered, the mask stopped in an arc around her mouth, exposing lips that had been painted blood red. She smiled, revealing too-white teeth, and lowered the hood of her cloak. Dark auburn hair ran in unbound waves down her back. "What brings you to our lady's temple today?"

Sanne resisted the urge to reach for Peacebringer. Until now, she'd only seen Zdesen's high priestess in the sunlight of the surface world. Here, in the garish light of the subterranean temple, courtesy of red-paneled skylights, the woman looked eldritch.

Ren stepped forward and bowed his head. "Good morning, High Priestess."

The two priestesses tittered to one another, pink lips smiling beneath the curved edges of their masks. The white-robed priestesses began to move again.

The high priestess smiled. "It's morning?" she said. "How lovely. And you seem to know me. Have you been here before?"

"No." The corners of Ren's eyes crinkled. "But I'm familiar

enough with temple customs and dress to guess at your elevated position, and it seems I was lucky."

The high priestess stepped forward. "Indeed. I am High Priestess Adarilen Vestel, rectoress of this temple, blessed of Zdesen. But we are the lucky ones to have such—" Her head bobbed slightly as she looked Ren up and down. Her smile widened, the tips of it almost reaching her mask. "—reverent visitors. Draw down your coverings. Let us see your faces."

"No."

The priestesses' heads swiveled to Sanne. "'No'?" Vestel repeated. "Our lady is the goddess of fear, the great equalizer. We are all the same in terror. We do not permit worshippers in our temple to hide their identities."

"Your faces are covered."

Vestel was irritated—Sanne heard it in the sharpness of her voice. "We have shown ourselves to our lady in other ways," she said. "She knows the depths of our fear, our weaknesses. She no longer needs to see our faces to know us wholly."

"How wonderful."

The two priestesses exchanged a look as Vestel stepped forward. "If you will not reveal yourselves," she said, pressing the tips of her fingers together, "we will have to ask you to leave."

"Our apologies, High Priestess." Ren lowered his hood and mouth covering. He shrugged his cloak back, revealing his armor and weapons. "We didn't mean to disrespect your lady."

Vestel shifted toward him. "A horned one?" She reached out a hand, her elongated nails pricking his jaw as she turned his head to the side. She wore a ring on her pointer finger, one with an ostentatious red stone in a silver setting, and it winked as it caught the light. The tip of a crimson-lacquered nail dragged down his tattoo. "I see. You are a long way from home, Nightmare." She turned her head to Sanne. "I suppose I know why *you* did not want to show yourself, then."

Sanne revealed herself as Ren had. Her plate seemed to glow. At the sight of it, one of the priestesses drew her lips back and hissed like an animal. Nightmares swore not to harm the living, yet Sanne considered throwing her into the sharp wall. "Do you blame me, High Priestess?"

Vestel smiled at Sanne, but there was none of the warmth she'd shown Ren in the expression. "Hello, Lady Nightmare. No, I do not 'blame' you. But I think you waste your potential by avoiding us." Her lips curled into something slick, as ingratiating as it was taunting. "Our lady whispers about you. You should visit her more often. You know she favors your bloodline."

Sanne, forgetting diplomacy, lifted her lips in a snarl. It mattered little that the palace and Zdesen's temple had maintained a tense peace ever since the Black Sun's exile—no one mocked her family like this, especially in front of an outsider like Ren. "You know nothing of my bloodline."

The three priestesses cocked their heads to the right. "The Black Sun," the priestess on the right said. "Is he not of your line?"

Fools. Idiots. Of course he was—that's why everything he did hurt so much. "He is an outlier," she snapped, coating her words in anger so she wouldn't cry. "My blood is blessed by Svetlen."

"So is his," said the priestess on the left. "To be blessed by one is to be blessed by the other. They are of the same body. The same heart."

"If you visited more, Lady, you would understand." Vestel stepped forward. Her scent washed over Sanne, battlefield-sweet. "Our lady respects you. Welcome her. Someone in your line of work could do great things with Zdesen."

Sanne stepped to meet the high priestess. She looked into her seven false eyes and scowled—no matter how she presented herself, Vestel was just a woman, a woman like Sanne, not a beast hidden behind a mask. Sanne would not be afraid. "That is heresy," she hissed. "I would *never*—"

Ren cleared his throat. "If I may interrupt, High Priestess," he said, lowering a sickle between the women, "we came here with a purpose."

Vestel did not turn from Sanne. "Other than disrespecting our lady?"

"Yes." The flat of Ren's blade clinked against Sanne's breastplate. He nudged, and she stepped back. "We'd like to ask some questions. We need your help."

"Oh. I see." Vestel's mouth quirked. "Does His Majesty the Radiant Sun know you're here?"

"Don't answer, Ren."

"Let him speak," the high priestess purred. "Don't hold his leash so tightly."

Ren's eyes flicked to Sanne. She nodded. "We're here in service of the king," he said. "There's an infestation of malevolent spirits in the palace, and we've been charged with rooting it out."

Vestel pointed at Sanne. "Allow me to guess. The Lady Nightmare believes we have something to do with it?"

"No," Ren said. He lowered his voice to the timbre of Vestel's. "She doesn't. I don't, either. But we're having problems with our prayer-spells. We've been speaking to each temple to see if they've had any difficulties with rituals or worship." He smiled. "We are all engaged in the service of gods, are we not?"

"We are, Nightmare, but—"

"Call me Ren. Please." He drew his hand over his chest and bowed. "In the name of our gods, can we not work together?"

Vestel eyed Sanne. "Will your handler agree to it?"

"His handler is here in service of the king," Sanne said. "The *rightful* king. She will do whatever is necessary to guarantee his peace."

"Do you believe I disagree with the Radiant Sun's place on the throne?" The high priestess tutted, shaking her head. "You're rather disrespectful to those you would ask for help, Lady Nightmare. But I understand asking for help may not come naturally to you." She extended a pale hand to Ren, her nails glinting red. "Walk with me, Ren. I would be happy to assist you."

Sanne moved forward as Ren did, but the two priestesses blocked her.

Vestel laughed. "Now, now," she said. "I won't hurt him. I won't *convert* him."

Ren held an arm out for Vestel. His eyes met Sanne's, and he widened them as if to say *trust me*.

She did—she had no other choice. Sanne crossed her arms and waited, watching as Ren and Vestel walked the perimeter of the cavernous chamber. She flexed the muscles of her back and shoulders to remind herself of Peacebringer's presence. If Vestel grabbed Ren and dragged him into the tunnels where the Black Sun had become corrupted, Sanne could probably reach them before Ren disappeared into Zdesen's clutches—probably.

One of the priestesses fiddled with her dress, a thread of which had escaped its seam. Sanne stared at the woman's hands. The pads of her fingers were pink and puffy, her hand shiny as if it had swollen too large for its skin.

"We spend our time cleaning," the priestess said, noticing Sanne's stare. She smiled, and her teeth were too white. "We don't have many visitors to minister to. Not anymore."

The other priestess glared at Sanne. "Not since—"

"If you speak of the Black Sun, I'll have you jailed for treason."

The expected rebuke never came. The priestess turned back around. Sanne pressed her lips together and took a mental count of the daggers strapped to her person. She hated coming here. When the Black Sun had been exiled for the second time last year—though this time by Cassander, not their father— many of Zdesen's priestesses had gone with him. Those who remained allegedly supported Cassander, but Sanne had never heard a priestess of Zdesen swear loyalty to him. The high priestess arm in arm with Ren was the same woman who'd overseen the Black Sun's oath-swearing trials; once he had broken his paladin's oath to Svetlen, she'd helped him swear it anew to Zdesen. Sanne had been present for the final of those trials, had seen the bloodshed the Black Sun rained upon the arena in Zdesen's name. She couldn't trust a woman who'd warped a devotee of Svetlen into something as monstrous as her cousin had become.

Before Vestel, the Black Sun had sworn his life to Svetlen and Svetlen only. If Zdesen and her priestesses could twist someone as devoted as that, what could they do to someone like Sanne? Sanne, whose worship was split amongst three gods instead of one?

She shook the thought away. Ren and Vestel came closer with every step, and Sanne strained to hear. He, by the gods, was laughing at something Vestel had said. Below the wicked edges of her mask, the high priestess was smiling. She placed another hand on his arm and squeezed conspiratorially.

"I will say this so the Lady believes it, too," Vestel said when they were close enough for Sanne to hear. "We've experienced nothing strange recently, but I remember having an interruption a few decades ago. Thirty years, perhaps? We were unable to pray, for a time. We felt as if we had been gouged out. Has anyone else reported that?"

Ren shook his head. When he looked at Sanne, questioning, she shook hers.

"I see. Then perhaps you are looking for answers too close to today. Perhaps this has all happened before." Vestel dropped her hold on Ren and turned to Sanne. Sanne couldn't see the woman's eyes, but felt their gaze as if she'd been pricked by dozens of tiny needles. "Have you considered that you're up against something a Nightmare cannot fight? Legend, not specter? We all have things in our past we hide from the light." She cocked her head on the last word, her tone turning saccharine. "We all know the stories of Naisvet, of the Prázeny Era. We've seen what happens when one feels that the gods are too powerful."

Anger, bright and hot like a tower of flame, licked up Sanne's throat. Of course the parasite's priestess was comfortable speaking of that heretical time, the brief era when the gods had been crippled. "Speak plainly or not at all."

Vestel's lips curled. "There is no speaking plainly to an Esclarmonde," she said. "You refuse to hear it. Now, Lady, I've said everything I intend to. It is almost time for our prayers. I must ask you to leave."

Sanne spread her fingers so she wouldn't form a fist. Zdesen's priestesses held ritual prayer at no specific time, bending the knee to their goddess only when their high priestess felt it appropriate. She and Ren were being forced out. "Of course," she said, though made no effort to warm her tone. "Thank you for your time."

"Thank you, High Priestess," Ren said, bowing again. He nodded to the women still flanking Sanne. "Priestesses."

A slow smile spread over Vestel's blood-red lips. Her parting words slipped out like viscera from a wound. "I wish you luck, Nightmares. Long live the king."

———

After the darkness of the subterranean temple, the brightness of the Celesty was blinding. It took traveling through the city, riding their Umbral mares up the winding forested path to the Stained Palace, and walking into her chambers for Sanne's eyes to stop smarting. Ren followed, matching her silence—Sanne had been too furious to speak during their return. She clung to the anger Vestel had stoked, clung to the heat and power and rightness of it. Descending to the parasite's temple had been horrible, and the mention of the godless Prázeny Era made Sanne want to scream. The era had been one of pure chaos, and the realm had moved past it. The gods had returned. Order had returned.

She ground her teeth. Her anger was just. Her anger was on behalf of her goddess, on behalf of her family. Zdesen's ilk spun truths into heresy, spiders using beautiful silk to weave traps for the faithful. Svetlen was the light, the undeniable truth, certainty shining radiant and unmistakable. How dare they mock her. How dare they mock Sanne.

Ren cleared his throat and let her chamber door swing shut

behind them. "So," he said, shaking the hood of his cloak loose from his horns, "are we going to talk about that?"

Sanne paced the sitting room. Her plate chimed. "What do you mean?"

"Well, it may be my own ignorance of such things, being the poor orphan I am, but that seemed like a very ignoble way for a noble to act." He eyed her, and when he spoke again, his voice was hushed. "Who do you serve, Sanne?"

She stopped. The gods, of course—what did he mean? "What?"

Ren crossed his arms. "The Order prioritizes neutrality in military and political conflict. You acted as if you wanted to gut Vestel alive. That's hardly neutral."

"I'm not just a member of the Order, Ren. I'm also an Esclarmonde."

"Are you going to war, then? If your king calls you to arms, will you use Peacebringer to smite the Black Sun?"

Sanne recoiled. Nightmares didn't harm the living, and they both knew it. Her war was in the palace—winning it was how she would help Cassander defeat the Black Sun, and he *would* defeat the Black Sun. "You wouldn't understand. Do you know what he's done to us?"

Ren pressed his lips together. "Yes. Your cousin, Casi—"

Sanne parroted Cassander's words without thinking. "We don't say his name."

Ren stared at her. He recited the facts of the war as if he'd been called on in a classroom: Cassander had risen to the throne when his father Oran had died; the Black Sun had challenged the ascension and claimed the throne for himself. He'd been dismissed and exiled, and fled to Nocovostvo, the kingdom of the night goddess Sumra. Nocovostvo's refugee laws had allowed him to establish a foothold there, where he dug his claws into the snowy mountains and hid from the fallout of his flight. Two Celestian citizens had been killed in the chaos of it.

Ren recounted the last twelve months of Sanne's life, twelve months of heartbreak and fury and betrayal, with a straight face and detached tone. His indifference made her anger cool to a bitter sorrow. He knew almost everything, and somehow it barely affected him. Sanne wanted to tell him the worst of it—that the Black Sun believed he was the eldest twin, not Cassander, and that their parents Oran and Annelore had lied to the entire kingdom about the boys' birth order. That the scorch mark across the Sohli Prophecy was because of the Black Sun's silver flames, that he'd defaced the prophecy and denounced it as lies. Yet the words wouldn't come. It was a ludicrous claim, and humiliating; it reflected poorly on the entire Esclarmonde line, that a king and queen would lie to their people so. Sanne didn't like to think about it.

"Knowing that, and knowing me," she said, "can you blame me for hating Vestel?"

He was quiet for a moment. Yes, they'd been apart for years, but Ren knew just as well as Sanne did what she was—a devotee, a woman who lived to serve the gods. Vestel sought to draw Sanne and the Celestial citizens into the parasite's fold; if Sanne went, she was afraid of what Zdesen would have her do. Zdesen was abhorrent, but she was holy, and a god was a god. Deep down, beneath the layers of Esclarmonde plate and Nightmare leather, Sanne knew that if Zdesen commanded her, she would have to listen.

Ren opened his mouth to speak, but there was a knock. A hand, gauntleted in gleaming white armor, opened the chamber door.

"I apologize, Lady," Vallen said, his bronze face appearing in the threshold, "but His Majesty has requested your presence. He wants a report on your hunt."

Sanne sighed. A god was a god, and a king was a king. She was commanded by both.

She dismissed Ren and went to meet Cassander.

"You went *where*?"

The war room's sconces blazed higher at Cassander's indignation, the golden flames almost reaching the ceiling. Sanne stretched out a hand and calmed them. "Zdesen's temple," she repeated. "No one saw us."

"And why, pray tell, did you go there?"

Sanne gave him the answer she'd rehearsed: that they—she was careful not to say it had been Ren's idea—had realized their prayer-spells weren't working, and thought it wise to speak to the temples in the Celesty to see if the issue was widespread. Leaving out Zdesen's temple would have overlooked the possibility that the palace's infestation was somehow caused by Zdesen, perhaps as a ploy to assist the Black Sun. Sanne didn't fully believe this last bit, as she'd never traced a hunt back to a divine origin, but Cassander didn't know how spirits manifested. She'd thought it might make him understand why they'd gone.

It didn't.

"Are you suggesting that the gods have retreated from us?" His eyes burned like embers. "That this infestation is some divine punishment because of my—" He swallowed. "The Black Sun?"

Sanne clenched her jaw and tried not to show her anger, though she knew her eyes blazed like his. "I would *never* suggest that Svetlen is punishing you," she hissed, pressing her hands onto the table where he sat and leaning forward. "She favors you, Cassander. You are the king she's chosen. No one else."

Cassander looked away first. The embers died to coals, and then to nothing. He dropped his head into his hands. "I'm sorry, Sanne." His voice was muffled, yet she still heard it waver. "I received word that meetings with Nocovostvo aren't going well. This war is...I am becoming someone I don't recognize. I'm sorry. You don't deserve this anger."

"I don't." She sat. Cassander had been twenty-eight when Oran died. He'd taken the throne two weeks later, not much older than Sanne was now. He'd been coronated with tears in his eyes, grieving a father and a brother amidst the birth of his reign. Sanne wondered which man he mourned more. "But neither do you."

War sounded simple in their history books, the right decisions and strategies so obvious when mapped out in black and white. But the histories never took into account that war was more than logistical; war was heartbreak and indecision and grieving someone who was still alive.

"I know your contract expires soon," Cassander said. "I know I've promised to let you go." He reached out a white-gloved hand to her. "But is there any way you'd consider staying?"

In Sanne's chest beat a heart of stained glass. Everything she loved, all she held close, was represented by a colored shard: gold for Svetlen, varicolored for Zikat, dark grey for Oddelen, burnt umber for the Order. Cassander's was sky blue, and it was these latter two that fought to be the largest. The leaden armature of her heart shifted each time a fragment changed in size, forever keeping her loves separate, never letting her loyalty to one mingle with the dedication to another. The Order's piece had been shrinking as of late, and she was afraid that if she stayed with Cassander, its shard would one day be swallowed by his. She was an Esclarmonde by blood, but the Order had forged her—it was something she couldn't turn her back on. It was something she knew Cassander wouldn't understand.

Sanne didn't know how to say this, so she said nothing at all.

9.25.626

She and Ren's hunt continued, the next four days an endless night punctuated only by Sanne's scheduled prayers. Each night brought them closer to the center of the palace, and, as Sanne had known it would, their prey grew in number and viciousness—they could barely exorcize a spirit before Marra, who Sanne recruited to scout, appeared and cried out to alert them of another. They fought well together, but their closeness was only martial. Ren had become distant since their trip to the Celesty, displeased that she'd become so embroiled in politics. He went quiet at any mention of Cassander, and it made Sanne want to shake him. It wasn't just politics for her. This was her family, her *blood* family, a compelled bond deeper than what ran between those who trained at the Keep. But how could he understand? He'd grown up an orphan.

He grew up free, Sanne caught herself thinking as she left the war room that night, ashamed that she had no news for Cassander. She hated not being able to reassure him, hated that she and Ren hadn't had time to look into Vestel's cryptic words, and hated that she was desperate enough to even consider the madwoman's incoherence. In her midday prayers, Sanne had begged Svetlen for guidance, but the goddess had been quiet—there were no guiding flares of heat or light. It seemed that Svetlen wanted Sanne to solve this on her own.

From the war room, she went to Ren's chamber. She'd ordered him to it that morning and sequestered herself in her own, intending for them both to rest. Though Nightmares trained to survive on little sleep, she and Ren hadn't done so for more than a few hours in the last four days. The exhaustion made them volatile. She hadn't realized Ren could be catty. Just that morning, he'd informed her that before taking this hunt, he'd made plans for the Solstice holiday in two and a half weeks and snapped, "Does the Order's princess think she'll be able to let me go by then?"

Sanne's patience had worn thin. After some shouting and swearing, she'd told him to go to bed and that she'd fetch him for prayers that evening.

He opened the door a minute after she'd knocked. His auburn hair was a mess—some longer pieces were snagged in his horns. "Good morning."

"Try again."

He rubbed his eyes. "Evening," he corrected. "Is it sunset?"

She nodded. Ren closed the door. He opened it a few minutes later dressed for the hunt. They walked to Oddelen's chapel in silence. The bags under his eyes were still present, but not as dark, and his bronze skin wasn't as sallow. He looked better, and Sanne hoped his attitude had improved, too.

They reached Oddelen's chapel, passed wrought-iron pews with dusky blue velvet cushions, and knelt at the altar. At the Keep, they'd sat in pews to pray, but that had been in a body of Nightmares so large that kneeling wouldn't have been suitable. Here, though, where she and Ren were the only two worshippers in the moonlight-filled chapel, they fit perfectly before the altar.

Sanne began to sing the ritual prayer, her voice hitting the bottom of its range and rumbling in her chest. Ren's voice, a baritone she'd forgotten how much she liked the sound of, joined with hers on the second line. As they sang, the notes left their chests and traveled into their throats and heads. The prayer ended with the breathy sound of a death rattle. In the Keep, hearing dozens of Nightmares make the sound had been comforting, the voices of many holding back the silence. In the Stained Palace, though, the quiet nearly swallowed them.

Ren whispered something in Oddelenic under his breath. Sanne fought the urge to listen and translate. Whatever he asked of the gods was not for her to know.

When he stopped, she spoke. "We both need to accept that we're not who we were eight years ago."

He didn't look at her. "I agree."

"I know you don't understand my place here. I know you don't care about the war. But I need you to accept those things, Ren, at least as long as you're here."

Ren turned to her. "No, I don't understand, and I don't care which of your cousins sits on the throne—my hunt will go on either way. But I care about you, Sanne." Their eyes met. "I see this wearing on you. I slept today. I rested today. Did you?"

She had, though not for as long as she'd meant to. Cassander had needed her.

"I worry you're playing too many parts," Ren said, his voice gentle. "For the Order, for your king, for your family." He paused.

From the way his eyes darted to her leather pauldron, which had been embroidered with the Esclarmonde sigil, and her tattooed hand, she had a sense of what he was going to say. "For yourself and your gods."

"They're your gods, too."

The deflection was quick, thoughtless. From Ren's deep sigh, Sanne could tell she'd disappointed him. "Not all of them. Not in the way that they're yours."

A bit of dead skin hung from Sanne's thumbnail. She ripped the skin away even though she knew it would make her bleed. She and Ren had been like siblings once. Sanne had a brother, but Becan was four years her junior; she'd been more of a second mother to him than a sister or friend. Ren had been different, someone her age on the same path whose companionship and advice actually meant something to her. She loved Becan, of course, but she'd chosen the brother before her. She felt him slipping away from her, too.

"I'm sorry," she whispered, because he was the only person who would let her say it.

He leaned over and hugged her, adjusting his hold so they wouldn't be pricked by one another's weapons. "I'm sorry, too."

Sanne wrapped her arms around him. She let her head fall into the crook of his shoulder and tried not to cry. Together. They would stamp out this infestation together, and she would ignore how much she was going to miss him when he was gone. "Are you ready to hunt?"

They left the chapel. It had started to storm. Rain cascaded down the stained and etched glass of the hall's windows, watery moonlight reflecting onto the night-black floor and ceiling. Lightning cut a jagged path along the sky. Thunder rumbled in its wake seconds later.

"So you have Solstice plans," Sanne said. Last night, they'd left off on the main floor, so she led them there now. "Are they with your mysterious correspondent?"

Ren fiddled with the strap of his pauldron. "Yes. She lives in Tanglewood."

"I see." Sanne let a few more of their steps echo down the hall before she asked, "Is she your lover?"

Ren ducked his head, but Sanne saw his smile. "I care for her."

Sanne knew that smile, that soft tone of voice—Cassander smiled at Malaia that way, spoke of her with the same gentleness. Ren was in love. "Tell m—"

Thunder covered her words. The boom of it rattled the windows. Sanne stopped—there had been no lightning, and the thunder wasn't stopping. The initial crack of it faded, but the resonance it left behind persisted. Ren drew a dagger. The blade hummed.

A chill ran down Sanne's back. The thunder conjured up the memory of a figure with pale purple eyes, of her skull colliding with the tile floor below the mezzanine. "I think—"

Thunder cracked loud enough to make Ren and Sanne to cover their ears. It wasn't the windows that rattled this time, but the sconces set along the wall. Tapestries drifted back and forth, their rods trembling. The sound hadn't come from the storm outside—it had come from the center of the palace.

The thunder rumbled in Sanne's chest, traveling through her ribs down her spine and into her gut. Her stomach twisted. A coldness spread over her as if someone had wrapped a chilled hand around her organs. Sharp pain spread through her as the frigid hand tugged; she gasped and lurched forward, pressing a hand to her stomach.

Ren grunted. When she looked over, he was also grimacing, though his hand had gone to his throat. "What in the three hells—"

The grip in Sanne's gut pulled her toward the center of the palace. "Let's go," she ground out. Ren followed. With every step closer to the palace's heart, the pain lessened, though it didn't disappear. Sanne was soon able to break into a run despite it.

The thunder sounded again, and the cold pull intensified as Sanne and Ren rounded a corner. The place it wanted her to go was unmistakable. "The throne room!"

They ran. Servants started to step out of their rooms, wondering at what they thought was only a storm. At a shout from Ren, they hurried back inside, away from the black-clad hunters barreling down the halls.

Ren and Sanne reached the throne room at the same time Vallen and some of his guards did. "This is ours," Sanne said. "Go to the king and queen. Keep them in their chambers until I've sent word that it's safe."

Vallen took one look at Ren, whose eyes already glowed red, and nodded. "You heard her." As he and his men bolted toward Cassander's chambers, Vallen shouted, "Be careful, Lady!"

Sanne muttered the spell for nightsight. When her vision washed red, she and Ren each took one of the throne room doors. Together, they swung them open and slipped inside.

A wraith twice Sanne's height hovered in the middle of the throne room, the fabric-like tendrils of its torn covering brushing against the dark tile circle inlaid into the floor.

"Well," Ren said. "Glad we rested."

The cold feeling in Sanne's gut turned heavy. The wraith's head—or what would have been its head—twitched to the side like a dog hearing a strange sound. Two pale purple eyes slid open in its false face. "*Hello again, plaything.*"

"I've fought this one before." Sanne drew Peacebringer and spoke her word, feeling a sliver of calm run through her pounding heart when the sword glowed. "It doesn't give up."

Ren drew his ax. "We'd be out of work if spirits did."

The wraith watched them as they moved to flank it. It remained still, its not-head twitching from side to side as if listening to an argument. "*What do you think you'll do?*" Its voice hissed like hot oil on sand. "*Kill me?*"

Ren shouted something at Sanne; it took her a moment to

realize he'd switched to Oddelenic. The dialect sounded out of place in a raised volume. "*It can speak?*"

Wraiths were the most intelligent of spirits, save apparitions, but most of them lacked the ability to form phrases. Grunts, curses, single words—that was how wraiths communicated their rage, not sentences. Not recognition.

Sanne opened her mouth to reply, but the wraith turned toward Ren and said, in perfect Oddelenic, "*It can.*"

Sanne gripped Peacebringer and drew a dagger with her other hand, clinging to her weapons to steady herself. Spirits walked the blurred lines between life and death. They defied the gods' order. How could this one speak their language?

Ren met her eyes across the room and nodded. At once, they sprinted at the spirit.

Thunder exploded outward from the wraith. Sanne stumbled. Her ears rang from the sound. The wraith cackled and raised its blackened bony hands. It still faced Ren, so Sanne cast darkdrape and hoped it would lose track of her.

"*Plaything,*" a voice whispered in her ear. "*You cannot hide.*"

It grabbed her braid and jerked her back, throwing her to the ground. She dissolved darkdrape and drove her dagger into the spirit's parody of a foot. She was rewarded with a howl.

Sanne scrambled to her feet, speaking her word again and willing Peacebringer to glow brighter. Before her stood a dark copy of herself, a void silhouette with lavender eyes. She had to be careful. She had to be vigilant. The last time this thing had taken her shape—

Across the room, Ren shouted. Sanne circled the spirit in front of her, allowing herself a glance past it to see Ren. He was locked in battle with a dark duplicate of himself, an ax of Nightmare steel clashing with an impossibly strong spectral copy.

Sanne's double blinked, its lids coming from the bottoms of its eyes to the tops. It drew a false Peacebringer. Sanne snarled—she had argued and fought and bled for her Nightmare blade. She would not be taken down by a mockery of it.

She knelt and swiped low, aiming for the back of the thing's knees—a weak spot in her own armor. The double leapt out of the way, but Sanne had expected that; she cast lightlance and drove the resulting radiant javelin through the thing's torso. Her double laughed. The spear of light disappeared. Sanne stared in disbelief as its radiance was absorbed by the spirit. Light flowed through it, illuminating false veins and flowing into a misshapen heart.

"*Good*," the double sighed. "*Give me more.*"

The false Peacebringer caught Sanne in the chest before she could block the strike. She teetered on her feet. Her armor had dulled the sharpness of the blade, but a liquid warmth seeped down her ribs beneath her shirt. Ordinary spirits didn't hit this hard. Fear wiggled into her heart, writhing about like a maggot in a corpse. By the gods. Her magic had strengthened it. "No spells!"

Ren drove his ax into his double's chest and shouted, "What?"

Sanne ducked behind the nearest column, desperate for some distance between herself and her double. "No spells!" She exposed herself long enough to throw a dagger at the advancing spirit. "They want it!"

Sanne's dagger flew back at her. She slipped behind the column at the last second. What was this thing? Wraiths didn't shift forms like this—ghouls did, but ghouls couldn't communicate with anything other than moans and malice. No spirits had eyes that glowed like this, either, and none of them fed on magic.

Ren's shout bounced across the tile to her. Sanne dove for her dagger, retrieved it, and turned, ready to defend herself on the way to Ren. But her double didn't descend. It, with its other half, had turned its attention to Ren. Two black blurs had entered the fight, blurs Sanne quickly realized were Ren's Umbrals. Kyr, his raven, dove at Ren's copy. Reia, his heeler, snapped at the heels of Sanne's double.

Sanne ran toward them. It was a good call—if they couldn't

use spells, they'd use everything else at their disposal. She whistled for Marra.

Sanne was back-to-back with Ren and half-covered in unblood by the time the gyrfalcon flew, shrieking, out of the shadows.

"Took her long enough!" Ren yelled.

Sanne couldn't deny it. The Umbral should have been scouting—where had she been? "Drive them together!" She tossed Peacebringer to the side. The feint worked. Her double lunged for the sword, creating an opening for Sanne to drive two Nightmare daggers into the mirror of her own chest. The spirit screamed, its jaw opening impossibly wide. Its breath reeked of death. Sanne screamed back.

She rotated in place, allowing Ren, who had driven his sickles into the shoulders of his spirit, to force it against hers. Kyr and Marra flapped their wings and slashed their claws against the spirits' faces. With twin roars, the spirits bled together. Their forms rippled, turning almost liquid beneath the daggers and sickles before reforming into the wraith. Ren shoved his weight into it and it collapsed to the floor, screaming so horribly that Sanne felt sick.

"How do we banish it, if our spells won't work?"

"Cut it up." Sanne knelt on its torso. The wraith shrieked and scrabbled at her, its claws cutting her leggings into ribbons. She pressed more of her weight onto her daggers. No spells meant none of her fire, and no way to burn the corpse. This was going to be messy. "*Quickly.*"

Ren wrenched a sickle free and raised it above his head. Before he could drive it into the wraith's neck, the spirit disappeared. Sanne hit the floor, the impact sending a shock into her knees and cut legs. She cursed.

The wraith cackled, hovering between Cassander and Malaia's thrones. The expansive tapestry behind the dais, a larger version of the one in Sanne's chambers, fluttered in some strange breeze. "*Almost. Try harder.*"

Ren roared in frustration. He drew his ax and charged before Sanne could tell him to wait. She scrambled to her feet, but was too slow and too late to stop Ren as he threw himself at the wraith. With a final crack of thunder, the spirit vanished. Ren disappeared.

"Ren!" Sanne ran up the dais, expecting to see him in a heap on the sliver of floor behind it. He wasn't there. Her voice took on a hysterical edge. "*Ren?*"

A hand appeared through a slit in the tapestry. "I'm here." Ren pushed the weaving aside. Blood covered the right side of his face, flowing from a tear at his hairline. "I need your firelight. There's some kind of room back here and I—" He winced and cradled his right arm. The tapestry fell back into place. "I lost my ax."

Sanne hopped off the dais. She lifted the tapestry, her stomach twisting. He'd fallen into the war room. He couldn't be here.

"I also need your help shoving my shoulder back in."

Gods above. "Let me see." Sanne raised a hand and called fire into her palm. None came. She furrowed her brow and tried again. It took three tries for golden fire to spark into her hand.

The war room came into vision around them. Shadows stretched tall along the walls. She didn't want to, but Sanne sent fire into the lamp in the center of the table—she'd need both hands to relocate Ren's shoulder.

"Your king will need a new door."

Sure enough, the wooden secret door, which had been treated to resemble white stone, hung from its hinges. A smear of red blood marred the center.

How was Sanne going to explain this? "Ren, are you—gods," she gasped, reaching a hand up to his horns. The tip of his left horn had cracked off, revealing the white interior. "Does that hurt?"

Ren's eyes widened. "Is it gone?" He raised a hand, visibly relaxing when he felt his horn and the extent of the damage. "Thank the gods. No, it doesn't. Everything else does, though."

His right arm dangled at his side, a concavity in his silhouette where his shoulder should have been. "You don't need me, you need a healer," Sanne muttered, but she took his arm and reconnected his shoulder.

Ren groaned, but was able to carefully move his arm again. "You don't look so good yourself."

Sanne took inventory of her own injuries. The cuts on her thighs throbbed and wept—she poked at one and her fingers came away bloody. Her scalp ached where the spirit had pulled her hair, and her knees pulsed with the aftershocks of falling to the floor. She opened her mouth to cast a healing spell, but remembered the spirit's pleasured sigh when she'd used lightlance and stopped. She leaned against the battle table. Ruhysvet spread before her. "What was that thing?"

On the other side of the room, Ren straightened, ax in hand. He glanced at the table, eyeing the little figurines Cassander had scattered within the borders of Jasniostvo and Nocovostvo. "This is your hunt," he said. "You tell me."

Before Sanne could respond, he turned away. Ren stepped closer to one of the maps pinned to the wall and frowned. "This is Tanglewood," he said, pointing to a red pin in Tmadrev Forest. "Why does your king—"

Marra swept into the room and cried. Sanne stilled and heard footsteps. If it was Vallen, she knew he would tell Cassander that they'd been in the war room. "We have to go!"

But they were too late. When they ran from the throne room, Cassander, Malaia, Vallen, and a small retinue of guards stood on the other side of the dais. There was no mistaking where she and Ren had been.

Sanne and Cassander addressed Vallen at the same time. "I told you to wait," she snapped as Cassander ordered, "Hold him."

Vallen obeyed his king. He and two other guards took Ren by the arms and dragged him from Sanne.

"He needs to see a healer!" Sanne cried, noting the pain that crossed Ren's face when the guards twisted his right arm.

Cassander raised a gloved hand to point at Sanne and then the war room. "Get inside."

"He needs a healer—"

"No—"

"Sanne, I'll be alright—"

Malaia rested a slim hand on Cassander's arm. "I'll see him to the healer's wing," she said, her voice soft among the chaos.

Cassander placed a hand on hers. "Are you sure?"

She nodded.

Cassander kissed her forehead and turned to the guards. "Let him go."

"Thank you," Sanne whispered as Malaia passed her. The queen gave Sanne a tight smile.

She followed Cassander into the war room. He stood just inside the doorway for a moment, rubbing a hand down his face as he took in the broken door. "You've disobeyed me."

"It was an accident," she said, hating that the truth sounded like an excuse. "Ren fell."

"Then you should have gotten him out immediately."

"I di—" Sanne clamped down on the lie before it slipped out. They'd been caught leaving. If they'd left as soon as Ren had fallen inside, they would have been seen going in, too.

Cassander shook his head in warning. "Think before you lie to me, Sanne."

She stayed quiet, fighting not to cover up her slip with another falsehood.

"Gods." Cassander began to pace. "I told you exactly where he was not allowed, and where do I find the two of you? Have you forgotten we're at war, Sanne? The information in this room could ruin us if seen by the wrong eyes."

"You needn't remind me," she said through grit teeth. "It wasn't my intention for Ren to come into this room. The spirit—"

"Should have died under your blade. Are you any closer to finding the source?"

"Not yet."

Cassander shook his head, laughing in disbelief.

"It's difficult to find it when we spend each night fighting until dawn," Sanne snapped. "We're trying, Cassander, but we're exhausted—"

"I thought you were the best."

Sanne recoiled. He hadn't raised a hand to her—he'd be stupid to—but his words made her cheeks sting nonetheless. "I'm sorry?"

He sighed. "I don't think you understand how excited my father was to contract you. 'Imagine it,' he said to me, 'the Order's best Nightmare coming home to serve her family. Imagine how powerful we'll be with both Svetlen's grace and the Order's might.' Where is that might, Sanne? Where is my Lady's power?"

Sanne shook her head. She and Cassander had grown up close enough for him to see how she conducted herself in battle. He knew her capabilities, didn't he? This was his anger talking, his fear, his disappointment. He didn't mean it.

She and Cassander stared at each other, the silence between them stifling. When Cassander spoke again, his voice was low.

"You know I don't trust Ren," he said, "and I would hate to lose my trust in you, too." Cassander stepped back. For a moment, Sanne didn't know the expressionless man who stood before her. "Get out. I don't want to see you again until this is done."

———

Zikat with the dawn, Svetlen at midday, Oddelen at night. It had been Sanne's routine.

She broke it by walking into Svetlen's chapel and falling to her knees beneath the altar. The chapel's stained glass usually draped her in rainbows, but in the pre-dawn hours, everything sat under a haze of blue. Shadows settled across the figurine of Svetlen before Sanne, their placement contorting the goddess's expression into a frown.

Sanne's breaths came in short gasps. The spirits were haunting the Stained Palace. They were haunting Svetlen's chosen king, distracting him at a time when he needed to be clear-minded. If he stumbled in this war, the Esclarmondes could fall. Jasniostvo could fall. Every bit of suspicion and casual cruelty that was cast on Zdesen's faithful would be thrown upon Jasniostvans tenfold, gleefully, by the Black Sun. Sanne's people would scream and bleed and die, and she'd be able to trace it back to this moment, this failure. The infestation wasn't just defeating her. It was defeating her kingdom—Svetlen's kingdom. She deserved for Svetlen to be unhappy with her.

Was that why Zdesen's high priestess had been the only one to offer advice?

You misunderstand my devoted, a voice whispered at the back of her mind. Her gut twisted. Zdesen's invisible claws tugged at Sanne's braid, stroking it in a performance of comfort. *Listen to me. Let me tell you what you seek.*

Sanne began to pray, speaking the Svetlenic dialect loud enough to drown out the parasite's voice. The claws pulled harder. Sanne's voice hitched higher. Her breaths shortened.

We are one, Sanne. We want the same things.

"No," Sanne whimpered. She swatted at the back of her head. Her hands passed through empty air. "No!"

Zdesen sighed, the exhale cool against Sanne's neck. *Very well.*

Sanne pressed her head to her knees and covered her head with her arms. Her prayers filled the small cavern she'd created, the space heating with her breath. A warm hand pressed against her back, one she knew she wouldn't see if she looked, and Sanne forced herself not to cry. The hand stroked her back, its soothing intent genuine. Sanne's breathing slowed. She raised her head and saw early morning light behind the altar. The figurine was no longer frowning at her.

Breathe, my child, a voice said. Though Sanne heard it in her mind, it sounded as if it came from the statuette. **Breathe. We have given you what you need.**

Sanne closed her eyes. She made herself take steady breaths. Svetlen rarely spoke to her, and she clung to the receding echoes of her goddess' voice, to the way she felt sunbeams on her face even though it was still mostly dark. "Thank you," she whispered.

The chapel was silent in response.

Sanne looked at her hands. The black swirls of her Nightmare tattoo were covered with blood: hers, Ren's, and the spirit's. She often considered bloodstained hands a sign of a good night's work, but now, the ichor on her hands was a taunting waste. The spirit had been hurt, but not killed. It still lived, and it would come back.

Cassander hadn't even asked if she was alright.

Sanne sat in the quiet chapel. She stared at the stone altar, let her gaze unfocus, and willed herself not to cry. Crying was for sorrow or heartbreak or sadness, not failure. Not for a lack of discipline, not for disobedience. Sanne didn't deserve to cry.

Her eyes welled with tears anyway.

10.1.626

Even with their increased healing speed—a blessing Zikat bestowed upon every Nightmare—it took almost a week for Ren and Sanne's wounds from the wraith to fully heal. It took only seconds for that healing to be undone by another spirit.

Sanne crashed into the oak bookshelf, thick tomes raining on her as she crumpled to the floor. The damn ghoul stuck its tongue out at her before cackling and darting away to find Ren.

Sanne grumbled, shoved the books away, and got to her feet. She loathed ghouls, had ever since one had taken two of the fingers on her right hand. It seemed the entire species had gotten a taste for her then.

"Sanne!"

She followed Ren's voice to the front of the library, where

he'd pinned the ghoul down between two overstuffed reading chairs. The spirit shifted forms beneath Ren's boot; it was Sanne's neck beneath the blade of Ren's ax, then that of a dark-haired woman Sanne didn't recognize. Thank the gods her eyes were black and not pale purple. The color had started to haunt Sanne's dreams.

Ren was already halfway through the banishment spell. Sanne waited for him to begin the second repetition of it before joining —they'd needed at least three repetitions the last few nights.

Tonight took four, as well as a desperate prayer to Svetlen that Sanne muttered between the lines of the banishment spell. The half-physical body of the ghoul deflated as its dark brown essence rose into the air. Ren murmured the slowwind spell, using the gentle breeze that came from his palms to shape the gaseous essence into a ball. "Where can I take this?"

Sanne led him into the hall. They weren't in the palace's grand library; they'd chased the ghoul to the secondary library, where the Esclarmondes kept the books that were too old or unfashionable to be displayed in the library open to visitors. They were a floor beneath the throne room, and the windows weren't floor-to-ceiling panes of glass here. Sanne reached up and opened one, allowing Ren to send the ghoul's essence into the open air outside.

In the library, the carcass had disappeared. A shadow clung to the place it had been; Sanne called flame into her palm and chased it away. She headed for the aisle where the ghoul had accosted her, intent on reshelving the books. Whatever librarian staffed this library would likely be horrified that two Nightmares had desecrated it. The least she could do was clean up after them.

Sanne gathered as many books as she could and began to put them back on the shelves. The books around her didn't seem to be arranged in any particular order, yet she couldn't shake the feeling that she was placing them incorrectly.

"That's not right." Ren came to her side. He took a book from the top of her stack and pointed to a little slip of parchment glued to its spine, a slip that had two letters, two numbers, and an odd symbol scrawled onto it. "This tells you how they're ordered."

Sanne stepped back to let him rearrange the books she'd improperly rehomed. "How do you know?"

A little smile crept over his face. "My woman in Tanglewood is a librarian."

"I see. And she put you to work shelving books?"

His smile widened. "It was the least I could do. I nearly destroyed her library exorcizing a wraith, so I tried to fix as much as I could before I left."

Sanne left him to it and settled into one of the reading chairs.

A few minutes later, there was a soft whump as Ren sat in the chair beside her, a book in hand. "I found this," he said, angling the spine toward Sanne. The book was bound in worn black leather. Its edges and cover script were a metallic red; the title *Stories of Naisvet* crept up the spine and shone like blood. When Ren opened the book to the title page, Sanne saw a flash of cream and oxblood marbled endpapers. "Vestel mentioned stories of the old world. Do you think this could have something to do with our spirits?"

Stories of Naisvet was where the Sohli Prophecy had come from; aside from it, Sanne wasn't familiar with the book's contents. After its translation, the prophecy had been excerpted and published in little pamphlets, and Sanne's schooling had never directed her toward the source material. The prophecy was enough, and Sanne couldn't imagine Vestel willingly looking to it for answers. "Doubtful."

"There's a bookmark in it." There was the sound of turning pages. "Oh."

"What is it?"

"The last person to read this book marked the Prázeny legend."

Sanne leaned forward. "Any particular part?"

Ren held the book out to her. His face was pale. "The part with the Stone."

Sanne took the tome and skimmed the current section, though she already knew the story. While ruling Naisvet, the old world, the gods had indulged every whim and allowed their peoples to ceaselessly fight for control. Their carelessness led to the Cataclysm, and the universe became enraged. As Naisvet had been the gods' creation, they'd been the universe's, and it felt responsible for their destruction. It decided that, as punishment, the gods would lose what they loved most—their power, for their world was already gone.

To do so, the universe first had to weaken them, and so the Prázeny Stone had been created. It purged the gods of their divinity and cast them out, then became sentient. It turned itself upon the apocalypse-ruined Naisvet to eradicate any remaining traces of godhood. Chaos had followed, greater than any havoc the gods had wrought on Naisvet. The Stone was an abomination.

"We hunt the reminders of that era," Ren said. He'd gone pale. "We compensate for that chaos. Do you think the Prázeny Stone could be here?"

The question hung between them. Sanne's first instinct was to laugh and deny it—she hadn't taken Ren for a fearmonger. According to legend, the Stone had been destroyed. The gods had returned with changed hearts; they built Ruhysvet from the ashes and cared for it well. Some doubted the legend's veracity, believing the Stone had simply gone dormant, but anyone who believed that parroted conspiracy and lies. The gods were alive in Ruhysvet, and how could they and the Stone both persist?

But as she sat with the idea, the terrible threads started to weave together: Vestel's suggestion to look to the past, the tenacity of the spirits, the decreased efficacy of their spells. The outlandishness faded the more she mulled it over. Spirits and spectral beasts defied the order set forth by the gods, existing in the grey area between life and death where Zikat and Oddelen's domains ended. It was why the two gods had created and ordained Nightmares; the holy gifts bestowed upon Nightmares placed them in the grey area with these spirits, part divine and part mundane as the spirits were half life and half death. If something in the palace was actively repressing the influence of the gods, it would follow that the unholy spirits were stronger and greater in number. It made sense that she and Ren's prayer-spells didn't work. Sanne remembered how the wraith had spoken to her both times she'd come against it. These manifestations even defied the Nightmares' order of things.

"If that's the case," she murmured, "how would we know what to look for?" There was another bookmark in the book, one of bright red ribbon. Sanne turned to the page it marked. "The legends say nothing—"

She'd opened to the Sohli Prophecy. One of its opening lines caused her words to die in her throat: "*A hollowing carved in blue and red.*"

Sanne read the prophecy in its entirety:

> *There will come a time when the gods are dead,*
> *A hollowing carved in blue and red.*
> *A pair of twin flames, from each one ray glows,*
> *The other bound by the weight of the stone.*
> *Mother of light, goddess of fear,*
> *Safeguard the truth and all we hold dear.*
> *From the reborn gods to the time of the end,*
> *A new king rises, the goddess his friend.*
> *The goddess' blessing, bestowed with intent,*
> *Upon the one who will make his ascent.*
> *King of the fire, king of the ash,*
> *King of the radiance, his rule forever lasts.*

Svetlen's rare words echoed in her mind: **We have given you what you need.**

How many times had she asked for guidance? How often had she begged to be shown the answer?

A hollowing carved in blue and red.

The weight of the stone.

The abnormal spirits all had purple eyes.

"I think you're right." She gave the book to Ren so he could read the prophecy. Her hands trembled. She couldn't believe it—but could she doubt Svetlen? They'd been led to this answer. It was no coincidence that this had been one of the books she'd knocked from its shelf, no accident that it had been Ren who'd come to help her. She'd needed fresh eyes to see what was truly happening.

"I think we've gotten very lucky," Ren murmured.

A laugh echoed in the back of Sanne's mind. *Tell him it's more than luck.*

Sanne shook her head. This had been Svetlen's providence. "I allow you no part in this, parasite," she whispered, turning her back to Ren. "I—"

I know what you've said.

As terrible as Zdesen's voice was, as awfully as it scraped in her skull, there was a familiar golden warmth beneath it. Despite Zdesen still hissing to be heard, despite what she now knew was causing the infestation, Sanne relaxed.

Svetlen was smiling on her.

10.2.626

Ren joined her for a late breakfast the next morning, having slept until the ninth bell. Sanne had risen with the dawn, as usual, but had whispered her lauds in a sun-lit alcove in the grand library. The librarians were also late risers, meaning that Sanne had been able to scurry between aisles unseen and unquestioned. She'd found an architectural plan of the palace and hastily sketched a copy before hurrying back to her chambers. She'd hung it on her wall by the time Ren ambled in, rubbing sleep from his eyes. They stood before it now as they ate.

"We're here," Sanne said, tapping the spot on the plan where her rooms were. The plan had aerial layouts of each of the palace's four floors, as well as the floor plans of the ancillary buildings on the grounds: the stables, armory, and dungeons. "We've fought spirits here"—Sanne circled the hallway of their first night's hunt with red ink—"here, here, here..." She circled eleven locations in total. Most of the spirits had manifested near the center of the palace; now, however, they could see that the ground and main floors had attracted the most prey.

"If we follow the logic that the Stone is attracting spirits," Sanne said, "we should concentrate our search for it on these floors."

Ren held a bunch of grapes in his hand. "We haven't gone to any of these areas," he said, popping a grape into his mouth and gesturing to the armory, stables, and dungeon. "Has nothing been reported there?"

"No. They aren't connected to the palace, which makes me think the Stone is within the palace walls. The dungeon runs underneath the palace, but can't be accessed from within it for security reasons. The stables and armory stand completely on their own."

Ren polished off the grapes and plucked one of Sanne's pens from the table—she'd placed them next to their breakfast while waiting on him. "It was a shrinking mist here," he said, writing the name by the only third-floor circle. "A bogle here, and that first ghoul here..." When he'd finished, each circle had a species of spirit by it. The circle around the throne room had been labeled "*Wraith?*" The question mark made Sanne uneasy, her breakfast turning cold and heavy in her stomach.

She picked up her pen and added three more circles around the areas her hunt had taken her before Ren arrived, the last one around the mezzanine overlooking the receiving hall on the ground floor. She took Ren's pen, blue ink instead of her red, and wrote "*wraith*" by the mezzanine circle. After a moment, she added, "*and ?*"

Ren's look was inquisitive, but Sanne also read worry in the furrow of his brow.

"It looked like what we fought in the throne room," she said quietly, "but didn't appear until the wraith had fled."

He crossed his arms and stepped forward, scrutinizing the map. Sanne moved back to let him think. She'd refilled her gold-rimmed coffee cup by the time he spoke.

"Earlier, you said that the Stone is attracting spirits." He looked over his shoulder at her, the morning light limning his profile and horns. "What if it's creating them, too?"

"Are you proposing an addendum to the Order's bestiary?"

He chuckled. "Do you want to keep this question mark alive long enough to study it?"

Sanne joined him at the map, her hands curled around her coffee. "No," she said. "If it really is some kind of new species or mutation, I want us to destroy it before it reproduces enough for the Triumvirate to know about it."

She met Ren's eyes, suddenly worried he would disagree—but it wasn't lying to the Triumvirate if they didn't know to ask about it. She had to think of Cassander, too, who'd be mortified to learn that the entire Order knew his palace had possibly spawned a new type of spirit.

Ren only nodded. "This is your hunt. I'll follow your lead."

Over the next few days, their hunt transformed. She and Ren used the day to rest and clean their weapons. Their personal arsenals now included small cloth-bound notebooks and charcoal pencils. For a few hours each night, once Sanne knew that Cassander and the librarians had gone to sleep, she and Ren cast darkdrape and snuck into the grand library to read whatever they could find on the Prázeny Stone. Unfortunately, it wasn't much—most accounts of the Prázeny Era had been passed down orally, if not lost to time completely, and the few transcriptions they could find made no mention of what happened to the Prázeny Stone. In one paragraph, the Stone was devouring ancient divinity; in the next, the mortal plane had been thrown into godless chaos. By the end of the page, the gods had returned and Ruhysvet was flourishing under their careful rule. The transitions were jarring. The plain language left no hints to be found. Their notebooks remained empty.

Sanne led Ren through the halls each night, the pair scouring rooms and hallways for any place that could hide a stone: alcoves, empty spaces behind tapestries, false flagstones, secret compartments in furniture. Sanne kept a fire burning in her palm, waiting for it to gutter out as a sign that they were close, but each night her golden flame was steady. Even with Marra scouting, they found and fought nothing. The palace was still and quiet—no spectral screaming or howling interrupted the sleep of those within. Whenever Sanne passed a servant or guard in the halls, she noted how their faces had a brightness she hadn't seen for some time, the happy glow granted by a good night's sleep. It tore at her heart. Of course she was happy that the Stained Palace and its people had a bit of peace, but with no spirits to hunt, she and Ren had nothing to lead them to the Stone. The peace would only last so long.

A third thing weighed on Sanne, too—Cassander. He deserved to know what they thought they were facing. She needed to report to him, furious outburst or not, but she couldn't find him. His throne, the war room, the sunny alcove on the third floor where she knew he liked to sit and think whenever he had a moment—they were empty every time she looked. Whenever she asked after him, his staff told her he was engaged. Sanne knew it wasn't true. Even when he'd become king, when he'd been consumed by grief and anger and the pressures of ascending, he had always made time to speak to her.

In return, she had always sought to calm him. The nightmares she fought for him were more than those that had given her Order its name: the fears of loss and usurpation, the anxiety that his people or even other Esclarmondes would abandon him and turn their favor to the Black Sun. She'd comforted him even when she had doubted, and her empty words had soothed them both. But now, when her words were urgent and heavy with certainty, he refused to hear them. Her stained-glass heart cracked under their weight.

All she could do was bring him a vanquished Stone.

10.4.626

After a light dinner and their nightly vespers, Ren and Sanne went to the ground floor of the Stained Palace to continue their hunt. Because guests seldom came to this floor—most visitors didn't go past the throne room or banquet hall, both of which were on the main level—the walls were considerably barer than those above. There were no tapestries woven with impressive detail, no busts of past nobility carved of dark-veined marble, no floor-to-ceiling windows, stained glass or otherwise. She and Ren cast nightsight as soon as they started patrolling; the small windows on this floor meant little moonlight to see by, and the orange-flamed torches weren't enough to chase away every shadow.

The walls down here were a red-toned, clay-like color that reminded Sanne of sun-dried earth. Coupled with the low ceilings, the color made her feel as if she was in a cave. As they walked the outer perimeter of the ground floor and descended a few steps to the next hallway, Sanne thought of Zdesen's temple. Unease settled into her stomach. When they'd first come to the secondary library, this floor hadn't seemed so—she felt ridiculous for thinking it, but *creepy*. She tried to remember all of the rooms on this level: extra pantries and storerooms, the secondary library, staff quarters, and miscellaneous studies. This floor was private— no public areas meant lots of good hiding places—and Sanne felt grimly hopeful. Their search of the upper floors had yielded no results. The Stone must be here.

She tapped the daggers at her thighs. She expected a fight worthy of the three hells once they found it.

"Do you know the distance from here to the Tmadrev Forest?"

Ren's voice boomed in the stillness. Sanne swiveled her head toward him. In the red haze of her nightsight, his Nightmare tattoo seemed to slither. "I'm not sure. I think it's a few days' ride just to reach the edge."

"Hm."

Sanne looked at her right hand, bending her remaining fingers and thumb. Her Nightmare tattoo remained still, the whirling slashes of ink void-like against her light skin. "When is she expecting you?" Sanne had tried to pry more information from Ren about his woman, but he'd been tight-lipped. She couldn't blame him. Whoever he chose to give his heart to had little bearing on their hunt. Matters of love, at least in a romantic sense, weren't often discussed among Nightmares. Many of Ren and Sanne's brethren, especially the older generations of hunters, had little use for it; if one had needs, they could be met for a night, but a constantly traveling hunter had no use for commitment. Sanne, however, had been raised at court, in a place where children grew up with stories of dashing knights who married beautiful princesses and noble guards who sacrificed their posts to dedicate themselves to the protection of one instead of the many. She didn't agree with the Nightmares' dismissal of love. Though distantly, she wanted it for herself, and she wanted it for Ren, too. "Solstice is in ten days."

"I'm not sure. I haven't been able to speak with her."

"Right." They'd gone down another hallway and turned inward, toward the palace's center, by the time Sanne spoke again. Cassander was already angry with her. What was one more transgression? "If we don't find the Stone tonight, I'll help you get a letter to her explaining—" She was going to say *your absence*, but stopped herself. She didn't want to promise he wouldn't make it. "Explaining why you've been unable to write."

Ren sighed. "Thank you. I hate to think it, but I'm sure she's worried."

"Better worried than angry, don't you think?"

"I suppose."

Their relationship wasn't romantic in the slightest, but Sanne wished Cassander would worry for her. "If I met her, do you think she'd like me?"

Ren chuckled, and a smile played at Sanne's lips. She hadn't been sure how he'd take the question, but her gamble had worked. "You'd give her ideas. Bad ones. She'd think she could become like you."

"On a royal payroll?"

"A hunter." He smiled, and his eyeteeth glinted in the light of the torches. "Gods, I can hear her now. 'Sanne did it, why can't I?'"

"Another female Nightmare sounds wonderful. I'd welcome her in the Order." Ren's woman was a librarian, but Sanne was the daughter of a duke. No one had expected her to take up a sword, let alone a Nightmare's mantle.

Ren rolled his eyes, but he was still smiling. "And that's why the two of you will never meet."

Sanne narrowed her eyes. She opened her mouth to reply, but a sudden pain welled low in her gut. An invisible hand buried itself in her organs and wrenched her forward. She wrapped her arms around her torso and gasped. A different kind of pain settled into her heart—the sharp prickles of fear. Sanne lifted a hand and called forth golden flame, hoping the manifestation of Svetlen's power would keep Zdesen at bay. The parasite loved to appear when Sanne was frightened.

"I don't hear any—"

Ren's words were lost to a rumble of thunder. As it had before, the sound sustained; Peacebringer and Sanne's daggers vibrated in their sheaths. The small window to their left rattled in its frame.

"It's here." She slowly straightened as the cold pain in her stomach—the announcement, she realized—eased.

Ren held out a hand to keep Sanne from moving and raised a finger to his lips. He gestured forward.

A few hundred feet in front of them, a figure drifted down the hallway. Though her nightsight tinted it pink, Sanne recognized it as the white-cloaked figure they'd chased on Ren's first night. As it approached a bend in the passage, Sanne swapped her nightsight for darkdrape, snuffed the fire in her palm, and crept after it. Ren followed on her heels.

The figure turned right. Ren and Sanne pursued it. The hallway deadened at a set of stairs, which created a switchback leading to the main floor. Sanne clenched her teeth. She suspected this figure had something to do with the Stone—but if that was the case, why would it return to the main floor when they knew the Stone wasn't there? Was her desperation making her weave connections out of false threads?

The figure stopped at the base of the stairs. She and Ren halted feet behind it, their darkdrape coverings holding firm. Ren's hand went to a sickle, but Sanne shook her head. *Wait*, she mouthed, exaggerating the shape so he could read her lips through the shadows.

Ren stilled his hand. The figure moved to the area beneath the stairs. It raised a hand, which was the same ghastly white as its cloak, and pressed its palm to the stone wall. A faint sound came from the figure, though Sanne couldn't make out the voice or any spoken words. Something she couldn't name shifted in the air around them, something that had her reaching for Peacebringer's hilt and preparing herself to hear Zdesen's low laugh.

A portion of the wall sank into itself. Dozens of stones around it followed, recessing into the wall with a horrible scraping sound. The stones swung open as one—a door.

The figure went in. The door began to close; before Sanne could decide what to do, Ren darted forward and grabbed its edge. He motioned Sanne forward. She ran inside and shoved her weight against the door to hold it open for Ren. She was little match for it, however, and her heels slid across the floor as it pushed her back. Ren slipped inside just as Sanne lost her grip entirely, and they were plunged into darkness as the door grated shut.

They switched darkdrape for nightsight as the stones settled back into place. Another passage came into form around them, as did a small landing at their feet. Steps away, a staircase descended into an even thicker darkness. The white-cloaked figure was nowhere to be seen.

Ren stepped close to her, eyes glowing red, and murmured, "Whoever built this palace had quite the penchant for secret doors."

With a small hiss, a bit of fire blinked into life in Sanne's palm —there were no torches down here, the darkness so absolute that even nightsight was little help. "Indeed," she muttered. The Stained Palace had been constructed by Heinrik, the first Esclarmonde king, and as far as she knew there had been no major modifications since. There was the hidden entrance to the war room, and now this—why had her ancestor needed such secrecy? Who made use of this passage now?

"Shall we?"

Sanne nodded, then said "Yes" out loud. They picked their way down the stairs, Sanne throwing her hands out to catch him from falling when the stairs ended before they expected. The floor at the bottom was level, but slick with runoff—when Sanne raised her flaming hand, they saw that the damp walls dripped with groundwater.

Unlit torches hung on the walls every twenty feet or so. Sanne found their placement strange; even if they'd been lit, they were so far apart that pools of darkness would still gather between the fires. Ren tried to lift one of the torches from its metal holder. It stuck.

"It's probably nailed—"

With a grunt, Ren ripped the torch and its holder from the

wall. Sanne looked down the passage, expecting the white-cloaked figure or a spirit to manifest, but nothing happened. Ren held the torch out to her.

"Gods above," she muttered, but lit it anyway. The flame sparked golden before settling to a mundane orange, revealing the jagged, rusty nails that jutted from the torch's holder. "Was that really necessary?"

"I wanted more light."

Sanne wished he hadn't destroyed Esclarmonde property to get it, but she understood. The golden fire in her hand only carried a few feet around her, leaving the passage's ceiling and most of the floor shrouded in darkness. If they'd been on the upper levels, or even the ground floor, for that matter, she wouldn't have minded, but she hadn't known this passage existed. She was just as blind as Ren was.

They continued forward, listening for any sound. Sanne kept alert for any new feeling in her torso. Though the cold had faded, it still felt as if something held her stomach and intestines in its taloned hands, twitching its fingers every so often to remind her of its presence.

A thought occurred, and she stopped walking. Ren continued for a few steps, but looked back when he noticed he was alone. "What are you doing?"

Sanne took a step back.

The pain in her gut, which had been manageable, rioted, falling on her as swiftly as the down swing of a blade. The flame in her hand sputtered. "We can't go back," she gasped, rushing toward Ren. The pain lessened with each step.

He turned the way they'd come. He made it two paces before his knees buckled. "Gods above." When he turned back to her, clutching at his throat, he'd gone pale. Nightsight flickered in and out of his eyes. "We must be getting close."

They continued on. Sanne didn't want to voice what she thought was happening—it seemed they were being led to the Stone, the pain guiding and correcting their path. What agony would they have to endure when they found it? Would she have her very essence torn from her as her gods had?

They reached the end of the passage. Ren's torch illuminated a tattered cloth hanging on the wall; he used the curved blade of a sickle to draw it back. The archway beyond led to a hallway, wider than the last, with barred-off cells on each side. Rats skittered through the walkway. The sound of their gnawing teeth echoed from every corner. In the distance, lit by the faint glow of torch fire, Sanne could see armored figures milling about and clattering their swords against the cell bars.

They were in the dungeon.

"So there is an entrance in the palace," she murmured. But why? If a prisoner discovered the passage and escaped, was it not a threat to the palace's security? To Cassander's?

To her right, Ren swore. She hurried toward his voice, but he met her at the open door of the nearest cell and whispered, "I'm fine. I think I just stepped on bones."

Sanne lowered her palm. Ren was right—his heel had gone through a brittle skull. She lifted her flame and shone it around the cell, half expecting to see a headless skeleton in shackles or another skull leering at her, but what happened was worse.

The golden fire in her hand, her gift from Svetlen, warped into a six-pronged arrow and guttered out.

In the little light from his torch, she and Ren gaped at each other. Her fire disappearing was one thing, but it being warped into a form she hadn't willed was another—she didn't like the thought of her fire being used. Sanne summoned more fire, but these flames didn't survive long, either. They were sucked toward the wall. When the fire collided with the stones, it billowed along the surface before disappearing. A sound like a contented sigh drifted through the air. This time, the absence of her flame brought back the pain in her stomach; judging by the wince that crossed Ren's face, it had returned for him, too.

When Sanne moved toward the wall, the pain eased. Nausea replaced it. Fear began to writhe in the corners of her mind, but she shoved it away. She ran her hands along the wall, feeling for what she knew would be there.

A stone gave way beneath her hand. As she'd thought, another door swung open. Sanne clapped a hand over her mouth to muffle the hysterical giggle that slipped out. How many of these were there? Why was her palace riddled with tunnels like an anthill?

She started forward.

"Sanne." Ren's free hand closed around her arm. "Let me go first."

"What? Why—"

"Please." She couldn't read his expression. "I have mundane fire. It'll just take yours."

There was more he wanted to say—she saw it in the set of his jaw—but he was right. She couldn't light their path, and if her fire had been ripped away, they'd likely lose nightsight, too. "Fine. But when we find it, follow my lead. We don't split up. We work together to fight whatever's down there, just like we did in the throne room." Sanne's hands shook. Why couldn't someone have recorded how the Stone had been subdued? Why hadn't the gods, or the universe for that matter, allowed mortals to preserve that part of the story? But the gods had persevered somehow. Sanne had to believe that, through she and Ren, they would again. "No spells. We have to do this with our strength."

Ren nodded. He clasped Sanne's forearm, closed his eyes, and began to pray.

She did the same. Their prayers were quick, hers to Svetlen and his to Zikat. As she followed him deeper below ground, Sanne tried not to dwell on the fact that she'd never seen Ren initiate prayer.

Halfway down the staircase, which wound in on itself like a coiled serpent, Sanne's prediction proved correct. She and Ren lost their nightsight.

The staircase deposited them at the mouth of a passage—one that had naturally occurred, if the jagged lines of the walls around them were any indication. Sanne peered around Ren, hoping to see the white-cloaked figure, but there was only darkness. They'd been right on the figure's heels—how had it escaped them?

The end of the passage was wide enough for Sanne to stand by Ren, so when he stopped, she came to his side. They stood at the edge of a large, rough-hewn cavern. Asperous walls of black stone stretched endlessly up; when Sanne stepped into the cavern and craned her neck, she saw that the walls tapered into a circular opening two or three stories up. Through the oculus, Sanne saw a familiar ceiling of richly colored stained glass.

They were beneath the throne room.

Ren's footsteps, though soft in his boots, echoed through the cavern as he followed her. Candles burned in the crags of the walls, having melted into dripping pools of wax. A thin shaft of light shone through the oculus, drenching a black stone pedestal in soft white moonbeams. Upon the pedestal was a three-legged stand made of gold. The stand held a lump of black rock.

Ren crossed his arms. "I thought it would be bigger."

Sanne agreed. The Stone was barely larger than her two fists held together. It resembled obsidian, but in the faintly flickering candlelight, shades of purple swirled beneath its glassy surface. A chill swept over her, leaving a heaviness she could only describe as begrudging—Svetlen recognized it. The knowledge was enough for Sanne to rock back a step, to stop holding back the fear she'd been trying to suppress. Before her was an atrocity, a despicable legend incarnate.

Why did she want to touch it?

"What should we do?" Ren asked, whispering as if they were playing hide-and-seek. "Do you think we can just shatter it?"

Sanne slid Peacebringer from its sheath. The sound of the blade's ring folded back on itself in the empty expanse of the cavern. The echo lasted unnaturally long. "I think we try to."

"No spells?"

"No spells." Then, remembering the enchantments in their weapons, she added, "No use of the word, either." The word was an invocation, something different than their spells, but magic was magic. She didn't want to risk it.

Ren drew his ax. He circled the Stone and stopped behind it. "On three?"

Sanne nodded. She lifted Peacebringer and counted.

On three, she swung Peacebringer from right to left, swiping the stand out from under the Stone just as Ren's ax fell upon it. At the faintest touch of steel, an invisible blast of force ripped out from the Stone. Sanne and Ren were thrown back. She slid along the cavern floor, her boots and gloves scraping against it as she tried to stop herself.

When Sanne got to her feet, she came face-to-face with a lavender-eyed entity. Wrongness emanated from it. The faint glow from its pale purple eyes illuminated a featureless face. The entity hovered before her, seeming to shift between gaseous, liquid, and solid forms. It had taken a man's shape, but a tendril snaked from the small of its back to the Stone—which, she saw with a sinking heart, was completely intact.

"*You found me.*"

It took a moment for Sanne to realize it spoke in the Svetlenic dialect—she'd been staring at its fingers, which were long and tipped in lethal-looking claws. She replied in the common language. "You led us."

"*You could have chosen not to come.*"

Behind the entity, Ren got to his feet. He crouched and crept toward it, keeping a wide berth around the pedestal. He waved his hand at Sanne in a way that meant *keep going*.

She raised Peacebringer. "Of course we would have come," she growled. "We're Nightmares. You're haunting my palace."

The entity chuckled, the sound low and rumbling. "*I know who you are, plaything. I see everything in this palace. I know everyone. I mark everyone.*"

Ren gave it no time to continue. He charged forward, ax raised above his head, but the entity flicked its wrist and Ren was ripped back. His ax hovered in midair, kept aloft by snaking tendrils of shadow.

"*How kind of you, horned one.*" The entity wrapped a hand around the ax and turned to Sanne. From the essence of its other hand, a false Peacebringer formed. "*Now, let us play.*"

Sanne's awareness narrowed to the thing in front of her and its weapons. The cavern faded, Ren faded, her fear faded—there was time to acknowledge nothing but the threat. It moved impossibly fast, taunting her every time it blocked a stab or evaded a slash. Sanne rolled to dodge Ren's ax only to feel the false Peacebringer cut across her back. She cried out. The entity howled—Ren had gotten to them and driven his sickles into its back. Sanne scrambled to her feet and locked crossguards with the entity; with a wrench, she tore the false Peacebringer from its hand and took it in her own. The black essence of it ate through her gloves and spread a cold fire across her skin.

Sanne reacted instinctively. Before she could think against it, she summoned golden fire to her palms—fire that was absorbed by the void blade. The entity threw its head back and laughed.

"*Good!*" it cried. A thick tendril erupted from its shoulder. The entity reached around and plucked Ren from its back, dangling him from his cuirass like one might hold a butterfly by its wings. "*Does he taste the same?*"

"Leave him alone!" Sanne took both Peacebringers in one hand and threw a dagger with her other. An undulating tendril shot from the entity, caught the dagger, and threw it back at her. Sanne rolled. The entity cried out—Ren had stabbed it again—and disappeared.

Ren groaned and got to his feet. Blood from his wounds covered his hands; when he retrieved his ax, its handle became sticky with red handprints. He reached for Sanne. "Should I strike it again?"

She took his hand and sheathed the true Peacebringer when she was back on her feet. Something, some low and horrible feeling, still buzzed in her. This thing had taken down the gods. Their fight had been too easy. "This isn't right," she said. "We didn't—"

Her left hand, which still held the false Peacebringer, throbbed with a sharp pain. Sanne looked down and screamed. Where her skin met the hilt, the golden light of Svetlen's warmth glowed—but Sanne felt no heat or relief. The light flowed from her into the dark hilt, which in turn pulsed with her leached radiance.

"Drop it!"

"I can't!" Her fingers remained curved around the hilt. When she tried to loosen them, a harsh pressure held them down as if someone had wrapped their hand around hers. Tears sprang to her eyes. A feeling, horrible in its peculiarity, spread through her. Her veins felt as if they were being emptied, a holy vessel turned on its side to let the anointing oil flow.

The light draining from her changed. Its goldenness faded to an orange, then a red, then a purple and blue and green essence— the bit of divinity bestowed on her by Zikat. This was what the Prázeny Stone had done to the gods in the ancient days: pulled out their essence, sucked them dry, eaten their godhood. And now it was happening to her.

Sanne turned her head and vomited.

The entity appeared before her. Its cackle echoed around the cavern, the sound raking claws down her neck and back. "*Sanne.*" Its laugh quieted to a contented sigh. "*You're delicious.*"

The divinity flowing from her changed colors again—a dark silver, the godhood of Oddelen, began to leave her. She howled. How could they have prepared for this? How could they have hoped to defeat it?

The entity shrieked. It and Sanne looked to see Ren behind the pedestal, his mouth open in a roar as he drove his ax into the Stone for a second time. The steel bounced off of it. Ren reared back again, but before he could complete his third strike, the entity raised a hand. Spirits of all kinds, from shrinking mists to wraiths, formed at the edges of the cavern. Each one had the same light purple eyes as the Stone entity.

"*Eat.*"

The spirits descended. Sanne was lost in the tempest, lost in the blur of bone hands and spectral claws and death-rattle screams and the stench of decay. She cowered. She fell to her knees and screamed for any god who would hear her.

But the false sword had done its work. She was empty.

As quickly as it had come, the spectral maelstrom faded. Cool air brushed against new cuts on her neck, back, and arms. Her braid hung heavy and wet with blood. Sanne wept, and even that small motion hurt.

The fingers of her left hand relaxed. The false Peacebringer fell silently to the floor. She drew her hands to her chest and fought to catch her breath, closing her eyes and hoping the darkness she'd seen in her veins had been a trick of the light.

It was gone. Every shred of her divinity was gone.

What was she now? Surely not a Nightmare.

Just a husk of a woman with an ichor-covered sword.

"Sanne."

The voice, Ren's, was too quiet. Sanne raised her head and screamed.

Ren hovered six feet from the floor, hanging limp like a child's discarded doll. One of the entity's dark tendrils jutted from his left side.

The entity laughed at her horror, laughed as Ren fumbled at the tendril and groaned. "*Now, now,*" it said, lazily contorting its fingers. The tendril buried in Ren curled in on itself. Its sharp tip pushed through his ribs. Bones cracked. Ren whimpered. "*You should have told me he was better. He's got an earthiness I quite like.*"

It dropped Ren. He hit the floor with a wet thud. The entity fell on him at an angle, supporting itself by driving one hand into the wound at Ren's ribs and the other into his hip. It lowered its mouth to Ren's stomach and unhinged its jaw. Currents of divine essence, green and multicolored and silver, began to flow into the entity's mouth.

Ren made no sound. He didn't move.

Sanne fought back a sob—she'd cry when they were out of here—and pushed to her feet. Peacebringer, the real one, was feet away. The entity was distracted, too engrossed in devouring Ren to notice what she was doing. The Stone was again in its stand on the pedestal, replaced by some spectral hand during the maelstrom.

"Please," Sanne whispered. "*Please.* Svetlen. Zikat. Oddelen, Sumra, Zatva." She wiped her bloody hands on her leggings and picked up Peacebringer. "*Anyone.*"

When she was in front of the Stone, she dug for any stubborn bit of divinity still in her. Godhood fed it, but the Stone had been defeated somehow. She had to try. Sanne spoke her word.

Invisible claws brushed back the hair that had fallen from her braid.

Peacebringer's blade glowed.

Before the entity could finish its meal, Sanne drove Peacebringer into the Stone.

Darkness exploded around her. It tore at her clothes and hair and hands, but she held fast. She stared at her glowing sword until her eyes ached. A roar filled her ears and she screamed to match it, letting every bit of agony and sorrow and fear color her cry until her throat too dry to make sound.

"*Sanne.*" The entity was inches from her, its mouth dangerously close to hers. "*What do you think you're doing?*"

"Go back to whatever fucking hell you came from!"

The entity laughed. She shouldn't have been able to hear it in the roaring darkness, but the sound crept down her spine and lodged there. "*Of course. All you had to do was ask.*"

The darkness vanished. Candles flickered around her like starlight. All she heard was her ragged breathing. Peacebringer's glow faded. She wrenched her blade from the Stone.

An inch-long fissure had appeared in it. The shimmering

purple flecks within the Stone winked in the candlelight. She'd hurt it.

As Sanne took in the motionless body on the floor, a matching crack opened in her stained-glass heart. There was no mistaking which shard suffered the rift—the true red one, the one that had swollen to rival those of Cassander and her gods.

The piece of her heart that belonged to Ren broke.

Sanne lost a day to the blur of a sickbed, memories coming to her unbidden as she drifted in and out of sleep.

Ren, bloody and blue-lipped.

Running through the palace halls, screaming for a healer. Forcing one to the dungeon at swordpoint when they wouldn't go. Helping the healer carry Ren to the infirmary because magic wouldn't work in the cavern.

Healers at her bedside.

Priests and priestesses at her bedside, muttering in blessedly familiar dialects.

A holy fullness no feast could ever compare to.

Dreams of lavender eyes. Waking up with wet cheeks.

Malaia and Cassander at her bedside.

That evening, when Sanne woke and her eyes stayed open for more than a few seconds, she sat up and assessed the damage. Her entire body ached, but the worst pain was at her back and on her left hand. She rolled her wrists. An ill feeling settled into her stomach when she realized the darkness she thought she'd imagined remained in her veins. Half of her fingernails were broken, and there was a deep gash beneath a bandage on her right forearm —it would pucker the skin between the swirls of her Nightmare tattoo when it scarred.

Sanne called her fire. Golden flame sparked in her palm.

She dropped her head into her hands and sobbed. Her godhood had come back. She was still a Nightmare.

The hair that brushed her fingers was damp, and the skin of her face felt fresh and soft. Someone had bathed her and dressed her in a soft white gown; she saw it when she lifted the sky blue blankets she'd been tucked into.

She was in the private wing of the palace infirmary, where the sickroom held four beds instead of the main chamber's dozens. Peacebringer and her daggers sat atop the chest at the foot of her bed. The bed to her right was empty, but the one to her left—

She gasped, throwing back her blankets and hobbling to Ren with an awkward, pained stiffness. Like her, he'd been cleaned. When she lifted his blankets, though, she saw he'd been dressed with considerably more bandages. Wide strips of white gauze, already spotted with red blood, wrapped around his ribs and shoulders. A sickly yellow bruise crept from below the edges of the bandages. The same darkness that ran in her veins bled through his, mapping out his arteries in shadow.

"Someone's feeling awfully forward."

Sanne threw her arms around him, ignoring the way the movement made every muscle in her arms and shoulders scream. "I thought you were dead," she said into his neck, unable to fight off the wave of tears that rushed forward. "Are you—"

"I'm alive." He smiled wanly. His lips were no longer blue. "That's all I can ask for."

Sanne drew up a chair and sat at his bedside. She stayed there for the next four days, keeping watch as the healers tended to Ren and he faded in and out of sleep. He'd suffered a punctured lung, three broken ribs, and immense blood loss, the healers told her, and though he was a Nightmare, his healing had initially been slow. Sanne believed it—a Nightmare's accelerated healing was a gift from Zikat, but the Stone had taken that from them. When the holy ones came back to the infirmary, this time to pray over Ren, Sanne sat in the corner and watched the godhood flow back into him.

On the fourth day, the healers told her she had a visitor. She didn't look at Cassander as he pulled a chair to her bedside. "I thought you didn't want to see me until this was done."

"It's hard for my Nightmare to tell me her hunt is finished when she's half-dead." She felt Cassander's eyes on her, but didn't turn. He leaned closer. "I'm so sorry, Sanne."

She looked at him then. Cassander's brown eyes were wet with tears.

"I shouldn't have dismissed you. I shouldn't have doubted you." He placed his hand on her bed, by hers but not close enough to touch. "I came as soon as I heard you'd been admitted. The healers weren't sure you were going to make it at first."

"No one told me that."

"They were afraid to." His throat bobbed. "I'm glad they were wrong."

She knew it wasn't her fault, but a shred of guilt tugged at Sanne's heart. Had she died, Cassander would have lost his third loved one in less than two years. Could anyone handle that much grief?

"And I'm proud of you," Cassander continued. He nodded to Ren. "You took the same beating as a male twice your size, and you're the first one on your feet."

"I'd hardly call this on my feet. I haven't left this room in days."

He smiled. "But you're awake, and you're healing."

Sanne couldn't find it in herself to smile back. "Has anything happened since...?"

"No, thank the gods. I don't know what we would have done." Cassander ran a hand through his hair, and Sanne realized he wasn't wearing his crown. "Whatever you rooted out seems to have ended the infestation."

"For now." She lowered her voice. "Cassander, I'm not sure if—"

Ren mumbled something in his sleep. His eyes fluttered beneath his lids.

Cassander stood. "You can tell me later," he said, resting a gloved hand on Sanne's shoulder. "Things have been quiet. You need to rest." He looked to Ren. "And so does he."

Sanne sighed. She supposed it could wait. The conversation she needed to have with Cassander would be difficult no matter when she had it—telling him a legendary stone was hidden in the bowels of the palace would sound incredulous no matter what. She'd accept the quiet. She'd accept the rest, and gladly, because when she went back to the cavern to put an end to the Stone, she was going to do it alone. "You'll be pleased to hear I'm sending him away as soon as the nurses say he can travel."

"Why?"

Ren stirred, his sleepy gibberish taking the shape of a woman's name. It wasn't the first time Sanne had heard it. "He has someone waiting for him."

Cassander gently squeezed her shoulder. "It's your hunt, Sanne. Do what you feel is best."

When Ren woke, Sanne sat alone at his bedside. "Think you're up for good?"

"For more than five minutes, yes, if that's what you mean." Ren pushed himself into a sitting position, and was able to do so without wincing. "I'm healing faster now. I can feel it. How long have I been out?"

"About four days."

His eyes widened. "When is Solstice?"

"In a week."

"Gods." He leaned forward, huffing out a breath and pressing a hand to his wounds as he did. Ren lowered his voice. "And the Stone? Did you destroy it?"

Sanne placed her hand on his. "Your hunt here is done."

Ren eyed her. "Really?"

She nodded. May the gods forgive her, and may the Order never find out she was lying. "It's gone." She rose and took a letter from her nightstand. She gave it to him to read. "I wrote to the Keep and informed them of your injuries. Because of their severity and how close you were to death, the Triumvirate has granted you leave until the spring equinox. Your options are to return to the Keep or, if you have somewhere in mind, go there and stay until your leave expires. You're not to hunt until then."

Ren tore open and read the letter. "And what did you tell them injured me so?"

She sat. "I believe my exact words were 'an entity not dissimilar to a wraith'."

He rubbed his thumb against the letter's edge. "Four months. Sanne, I can't go that long—"

"You can." They'd almost ceased to be Nightmares, and for Ren, that was all he knew. Sanne couldn't be the reason he was torn from the only place he'd ever belonged, and she knew that if she let him stay, he'd realize that the Stone remained. He'd try to help her destroy it, but this wasn't his war to wage.

A flare of heat spread through her, hotter than the warmth that came when Svetlen smiled on her. Sanne knew in her heart what it was: a warning, and a confirmation. She couldn't keep Ren here. She couldn't expose him to this again. He had to go.

"Sanne—"

"We're Nightmares. You know what that means."

Ren sighed. "That I can't defy a direct order from the Triumvirate."

"That someone always needs us more." Sanne forced a smile to her lips. He'd earned this reprieve. He'd earned the right to worry about nothing more than his woman. "And right now, Morgaine needs you more than I do. Go to her. Go rest."

10.8.626

Away from the suppressive influence of the Stone, Ren healed rapidly. Early the next morning, Sanne received word that he was cleared for travel.

When she met him outside the front gates after breakfast, he looked considerably better than he had the day before. With how gaunt and pale he'd been then, he looked far from healthy now, but Ren had just enough color in his cheeks that Sanne could convince herself it was alright for him to go. He'd dressed for traveling in a thick tunic and leggings of black wool, one of his sets of leather armor, and black gloves. He'd fastened a woolen cloak over his shoulders, and a cowl hung loose at his neck, ready to be drawn over his mouth and nose to ward off cold winds.

He was slinging a saddlebag over Reia's rump when Sanne approached. Her greeting was lost to the sound of clinking glass. "What's in there? Did you rob our liquor stores?"

"They're tinctures for pain," Ren grumbled, tightening the saddlebag straps. "Your nurses made me take them. They said I shouldn't strain myself by casting healing spells."

Sanne eyed the way he checked his tack. He moved slower than usual. "I'm inclined to agree." She shrugged the bag she'd been carrying from her shoulder and held it out to Ren. "This is for you."

He opened the bag. "Books?"

"For her," Sanne amended. "It's Solstice. You'll need a gift."

To Sanne's relief, Ren dug past the books and held up a heavy coin purse. "This feels like much more than I negotiated for," he said, tossing the pouch up and down.

"It's a hundred extra."

He stared at her. "A hundred? How did you pull that off?"

Sanne shrugged. "Cassander won't miss it," she said, "and you can't hunt for four months. This should help lessen that blow."

Ren ran his fingers over the pouch's cinch closure before packing it and the books into a saddlebag. The red edges of one of the books winked in the sunlight. Ren checked the tack once more before turning to Sanne. "Are you sure you'll be alright?"

She nodded. She'd damaged the Stone, which meant it could be destroyed, and she had her gods back. She knew what to expect now. She could protect her palace and king, and she would protect Ren, too. "I'm healing. I'll be alright, in time. You need to get going."

Ren glanced at the open gates. A softness passed over his face, a longing that Sanne knew in name only. "I do." He pulled her into his chest, wrapping his arms around her and squeezing, though the embrace was tight enough to hurt them both. Sanne didn't mind the pain. "Thank you, Sanne."

"Of course."

Ren was the first to let go. "Don't let it be three years before I see you again," he said, using a block to mount Reia. Kyr settled onto the mare's rump.

Sanne laughed, and was relieved to find that it sounded genuine. "I wouldn't dream of it."

With a final wave goodbye, Ren spurred his mare forward.

Sanne watched him go. Her heart ached as his silhouette grew smaller, and she knew what the discomfort was: her stained-glass heart was reforming itself again. The fragments shifted and competed for space, a feeling Sanne knew well, but her shards had a new contender: the bright red piece that was Ren's. Its crack was healing, and it was growing. Sanne sighed and let it. She'd made the right choice in sending him away. The war she waged was now for him, too.

When he disappeared from sight, Sanne went to her chambers and marked the loss of one hundred gold from her account books.

THE EIDOLON

It was a beautiful day in the Celesty, but the blood made Sanne feel sick.

She turned her head as the royal entourage rode through the butcher district. She was spared the sight of the pig's hot blood running down its flesh, but not the smell—a metallic, bitter scent that made her decide she'd abstain from bacon and chops for the foreseeable future. In the month since Ren had left the Stained Palace, only half-healed and still bleeding, Sanne hadn't been able to see the color red without her stomach twisting. It meant no wine, no winter berries, no red sauce—even using nightsight sent waves of nausea through her, and tending to herself during her cycle the week prior had nearly sent her into a panic. She'd been a Nightmare hunter for nine years and had never responded to a hunt like this. She'd always been so good at recovery.

But until last month, Sanne had always worked alone. The only blood she'd had to cope with seeing had been her own.

The rumps of Cassander and Malaia's horses swayed in front of her, their braided tails sweeping back and forth. Malaia's black hair, unbound beneath her golden tiara, swished in time. Sanne lifted her face to the pale winter sun and breathed deeply, closing her eyes and letting Marra, who'd taken the shape of a dappled mare, carry her forward. The butcher stalls were behind them now. The air around her was cold and crisp and clean-smelling, and the sun warmed her face. Svetlen wasn't quite smiling on her, but it was always harder to feel her goddess in winter. Sanne let herself be content with the small bit of warmth she'd found.

Cassander and Malaia were chatting, and Sanne watched her cousin draw his wife's gloved hand to his lips and kiss it. The king and queen took monthly trips into the Celesty as a goodwill measure, reserving the first Odsden of each month for the sojourn. The trips had been Malaia's idea, implemented upon her coronation as queen; her parents ruled the Karilan Atoll, an island nation off Jasniostvo's southern coast, and they had done the same. Malaia had grown up forging bonds between her royal family and the island's artisans, bonds that led to a steady flow of funds and commissions between the Atoll's royalty and its people. Cassander had scheduled the first trip into the Celesty the week after he and Malaia's honeymoon, and the tradition had persisted.

Sanne had never been invited before—what purpose would the Lady Nightmare serve on a shopping trip?—but Cassander had insisted that she deserved the break, and she hadn't had it in her to refuse. She rode at the back of the royal party, a guard on either side of her. Captain Vallen rode in front of the king and queen, and he'd arranged his guards around them. The guards wore shining white armor, deep yellow feathered plumes rising from the tops of their helmets. Their horses' caparisons were sky blue, the edging cream; barding made of golden scale mail jangled brightly as the horses walked. Marra tolerated none of these adornments, only the shadow-tack that every Umbral wore, but Sanne didn't mind. She shone enough, for she wore her golden plate. Her sky blue cloak was spread over Marra's rump to keep it from dangling around Sanne's feet, and she'd braided her hair half-up, letting the rest of it fall golden and loose around her shoulders. This may have been a pleasure trip, or at least as close to one as a hunter like her could have, but she knew good and well that the eyes of the Celesty would fall to Cassander, then Malaia, then her. The crown had an image to present and preserve, and she knew her part. It was a role Sanne had played, in one way or another, since childhood.

The party reached the merchant's district and halted in the center forum. As in the temple district, the large stained-glass pavilion overhead cast shards of colorful light onto shopkeepers and patrons. Vallen and Cassander dismounted. Cassander went to Malaia's gelding and helped her down. Sanne shifted her weight to her left foot and swung her right leg over, dismounting the way she and Marra had perfected at the Keep. It was quite impressive when done correctly—halfway through the dismount,

Marra transformed into a gyrfalcon, leaving Sanne to drop lithely to her feet. She noticed the guards watching, though they turned to the king and queen as soon as Sanne's feet hit the ground.

"That's my grumpy girl," she said to Marra, extending her arm. The Umbral perched on Sanne's forearm and ruffled her feathers. She allowed Sanne to stroke her beak only once before snapping at Sanne's finger. "Enough. I only have so many fingers left."

Marra stared at her.

"I'll call you when it's time to return." Sanne quickly rose her arm so Marra would take flight. "Go find yourself a fat Celesty rat."

The Umbral shrieked and soared into the sky. She passed through the dome and was soon out of sight.

"Such fascinating creatures you Nightmares have." Malaia smiled as she approached Sanne. "The Atoll has many strange beings, but nothing like your Marra."

Sanne's returned smile was polite. "Thank you, my queen. She's a great asset."

Cassander appeared with a fur shawl in his hands and draped it over Malaia's shoulders. "Here you are, my love," he said, pressing a kiss to her temple.

"You've attracted quite a crowd." Sanne nodded to the people gathered at the forum's edge. Some whispered behind cupped hands, while others—mostly children—pointed outright at their king and queen. The palace guards who'd accompanied them had arranged themselves in a loose circle around Sanne, Cassander, and Malaia. Vallen stood steps away. "Is this normal?"

Cassander faced the crowd, smiled brightly, and raised his left hand in greeting; his right was wrapped around Malaia's. Those under his warm gaze beamed and waved back. "Yes," he said, "but there seem to be more than usual today."

"Our anniversary is in a week," Malaia said, looking up at her husband. "We weren't able to invite many of the people to the ball. They may want to congratulate you."

"Congratulate *us*." Cassander raised her hand to his lips. "Or perhaps they saw we're accompanied by our Lady Nightmare."

Sanne knew it was possible, which was good—optics were part of the reason her late uncle had contracted her. Residents of holy cities like the Celesty knew little about the Order of Nightmares, only that they were devout and powerful; when Oran had heard of Sanne's skill at the Keep, he'd seized the opportunity to bring her home. To the people, she was an example of Esclarmonde strength and power—look how their king had convinced the Order to bend their rules and let her settle in the Celesty, where she'd serve the throne instead of the realm. Now that Oran had passed and the Black Sun had reared his head, however, there was another layer to Sanne's royal employ: look how the rightful king retains a Nightmare in golden plate. See how blessed he must be. "Perhaps," she said. "But I hope it's the former."

"No sword today?"

Sanne tensed her shoulder blades reflexively, feeling for a scabbard that wasn't there. "Not today, no. Only two daggers."

Cassander chuckled. "It's a peaceful trip, Lady."

"I understand." She gave him a small smile and hoped her tone was acceptably teasing. "But a Nightmare is always prepared for danger, my king."

He smiled and reached for her. They clasped forearms. "I hope you enjoy this time," he said. "I think it will be good for you to feel Svetlen's light on your skin."

"Thank you. I agree." Since having her godhood torn from her, Sanne had been terrified of feeling that cold emptiness again. It touched her to hear that Cassander wished the sun upon her. "Now, where do you like to visit first?"

———

Sanne soon realized a drawback of spending most of her time among the Order, on a hunt, or within the walls of the Stained

Palace, where a servant could be summoned to see to her every need: she'd lost her taste for shopping.

As a child, she'd loved shopping with her mother Rinnekeh. Much like Cassander and Malaia did now, they'd made a day of it: a special breakfast in the morning—Sanne was allowed coffee on shopping days, which made her feel so grown-up—and then a ride from their estate into town with only the two of them in the carriage. There was no father to distract Rinnekeh and no little brother to annoy Sanne. The shopkeepers had doted on her, bringing her sparkling jewels to try on while her mother was fitted for dress after dress. She now knew they'd only done it to please Rinnekeh and hopefully make a sale, but Sanne still remembered those days fondly. The world had been bright and shining and safe.

The shopkeeper she stood before now tutted. Sanne had put a ring on her left finger to test its size—now that the darkness in her veins had faded, she wanted to treat herself to some jewelry— which prompted the silver-haired human woman to say, "Not that finger, my lady. Let's keep that free for a husband, yes?"

Sanne lifted her bare hands, showing the shopkeeper that she only had a thumb, pointer finger, and middle finger on her right hand. "I have no other ring finger on which to try it, madam."

The woman paled. "I see." Her wide eyes locked onto Sanne's swirling Nightmare tattoo, which spread from the place where Sanne's ring and little fingers had once been. "Forgive—"

Bells tolled through the district center, sounding twelve times. Sanne looked to the sun—how was it already noon? "Good day," she said, turning on her heel and leaving the shopkeeper stumbling over an embarrassed apology.

The temple district was a street away from the jeweler's shop. Sanne decided to walk to Svetlen's temple instead of summoning Marra, enjoying the brisk sound of her boot heels on the cobblestones. She greeted those she passed on the way, especially a gaggle of teenage girls whose jaws dropped when they saw her.

"The Lady Nightmare," Sanne heard them whisper as she

approached. They had good eyes—when she wore her plate, the only Nightmarish things about her were the black lining of her cloak, her black gambeson and leggings, and the tattoo swirling up her right hand. They were lucky they'd seen it, as Sanne hadn't yet replaced her gloves.

"Good day," she said as she passed, wishing she'd brought Peacebringer after all. She would've liked to show them her Nightmare steel.

"Good day," they echoed, turning to one another and giggling.

"Long live the king!" one of them shouted after her.

Sanne smiled. It was good to see the people's support. "Long live the king."

"Long live the Order!"

Sanne stopped in her tracks. Was the longevity of the Order truly something the people wished for? Even as the first female Nightmare, and even as one of the best Nightmares regardless of gender, Sanne had never felt particularly revered for it. Her place in the Esclarmonde bloodline, yes, but not her place in the Order. Someone needed a Nightmare, they hired and paid them, and that was that. Most saw Nightmares as honed tools to be wielded, holy instruments crafted to do a job they could not—or so Sanne had thought.

She, after all, had seen the Order as more than a sharp blade.

She turned back to the girls. She didn't wear Peacebringer, but there were two serrated Nightmare daggers beneath her breastplate. She drew one and tossed it into the air with a flourish so the girls could see its marbled steel-and-copper blade. They gasped. Sanne grinned, sheathed the dagger, and turned to go, though not before agreeing wholeheartedly, "Long live the Order."

———

Cassander, Malaia, Vallen, and the guards had already started the noontime prayer when Sanne slipped into the royal family's chapel. She sat behind Malaia and found her place in the orison with little effort, though she spoke more quietly than normal. So often she prayed alone, and it lifted her spirits to hear others join in. She especially wanted to hear Cassander pray—she suspected this was the first time he'd done so in months.

She'd joined at the end of the prayer; Cassander and Malaia rose only minutes later. "Are you coming with us?" Cassander asked.

"Not yet." Sanne stood. "I need to speak to Svetlen more."

The look in his eyes made her heart sink. "Take all the time you need," he said. "We will be easy to find once you're done."

Sanne thanked him. She walked to the front of the chapel, knelt before the altar, and discarded her weapons. When she heard no more footsteps, Sanne dropped her head and let the tears rush forward. A prayer in the Svetlenic dialect fell as her tears did. She knew that look in Cassander's eyes: pity. He'd watched the holy ones pray the godhood back into her, after all. Their conversation after Ren left the Stained Palace, when Sanne knew she could no longer put off telling Cassander about the Prázeny Stone, had been fraught. She'd gotten silence, not the shouting or panic she'd expected. Cassander had sat in the war room, his fingers tented together, for a long time before he'd said, "Take me to it."

Sanne had refused. "You are my king," she said, "and Svetlen's chosen. Her blessing beats in your heart, Cassander. I can't expose you to it."

"But you—"

"I can be repaired." And she could be. She had been. Now that her godhood had been restored, the air in her lungs felt fulfilling, the blood in her veins once again life-giving. The power of Zikat and Oddelen hummed in her, and Svetlen again shone light into her stained-glass heart. She could shoulder this burden for him. She *would*. It was a Nightmare's job, not a king's, to be haunted. "I've damaged it, which means I can destroy it. Just be careful who you send to the dungeon."

He'd stood and done the last thing Sanne expected. Cassander had hugged her.

His gratitude had rained down on her for the last month, manifesting as little gifts delivered to her room: whetstones, velvet hair ribbons, golden barding for Marra's reins, books and dagger sheaths and dinner invitations. Sanne had accepted them all. She'd had time to enjoy them all, too, for the spiritual activity had all but stopped since the night she and Ren had fought the Stone. He'd been granted a four-month respite, and Sanne had gotten a little leave of her own. The Black Sun's activity had quieted, too; she and Cassander had been able to spend time together as family, not a king and his lady. Their dinners were less formal, his words said less from frustration and exhaustion. She'd started telling him about the Keep, swapping stories of her Nightmare training for tales of what he'd undergone when swearing his oath.

What she'd yet to tell him though, was that their small peace had ended last night.

The hardly-healed gash on the back of her neck ached—concealing it had been the real reason she'd worn her hair this way. A lavender-eyed ghoul, a manifestation of the Stone, had caught her by surprise just after midnight.

She reached for the bronze statue of Svetlen atop the altar, the sandals of which had been rubbed to a brighter color by supplicants like her. Something stirred in the shadows.

Sanne reached for a dagger, yet it was only Marra. The gyrfalcon hopped across the white tile floor with a folded note clutched in her beak.

"What have you got?" Sanne wiped the tears from her eyes and unfolded the note.

Lady,

Are you intending for me to assume you've died?
I know that isn't true.

We need to speak about what's happened. I know what you found.

This has all happened before.

Descend.

- A.V.

Sanne crumpled the note from Zdesen's high priestess in her hand. The wave of anger that came wasn't enough to stop more tears from falling. Though she hadn't hunted for the last month, she'd gone nights without sleeping anyway, combing through both palace libraries for any information she could find on the Prázeny Stone. She'd found nothing new. She'd become desperate, and then the high priestess had started sending notes—somehow, Marra had learned she could slip into Zdesen's temple, and Vestel had seized the means of contact. She pestered Sanne to meet, though every note was tauntingly vague. Sanne was haunted by the question of how much Vestel knew.

She knew she could descend to the temple. She could use her position to force Vestel to tell her everything.

So why don't you? Zdesen whispered. A rush of air brushed the wound on Sanne's neck. *Tell me, Sanne.*

The reason was simple. She'd discovered something that resisted all offense, that could destroy the gods and their faithful if she didn't carefully hunt and destroy it. Sanne was afraid. Descending to the goddess of horror's temple in this state would be like tracking a bear while draped in honey. Sanne hadn't hunted in weeks, but she was tired. She was lost. If Zdesen appeared while Sanne was in that wretched place, she was afraid she'd be manipulated as the Black Sun had.

She pressed her palms to the floor and implored Svetlen to aid her.

The temple was quiet.

"Please," Sanne begged. Her tears dampened the floor. "Please, bright one—"

A warm hand ghosted across her back. Its second pass was firmer, more intentional. The divine comfort only made Sanne cry more.

There's more help you can ask for, you know. A second hand joined the first, though its touch was cold and rough. Sanne threw her hands over her head and shuddered.

The goddesses spoke as one, a stomach-twisting harmony urging Sanne to **Go below**.

She stared at the floor, thinking of the cavernous temple beneath. They had never spoken to her together before. Why both goddesses at once? Why now? She didn't want to descend, but if Svetlen was now telling her to go—

"My lady."

She lifted her head. Vallen stood behind her, hands clasped behind his back. "His Majesty asked me to fetch you," he said. "It's time to return to the palace."

A coward's relief flooded Sanne, chased by shame moments later. "Thank you, Captain." She collected her weapons, sheathing them and wiping her tears before she turned to Vallen. "Let us not keep him waiting."

The goddesses were silent as Sanne left the temple.

———

On the trip back from the Celesty, Sanne resolved to tell Cassander of the Stone's resurgence that night. She thus expected a bad evening.

She hadn't prepared for a confrontation, however. When she entered the war room, Cassander wasn't alone.

He looked up and smiled when she entered. The Eclipse, though, just stared at Sanne, her amber eyes stoic over her mother-of-pearl mask.

"Forgive me," Sanne said. Peacebringer was at her back again, and Sanne fought the urge to draw it. "I didn't realize I'd be interrupting."

"You're not. I thought it wise for the three of us to speak now that the Eclipse has returned. Help yourself to a drink, Sanne." Cassander motioned to the sideboard, upon which sat two trays of drinks: a porcelain pot and teacups on the left, a crystal decanter and rocks glasses on the right.

"Lovely. When did you return, Eclipse?" Sanne asked, walking to the sideboard. "How did you fare in Nocovostvo? Although —" She tilted her head, feigning confusion. "I don't see the Black Sun chained at your side, nor the Red Sky. Did your negotiations fail?" Two months ago, the Eclipse had been sent to Nocovostvo, the refugee kingdom where the Black Sun had established his army and foothold, to negotiate his extradition with Queen Yvaine. Sanne hadn't expected the talks to bear results, but Cassander had been desperate to try, so she'd held her tongue and enjoyed the Eclipse's absence.

Cassander frowned. "Sanne—"

"I relished the opportunity to serve my king," the Eclipse sneered, "and to prevent this war from spreading. What did you accomplish in my absence, Lady? Saving a toddler from the monster under his bed?"

Sanne poured herself a drink. "As always, you remain ignorant of my importance," she retorted, cutting her eyes at the Eclipse. She wished she'd kept her plate on instead of changing into a Nightmare's leather armor—she knew the Eclipse was jealous of her golden plate, which marked her as an Esclarmonde by blood. The Eclipse's plate had golden details, as did the mask that covered the lower half of her face, but the armor itself was bone white. As Sanne's armor was indicative of her position, the Eclipse's was indicative of hers: tied to the king, in service of the king, but not blood related. "I take it you haven't heard what I faced in your absence?"

The Eclipse scowled. "No, Lady. His Majesty hasn't told me."

Sanne hid her smile by taking a sip. Smooth whiskey burned

across her tongue. "I see." She knew she shouldn't taunt the Eclipse, especially in front of Cassander, but she itched to put the elven woman in her place. No other kingdom had a position like the Eclipse, who split her time between serving as Cassander's personal bodyguard and as his representative in foreign affairs. As an eclipse concealed the sun, the royal Eclipse was meant to cover the king, whether that be from an attack or being seen in his stead at a foreign court. Only the king was allowed an Eclipse; when Cassander had taken the throne, he'd discharged Oran's and chosen his own. He'd selected her from the most devout of Svetlen's priestesses, as was tradition, and sent her to be trained by the Aurorals, Jasniostvo's regiment of elite soldiers.

Sanne didn't know her name, but her name wasn't important —the female she'd been had ceased to exist the moment she donned the Eclipse's mask and wrapped her hand around Saroszy, the sword every Eclipse wielded. All Sanne knew of this Eclipse was that she was a bronzed elf, the elven species native to Jasniostvo, and that her devotion to Cassander was absolute. Like a Nightmare hunter, the Eclipse could be considered a holy role: Nightmares worshipped Zikat and Oddelen and, in theory, the Eclipse worshipped Svetlen. Cassander's Eclipse, however, worshipped him.

"Tell her, please, Sanne," Cassander said. He drank from his own glass of whiskey. "And then I'd like us to discuss what you needed to tell me."

Sanne recounted the events of the past month for the Eclipse: her difficulty banishing spirits, Ren's assistance, the discovery of the Stone, its feeding, and the subsequent quiet. The Eclipse remained stoic through it all, and her indifference infuriated Sanne. She reined in her anger, though—it mattered what Cassander thought, not his votary. It was Cassander she was fighting the Stone for. "What I've needed to tell you, Cassander, is that it's returned."

He paled. "When?"

"Last night."

Silent minutes passed as Sanne and the Eclipse waited for his reaction, his decree. He'd given orders so easily when she'd last hunted. Sanne hadn't expected the frightened, rudderless look that passed over Cassander's face before he turned to her and said, "The ball for Malaia and I's anniversary is in a week."

"Yes."

"The Stained Palace will be full of guests."

"Yes."

"What should we do?"

Sanne opened her mouth to answer, but the Eclipse spoke first. "If I may, my king," she said, "is the Lady Nightmare truly equipped to defeat this? It sounds like no creature or spirit. Is it under her purview?"

Sanne's jaw ticked. "Did you hear a single word I said?"

Cassander pinched the bridge of his nose. "The Stone has appeared in my nightmares," he whispered, "and nightmares are what Sanne hunts, so, yes, she is qualified to handle this. I know she will fight it until her last, if necessary."

It wasn't a question, but Sanne nodded when Cassander looked at her anyway.

"So I will ask again," he continued, glaring at the Eclipse, "what Sanne thinks we should do?"

She'd mulled this over during some of her sleepless nights. "The Stone feeds on godhood, and when it drained me, I was healed by holy ones praying over me," she said. "As they did centuries ago, our gods prevailed over the Stone's effects. I believe, therefore, that it would be beneficial to have the high priest and priestesses of the Celestian temples arrive now, so they can be a holy presence here in the days leading up to the ball. We can ask them to prepare the palace chapels for your guests to disguise the true reason for the request. And because they're of the Celesty, we have little reason to question their discretion or loyalty to you."

"You're proposing preventative measures, then?"

Sanne nodded. "And I'll continue my hunt, of course. I don't know if I can destroy the Stone before the ball—it may not be safe to—but at the very least, I'll keep its manifestations at bay."

Cassander thought for a moment. "It's a start."

The Eclipse cleared her throat. "*All* of the holy ones, Lady?"

"That's true," Cassander said. He lowered his voice. "Do your plans include bringing the parasite's priestess into the palace?"

Sanne swirled the whiskey in her glass. She didn't like the thought any more than Cassander did—Zdesen was persistent enough as it was, and Sanne hated to think what effect Vestel's presence would have on the goddess' attempts to seduce her. It also posed a great security risk; Sanne knew Cassander questioned Vestel's loyalty and suspected her of being an informant for the Black Sun. Most of Zdesen's priestesses had fled with him upon his second exile, but the high priestess, for reasons unknown to the crown, had stayed. Sanne shared Cassander's skepticism, but, "It would be a great offense if we excluded her."

The Eclipse crossed her arms. "The Lady is right," she said, and Sanne had the suspicion she was grinding her teeth beneath her mask. Good. "Her exclusion could provoke the Black Sun to further action if word of it reached him."

"Yet he rejects Svetlen entirely," Cassander muttered. He rubbed his face with his gloved hands. "I'll allow it, but she is to be watched. Closely. We'll assign guards to each of the holy ones to avoid seeming suspicious."

The Eclipse nodded. "I will notify Captain Vallen to pull some of his guards."

"No need. I'll tell him." Cassander drummed his fingers against the table as he looked around the war room, taking in the maps on the walls, the plans and supply lists scattered on desks—all the information that could be passed to the Black Sun if they weren't careful. "I want to handpick each guard."

"Of course, my king."

"My hunts are nocturnal," Sanne said, "so I'll guard a holy one during the day, if needed."

The Eclipse was not to be outdone. "As will I."

"Thank you both. You've given me much to think about." Cassander stood and refreshed his whiskey. "The two of you are dismissed."

Sanne rose. The Eclipse began to protest, but Cassander raised a hand.

"I need to think," he said. "Eclipse, your queen has missed you. Go tell her you've returned. And Sanne?"

"Yes?"

"Go rest." Purple smudges had settled under Cassander's eyes. Sanne didn't think they'd been there at the start of this conversation. "I need you at your strongest."

11.9.626

The holy ones arrived two days later. Sanne, having just completed her morning lauds, stood next to the Eclipse in the Stained Palace's receiving hall. Vallen's four best guards filled out their line.

"We're honored that you've all agreed to join us in celebrating Malaia and I's anniversary, and that you've blessed us by arriving early," Cassander said. He gestured to Sanne and the others. "Captain Vallen and I have chosen a detail of guards for each of you to guarantee your comfort and safety."

"We've also appointed a head to each detail," Vallen said. "They're chosen from our best fighters in the Celesty."

Sanne's breath caught in her throat as the six holy ones, a single priest and five priestesses, approached. High Priest Hazecu was from Oddelen's temple; his black skin, long white hair, and pale gold eyes identified him as a gloam elf, the elven species created by the death god. The five high priestesses were a mix of elven and human—Sanne counted three pairs of pointed ears, one pair of ears round and short enough to be fully hidden beneath hair, and a set whose points were just enough to show through a half-elf's purple crown braid. Each elven species was represented: Oddelen's gloam, Zikat's prismatic, Sumra's shaded,

Zatva's horned, and Svetlen's bronzed. The only fully human holy one was Adarilen Vestel—Zdesen had refused to create an elven race.

"Captain, if you'll make the introductions?"

Vallen stepped forward. "As you wish, my king. High Priest Hazecu, you will be accompanied by Lieutenant Elas Reilen."

The gloam elf stepped forward, his white robes swishing across the floor. "Hello, Lieutenant."

Vallen continued down the line. High Priestess Rada was a prismatic half-elf, with periwinkle skin and amethyst eyes; High Priestess Cardaril, of Sumra's temple, was a shaded elf wrought in grayscale; and Sanne remembered the horned High Priestess Lirwood—she'd seen her embracing Ren in the Celesty only a month ago.

By the time Vallen reached Sanne and the Eclipse, only two priestesses remained: High Priestess Sohli, the bronzed elf who presided over Svetlen's temple, and Vestel. The latter smiled at Sanne, her red lips slick with lacquer.

"And for you, High Priestess Sohli," Vallen said, "we felt it was only right for Svetlen's high priestess to share the same guardian as Svetlen's chosen king. The Eclipse will see to your wellbeing."

Though Sanne hated the Eclipse, she'd spent enough time with her to know her tells, to read her body as if it was Sanne's own. She suspected she was the only one who noticed the Eclipse's slight deflation. "It's my honor, High Priestess," she said, stepping forward and offering Sohli her arm.

They followed the rest of the holy ones and their guards, though Sanne didn't watch them go—her heart beat too loudly in her chest. Her vision narrowed too sharply to the masked woman in front of her. She could imagine Cassander's reasoning: Vestel couldn't know just how threatened by her he felt, and to assign the Eclipse to her would have planted that seed in her mind. Sanne was a safer choice, close enough to Cassander to show sufficient deference—Zdesen was, after all, part of Svetlen, and Jasniostvo could be argued to be her kingdom as well. To publicly suggest as much would be heresy, but Sanne understood why someone would try to claim it as truth.

"Finally, High Priestess Vestel," Vallen said, standing at a healthy distance from her, "you'll be accompanied throughout the Stained Palace by—"

"The Lady Nightmare." Vestel's smile grew. "How you honor me, my king."

Sanne pictured the sun, imagined the sensation of staring right at it. Svetlen's light would burn away her fear before Vestel or Zdesen could take advantage of it. She offered the high priestess her arm. "It's my pleasure, High Priestess."

Vestel's nails, black today, clicked against Sanne's golden armor as they left the receiving room. A servant appeared from the shadows and gestured for them to follow her.

"If I could be shown to my lady's chapel, please," Vestel said. "I would like to thank her for the safe journey." Her grip tightened on Sanne's arm. "Such dangerous times we live in, yes? We shouldn't take uneventful travels for granted."

The maidservant looked to Sanne. "My lady?"

Sanne nodded. "You may go."

The maidservant scuttled away with her head bowed. Sanne didn't blame her.

She steered Vestel toward the chapel wing, keeping them in the middle of the hall. Sanne didn't like the thought of Vestel brushing against the walls or touching any art they passed—she could hardly stand the high priestess' bare hand on her armor. She was going to thoroughly polish it later. The high priestess belonged to Zdesen, so she did not belong in the Stained Palace. Nothing of the parasite did.

"I've been trying to contact you," Vestel murmured. "I know you found it. You reek of fear."

Sanne pressed her lips together.

"It is a sweet smell," the high priestess continued, "and earthen. Like sage."

Only another flight of stairs and one more passageway, and

then Sanne could usher Vestel into the chapel and have a moment's relief. Divine claws tapped along Sanne's armor—she heard it in her mind. Vestel's presence was drawing Zdesen closer.

"Are you not going to speak to me, Lady? After I was so helpful to you and your companion?"

Only the passageway remained. *How did you know*? Sanne wanted to shout, but she bit her tongue. The passageway was too public, and Vestel had arrived too recently. Sanne couldn't make the high priestess immediately feel suspected.

"We've reached Zdesen's chapel." Sanne dropped Vestel's arm and opened the door for her.

They entered. Vestel's lips curled in disgust. "It's quite small," she said, running a finger along the back of a black pew. A clean streak was left in the dust.

Vestel was right, but Sanne saw no issue with the chapel's size —no one in the Stained Palace worshipped Zdesen, not anymore, and Vestel should've been grateful that Cassander allowed her to use it at all. He'd had it barred after the Black Sun's second exile. "Does that shock you?"

"No. But it displeases me nonetheless." Vestel walked down the red-carpeted center aisle, past the single row of pews, and paused before the dark metal altar. She inclined her head to the misshapen statue on it before turning to Sanne and adding, "Yet I will make do. After all, my lady isn't contained by the walls men make for her."

Sanne thought of the Black Sun. She thought of her own stricken mind. "Indeed she is not."

Vestel strode down the center aisle to Sanne. She lifted a hand, and when it landed on Sanne's cheek, she struggled not to recoil. "Does my lady still speak to you?"

Sanne clenched her jaw so tightly her head began to hurt. She stared at the high priestess' black bone mask. How did she see? There were no slits to look through, no cleverly hidden mesh panels to conceal the eyes. What color were her eyes? Blue? Green?

Brown like Sanne's? Black and red like the Black Sun's eyes had turned after he swore himself to Zdesen?

"I see," Vestel said, tutting. She dropped her hand. "It's no matter that you don't want to tell me, Lady Nightmare. You and I will have much time to talk." She turned on her heel and walked back to the altar, waving a hand. "You are dismissed. I need to pray."

Sanne slipped from the darkness of the chapel into the prismatic light of the corridor. She closed her eyes until her nausea passed. Though she ached for answers, she didn't want to admit needing Vestel's help—when would the high priestess consider the favor repaid? Sanne didn't want to be tied to her. She didn't want to become like the Black Sun.

She stared at her right hand. Beneath her Nightmare tattoo, her veins had once been shadowed. Yet her gods had returned to her, and the darkness had faded. That was what she needed to remember: she was a Nightmare and a blessed Esclarmonde, and her gods would always make her well.

She kept a small golden fire burning her palms until Vestel was done.

11.10.626

The first ball guests arrived the next morning.

Sanne heard them before she saw them. Their voices bounced across the polished white floors as she walked from Zikat's chapel to her chambers. She paused in the entryway of the receiving hall, grateful she didn't yet wear her plate. Shadows were rare in the many-windowed rooms and halls of the Stained Palace, but it was early enough in the day that bits of night could still be found hiding in corners. Sanne cast darkdrape and slipped into one to see who had arrived.

Malaia dashed across the receiving hall, still in her dressing gown and slippers. "Mother!" she cried. "Father!"

A couple, with hair as night-black as Malaia's and the same

sepia-toned skin, quickened their own steps to meet her. "My little princess," the man said, wrapping his arms around his wife and daughter and pressing a kiss to the latter's head. "We've missed you so much."

"Queen," the woman corrected, though she laughed and embraced her daughter too. "She is a little princess no longer." Sanne had attended Cassander and Malaia's wedding, though she hadn't gotten any closer to the Akaris than she was now. Chieftain Khal Akari and his wife, Chieftess Lea Akari, had been seated in the frontmost pew of the temple; they'd spent the ceremony weeping happily over their daughter's marriage. "Look how long your hair has gotten!"

"She grows more beautiful every day, does she not?" Cassander called, striding into the receiving hall to greet his in-laws.

The Akaris opened their arms to him. Cassander disappeared into a mass of dark curls, richly embroidered traveling robes, and warm laughter. Sunlight streamed in through the arched windows of the hall and shone on the little huddle.

Sanne leaned against the wall. This was what she'd remember in the nights to come. The Stone had been blessedly quiet the night before, but with yesterday's influx of holy ones and the stream of guests who were set to arrive, all with hearts full of faith and holy awe, Sanne knew she was going to have many sleepless nights. But this, this happiness and familial love and devotion—protecting honest things like this was why she hunted. It made the exhaustion worth it. Cassander had lost so much; it was only right that the Akaris embraced him as one of their own, and it was only right that Sanne, one of the few faithful blood relatives he had left, would fight to preserve what little family he still had. Even his own mother had left the Stained Palace.

"Let me show you to your chambers." Malaia took her parents by the hand. After a kiss from Cassander, the queen disappeared with her parents down the hall.

Cassander turned and noticed Sanne, raising a hand to her in greeting. She fell into step beside him. "Have you heard from your mother?"

Cassander lowered his voice—a servant was approaching. "A letter from yours arrived last night," he said. "Neither my mother nor your parents are coming. Your mother worries it will be too great a strain on mine."

Annelore, Cassander's mother, had suffered a nervous breakdown when Oran died. She'd recuperated in just enough time to see her sons declare war on one another. The new grief had consumed her. When her doctors recommended that she get away from the Celesty, Sanne's parents had offered to host her at their country estate. Annelore had never returned.

"I'm sorry," Sanne said, though part of her was relieved. The mention of her parents called up a humiliating memory: her father Olek and brother Becan at the gates of the Keep, telling her they'd arrived to bring her home. They hadn't thought she would last more than a year in the Order. "But perhaps it's for the best."

The cousins fell quiet. Sanne realized Cassander was going to the war room. Yes, it was for the best that she and Cassander's parents would stay away. He needed to plan for his brother's eventual attack, and he couldn't do that if he was tending to his mother and hearing her weep over what had become of her boys. Sanne needed to destroy the Stone, and she couldn't do that if Becan and her parents were questioning her life's path. Cassander deserved the chance to reign without a mother's grief hanging over him. Sanne deserved to be taken seriously.

She left Cassander outside the war room and went to her chambers to get ready for the day. For the Order, the Lady Nightmare was enough. The Lady Nightmare was extraordinary.

But before the Stone, she'd fallen.

In Cassander's service, she'd fallen.

She picked up Peacebringer and ran her fingers over the blade. It needed to be sharpened. The next time she stood before the Stone was going to be the last.

———

Sanne was grateful for the thunder and the lavender-eyed ghoul that manifested that night. She didn't mind its howls. She didn't mind the way it gibbered and clawed and slashed her cheek open in three stinging places. She didn't mind that it took the form of Ren, then Cassander, then a man who was Cassander but ruined—a man with silver-blond hair, whose eyes had black sclerae and red irises. She didn't care that three of the holy ones, Hazecu and Lirwood and Vestel, heard her shout her word and opened their doors to see her drive a glowing Peace-bringer into the ghoul's torso. She didn't mind that it took her almost an hour to recite the banishment spell enough times for it to work; if anything, she welcomed the way her throat dried and her voice scraped against itself until nothing came out at all.

It gave her something easy to think about: hunt, slash, cast, dodge, kill.

It gave her a reason to fall to her knees in Svetlen's chapel, a gnawing pain knotted in her stomach. Emptiness whipped at her like a cold wind.

It gave her a reason to pray, and pulled between Cassander and the Stone, that was all she could think to do.

———

She stood at her post outside Vestel's door, bloody and mute, until dawn.

"You look like you've crawled from the third hell," the Eclipse said, passing by to take her post outside of High Priestess Sohli's room. Five guards followed.

Sanne kept her mouth shut—she wasn't sure if words would even come out if she tried to speak—and resisted the urge to knock the Eclipse into said third hell. Her copper-colored hair was neatly braided in a single plait down her back, her eyes were bright and alert, and her white armor gleamed. She'd evidently had an easy night.

Sanne stepped aside so the guard relieving her could take her place outside Vestel's door. With a nod of gratitude to the guard, she walked away without a word.

As there was each morning, a tray with a coffee press and cups waited in Sanne's sitting room. She decided to take her coffee in the bath and set a little table by the tub to rest the tray on while she soaked. The table was inlaid with mother-of-pearl, the same material as the Eclipse's mask.

I relished the opportunity to serve my king and to prevent this war from spreading, the Eclipse had snipped, and yet she'd failed. The Black Sun hadn't been dragged home. The Eclipse hadn't even negotiated the extradition of his commander, the Red Sky, or any other supporters. Cassander wanted to stop the civil war from involving other kingdoms, yet it seemed this was inevitable. Nocovostvo's refugee laws were ironclad—would Cassander's attempts to subvert them trigger retaliation? Would Cassander send men to Nocovostvo to retrieve the Black Sun by force?

Sanne's head swam. She closed her eyes and slipped under the cooling bathwater, forcing herself to think of the spirits she'd banished and the Stone that waited in the dungeons. That was her fight. That was her place in this war.

A muffled thud came from the world above. Sanne broke the surface of the water, drawing her arms across her chest.

A maidservant had entered. "Apologies, my lady, but High Priestess Vestel has called for you."

To drag Sanne into Zdesen's chapel again, no doubt. "Thank you. I'll go to her once I'm dressed."

The maidservant nodded and cleared away the coffee tray before taking her leave. Sanne dressed quickly, casting a forlorn look at her bloodied and sweaty Nightmare armor as she strapped into her plate. She'd have to ask someone to clean it before it stained.

The receiving hall buzzed with activity—Sanne heard the

din of its small crowd well before she reached it. She kept to the edge of the hall, hoping to slip past without a fuss. Cassander was in the center of the room, shaking hands and warmly greeting the arriving guests: King and Queen Villari of Zijustvo, Queen Aster Nettal of Rastlinostvo, and a Znoviostvan court official in a dark blue suit. They rotated around Cassander like the sun he was, their travel fatigue melting away from a moment in his orbit. He looked as if he didn't have a worry in the world.

Sanne desperately wished that could be true.

Hurry on. One of my faithful needs you.

"Leave me alone," Sanne grumbled. When this was over, she was going to lock herself away and sleep for days so no mortal or god could reach her.

You are the Lady Nightmare. You set an example. Act like it.

"And it is my example, not yours. I order you to leave me alone—"

Why? Because you fear me?

"I have more to fear than you." Yet they both knew it wasn't quite true.

How tired you must be from fighting me.

Sanne paused and bowed her head. "Svetlen—"

Zdesen's sigh blew back Sanne's loose hairs like a gust of wind. *Run as you always do. Yet your time is coming. You will tire, and you will fall, and I will be the one to catch you.*

Sanne murmured a prayer as she hurried away, the Svetlenic dialect falling from her lips as she disappeared from the receiving hall in a flash of gold.

"You sadden me, Lady."

Sanne's back was to the altar, so she was free to roll her eyes. "I'm sorry to hear that, High Priestess."

Vestel clucked her tongue. "A lie, even coming from a noblewoman's pretty lips, is still a lie. Didn't your mother teach you that?"

"I'd ask you not speak of my mother."

"I see. My deepest apologies."

She began to pray again. Sanne did, too, whispering in Svetlenic so she wouldn't have to hear the low, fluid hissing of Vestel's Zdesenic. She told Svetlen about her worries, her desire to run from the Stained Palace the moment the Stone was vanquished for good, and the guilt this desire stirred in her. She wasn't Ren. She wasn't their brethren. She wouldn't serve the Order like most Nightmares because she was no ordinary Nightmare—they would run, but Sanne would stay.

"I've finished."

Sanne flinched. Vestel stood behind her, hands clasped beneath the folds of her dark robe. "Where would you like to go now?"

"Nowhere." Vestel motioned at the nearest pew, but Sanne didn't move. "Very well. I can wait. You know that here and my chamber are the only places I need to be."

"And what are you waiting for?" Sanne asked, though she knew.

"You have things to ask me."

So ask them.

By the slick smile that crept across Vestel's face, Sanne knew she'd heard the parasite, too. She glanced at the chapel door. There were many things Sanne wanted to know—what Vestel had done to the Black Sun, what Vestel and Zdesen wanted to do to her—but she settled on the question most relevant to the matters at hand.

"The disturbance you told Ren and I about. Did you know it was the Stone?"

"I wasn't sure." Vestel's red ring glimmered as she stroked the edge of her robes. "As I told you, my fellow priestesses and I experienced an unexplained loss of holy connection three decades ago. A few years before, one of Svetlen's priestesses, Lara, translated a prophecy—you're familiar with it. The late king was very taken by it."

Sanne nodded. The "Lara" Vestel spoke of was Lara Sohli, the current high priestess of Svetlen's temple.

"Well, other than the purpose the late king made it serve, Lara didn't think much of the prophecy. Our loss, though, made her see its words in a new light. Zdesen's priestesses used to mingle with Svetlen's, and Lara shared it with us—she and I were the same age then, barely eighteen. We already had the 'twin flames,' she said, and she was afraid we were being affected by 'the weight of the stone.' 'The gods are dead,' she told us, 'just as my prophecy said. They won't speak.' She was convinced that we were somehow being devoured by a Prázeny Stone." Vestel sighed. "Lara was an anxious little creature when we were younger. We didn't believe her at first, but as weeks passed with our prayers going unanswered, I started to listen. I took charge and began requesting books so I could do some research, but before I received anything, our connections were restored."

Sanne looked at Vestel's hands. Other than being discolored from age, they were pale—not shadowed like Sanne and Ren's had become after the Stone drained them.

"We were never attacked as you were," Vestel said, "just...affected. I would wake in the middle of the night from stomach pains."

"Were there spirits in the temple?"

Vestel shook her head. "Only the pain, and only the quiet. When my lady returned, it was as if nothing had happened. We recovered and we carried on, but I never forgot. And then, almost thirty years later, you and your horned one came into my lady's temple reporting the same silence." The high priestess smiled, showing her white teeth. "I had an opportunity to get some answers, and you were kind enough to confirm my suspicions."

Sanne wanted to strike her. Anger flared in her stomach where there'd once been nothing but cold. She'd suffered for Ren and Cassander and her gods, yet Vestel had made her suffer for

Zdesen, too. For Zdesen, who reveled in fear, who loved to twist and taunt and take. "You used us."

"Yes. I won't deny it." Vestel paused. "But you cannot say my lady and I weren't helpful."

Sanne stepped closer. Vestel was taller than she was, but Sanne didn't care. In this palace, she outranked the priestess, and she wanted Vestel to know it. "You weren't—"

"Lady."

Sanne whirled. The Eclipse stood in the doorway of the chapel. "I must interrupt. Her Majesty asked me to tell you that the dressmaker is done with her ballgown and is ready to make the final adjustments on yours. Your presence is requested."

Sanne stared at the Eclipse for a moment, the tirade she'd been ready to unleash on Vestel dying on her lips. "I—yes. If you'll escort High Priestess Vestel back to her chambers, I'll meet the dressmaker now."

The Eclipse nodded and held a hand out. "High Priestess?"

Vestel smiled innocently at Sanne. "A new dress? How lovely. You'll be a vision, Lady." Her parting words were saccharine, the threat beneath them only for Sanne to know. "You'll make each of your gods very proud."

11.13.626

It was the night before the anniversary ball, and Sanne couldn't sleep.

The cause of her insomnia was twofold: she wasn't permitting herself to sleep, as she needed to be absolutely sure that the palace was spectrally silent, and she couldn't quiet her mind enough to rest. Vestel had used her as a pawn, and Ren, too. Now that she'd gotten the confirmation she wanted, what was she going to do with it? Would she try to take the Stone for herself? For her beloved lady?

For the Black Sun?

Sanne shuddered at the thought of the Stone in the hands of

Zdesen's faithful. Svetlen's light had been absorbed by the void rock so easily. She could only imagine the destruction that would rain down upon Jasniostvo if the Black Sun rendered Svetlen's faithful powerless. And the Order, with its pair of gods—would her cousin seek to destroy it, too?

She called holy flame into her palm and held the little golden blaze to her chest to comfort herself. The Stone had to be destroyed. It was the only way forward.

Her first patrol was uneventful. When the bells tolled three, Sanne walked the palace again. She started on the third floor and worked her way down like she had with Ren. The soles of her boots padded softly on the flagstones and runner-covered hallways. She wanted to run to the Stone and destroy it, but it was too risky—only the gods knew what would happen if the entity broke loose and fed on the holy ones.

Nausea washed over Sanne. No, she knew, too.

She slumped against the nearest stone wall and slid to the floor. The hideous feeling of being siphoned washed over her. A cruel cold settled into every bone and tendon and artery. A jumbled prayer fell from her lips, the dialects of her gods stumbling and falling into one another: Oddelenic, Svetlenic, Zikatic, and over and over again until the panic passed.

When Sanne lifted her head, the white-cloaked figure stood at the end of the hallway.

Its back was to her, so Sanne was able to rise, cast darkdrape, and follow without being noticed. The figure drifted down hallways, down stairs to the ground floor, and made no sound as it approached the secret entrance to the dungeons.

Sanne scowled. She would not lose it again.

She hissed the spell for lightlance and drew its ward in the air. She hurled the radiant spear, hoping to pin the cloak to the wall with it, but the figure dodged and rolled. White light flared in Sanne's vision and she cried out, temporarily blinded.

When her vision balanced again, the figure was gone.

Sanne swore. Who was it? *Who*? They had led her to the

Stone's threshold not once, but twice now, and had escaped her each time. Sanne was a hunter, the best in the Order. She wasn't supposed to permit escape.

She stepped toward the secret entrance. Could she open it herself? Was that where the figure had gone?

Heat burned on her skin, the warmth concentrated on her sternum. An unseen, though gentle, force pushed her back.

Not yet.

Svetlen and Zdesen spoke in unison, only the second time Sanne had ever heard them do so.

"Why not?"

Only Zdesen answered, and Sanne felt the words like a knife through her heart. *Because we know what lies below. And you are not ready.*

11.14.626

Esclarmondes wore golden plate armor into battle. Nightmares wore leather armor when they hunted. Sanne, however—whose battlefield was tonight a ballroom—wore a dress.

She also wore weapons, of course. Beneath her skirt, she'd strapped two daggers to her left thigh, and her dress had been designed to allow Peacebringer to fit in a hidden sheath down her spine. Its opal-laid hilt rested against her shoulders, camouflaged as a piece of metalwork that was simply part of her gown. As she milled about the ballroom, accepting condolences that her parents hadn't been able to attend, no one looked at Peacebringer twice. Most nobles were far too focused on her tattoo and missing fingers.

Sanne didn't mind the attention. She'd actually quite missed this: a reason to wear lip and cheek pigments, to put pretty things in her hair, to slip into a beautiful dress instead of plate or leather. Cassander had gifted her the hair combs, two golden suns studded with sapphires; she'd swept the top portion of her hair back with them and left the rest, which was wavy from being eternally braided, loose. The flowing skirt and right half of her dress' bodice were the same sapphire color as the stones. The rest of the bodice and the dress' high neckline were of a shimmering fabric that winked blue and red when light shone on it. Gold piping fragmented the panels of her gown. The dressmaker had clapped her hands and declared that Sanne looked like a butterfly; Sanne had held her tongue, but greatly disagreed. She thought she looked celestial.

She took a glass of sparkling wine from a passing tray, though she didn't drink—beautiful gown or not, she was here as a Nightmare, not a lady. When she focused, she could hear low rolls of thunder beneath the playing of minstrels and chatter of ball guests.

If she looked for it, she could see signs that something was amiss in the Stained Palace: bronze-armored Aurorals were posted along the perimeter of the ballroom, and some of the guests swirling about the dance floor were really Vallen's guards dressed in borrowed finery. Cassander's post-banquet welcome, which had started off the dancing, had been incredibly brief. He'd held Malaia's hand too tightly, as if afraid someone was going to tear her away. Sanne had seen the queen struggling not to wince, and Cassander repeatedly and apologetically kissing Malaia's hand when the dancing had begun.

The Eclipse stood near the front of the room. Like Sanne, she'd changed for the occasion, but unlike Sanne, was still in plate. The Eclipse's ceremonial plate was the same design as her usual armor, but a polished black instead of white. She looked every bit her namesake, void-like and dark, as Sanne approached.

"Lady."

"Eclipse."

A tense silence stretched between them, persisting despite the music and wine-tinged laughter of the guests. Sanne watched them dance. Women's gem-colored dresses swirled and snagged on the legs of the men who swept them around the floor. It was a beautiful sight. Cassander had employed mages to conjure sunlight; instead of muted moonbeams, the stained-glass ceiling cast vibrant multicolored light as it would in the day. A woman in a white dress was clothed in green, then yellow, then purple as her partner spun and dipped her.

The song changed, and the crowd parted as Cassander led Malaia to the middle of the floor. He bowed. Malaia giggled and took his hand, and the two began to dance. After a moment, Sanne looked away—the softness in Cassander's eyes felt too intimate for her to be seeing.

"Have you noticed anything amiss?"

"No," the Eclipse answered. "The night is going well. Have you seen anything?"

"No." And it worried her. The Stained Palace was full of faithful: the holy ones, the realm's other rulers, nobility Sanne knew bowed the knee to at least one god. She didn't want an attack, of course, but it had been so long without activity. A quiet spirit was a scheming one. What was the Stone waiting for?

The crowd shifted. For a moment, Sanne could see through it to where the six holy ones stood along the wall, chatting with nobles from their gods' respective kingdoms. Vestel, however, stood alone. Her head swiveled. The seven white eyes of her mask bored into Sanne. She raised a hand in greeting, her large red ring winking in the light and her white ceremonial robes flowing as she moved—were they white enough to glow in the darkness of a secret passage?

Zdesen's priestesses used to mingle with Svetlen's, Vestel had said. The Eclipse had been chosen from among Svetlen's priestesses, and Sanne had no real idea of how old she was—the bronze skin around her eyes wasn't wrinkled, but elves aged slower than humans did. Had she been among the priestesses when Sohli translated the prophecy? Had she felt the emptying? She'd been calm when Sanne told her about the Stone—was it because she'd already felt its effects?

"How old are you, Eclipse?"

The Eclipse kept her attention on the crowd, but scowled for a moment. "How old are *you*, Lady?"

By the gods. This wasn't the time for the Eclipse to feign offense. "Twenty-seven."

"I'm twenty-nine."

Too young to have been a priestess with Sohli and Vestel, then—and younger than Sanne had realized. She cleared her throat, abandoned the thought, and changed the subject. "The king and queen look lovely, don't they?"

The Eclipse nodded. "Indeed. His Majesty glows with divine light."

A familiar cold pain flared in Sanne's stomach, webbing itself between her legs and up her back. Gods. It was coming. She dug her fingers into her palms and said, "He's lucky to have you."

The Eclipse turned to her, confusion written across her brow—Sanne could count the kind things she'd said to the Eclipse on her right hand—but it smoothed when she saw that Sanne wasn't sneering. "It is I who am lucky to have him. He is everything." The Eclipse's hand brushed Saroszy, which hung at her hip. "He deserves my protection."

Sanne followed the Eclipse's gaze to the middle of the ballroom, where Cassander and Malaia swayed. The Eclipse's eyes burned with emotion, and Sanne recognized the flames: admiration, devotion, infatuation. Obsession.

Yet the flames died a second later. The Eclipse's gaze sharpened. "Do you see the dark cloak?"

Sanne swept her eyes over the crowd. Dancers moved about the room in undulating steps and patterns, and it was the irregularity in motion that Sanne noticed first: a figure in a black cloak strode, out of time with the waltz, through the center of the ballroom. Its head swiveled to the right, toward the holy ones, before swinging left toward the Eclipse and Sanne.

Two pale purple eyes glowed beneath the black hood.

An invisible hand curled around Sanne's innards.

"Dance with me," she muttered, setting her empty wine flute on a passing servant's tray.

"What?"

"I need to get close, and I don't want to frighten anyone. Dance with me."

The Eclipse frowned, but took Sanne by the hand. They slipped into the waltz. Bits of conversation flew past Sanne, discussions of mundane things: preferred ateliers, which breed of horse to buy, whether investing in oakwood or birchwood was more prudent in this economy. She ignored it all. The Eclipse moved them closer and closer to the cloaked figure, and Sanne flexed the muscles of her back. Peacebringer's blade dug into her skin. The entity liked her. She'd lure it away from the crowd, draw it into seclusion like a scheming lover, and then strike.

The waltz approached its climax. Strings screeched as the minstrels played faster and faster.

They were steps away when Sanne leaned close to the Eclipse and murmured, "Find Vallen. Get the king and queen out of here."

The Eclipse dropped her hands from Sanne's waist and slipped away.

Sanne whispered a desperate prayer to Svetlen, though she already felt the goddess' warmth seeping from her. The coldness in her stomach lurched against her lower spine—the cloaked figure was behind her.

Sanne turned. The golden rings she wore flashed purple beneath its gaze when she offered her hand. "Would you care to dance?"

The entity raised its head. Its eyes glowed in a featureless black void. "*Sweet Sanne.*"

A wave of cold rippled outward from the entity. The dancers around Sanne stilled. A woman behind her screamed.

The entity lifted a hand to take Sanne's, but the false hand melted into three whips of shadow. "*I thought you would never ask.*"

Sanne whirled, shouting at the crowd, "Go!"

The Stone entity threw back its cloak. The fabric, which Sanne now saw had been tightly woven strands of shadow, melted into it. The entity's body began to writhe and pulse beneath its outermost layer, reforming itself from a vaguely human shape into the torn, sagging form of a wraith. Thunder boomed, though there'd been no lightning.

Sanne tore Peacebringer from its sheath and thanked the gods she'd had the dressmaker cut two high slits in her skirt. The crowd, approaching hysterics, surged to the edges of the room. Women's cries pierced the air.

An undulating black tendril struck one of the hired mages in the chest. Sanne pirouetted to gain momentum and severed the tendril before the entity could begin to feed. The conjured sunlight flickered out, and the ballroom plunged into shades of eerie silver.

The entity roared and shot a spiked tendril toward Sanne. She froze for a moment—this was how it had gotten Ren—before remembering herself and diving away. But the hesitation cost her; when she rose to her feet, blood poured from a tear in her side. Her dress was ruined in seconds.

"What are you waiting for?" Sanne shouted at the crowd. They stared blankly back. Guards tugged at the nobles, but the guests seemed rooted in place, transfixed by the spectacle of a Nightmare's hunt unfolding before them. "*Get out!*"

The entity rose to the ceiling, hovering in the center of the twinkling brass chandelier. Cream-colored candles burned with golden flame—Svetlen's flame—and the entity breathed deeply, sucking the fire into itself. "*Yesss,*" it hissed, sighing with pleasure. "*A little taste before I feast.*"

Across the ballroom, Cassander pulled Malaia into a corner and shielded her body with his. Sanne summoned Marra and raised Peacebringer.

Her Umbral must have sensed Sanne's urgency, as she appeared immediately. Marra pressed her wings to her sides and barreled toward the entity, shrieking as she flew. The entity howled and turned to face Sanne.

"*I didn't want to hurt you*," it snarled, pointing a hand that dripped decayed skin at Sanne. "*But you seem intent on dying tonight, Nightmare.*"

Cassander lurched forward. "Sanne, *no*—"

"Get out!"

The entity shot at her like a dark meteor. She gripped Peacebringer and waited, waited, waited—

At the last second, she sidestepped, spun, and plunged Peacebringer into the entity's back, putting her entire weight behind the thrust. Unblood, slick and dark and shimmering in the moonlight, spurt onto her. The entity writhed, its howl of pain like wind rushing through a narrow pass. Its claws scraped Sanne's legs and arms, but she held fast. "I will send you to the lowest hell," she snarled. Sanne drew her lips back and spat. Her saliva landed in one of the lavender eyes and sizzled.

The entity hissed. One of its tendrils slipped into the cut at her side and thrashed around like a tongue between teeth. Heat burned around the wound—Svetlen's heat, sucked toward the tendril. "*Then come find me.*"

It disappeared. Sanne, with nothing to support her, fell. Peacebringer clanged against the slick tile. Blood, hers and the entity's, pooled around her. No one spoke. No one came forward to tend to her. The only sounds in the room were scattered sobs and Sanne's heavy breathing.

She stood and slowly turned, a snarl playing at her lips as she swept the crowd for someone who would *fucking listen to her*. How foolish were they, to just stand by and watch? Didn't they understand they could have died? "Captain." She raised her tattooed hand and pointed straight at Vallen. A drop of unblood fell from her extended finger. "Get the holy ones to their chambers."

He nodded. His path to the holy ones took him through the rivers of blood. They stained the bottom of his white cloak.

"Eclipse. Get our king and queen to safety." Sanne adjusted her grip on Peacebringer—she shook with rage. It was time to end this. "And the rest of you!"

She shifted Peacebringer into one hand and pointed it at the gawking crowd. Sanne cast nightsight, and a small part of her relished the way some nobles cowered when her eyes began to glow. They wanted to see the Lady Nightmare in action? They wanted to see her angry? Fine. "Visiting nobles. Esteemed guests. Go to your chambers, and by the gods, *stay there*. I won't have you getting in my way."

With a cry, Marra dove from the chandelier and soared through the ballroom doors to the dark hall beyond. Sanne adjusted her grip on Peacebringer with a flourish, drew a dagger, and followed.

It was time for the Lady Nightmare to bring down her prey.

———

She didn't stop until she stood before the Stone's pedestal. Her lungs burned. The gash in her side wept. A coldness shifted around in her, chased by coils of heat that flared erratically as if panicking—her godhood seemed to have found a mind of its own.

The entity, cloaked in itself once more, hovered in front of her. A translucent shred of shadow led from the small of its back to the Stone. Two hands, one with only three fingers, reached up and lowered its hood.

Sanne beheld a dark copy of herself, the glow from its lavender eyes illuminating lips drawn back from too-familiar teeth. "Do you think taking my form will slow me?" she snarled. "I've hunted wretches like you for nine years, spirit. I've gutted copies of myself more times than I can count."

The other Sanne laughed, though it was the rasping chuckle of the entity. "*Sweet Sanne,*" it said. "*You have hunted nothing like me. And it is* I *who will be gutting* you."

Her nightsight disappeared. The onslaught began, but this time, Sanne was ready. She anticipated the entity's false Peacebringer and blocked its strikes with the true sword, disengaging as quickly as she could to keep the void blade from touching her. Marra appeared from the shadows and dove at the entity, her body a blur through the oculus' beam of light as she flew.

Sanne's heart pounded in her chest. As she spun and blocked and slashed and dove, she imagined the shards of her heart dedicated to her gods glowing with light: golden and parti-colored and dark grey. Their three-part blessing of light and life and death spurred her on. She was mortal and divine and the area in between, and she fought in service of the gods. She would drive this blasphemy back in their name. She would protect her king, her poor cousin who'd lost so much. She would honor the Order and her gods and *herself*, the Lady Nightmare, the first and only one.

Sanne aimed Peacebringer and her daggers at the places she would have bled the most—upper thigh, inner wrists, her throat —and was rewarded for her cunning with the entity weakening. It backed into the steps leading up the pedestal's dais, stumbled, and fell. Unblood coated the stone floor.

A laugh, half relieved and half crazed from exhaustion, slipped out of Sanne as she advanced. "I told you, spirit." Her throat scraped, but she swallowed and continued on. "Do you feel it? Hell is opening for you."

The shadow Sanne shook its head. "*Cruelty is very unbecoming, Sanne.*" It pushed itself onto her elbows. "*You are too pretty for it. Too sweet. Your taste—ah, I remembered it fondly while I regained my strength. Though I wish he'd kept the horned one around.*" The form on the dais became Ren's, chipped horn and all. The entity sighed. "*He tasted divine.*"

Sanne had heard enough. With a cry, she stabbed Peacebringer into the entity's chest.

Something pierced her side in the same moment.

A copy of one of her serrated daggers, formed from wisps of

tenebrous essence, jutted from her side. The wound didn't bleed or burn as if her skin had been broken, but Sanne was overcome with immense, needling pain.

She screamed. The entity cackled and reached for the dagger; when its hand touched the hilt, the two morphed into one continuous spear of darkness, the tip of which was now embedded in her. It started to pulse. Horror flooded every one of Sanne's senses, the feeling so primal that all she could do was keen. A thread of golden light slipped down the tendril, lining it like a vein.

Cold rushed into her, the numbness of it starting at her fingertips and spreading toward her core—her heart. Sanne howled. This was hell, every level at once, to watch her godhood be stripped like this. The golden light changed to Zikat's color-shifting essence. Sanne's lungs spasmed, searching for air that was no longer there. Out of the corner of her eye, she saw the entity kneeling at her side, its jaw unhinged and its eyes rolled back in pleasure as it fed.

Cassander. Malaia. Ren. They would know she had failed.

Svetlen would know she had failed.

Sanne crawled up the dais. Her vision darkened with each second, and she no longer knew where the entity was—only that it was connected to her. It was watching her. It was feasting on her.

"Marra?"

But the gyrfalcon didn't come.

The godhood draining from her was now dark silver—Oddelen's essence. After this, there would be nothing left.

"*I told you,*" the entity murmured, its breath rank and cool against her ear. "*How does it feel to be gutted?*"

All she could see was her right hand, the tattoo bleeding into the dark and her veins again ruined, and the hilt of her sword. Peacebringer. If she could only get to Peacebringer—

But she was too late.

The entity's proboscis retreated from her. A contented sigh

filled the air around her. "*A Nightmare's divinity.*" The entity drifted toward the Stone. Sanne couldn't lift her head to see whose form it wore. "*Delicious. You've spoiled me for everyone else, Sanne. I hope that is some comfort.*"

It slithered into the Stone without another word. Sanne laid on the floor in a heap, empty and shaking and alone.

Up. She had to get up. She had to keep fighting. She had to warn Cassander. He—

Gods, her head ached.

Whose blood was she covered in?

What was pecking at her hand?

SANNE!

The voice was familiar. It echoed in her mind like a god's, but wasn't that impossible? Hadn't they left her?

GET UP!

No. Her gods hadn't left her.

They'd been taken.

Dull claws raked across her cheek. A palm she couldn't see struck her.

"Svetlen?" Even speaking her goddess' name hurt.

You wish. Let me in, Sanne.

"I can't—"

Yes. Zdesen's voice sounded ragged. *There's something it fears. We can hurt it, you and I.*

Sanne pushed herself up to a half-sitting position. It took extraordinary effort, and the pain was excruciating. "You're a parasite," she spat, blood flying from her split lip when she formed the "p." "You feed on fear—"

Svetlen is afraid. Do you think I consume her?

Sanne fell silent.

Svetlen is afraid, Zdesen repeated. *I can feel it. Her heart beats as mine, and its pace is so fast, Sanne. Lend me yours.*

Let me in.

Her goddess was afraid. Cassander was afraid. Everyone she

served in the Stained Palace, every guard and visiting noble and royal she'd pointed her sword at that night, was afraid.

And Sanne could fix it.

She shoved herself onto her knees. Her face was wet, though she didn't know if it was from blood or tears. "Zdesen." Though she tried to keep her voice quiet, it echoed like a shout in the cavern. She winced at the sound of the parasite's name on her lips —it sounded *right*. Sanne spread her arms and closed her eyes, tilting her head back as she'd seen the Black Sun do at his oath-breaker trial. Her voice trembled, and she hoped Svetlen would forgive her. "Help me."

———

The holy vessel that had been Sanne Esclarmonde rose to its feet. When the entity erupted from the Stone and howled at her, she roared back, and the sound rattled the Stone on its pedestal.

The vessel spoke the word of its blade. The Nightmare sword glowed, though its aura was different—still golden and warm, but now rippling with a silvered darkness that slithered beneath the glow. The entity dove, but the vessel was faster. Its blade connected with the Stone hard enough to slice off a piece, which skittered along the bloody floor into a dark corner.

The entity, stronger from its feeding, threw the vessel into the craggy wall of the cavern. It was just as well—Zdesen felt her lended time in the vessel ending. She slipped half-out of it and stroked its blood-matted hair, using the last of her reserves to hurl a bolt of dark energy at the entity. It shrieked and disappeared into the Stone. Before her hold on the vessel deteriorated—she felt it fighting her presence—Zdesen allowed herself a moment of satisfaction. Her deformed mouth curled into what, for her, passed as a smile.

Everything feared something.

Maybe now, this vessel would no longer fear her.

———

Sanne opened her eyes to a room full of darkness and pain.

Countless times after a hunt, she'd woken in a sickbed and immediately pushed herself up to see what injuries she'd sustained. Now, though, just holding her eyes open was too much to bear. The pain was all over, and it was varied; dull aches hovered at the back of her skull and along her spine, needle-pricks danced along her cut-up arms and legs, and hollow pangs pulsed in her stomach. She shivered despite the blankets piled on top of her.

"You're awake."

Sanne turned her head. Ren sat at her bedside, his face drawn. Had he been crying?

She shoved herself up and gasped at the pain, but managed to choke out, "You shouldn't be here. You can't be here, Ren, the Stone wants you—"

He reached out a hand. "But I'm not here, Sanne."

The hand that settled on her leg belonged to a different male, one with tousled, sand-colored hair and hazel eyes. He rubbed his thumb along her knee. A tiny thrill ran through her at his touch, followed by the memory of him crawling into her bed at the Keep when they'd been younger.

"Baer?"

"Why did you go, Sanne?" he asked. His voice wavered as if he was holding back tears. "This wouldn't have happened if you hadn't left the Keep."

Her heart cracked. Even now, nothing had changed? "I had to go." Her throat was raw. "My family needed me."

"But I nee—" Baer drew his hand back. He tipped his chin to the ceiling and took a deep breath. "I wanted you to stay. I wanted us."

Sanne's lower lip quivered. "Why didn't you say as much then?"

"Would it have mattered?"

Sanne wanted to scream. Of course it wouldn't have mattered —someone always needed a Nightmare more, and a Nightmare always had to go. The teaching sounded lovely and self-sacrificing, and it was, but it had also taught every Nightmare how to run. Baer, of all people, should have known that.

She dropped her head into her hands. She didn't want him to see the tears welling in her eyes. She didn't want him to see that he might have been right—maybe she shouldn't have left.

"You still wear your hair the way I showed you."

Sanne lifted her head and sobbed. Tovar sat by her now, his black skin and white hair almost glowing in the slight moonlight. He pulled his braid over his shoulder to show her, a boyish grin spreading over his face. Gods. He looked like a child—but the last time Sanne had seen him, they'd been eighteen. He *had* been a child.

She had no idea what Tovar had looked like as a man. His casket had been closed.

Sanne burst into tears.

"Oh, Sanne." The bed creaked, and cool arms settled around her. "It's okay." Tovar rested his chin on her head. "I don't hurt anymore."

It was wrong for Tovar to be comforting her. He'd been the smartass, the insufferable one, the friend who'd always made horrible jokes and ignored how everyone rolled their eyes at him. Sanne didn't need him to be comforting. She needed him to be real.

She tried to wrap her arms around Tovar, but her touch passed through him.

Sanne woke, truly woke this time, and cried out.

As it had been in her dream, the room was dark. Her body ached and throbbed and stung. But there was another pain, too, one she hadn't felt in the dream—her eyes burned with a cold fire, as if she'd touched them to ice. The moonlight in the room was too much to withstand.

"Lady?" It was a male's voice. She gasped, expecting Ren or

Baer or too-young Tovar to lean over her, but it was Vallen. He still wore his white armor from the ball. "You're awake. How are you feeling?"

She couldn't pretend. Tears sprang to her eyes. "Empty."

Vallen turned to the figure at his side. From the silver-lined silhouette, Sanne guessed it was a healer. "Fetch the holy ones."

Sanne closed her eyes—holding them open hurt. "Cassander," she rasped, "is he—"

"He and the queen are safe. None of the guests or holy ones were hurt." A gauntleted hand lowered onto her bandage-wrapped one. "You did well."

"Can I see him?"

"You need to rest," a female voice said. "Thank you for notifying us, Captain. We'll see to her."

"Where are the others?" Vallen was frowning. Sanne heard it in his voice. "And why is *she*—"

"We will see to her," the female repeated. "The others will join us."

"Very well." He was displeased, but an order was an order. "Good night, High Priestesses."

There was a soft clanking as Vallen left the room, and then silence. Sanne sensed two presences around her, one on each side of the bed.

"We've been waiting for you to wake," the female voice said. A hand, too warm to be an ordinary mortal's, lightly grasped Sanne's. "We've come to pray over you."

Sanne opened her eyes. High Priestess Sohli held her hand. A faint golden light emanated from her bronze hair and shimmering skin. Some of the cold melted from Sanne's eyes, though looking at the light hurt.

"'We'?" Sanne tried to sit up. She expected to find Hazecu or Rada, but it was Vestel who sat to her right. Sanne shook her head and looked at Sohli with wide eyes. "No. I don't want her to pray over me. I need Hazecu and Rada. I worship Zikat and Oddelen."

Sohli and Vestel exchanged a look, their mouths pressed into thin lines. "We didn't think you'd want them to see you like this," Sohli said.

Dread crept into Sanne's gut. "What do you mean?"

Sohli brought holy flame into her palm. Vestel took a silver mirror from the bedside and held it up for Sanne.

Her bottom lip was split, and there were cuts along her hairline and eyebrows—that was normal. She'd come to expect those injuries after a hunt. That wasn't what made her scream, what made Vestel clap a hand over her mouth to muffle the sound.

It was her eyes.

Before the Black Sun had sworn himself to Zdesen, his eyes had been green instead of she and Cassander's brown—when they were children, it had sometimes been the only way Sanne could tell her cousins apart. But when he'd sworn his oath anew, when he'd offered himself as a temporary vessel for Zdesen's power in his final trial, he'd left the encounter with horrible black and red eyes. It had made Sanne sick to look at him.

It made her sick to look at herself.

She shoved the mirror away and retched over the side of her bed, screwing her eyes shut and weeping. Her eyes had changed. The sclerae were black.

Vestel rested her hand on Sanne's knee. "You succumbed."

"I had to!" Sanne cried, wiping her mouth even though she hadn't vomited. By the gods. Vestel sounded proud. "The gods were—I was—" She dropped her head into her hands and sobbed. What had she done?

You're being dramatic, Zdesen murmured, but her terrible voice had none of the derision Sanne had come to expect.

"I had no choice," Sanne said, her voice muffled by her hands —her hands, which were again webbed with shadowy veins.

"It may fade," Sohli said gently. "That's why I've brought High Priestess Vestel."

When Sanne looked up, however, the downward turn of Vestel's lips seemed doubtful.

"Will you let us pray?" Sohli asked.

Sanne's gaze fell to the holy fire burning in Sohli's palm. She welcomed the pain in her eyes, her ruined eyes, when she beheld the golden flame. Svetlen's light would cleanse her. Svetlen's light would purge the parasite. "Yes."

Zdesen hummed in distaste. *You're wrong. Svetlen cannot destroy what is part of her.*

"Let Svetlen tell me that," Sanne muttered.

The high priestesses exchanged another look, but neither spoke. Sohli handed Sanne a pain tincture, one that tasted horrible when Sanne swallowed it. She took the second vial Sohli offered and downed it without hesitation when the high priestess said it was a sleeping draught. Sanne didn't want to be awake. She didn't want to think.

She fell asleep to the disharmonious sound of Sohli and Vestel's prayers.

———

Sanne dreamt again, and she wasn't supposed to—not so soon. Nightmares weren't supposed to have them.

She stood before the entity, and its form flowed between the shapes of everyone she'd ever disappointed: her parents, Becan, Ren, Baer, Tovar, Malaia, Oran, Cassander.

"*Little Nightmare girl,*" they—it—said. "*Well—a Nightmare no longer. How does it feel, Sanne?*"

Horrible. Indescribably horrible. "Show me what you really are," she said, too exhausted to shout.

The Stone entity returned to its original state: a faceless, vaguely male figure with luminescent lavender eyes. "*I am this,*" it said. "*I am hungry.*"

"What do you want?"

"*To feast.*"

Sanne swallowed and took a step forward. "Who brought you here?" she asked, suddenly afraid to hear the answer. "Who do you serve?"

Something writhed in the entity's face. By the light of its eyes, Sanne saw the sharp corners of a mouth curl into a smile. *"The universe, once. But now I serve man."*

11.16.626

"Sanne—"

"My king." Sohli's voice was firm. "She's resting. We have been praying—"

"She serves gods other than Svetlen." Cassander's voice pitched higher. "Where is High Priestess Rada? High Priest Hazecu? Sanne is a Nightmare. She needs a Nightmare's godhood."

Sanne opened her eyes, though the movement was slow. Her eyelids felt heavy as stone.

"Close them," Vestel, close by, hissed.

Sanne didn't, but she kept her head down as she sat up. "Cassander?"

She saw his boots step toward her. "Sanne!"

Sohli raised her arm so her tan robes blocked Sanne from Cassander and Malaia's view. "We must prepare you for what's happened."

"What do you mean?" Cassander was indignant. "She's alive. What could possibly be—"

He pushed past Sohli and looked at Sanne before she could prepare for it. Their eyes, which had once been the same, locked.

In Sanne's chest beat a heart of stained glass, but it was Cassander's heart she heard shatter.

"Sanne." His face was white as bone. "What have you done?"

So the high priestess' prayers had failed. She was still disfigured. The proof of her failure remained. Everything she could have said—*what I had to do* or *I survived* or *I tried* or *I'm sorry*—died in her throat. "Cassander—"

His shock disappeared. Fury replaced it. "What have you done?!" he bellowed, white-gloved hands clenching into fists at his side. Disbelieving laughter fell from his lips. "You know what that parasite seeks to do!"

A cold haze settled over Sanne. By the way she straightened, Vestel felt it, too—Zdesen was listening. Vestel cleared her throat. "My king—"

"You," he snarled, pointing at Vestel. "I should've had you removed from your position the moment my brother broke his oath. Has it become your mission to destroy my family?"

"Cassander."

He whirled back to Sanne. She was grateful that no candles burned in the room—his fury would set them all on fire. She had to make him understand. She had to calm him. "I conducted my hunt as I always do," she said, "in service of you and in service of the Order and the gods—"

"Which ones?"

"You know which ones. Svetlen, Zikat, and Oddelen."

Zdesen chuckled. *And now me.*

Cassander scoffed.

"Look at me," Sanne said, leaning forward. Though her muscles cried out in protest, she held out her arms so Cassander could see the dark veins peeking through her bloodstained bandages. "You know what I fought. You know what's happened to me. Cassander, it was—" A fresh wave of tears came, but she fought them back. She would not cry in front of him. "It was worse this time. I thought I was going to die—for all I know I *was* dying—and all I could think was that I had to warn you. The gods had been taken from me. I felt Svetlen's fear, and I—"

Cassander shook his head. "You serve other gods," he said, and Sanne wanted to scream. He wasn't listening. "You could have cried to Zikat for assistance, or Oddelen. Zdesen—" He froze. When he spoke again, his voice was as low and menacing as Sanne had ever heard it. "She's been after you."

Sanne looked down. The quilt that had been laid over her was black and embroidered with golden suns.

"She has a soft spot for you, doesn't she?" Cassander came to her bedside and leaned down. His face was inches from hers. She didn't recognize the inhuman look in his eyes, and had the fleeting fear that he'd sink his teeth into her like a ghoul. "How long, Sanne?"

"I will not and do not pray to Zdesen—"

Please. You already do. I hear everything Svetlen hears.

"You may not now, but you will!" Cassander shouted. He straightened. "You'll have to! Have you forgotten that *we've already seen this happen*?"

She hated how broken her body was. She wanted to defend herself on her feet. "I am nothing like the Black Sun," she hissed. "I will resist—"

Cassander barked out a laugh. "By the gods. What am I supposed to do with you?"

She had given his throne the last three years of her hunt. She had kept his secrets from the Order. She had risked her life for him. She had been torn from her gods twice for him. What would ever be enough?

"You could believe me," she said, her voice shaking with unshed tears. Her words seemed to roll like thunder in the quiet room. "You could trust me. I hurt it again, Cassander. I broke a piece off. I'm making progress." She was an Esclarmonde, tied to him by blood. She was the Lady Nightmare, the first and only of her kind. She was made of fire and devotion, and she burned to fix what she'd broken. "Let me heal, and I will try again."

He turned his back to her. Cassander pinched the bridge of his nose and began to mutter beneath his breath. Sanne recognized the cadence of the Svetlenic dialect, though it was interspersed with phrases in the common language—but that was alright. He was trying. "You would do this again? Expose yourself to it, for me?"

The human part of her wanted to press her hands to her head and scream, but the divine part of her—well, the part that would soon be divine again—was heavy with certainty. "Yes. You're my king, the rightful king. I protect Svetlen by protecting you."

Cassander stared at her for a moment, then turned to Sohli. "Get Hazecu and Rada in here." He waved a hand in Sanne's direction. "Fix her. I want the darkness in her eyes gone."

Sohli and Vestel exchanged a look. "We're not sure if that's possible, my king—"

Zdesen tutted. *It isn't.*

"Find a way, High Priestess. Your king commands it." Cassander left the room without another word. Sanne stared after him.

A soft touch brushed against her hand. "I'm sorry he's reacted this way," Malaia said. Tears glistened in her dark eyes. "Thank you for protecting us. I want you to know that it does not go unappreciated."

"Thank you, my queen."

Malaia knelt at Sanne's bedside. "I will speak to him, see if I can calm him. If there's anything I can do for you, Sanne, to make your healing more comfortable, please notify me."

Sanne knew she wouldn't, but she nodded anyway and thanked Malaia again. The queen smiled sadly and followed Cassander, her footsteps silent on the tile floor.

The high priestesses left after a time, too, when they realized Sanne wasn't going to speak.

Only when she was alone did she let herself cry.

11.19.626

Sanne passed the next three days in a blur of sleeping, sobbing, and rotting in bed while one of the holy ones prayed over her: Rada with the dawn, Sohli at midday, and Hazecu at dusk. It should have comforted Sanne to have her holy schedule once again, to feel the godhood returning to her bit by bit, but she only felt wrong. Zdesen's blessing, once welcomed in, had carved out a place for itself. There was a new hollow in her heart, an opening for a dark bit of stained glass, and the blessings of her three gods couldn't fill it.

Her mind recovered faster than her body did, leaving her trapped in bed with a growing anxiety and no way to seek recourse. When her eyes finally stopped aching, she spent hours staring at the door of her bedroom, waiting for Cassander to walk in and apologize. She asked each holy one for news, either of him or of activity in the palace, but they just shook their heads and began to pray. Sanne should have expected it. Of course Cassander would keep his movements quiet. And why would there be any spiritual activity? The Stone had gorged itself on her.

On the third day of her bedrest, Sohli brought a tray of fruit and honey when she came for midday prayers. "I thought you deserved a small treat," she said, and pulled up a chair.

"Thank you." Sanne pushed herself up and reached for a bowl of berries. Her mouth watered. The healers had only brought her unsalted chicken and porridge to eat, not wanting to upset her stomach while her body was healing, but she felt stronger today. She was allowed a bit of sugar.

Sohli set two corked vials on the tray. "Your tincture and draught first."

She sighed but complied, setting the berries down and swallowing the tincture. Thank the gods she was healing—she wouldn't be able to bear this taste much longer.

The drowsiness came immediately. Sanne set the bowl on her lap and reached for Sohli's outstretched hand. The priestess' touch was warm, her voice soothing as she beseeched Svetlen to spare some godhood for Sanne. Sanne's eyes drooped. She stared at the berries to keep herself awake: red raspberries, shining strawberries, pomegranate seeds swelling with juice. They were bright against the muted blue of the bowl. A line slipped, unbidden, into Sanne's head.

A hollowing carved in blue and red.

"High Priestess?" Sanne asked when the priestess had ended her prayers. She wanted to hear the prophecy. She needed to be reminded of the truth. Sleep danced at the edge of her mind, but

Sanne refused to take its hand and join the waltz. "Cassander's prophecy. Will you tell it to me?"

Sohli brushed a lock of hair back from Sanne's forehead. "Of course, Lady. I imagine it brings you great comfort in times like this.

> *There will come a time when the gods are dead,*
> *A hollowing carved in blue and red.*
> *A pair of twin flames, from each one ray glows,*
> *The other bound by the weight of the stone.*
> *Mother of light, goddess of fear,*
> *Safeguard the truth and all we hold dear.*
> *From the reborn gods to the time of the end,*
> *A new king rises, the goddess his friend.*
> *The goddess' blessing, bestowed with intent,*
> *Upon the one who will make his ascent.*
> *King of the fire, king of the ash,*
> *King of the radiance, his rule forever lasts."*

Sanne yawned and frowned—all she could think of was Vestel. "It scared you once, didn't it? The prophecy?"

Sohli had been stroking Sanne's hair, but her touch stilled. "What do you mean, Lady?"

"Vestel told me what happened to you decades ago." Sanne popped the last raspberry into her mouth and settled against her pillows. The berry's flavor washed over her tongue. "How you thought you'd been exposed to a Stone. After seeing what happened to me, do you think that's what happened back then? Isn't it odd that Cassander's prophecy mentions a Stone?"

"I'm not sure what you mean, Lady," Sohli said, her voice gentle. "Vestel misremembers, I think. You've gone through so much. You may be confused."

Sanne yawned again. "Maybe." Sleep pirouetted closer, beckoning Sanne to join its dark dance. It would be alright to waltz a few steps, wouldn't it? Oddelen presided over sleep, and he was good. Sleep was good.

"Rest, Lady. The world will make sense once you rest."

Sohli's hand was warm and comforting against her hair, the loving touch of a mother on a sick child, and Sanne fell fast asleep.

11.20.626

Sanne was out of bed and halfway to her mirror before she realized she was standing. She stilled, expecting an ache or stab of pain to come with the realization, but there was nothing. A relieved, awestruck laugh slipped from her. Sleep was good. Her gods were good.

She drew her robe tighter and continued to her full-length looking glass. For the first time in days, she wanted to braid her hair, and she wondered if the cuts on her face had healed as well as the ones on her arms and legs had—her limbs now bore thin slivers of new tissue instead of dark red rips.

Any bit of joy and relief Sanne felt vanished when she saw her eyes.

She leaned close to the glass and rolled her eyes for a better look. Her heart sank. When she'd first seen Zdesen's stain, it had resembled a drop of ink in water. Her sclerae had still been bright at the edges. Now, though, the darkness had spread. Sanne only saw white if she rotated her eyes enough to look at the very bottom of them. She turned from the mirror and sighed. Maybe the darkness would fade when she was able to visit the chapel and ask Svetlen to burn it away herself.

A little gold table to the side of Sanne's mirror held her favorite cosmetics and some hair clips; she divided her hair into quarters and reached for one, ready to begin braiding, but her hand knocked against an unfamiliar bottle. When she unscrewed the top of the dark glass vessel, she pulled out a dropper. A note rested beneath the vial.

Your king asked that I deliver this concoction to you. The healers believe it will brighten your eyes until High Priestess Sohli and I find a more permanent solution.

- A.V.

Sanne used the dropper to squeeze a bit of the milky white solution into her eye.

"Gods!"

It stung, but it worked—the darkness writhed about in her eyes like maggots in flesh, but she felt it retreat. When Sanne looked into the mirror, her sclera was white and clear as if she'd never succumbed at all.

She put the solution into her other eye before she lost her nerve. She'd bear the pain for some normalcy. Sanne finished braiding her hair and dressed in a sky blue tunic and dark leggings. She strapped a dagger to her thigh and left her room for the first time in days.

It was midday, and the halls of the Stained Palace were awash with color and light. Taper candles of every color burned in the halls without windows, in wall sconces and in brass candelabras on sideboards. Sanne inhaled the acrid odor of burning wicks and heat, grateful to smell something different. Her room stunk of sweat and the mustiness of a sickbed.

Voices carried down the corridor as she approached the receiving hall. She crept up the stairs to the mezzanine over-looking it, taking care to stay half-hidden in shadow as she looked onto those speaking.

Cassander and Malaia embraced the Akaris. Two brown trunks sat by the door. Four footmen waited for the royals to finish their goodbyes.

Malaia stepped back and wiped away tears. Her mother did too, clasping her daughter's hands and murmuring something

Sanne couldn't hear. She averted her eyes, jealousy simmering in her stomach.

Chief Akari clapped Cassander on the back, drawing him into a hug like he was just the chief's son-in-law and not also his king. "I have good soldiers waiting for my orders," he said. They separated and shook hands. "I'll send them to the Celesty as soon as we arrive home."

Cassander's response was too low for Sanne to make out individual words, but it was a question.

The chief nodded. "The plans are with the Eclipse. Work will begin as soon as we receive your approval."

Heat, pointed and intense, flared in Sanne's ribs. She gasped, clapping a hand over her mouth and ducking into the hallway in case she'd been heard. What was Svetlen warning her about? The mention of soldiers was concerning, yes, but Jasniostvo *was* at war —it made sense that Cassander would request soldiers from the kingdom's territories. The plans were no doubt related to the military assistance, but what were they for? Funding? Establishing a supply chain? Weaponry?

The voices in the receiving hall quieted. Sanne heard the grand doors open, then close after a few moments. She stepped onto the mezzanine and saw Cassander pressing kisses to Malaia's forehead. "We'll see them again soon, my love," he said. "Less than a year to go."

Malaia nodded, her face buried in Cassander's chest. Sanne crept forward, but before she could hurry to the other side of the mezzanine, Cassander looked up and saw her. Their eyes again matched, but Cassander just scowled.

"Let's go have lunch," he said to Malaia, and lowered a hand to the small of her back.

Sanne watched them go. Her hands trembled. She'd fought her way through Nightmare training. She'd lost two of her fingers. She'd lost one of her best friends and her parents and her uncle and a cousin and now, it seemed, the other one, though all she did was fight to hold onto him.

She didn't know how much more suffering she could take.

11.21.626

Sanne's hunt made her look like a madwoman.

She stalked the halls in the early hours of the morning with her arms crossed and eyes glowing red, muttering to a creature of shadow that the untrained eye wouldn't be able to see. If Sanne was honest with herself, she would've admitted that she missed Ren, and that was why she hadn't let Marra scout. She was tired of hunting alone. But Sanne didn't know how to be honest with herself, not anymore, so she'd summoned Marra and told herself it would be helpful to have something to talk to—even if that something didn't care what she had to say.

Sanne recounted everything she knew to Marra, ticking off each point on her fingers and ignoring how the gyrfalcon's beady eyes seemed to narrow each time Sanne started a new sentence. There was a Prázeny Stone beneath the palace. It fed on godhood, and was therefore a threat to Cassander, Sanne, any faithful person living in the palace, and the gods themselves. Sanne didn't know who put it there or why it was being kept active—though she believed it had something to do with Vestel.

"And on top of all that, you keep disappearing," Sanne said to Marra, who'd perched on Sanne's lifted forearm. "Where do you go?"

Marra fanned her tail feathers and snapped, her beak closing inches from Sanne's nose. Sanne sneered in return and flung Marra into the air, letting the gyrfalcon fly away for a moment's peace.

The Stone, the prophecy, Vestel, and now the plans Cassander had received—it all swirled about in her mind, a maelstrom of loose ends and hazy theories. Earlier that day, Sanne had tried to find Sohli or Vestel. She'd run into the Eclipse instead, who'd informed her that Cassander had sent the holy ones back to the Celesty. "And you'll want to administer another dosage of your drops, Lady," she'd sneered. "I can see the para-site's mark."

The only way Sanne could redeem herself now was to destroy the Stone. The anniversary ball was over. The holy ones were gone. The only thing stopping her was her own weakness.

She turned a corner. The hallway before her stretched long and dark, but at the end, something bright swayed from side to side.

The white-cloaked figure had reappeared.

Her hand curled around Peacebringer. Sanne was tired of guessing its identity. She was tired of theorizing.

She wanted to *know*.

Sanne cast darkdrape and followed the figure, silent as death and dark as night. It led her to the staircase, to the dungeon, to the secret passage below it. Her nightsight disappeared, and in the dark, Sanne's certainty wavered—it had been hard to assess the height of the figure from a distance, but this close, Sanne realized it was taller than she'd thought. Vestel was an average height—could it be the Eclipse, who was tall and slender and always armored in white? Would she use the Stone for Cassander?

They reached the cavern. Sanne paused in the mouth of the passage to see what the figure would do.

The entity manifested behind the Stone's pedestal. "*How kind of you to come. My pangs were just beginning.*"

The figure lifted its hands, removed its white gloves, drew a dagger, and slit the heel of its right palm. Blood welled in the cut, the red liquid gleaming in the white light from the oculus. The figure pressed its weeping, dark-veined hand to the Stone.

The entity sighed, its head falling back. Its pleasure was momentary, however; the entity narrowed its lavender eyes at the figure. "*This again?*"

The figure murmured something too low for Sanne to hear—too low, because the voice was too deep to be female.

"*I grow tired of feasting on meager amounts of one-note blood,*" the entity said. "*I want what I was made for: godhood, mixed godhood. Its taste is unparalleled. The ones you sent me were delicious—oh, the flavors! Citrus and vanilla and malt, and a bit of earth."*

The figure cleared its throat. "There is another flavor still," it said, "one you have yet to taste."

Its voice. Sanne knew it. She bit into her hand so she wouldn't vomit.

"Oh, but I have. Anise with the faintest hint of woodsmoke, yes? I taste a bit of it in you." The entity raised a dark finger and pointed at Sanne. *"But I taste it more in her."*

The white-cloaked figure turned.

Cassander's brown eyes were dark in the candlelight. "Put the blade down, Sanne."

Her heart rattled in her chest. The ringing in her ears sounded like shaking panes of glass. "How—" Her vision blurred with tears. She adjusted her grip on Peacebringer. "How, Cassander? *Why?*"

He held out a hand. "Come here."

She stayed where she was. His blood disappeared into the Stone, absorbed to the last drop. "What are you doing?"

The entity's eyes glowed brighter. *"He is tending to me,"* it said, drifting closer to the Stone. *"As he always has."*

Sanne dug her fingers into the heel of her palm. It hurt. This was real. "What is it talking about?" she hissed at Cassander. "Are you feeding it?"

Cassander raised his hands. His veins were shadowed like hers. Blood dripped to the cavern floor. "It has to be pacified, Sanne."

"How long have you been—?" She couldn't finish the sentence.

"It's been in the palace for almost thirty years," Cassander said. His voice was calm, steady, as if he'd simply been caught reading too late into the night. "But I've fed it since I took the throne."

"Why?" He'd known the entire time what hid in this cavern, and he'd let her face it not once, but twice. *Twice* she'd been torn from her gods. She'd endured that hollow pain for him, thinking she would shoulder it so he wouldn't have to suffer that emptiness —but he'd known it all along. "It will ruin you—"

"It won't." Cassander stepped closer, his hands still lifted as if he was calming a spooked animal. The entity slithered back into the Stone. "Let me explain."

"What's there to explain?" Her voice pitched to an almost hysterical level. "You know what this thing has done to me. To *Ren*—I almost lost him to the Stone! How can you sustain it? Why didn't you tell me you knew about it? Cassander, by the gods—" She swallowed. She didn't want to ask this question. "This Stone is a divine affront. You know what the legends say, don't you? It ate the gods' divinity in the old days. Why would you betray Svetlen this way, when she's chosen you?"

"I know what it is," Cassander said, walking down the dais toward her. "But you were never supposed to. I had always been enough to keep its entity contained. It had always obeyed me. When the spirits started manifesting, I truly didn't know they were born of the Stone. You must believe me."

Sanne shook her head. He'd sat at her bedside the first time she'd had the godhood prayed back into her. He'd seen her veins. "Even if you didn't know at first, you knew by the time Ren left. You knew what I would be facing alone."

"You were content to face it alone—"

"Because I thought I was doing it for you!" Didn't he understand? He was her king. Her blood. Her family. She would have done anything he'd asked, not just because her contract demanded it, but because she loved him. Svetlen loved him. "Not because of you! I thought I was protecting you from something that would strike down Svetlen's chosen king. I thought Zdesen and her ilk were working against you!"

Cassander's face twisted into an ugly sneer. "*They are,*" he snarled, seizing her face in his hands. His palm was sticky against her cheek. "That's why we need the Stone. You were there when the Black Sun swore his oath to Zdesen. Don't you remember the destruction he wrought in his final trial? How powerful her influence made him?"

She remembered how the Black Sun had stood against a horde of monsters before being commanded to invite Zdesen in. He had. He'd gone without sleep for a week, and the parasite rewarded his submission with everything his exhaustion made him lack: awareness, cunning, strength, magic, endurance. Power. She'd revived him, and it had been a slaughter. The arena had become slick with blood. "Yes."

She saw herself reflected in the whites of Cassander's eyes. "I'm trying to stop that from happening to us," he hissed. "He wants the throne. He would take my queen." His eyes searched hers, but Sanne didn't know what he was looking for—understanding? Sympathy? Surrender? "You know how my brother is. You know things will only get worse. The Stone is going to be used as a weapon of war. Zdesen's influence will be drained from him and his traitorous army, she'll be cast out, and we will be victorious. That's why I sustained the Stone, and that's why I need you."

No. She couldn't allow the gods to be used like this—to be drained from their faithful to power their own destruction. It was sacrilege. A god was a god. Sanne tried to shake her head, to tear herself away, but Cassander held her too tightly.

"I was enough for the Stone until a month ago. It got a taste of you, and suddenly I wasn't good enough." His voice dripped with resentment. "It woke up hungry, but only for you. It wanted Nightmare godhood." His nails dug into her skin. "So when you offered to continue your hunt for it, of course I let you. I had nothing to fear. You would be busy, and it would be fed. You can't defeat the Stone, Sanne." He began to laugh. "We can subdue it, but there's no destroying it. We can only use it."

She put her hands on Cassander's chest and shoved as hard as she could. He stumbled, the edge of the cloak tangling in his feet. Sanne raised Peacebringer and charged the Stone—this *thing* had corrupted Cassander—but the entity shot from the Stone and wrapped itself around Sanne. She cried out and thrashed, but it was too much. The entity twisted around her like ropes and threw her to the ground at Cassander's feet.

"*I want her. Let me eat.*"

Cassander shook his head. "She's only had days to recover. Wait. Let her divinity ripen again."

Ripen, as if she was a fruit to be sliced and served on a tart. She wanted to vomit. "You know what's happened to me," she said. "How I've been ruined. Why do you think the Stone, when you unleash it, won't also hurt you?"

Cassander smiled. "Every good poisoner knows to build up a tolerance."

Conviction sparked in his eyes, and Sanne understood that the Stone hadn't done this to him. She wasn't going to save herself with reason. "This is madness."

"This is war." He knelt at her side. "I've been thinking, Sanne, and I need to revoke a promise I made to you. I can't set you free of your contract." His gaze ran over her bound body, over the leather armor and tattoo that marked her as a Nightmare hunter. "I'll need someone with your strong faith by my side in the coming years. The Stone needs you, too. It's become accustomed to regular feedings."

Her stomach twisted. "I won't be its sustenance," she hissed. "I won't let you use me—"

Cassander picked up Peacebringer. "I'll ensure the chapels are staffed with holy ones to restore you. It won't be so bad."

"You can't ask this of me. I'm your cousin—"

His eyes flashed. "I'm not asking. And you are my subject."

She almost wished he'd stabbed her. It would have hurt less than the revelation before her, that he'd never cared about her as much as she did him. Sanne felt her godhood writhing about, Svetlen's heat flooding her back in an attempt to get away from the Stone. "Cassander, *please.*"

"*I want to eat, king.*"

Cassander drew the hood of his cloak over his head. He

slipped white gloves back onto his shadow-veined hands and rubbed his thumb along Peacebringer's pommel. "Very well. But only a taste."

———

Sanne regained consciousness in just enough time to see a cell door close in front of her. Vallen locked her in, his expression as blank as if she was a common criminal.

"Vallen!" She scrambled to her feet. Her vision swam. "Let me go. Cassander is—please, Vallen, you have to let me out."

He turned on his heel and walked away.

"Vallen!" Her scream echoed down the dungeon hallway, but the captain didn't stop.

Sanne rattled the iron bars, tested the door, kicked at the lock —nothing. She leaned against the bars and cast nightsight to inspect the cell around her. It took two repetitions of the spell for the redness to color her vision. Her heartbeat, which was painfully quick, slowed a bit. She was weak, but she still had her magic. The Stone hadn't taken everything.

The cell she'd been thrown into was at the end of a dark hallway. Every cell around her was empty—she could see straight through the bars to the cells at the far end of the hall, and she neither heard nor sensed anything to indicate the presence of another person. Roots grew along the walls. Groundwater ran down the stone. The cell grew cold as Sanne walked toward the wall, and she stumbled as if jerked forward. Dread coiled in her. She called holy flame into her palm and reached for the stone.

The flame was sucked into the wall's crevices, and Sanne recognized her cell. The Stone hadn't taken much this time. It was likely still hungry, and here she was, being preserved for it like a cut of meat.

Flames, golden then orange, blazed to life in the sconces hanging along the walls. Her vision washed pink and white, and

Sanne recalled nightsight. The sounds of booted footsteps and clanking metal echoed toward her.

The Eclipse came to a stop in front of Sanne's cell, a flame in one hand and a large, bulky sack in the other. Her white armor was pristine despite the grime of the dungeon. Saroszy was at her hip, and a second sword hung at her back. Sanne's heart twisted when she saw the opals in its hilt.

Sanne lunged for Peacebringer. "Let me go!"

The Eclipse swatted at Sanne's hand with her fire. "I don't negotiate with those who have betrayed my king," she said, raising the torch and peering into Sanne's eyes. "Disgusting."

Rage, white hot, rolled over Sanne. She no longer felt the writhing in her eyes—the drops had worn off again. "Let me go."

"Put this on." The Eclipse shoved the sack through the bars, twisting it until the contents had shifted enough for it to slip through. It fell to the floor with a clatter, the burlap cut open to reveal a wink of gold—Sanne's Esclarmonde plate.

"Why?"

"This is a serious occasion. You need to remember who you are." The Eclipse stared at Sanne. Sanne stared back. "Well? What are you waiting for?"

Sanne glared at the Eclipse as she removed her leather armor. Her daggers had been stripped from their sheaths, and she missed their weight. The Eclipse hadn't brought her any clothing, so Sanne remained in her black tunic and leggings as she buckled herself into the shining plate. She'd been given Peacebringer's scabbard, too, but it hung empty at her back.

"She's ready, my king."

Cassander appeared in front of the cell. He wore his Esclarmonde plate, too, and his golden diadem sat atop his blond curls. He was a vision in the armor, a shining vision of grace and health and power. Though there was no sunlight this far below ground, his armor reflected the firelight onto Sanne. Her plate reflected it back, and the two Esclarmondes seemed to glow.

He held a familiar piece of parchment and a quill out to her. "Sign your contract."

"No."

"I'll let you go back to your room if you do," he said. "Think about it: your bed, your clothes, your weapons, a warm bath and hot meals. The holy ones have already been notified that you need them. High Priestess Sohli has returned, and is waiting to fill you with Svetlen's light again."

Sanne drew her lips back. "How dare you speak Svetlen's name," she spat, "you, who would forsake her for the slightest bit of control—"

"Quiet!" Cassander snapped. "Sign the fucking contract, Sanne."

"No!"

"Fine." He rolled the parchment back up and gave it to the Eclipse. "Then I'll be sure to have your Order sign it. I'll tell them you've fallen ill and cannot sign it yourself. I'm sure you remember, from when you signed it with my father, that only two of the three parties need to agree?"

She did. The Order had wanted the ability to recall her, but now she wondered, deliriously, if they'd known something she hadn't. "They wouldn't sign me away without asking me—"

"Then I'll contract someone else."

Sanne barked out a laugh. By the gods, she was tired of being threatened by Cassander. She was tired of dancing around his needs. What good had it ever done her? "The Order doesn't regularly contract Nightmares. I was an exception made for your father because of our position. You know that."

"Then I'll invade your Keep and take a replacement by force." His eyes flashed. "Maybe Ren."

"You'd have to find it first." Sanne's voice shook. She didn't want to add to her list of lies, but it was the only way she could think to protect the Order—to protect Ren. "I don't even know where they are."

Cassander watched her for a moment. She'd started to cry

again. Were the tears making her dark eyes glitter in the light? Were they making tracks through the dirt on her face? "You really won't sign?"

"No."

"Very well." Cassander held out a hand. The Eclipse gave him another scroll. He opened it and began to read. "'Sanne Olekria Bastillen Esclarmonde, Lady Nightmare sworn in service to the Crown of Jasniostvo, you are hereby charged with high treason and heresy—'"

"*What—*"

"'—for your actions against His Majesty King Cassander Annen Calara Esclarmonde, the Radiant Sun of Jasniostvo. You are accused of the following: doubting the Sohli Prophecy, therefore questioning His Majesty's place on the throne and challenging the goddess Svetlen's grace and providence; allying with a suspected accomplice of the Black Sun, traitor to the throne and implement of the dread goddess Zdesen; tampering with Jasniostvan royal armament; and exposing an outsider to the Crown's secrets.'" Cassander lowered the scroll. "How do you plead?"

"Plead?" she asked, her throat thick. Three years of service. Three years of standing at Cassander's side, watching Oran die and the Black Sun betray his family, and comforting her king through it all. Three years she should have been serving the Order. Three years of her life she had sacrificed for her bloodline and her goddess, all to be desecrated by one word: heresy. "Is this my trial as well?"

Cassander pressed his lips together. "I offered you a way out. You refused to take it."

"My king!" Vallen shouted. "We've found her. She was in her temple."

Cassander and the Eclipse moved aside. He gestured to the empty cell across from Sanne's. "Good. Bring her in."

Vallen and a small retinue of guards dragged a body down the hall. They threw it into the cell, where it fell against the stone floor with a thud. A sharp crack echoed through the dungeon.

"I must thank you, Sanne, despite all of this," Cassander said. "You've given me an undeniable reason to finally arrest this filth."

The body in the cell rose to its feet. Black robes settled around it. A bone mask, painted black except for seven white eyes, fell to the floor in halves.

"You've arrested a high priestess?" Sanne gasped. She rushed to the bars. Vestel's shoulders shook. "Cassander, no king has ever done this. The gods will be furious—"

"Do you think the gods care about Zdesen?" The question was for Sanne, but Cassander directed his words to Vestel. "She is a leech, a parasite soiling the back of our bright lady's head. Svetlen will not begrudge me for this. High Priestess Sohli is ready to beg for my absolution."

Sanne tensed, waiting for Zdesen's claws to tick down her neck, but nothing came.

"Leave Sohli out of this," Vestel said, her back still turned. "She has suffered enough for your throne."

"Sohli doesn't remember her suffering," Cassander said. "She looks upon me with great favor. It's something I'm sorry, Vestel, that you could not do." He stepped to the bars of Sanne's cell. "Because I'm feeling merciful, Sanne, I will give you the night to think. You know what you've done. You know the offenses you face, and you know what you can do to be forgiven." He pushed the contract through the bars. "Sign, and you won't be written into history as a traitor. Your plate will mark you as a loyal Esclarmonde instead of the shining heretic you have become." He reached through the bars, cupping her face and lowering his voice so only she would hear his parting words. Only she would see the mask slip, see his eyes shining with tears. "I've lost so much, Sanne. Don't make me lose you, too."

11.22.626

Vestel's eyes, as it turned out, were blue.

She sat on the floor of her cell, twisting her ring with the ostentatious red stone around on her finger. Marra, who'd hopped from the shadows without Sanne calling her, sat on one of the folds of Vestel's robes. Sanne had expected the high priestess to either be stunningly beautiful or excessively ugly; in truth, she was quite plain. Her eyes were big and long-lashed, her cheekbones high, yet her lips were thin and her nose slightly crooked. She looked like any citizen Sanne would have passed in the Celesty, someone whose appearance wouldn't warrant a second thought.

Sanne found it a bit comforting.

The prisoners hadn't spoken to each other since Cassander and his entourage had left the dungeon—they'd bowed their heads and prayed to their goddesses, Sanne slipping out of the Svetlenic dialect only to huff at Marra for choosing Vestel over her. Perhaps her traitorous bird had been spending her time with Vestel instead of scouting.

When she returned to her prayer, she continued it until her throat rasped and the words became stuck. When she couldn't speak anymore, she cried. Svetlen would see her tears. So would Zikat, and Oddelen, and maybe one of them would comfort her. Maybe one of them would rebuke the crawling cold she felt seeping out of the cell's far wall. The Stone wanted her, and it was reaching for her. Sanne knew that if its pain-ridden fingers wrapped themselves inside of her and pulled, she would have to go.

It could have been minutes or hours, midnight or dawn. The dungeon had no windows. Sanne had no way to know.

"Your suspicions are correct," Vestel said, her voice soft in the quiet. "I've communicated with him."

Sanne sighed. The admission should have surprised her, but she doubted little could anymore. "Does he know about the

Stone, then?" Would the Black Sun's forces one day invade the Stained Palace to find her half-rotted in this cell?

"It's been a while since I've written. It isn't easy to get word out of the Celesty without someone else knowing."

A chill crept into Sanne's belly and stroked, the sensation like a finger running up and down her intestines. Heat pooled around it, drawn to the cold. A god was a god, therefore a priestess was a priestess, and Sanne desperately needed comfort. "It's reaching for me," she blurted, tears rushing to her eyes. "It's hungry."

Vestel gripped the bars of her cell. "Fight it."

Sanne grabbed her cell bars, too, hoping it would keep her from following the cold pull into the sub-dungeon. "I'm scared, Vestel. He's going to keep me here. He's going to use me to feed it, and then he'll—" Sanne sobbed and let her head fall against the iron bars. "He's going to use me to wipe away the gods' power. He wants to use the Stone to cripple the Black Sun. He doesn't care that it wants every kind of godhood. He thinks he can withstand it, but the rest of us—" She choked on her words. Cassander hadn't felt the raw emptiness like she had, missing the divinity of three gods to his one. He hadn't known how weak she'd felt. "We need the gods."

"Sanne."

She looked up. Vestel was reaching for her.

"You're not going to like what I have to say, but you must listen." Vestel's eyes were wild. "You must take this information to the Black Sun."

Sanne felt the color drain from her face. "What? You know I can't go to that traitor—"

"Be careful with that word. It fits you now, too." Vestel withdrew her hand. The distance between them was too great. "You must tell him what Cassander plans to do. He is one of my lady's most faithful. Together, they may be able to stop this. I can do no more." She gestured to Marra. "There are tunnels leading from here to my lady's temple. Your cousin used them. Your bird knows them."

Sanne shook her head. "If I get out of here, I will stop Cassander. And I won't need to ally with the betrayer to do it."

"Who will you rally?" Vestel snapped. She jabbed a finger at Sanne's eyes. "My lady has marked you. Who will come to your aid other than him? Who will understand what you've been through other than him?"

Sanne closed her eyes. She waited for the taunting remark from Zdesen, but none came—they were likely too close to the Stone. Any manifestation of a god would surely be sucked into it.

"Who will believe Cassander's true plans, other than him?" Vestel's voice was barely a whisper. "Cassander is golden. He is beloved. We were both at the ball. We both saw the kings and queens who came to support him during his time of great trial. Who will you rally?"

"You're manipulating me—"

"I'm trying to free you! You are a Nightmare. You understand what it is to have a divine call, a holy cause. We've been watching you, Sanne, my lady and I, and she has use for you. Go to the Black Sun." Vestel lifted her hand, which sparkled with the red stone. "Use the tunnels to flee to my lady's temple, and shatter this ring. It will take you to him."

Despite her fear, Sanne's lip curled. "No. Svetlen has use for me, and Zikat, and Oddelen—"

"So what is one more goddess?"

"This goddess is a parasite!" Sanne's shout echoed in their cells. "Zdesen took the blessed light given by Svetlen and used it to reveal the horrors lurking in the world. She manipulates Svetlen's domain to increase her own."

Vestel was quiet for a moment. "Svetlen's light only showed what the gods had created," she said, "and my lady was born of their fear. Why don't you blame them for her existence? They created the horrors of this world, and Zdesen was made to help them cope. You fundamentally misunderstand her, yet you curse her at the top of your lungs." She turned her back to Sanne. "You blaspheme. Perhaps you are a heretic."

"I am no such thing."

"Then you're a coward, too afraid to face the truth."

Sanne wiped the tears from her eyes. Fine. Given the choice, she'd rather be a coward. "Cassander is the first-born son. He sits on the throne by that right as well."

Vestel sighed. "Even if you don't believe the Black Sun's claim that that's a lie," she said, "would you let a matter as stupid as primogeniture put someone on the throne who would threaten our gods? You're too afraid of men and their laws. It would do you good to—"

Firelight flickered in the sconces, shifting from orange to gold. Sanne and Vestel leapt to their feet. Guards charged into Vestel's cell. Cassander watched as they seized the high priestess and opened Sanne's cell door.

"You," Cassander growled, jabbing his finger into Vestel's face as she was dragged past him. He clutched a note in his hand. "You and your goddess have ruined my family, yet you keep trying to take what little I have left. I should have done this years ago."

"Cassander, what—"

He shoved the crumpled note at Sanne, a half-written missive that read, *Go to the Black Sun. He knows you have—* "The Eclipse found this left in the priestess' guest chamber. She was writing to someone." He glared at Sanne. His eyes were wild. "You, perhaps?"

Sanne paled. What was the note supposed to say? *He knows you have found the Stone*? "I don't know—"

Cassander strode into Sanne's cell with the Eclipse at his heels. "You have hours to decide, Sanne," he spat over his shoulder, grabbing Vestel by the collar. "I'll pardon you if you cooperate. This doesn't have to hurt."

He opened the secret passage to the Stone, and he and Vestel disappeared inside.

Sanne screamed and threw herself at the entrance. The Eclipse grabbed her by the braid and threw her into the cell bars. "You should be grateful this is happening," she hissed. "She will help us bring down the Black Sun—she, the woman who made him. Isn't that beautiful, Lady? Don't you see the poetry?"

Sanne could only cry. She didn't dare speak Vestel's name.

The cold clutch around her innards loosened and, too quickly, disappeared.

It was done. The Stone had been fed.

The Eclipse released her. Sanne collapsed. She didn't like the sensation that hung in the air now, a heaviness she'd only felt when past hunts had taken her to fresh graves. It was the heaviness of Oddelen's thick robes settling around his newest charge and ushering them into his arms. It was the heaviness of death.

Vestel had been drained of her divinity before the end. Had she felt Oddelen's comfort? Or had she died alone?

The corpse was dumped in Vestel's cell—Sanne heard rather than saw it, for she couldn't bear to look. Footsteps retreated from her cell, and the entrance to the Stone ground shut.

"Hours, Sanne. I don't want you to meet this fate."

Metal clattered to the ground in front of her. "Another option to save yourself, if signing the contract isn't good enough," the Eclipse sneered. She leaned down. "My king is adamant that it must be you, but I'm not convinced. Take the coward's route, Sanne. We will find another Nightmare."

———

Sanne sat in the dungeon, alone with a corpse. It had already started to smell.

If she was crying, she couldn't tell. Everything was numb.

Her mother, her father, her brother, the trainees and instructors at the Keep who'd doubted her place there, so few yet so vocal—they'd been right, in the end. She'd broken. She'd failed.

Peacebringer rested across her lap. Her plate was cold and heavy against her skin. The Order, the Esclarmonde line—she'd had supporters in them, too, but it did her little good now. There was Baer, but she'd broken his heart. Ren was gone and happy. The Black Sun was a traitor, and Oran and Tovar were dead.

Sanne closed her eyes. If she died in this cell, who would welcome her to the other side—Oddelen or Tovar?

A hollow ring came from her golden vambrace. Marra had tapped it with her beak.

"Stop," Sanne whispered. "I probably don't have much time left. You don't have to stay."

The Umbral's pecks increased in number and tempo. The tinny clangs rang in Sanne's ears.

"Marra, I said stop!" Sanne opened her eyes.

A dark figure hunched over the body in Vestel's cell. Sanne froze—there was no way the figure hadn't heard her. Was it the entity? Had it come to scavenge for remains?

The figure drifted into Sanne's cell. It remained cloaked in shadow until it raised a hand. The fire in the nearest sconce blazed brighter. The light shone golden, then silver, then a combination of both.

Vestel hovered in front of Sanne, her mask reformed. Her lips shone blood red, and her voice was sweet as sun-warmed honey. **Hello, my child.**

Sanne's mouth went dry. It was Vestel, but not—the priestess' hair had been auburn, yet this being's hair fell long and blonde from its hood. Golden curls brushed against the black mask. "Svetlen?" Sanne whispered, shifting Peacebringer and rising to her knees. "Is it really you?"

Vestel's mouth smiled. **Not** *quite*. The second word was a yowl, the voice twisting into one Sanne had only heard in the back of her mind.

Vestel lifted one of her hands, the skin of which had shriveled and sagged, to her other, which was tan and smooth. The shriveled hand worked Vestel's red stone ring free and dropped it. The ring fell, slowly, to the floor at Sanne's feet.

The shriveled hand rose to the bone mask. It fell to the

dungeon floor and shattered. Vestel's other hand, now faintly glowing, reached for Sanne.

Sanne beheld the shifting faces of the joined goddesses. She wanted to scream. She wanted to cry. She wanted to throw her arms around the goddesses' waist and sob into the folds of their robe like a child.

But all she could do was stare—stare and finally, finally, understand. The same body housed each goddess. The same heart beat in each chest. A god was a god. Holy was holy. Svetlen was Zdesen and Zdesen was Svetlen, and Sanne was theirs. She'd been a fool to let her king tear them apart.

The eyes behind Vestel's first mask had been blue. The eyes behind this one were black and red, the sclerae dark as midnight shadows and the irises red as blood.

Our child. You are ready.

The gap in Sanne's stained-glass heart filled in with a new shard: dark brown and slick like a spirit's unblood.

Sanne reached up and took the goddesses' hand.

THE SHINING HERETIC
(OR, SANNE ALONE)

Esteemed Members of the Triumvirate,

I'm writing to notify you that I've abandoned my contracted post in the service of King Cassander Esclarmonde of Jasniostvo. I did not make this choice lightly. I request a meeting with you as soon as possible to discuss the circumstances of my desertion. I don't feel safe putting the details in writing, but a great danger to the Order is being cultivated in Jasniostvo. Where is the Keep currently located?

If you receive the documents to renew my contract before we're able to meet, I beg you not to sign them. I beg you not to send any Nightmares to the Stained Palace, the Celesty, or the surrounding areas. At the least, they would be at risk of mortal or divine injury, and at most, doing so would jeopardize their lives. The gods know I fear for mine.

Sanne Esclarmonde
11.23.626

SANNE,
YOUR LETTER WORRIES US GREATLY. IT MAY COMFORT YOU TO KNOW THERE ARE NO NIGHTMARES CURRENTLY IN OR NEAR THE CELESTY, SAVE YOU. WE'LL ADVISE ANY NIGHTMARE WHO GETS CLOSE TO THE AREA TO EXERCISE THE UTMOST CAUTION.
WE'RE LOCATED IN TMADREV FOREST, APPROXI-

MATELY THIRTY-FIVE MILES SOUTH OF THE ZIJUSTVO-
JASNIOSTVO BORDER. MARRA WILL SHOW YOU THE WAY.
HAVE US NOTIFIED UPON YOUR ARRIVAL AND WE WILL
MEET WITH YOU IMMEDIATELY.

WE'VE RECEIVED NOTHING FROM YOUR KING AT THIS
TIME. WE'LL SIGN NOTHING UNTIL WE SPEAK WITH YOU.
HURRY HOME.

SIGNED,
SER BERRICK TMARREY
SER CRANNOC MERD
SER REDDIN CAZRET
THE TRIUMVIRATE OF THE ORDER OF NIGHTMARES
11.24.626

Sanne tucked the letter into her pocket, grateful she'd seated herself in the darkest corner of this grimy tavern—no one had seen Marra melt from the shadows and drop the letter in Sanne's lap. She was too far from the Celesty to think anyone was actively patrolling this border town for her, but she didn't want to take her chances. She'd concealed her Nightmare tattoo and missing fingers by stealing gloves from a cart on the side of the road and stuffing grass into the empty ring and little fingers, and she'd stashed her Esclarmonde plate in Marra's saddlebags, but there was little she could do to hide her eyes. Her sclerae were still black as night, and Sanne knew they'd never be white again. She would always bear Zdesen's stain—yet the thought didn't turn her stomach quite as much.

She tugged the hood of her cloak farther down and sipped her terrible ale, watching the others in the Drunken Twig talk and flirt and work. The night had the air of habit about it: laughter came easily, and the two barmaids knew whose grasping hands to shy away from. These people knew one another. They'd remember an outsider. Sanne wouldn't be able to stay long.

Her food came, steaming vegetable stew in a chipped bowl.

"Thank you," she said, trying to smile without lifting her eyes to the barmaid. She hoped it didn't make her look freakish. Women remembered those who frightened them, and Sanne wanted to be forgotten as soon as she slipped outside.

The barmaid walked away, and Sanne took her first bite. The stew wasn't seasoned and the vegetables were far from cooked, but the food was hot, and that was all she wanted. Because of Svetlen's grace, the Celesty was always warm; Sanne was therefore ill-suited to handle the cold. She couldn't seem to stay warm. Even the small fires she built each night, holding her hands so close to the orange flames they almost burned, were little help.

She finished her stew and drank the hot broth. Sanne tossed two silver coins on the table and rose to leave.

The door of the tavern opened. "Good evening!" a voice called. The tavern patrons cheered in response, and the door swung shut as an elven bard strode in. His eyes, the color of the dregs in Sanne's cup, swept over the room and settled on the barmaid who'd served her. "I've come to play for my dinner, sweet Gracen, as a man must eat even when he has no coin."

Gracen rolled her eyes, but the smile on her face told Sanne this wasn't out of the ordinary for the Drunken Twig. She gestured to a raised circular platform in the corner. The bard stepped on and started to tune his dulcimer, giving Gracen a toothy grin when she settled a flagon of ale at the foot of the platform.

"Thank you, my dear." He strummed his instrument a few times; satisfied, he addressed the crowd. "Good people! I bring my usual repertoire, which you all know so well, but also news of the realm. What shall I sing of first? Love? Regret? The deeds of famed explorer Sir Lissan Rivasi? Or the upset recently suffered by our own dear king?"

Sit down, child.

Sanne obeyed her goddesses' order. Zdesen's invisible claws wove through her braid, and Sanne's first impulse was no longer to tear herself away. "Is this about—"

You? Yes.

"What's happened to our king?" one of the lusty men said, leaning forward and scowling.

The bard smiled indulgently and picked out a tune on his dulcimer. "A tragedy, my friend. Our young king faces another betrayal." He began to sing:

> *I sing to you a tale, my friends, a tale of deepest woe,*
> *A king blessed by the light, whose misfortune only grows,*
> *A father, a mother, a brother, all lost,*
> *And yet, there is more to come,*
> *For his Lady he's lost, a Nightmare he lives,*
> *The damage cannot be undone*

Sanne closed her eyes against the sickening feeling that rushed forward, against the memories of Ren half-dead and purple-eyed spirits and Cassander's instruction that the Stone let her *ripen.*

The bard continued:

> *I sing to you a tale, my friends, a tale of blasphemy,*
> *The Lady Nightmare led astray, Zdesen's now is she,*
> *Golden her plate, yet black are her eyes,*
> *A mark as Black as the Sun,*
> *The Heretic shines, the Heretic flees,*
> *To the Order they say she runs*

Sanne dug her nails into the table. She forced herself to take steady breaths. Word had spread so quickly. She didn't recognize this elf, but she didn't put it past Cassander to have hired bards to spread a curated version of events throughout the kingdom. As she'd fled the Celesty, sneaking through back alleys in the dead of night, she'd heard whispers of someone called the Shining Heretic—someone she'd swiftly realized was her.

"She's power-hungry," a woman muttered to her companion

over a bottle of ale. "I heard she made offerings until the parasite blessed her."

"I heard she wants to help the traitor overthrow our king," her companion replied. "And that she's been spying for him." She swallowed the ale and chuckled ruefully. "She claimed to be so holy."

Sanne's identity, her personhood, had been stripped just as the Black Sun's had. No more would the Celestian people speak of Sanne Esclarmonde, the Lady Nightmare. As far as they were concerned, she'd died in the Stained Palace, and the Shining Heretic had writhed from the corpse like a well-fed maggot.

Yet it was just as Sanne had told Vestel: everything Cassander had charged her with, she'd done. The people just didn't know why.

The bard launched into the third verse of Sanne's dirge.

I sing to you a tale, my friends, and beg you to take heed,
The Heretic has come undone, has disobeyed her creed
She hears no reason, will give no grace,
Her blade will run you through,
I say, my friends, be on your guard,
She could be behind you!

Sanne held her breath and prayed no one looked to her corner.

Scowls twisted the faces of the patrons and barmaids. One of the drunkards curled his hand around his flagon until his knuckles whitened. Sanne sat in the corner as her reputation died, her cheeks flushing as the fury the Jasniostvan people felt toward the Black Sun sparked and began to burn her, too.

"The Order will cast her out, if they know what's good for them," a crone called from her rickety table.

Gracen spat on the ground. "I hope the traitor kills her."

Sanne could bear it no longer. She darted from her dark corner and fled into the cold night. She reached back and wrapped her hand around Peacebringer's hilt, ready to defend herself, but only the patrons' shouts followed her.

When she heard the tavern door slam back into its frame, she cast darkdrape and melted into the shadows. A few hundred feet from the tavern were the outskirts of Tmadrev Forest. Sanne entered the tree line, slowed her pace, and tried to control her breathing so her panting wouldn't give her away. She made sure to step in preexisting footprints. She wanted to disappear. She needed to disappear.

When she reached the boulder she'd chosen as her campsite for the night, Marra already perched atop it, preening. The woods around them were still and dark, but the trees were spread out enough to allow soft bits of moonlight to drift through the canopy. With a plead to Marra, her shadowed saddlebags appeared and fell to the snowy ground with a clank.

Sanne sat, trying to ignore how her fingers burned from the cold despite her stolen gloves, and accounted for each of her things: her Esclarmonde plate, her other three daggers, a fat pouch of gold, and two small loaves of stale bread.

Sanne ran her fingers over the saddlebag's flap. How she'd left the palace with any of this in her possession was one of the mysteries of her flight. From the moment she'd taken the goddesses' hand, she'd lost hours. Sanne had come into herself atop Marra's back, clutching the reins for dear life as Marra galloped from the Celesty in the blue pre-dawn. Flashes of memory had come back over the last few days—she'd watched the midday sun warm an icicle enough for it to drip and remembered the sweat rolling down her back as she barreled through the Stained Palace, stopping in her chambers only long enough to grab her daggers and a mysteriously packed bag. She'd shifted oddly in the saddle and felt the spasm of a sore muscle in her shoulder, and remembered ramming herself into the wooden door that led from the chthonic palace tunnels into Zdesen's temple. She'd found a skinny rabbit half-dead in a trap and snapped its neck—it was a mercy, she'd told herself, even as she butchered it for a desperate meal. The rabbit's blood on the snow reminded her of the crusted blood she'd found beneath her gloves.

"You have to tell me if I killed someone," she muttered, not for the first time.

A creaking sigh drifted around her. *You didn't.*

"I must pray for absolution if I did," Sanne continued, though Zdesen already knew. "Even if I hurt someone, I should pray. Nightmares aren't meant to strike the living."

Pray, then. Zdesen's voice faded away. *But unless my cousins smite you where you stand, I think you can consider yourself forgiven.*

Sanne closed her pack and set it on the cold ground. She snuggled into her cloak and whispered a prayer for forgiveness to Zikat. Teeth chattering, Sanne switched to the Oddelenic dialect and rushed through her vespers—the sun had set while she was in the tavern, and even in the wilderness, she would not abandon her prayers.

The last holy words Sanne spoke for the night were an entreaty to Svetlen, a plea for her goddess to wrap her in warmth as she slept. Sanne was too afraid to build a fire—this close to a town, she didn't want to chance being seen, and she wasn't sure the wood around her was dry enough to spark. She didn't dare call her holy fire, either—not after what it had become.

She laid beneath the boulder and rested her head on her pack. Sometime in the boulder's ancient past, something had struck it; the resulting angled edge made a slight overhang, one that would protect Sanne from any falling snow if she curled up just right. Marra hopped from the top of the boulder, settled into the crook of Sanne's legs, and tucked her head beneath her wing.

The moment before Sanne fell asleep, Zdesen showed her another shred of memory from her flight: the palace guards standing motionless as Sanne ran past, their mouths open in gaping, silent screams.

I distracted them, the goddess whispered, her voice as close as if she'd curled up next to Sanne. *You know what I want in return. Go to my champion.*

"I know," Sanne whispered. She shuffled back against the boulder, wedging herself against it in hopes that her body heat would somehow warm the stone. "And I'll do it."

Vestel's ring was cold against Sanne's breast, where she wore it on a red ribbon for safekeeping. She closed her eyes; instead of seeing Vestel's hollowed corpse like she usually did, she saw the Eclipse sneering over her, dropping Peacebringer at her feet. *Take the coward's route, Sanne. We will find another Nightmare.*

A dead woman had charged Sanne with informing the traitor of Cassander's plans. Sanne's new goddess had done the same. But there were others who needed to know first—an entire Order of them.

"But he'll wait," Sanne said, ignoring Zdesen's irritated chuff. She drew her hood over her neck and face. If someone came upon her while she slept, hopefully they'd just pass her by. "There's something I must take care of first."

11.25.626

When Sanne shivered awake, Marra appeared and dropped a letter into the snow.

Sanne mumbled through her morning lauds to Zikat, pausing between each line to huff into her hands. Her breath smelled horrible—everything about her smelled horrible—but the exhalations warmed her enough to wiggle her fingers and open the letter.

> SANNE,
> IT'S BEEN TOO LONG. I'M SORRY I DIDN'T WRITE SOONER.
> I'M AFRAID FOR YOU. THE TRIUMVIRATE IS DEBATING CALLING EVERY ACTIVE NIGHTMARE TO THE

KEEP. THEY WANT US TO GO TO GROUND. YOUR NAME WAS MENTIONED IN THE DISCUSSION OF WHY, AND SO WAS REN'S, AND THEN TMARREY SAID THAT HE FELT ZIKAT WAS URGING HIM INTO ACTION.

I KNOW REN WORKED WITH YOU IN JASNIOSTVO IN THE NINTH MONTH. I'VE READ HIS REPORT, AND YOUR LETTER ABOUT HIS INJURIES. WHY THE VAGUE LANGUAGE? WHY HAVEN'T YOU SUBMITTED A REPORT? THAT IMPLIES THAT YOUR HUNT ISN'T DONE—THOUGH REN SAID IT WAS—AND YOU WOULDN'T LEAVE SOMETHING UNFINISHED. I KNOW HOW MUCH YOUR CONTRACT MEANT TO YOU. WHAT'S HAPPENED?

I'M GOING TO TRY TO PERSUADE MARRA TO TAKE THIS TO YOU THE NEXT TIME I SEE HER. I HOPE IT'S NOT TOO LATE.

WITH EVERYTHING THAT HAPPENED, SANNE, I WANT YOU TO KNOW I STILL TO I STILL CARE FOR YOU PLEASE WRITE BACK. I'D LIKE TO KNOW YOU'RE SAFE.

BAER
11.25.626

"Too long." Despite their cold-induced dryness, Sanne rolled her eyes. It had been three years, almost to the day, since Baer had last spoken to her.

Yet when she read the letter a second time, she had to tamp down what surged forward: the sorrow, the shame, the guilt, even the longing she'd made herself kill. In the Stained Palace, there had always been something to keep her busy, even at the start of her contract: Cassander and Malaia had married at the end of that year, and the Esclarmonde family had fallen to pieces shortly after. The Black Sun had made his claim for the throne, Oran had rebuked and exiled him and then died. When Cassander took the throne, there'd been hope that he'd be able to pacify his brother in a way their father had not. Sanne had shared that hope—the twins had loved each other once, of course, and Cassander knew his brother in a way no one else did. But it hadn't worked. Negotiations had soured. The Black Sun declared war on Cassander and returned to Nocovostvo. Most of Sanne's time had been spent caring for her shattered family, her hunts few and far between in a city as holy as the Celesty. Until Ren had come, memories of the Keep and those she'd left behind had slipped away.

Here, though, with only the snow and naked trees and milky dawn light to keep her company, Sanne had little to distract her from thoughts of Baer. She deflected as much as she could, setting her mind to her breakfast of tough bread before packing her meager belongings into the saddlebags. The morning was still. No hares or squirrels ran about, no birds chirped. Sanne told herself they were sleeping, but they also could have been frozen. Not every creature had the goddess of light's fiery devotion burning in their heart—though Sanne still felt cold.

She double-checked her things, grateful for whatever weird enchantments had been woven into Marra's strange saddlebags that allowed them to hide the gleam of her plate. She didn't know how far she was from the Keep—Zdesen's strange assistance hadn't included packing her a map. Even if the goddess had, though, Sanne didn't know where she was. She didn't know the name of the town she'd supped in. She could only trust that Marra would get them to the Keep as quickly as she could.

She hated feeling so blind.

Marra, having shifted forms to a speckled mare, huffed. Her breath formed white puffs in the air. She swung her velvety black snout into Sanne's side. She'd finally allowed her tack to manifest —she had a habit of putting it off for as long as possible—and Sanne swung herself into the saddle. The letter from Baer was still clutched in her hand.

Sanne read it once more before tucking it into the nearest saddlebag. "The faster you get me to the Keep," she said to Marra, "the sooner the saddle and bridle come off."

The Umbral mare snorted and started forward, weaving through the trees at a canter. Sanne let her run while they still could. Up ahead, the trees thickened, great enough in number to block most light even though their branches bore no leaves. Tmadrev Forest was a wall of darkness and silence. Sanne was relieved to let it swallow her.

———

Sanne had met Baer Enorry when she'd met every other Nightmare: at age fifteen, when she'd arrived at the Keep. They were the same age, and though he was young and cocky, the housemasters had trusted Baer enough to have Sanne room in his suite. There'd been two other trainees living there, a shaded elf called Tovar Moriya and a horned elf named Ren. She'd expected the three of them to shut her out—from the way she saw bits of the others in the way each one moved and talked, she could tell they'd been friends for a time, and she'd been warned that some of the trainees might resist her presence among them—but they'd welcomed her. They ate and studied and sparred and trained together, and the boys' trio became a quartet. They didn't judge her devotion to Svetlen as the other trainees did. They didn't pry for information about her noble family. They didn't question her desire to trade a comfortable court life for the cold and lonely calling of a Nightmare hunter. They'd just accepted her.

Sanne, who'd argued with her parents for months about joining the Order, had never known such easy acceptance. It didn't stop her from trying to earn it, though. She was an Esclarmonde, and even if she told herself she didn't care what her family thought, she did. She wanted to spite her parents and little brother. She needed her uncle and cousins, who'd supported her wish to become a Nightmare, to be proud of her.

Tovar and Ren hadn't understood her burning need to please her family. Tovar had run from parents who saw their children as mouths to feed and objects to beat when they were angry, nothing more, and Ren had come from a Grey home. They'd been content simply to find security and companionship in the Order.

Baer, though—Baer understood.

Though he hadn't come from an elite family like Sanne had, an ambition she'd only ever seen among nobility burned in him. Baer wanted to be one of the Triumvirate, one of the three senior hunters who governed the Order of Nightmares, and that desire had shown in every swing of his shortsword and every moment he'd spent studying. When they'd been asked to choose their Nightmare distinctions, Baer had chosen Duokrist like Sanne— the most dangerous of the three options. Nightmares of that distinction hunted spirits and spectral creatures in equal measure, whereas the other two distinctions, Apprazit and Tvura, focused on one or the other. Duokrist hunters faced the most danger, yet also the most chance for renown. Baer, like Sanne, hadn't been able to resist.

As the four of them had gone through their training, Sanne had come to see them all as her best friends. For Baer, though, she'd started to feel something more. She didn't remember the first time she'd kissed him, or making the decision to—it had just happened, as easy and thoughtless as taking her next breath. She only remembered that some nights, Baer would sneak into her room after Ren and Tovar had fallen asleep, and would be gone before first light. Somewhere within those nights, when they'd been seventeen, she'd lost her maidenhood to him—something she felt no shame for, because she'd been his first, too.

They'd kept their relationship a secret from Ren and Tovar for almost two years, both loving the others too much to risk upsetting the balance of their four-way friendship. It bothered Sanne more than it bothered Baer, and just when her agony over whether or not to confess was at its greatest, the four of them finished their training and were thrown into the hunt. Over the years, the hunt claimed two of Sanne's fingers, then her friends. Ren and Tovar's letters slowed, then stopped, and so did hers. Her friendship with Baer survived, but only just. If their paths crossed whenever they returned to the Keep, they'd fall into bed for the night and go their separate ways in the morning. Sanne didn't mind—Baer was a homecoming, in a way, and a reminder of how far she'd come—but he grew dissatisfied with the way they always broke apart. He asked her to be his one night, whispered it across the rumpled sheets when she was moments from sleep. A lone candle had been burning, and Sanne had watched the way the flame flickered in Baer's hazel eyes. He'd been so hopeful that even the little flame had seemed to dance with anticipation.

Sanne had said no. She'd fled before morning. The affection she felt for Baer wasn't the love he wanted; she was fond of him, but not in love, and it was the latter she'd seen behind the hope in his eyes. She couldn't give him a yes, couldn't give him a "maybe one day." So she'd said no, and she'd run. They were Nightmares, after all. Someone had needed her more.

Baer wrote to her twice after that. She responded to each letter days later, painstakingly crafting her replies to read as platonically as possible. They were adults now, no longer love-hazy teenagers, and she'd wanted to disentangle herself from Baer. It had worked, for a time. He no longer signed his letters with "love" or "yours," and she stopped daydreaming of his skin on hers.

But then Tovar died. Tovar died, and the quartet was again a trio, and the survivors held each other and sobbed in their old suite where he used to finish Baer's sentences and braid Sanne's hair. They slept in their old rooms. Baer had come to Sanne in the dead of night, his face still wet with tears, and she'd let him in. She'd been hoping for it.

They'd woken to find Ren gone, and had found comfort in each other again that afternoon. Sanne stayed at the Keep with Baer for a few weeks, knowing she needed to go but unable to, until the letter came: Oran Esclarmonde, her uncle and the current king of Jasniostvo, wanted to hire her as the crown's

Nightmare hunter. It had been a gods-send. She'd accepted, desperate to get back to her hunt and distract herself from the sadness that clung to her like a half-shed skin. But there'd been another reason she'd said yes, one she told no one. Baer wanted her to linger longer and longer in bed each morning, and she was afraid if she didn't break from him soon, she never would.

He hadn't taken the news well. Sanne didn't like to think of the things he'd shouted at her, how his face had turned red and how, halfway through his tirade, he'd stopped and stared at her as if she was a stranger. The silence had been worse than the shouting. She understood his anger. He'd lost his best friend, then another close friend, and now he was losing her, too—but he'd still had no right to scream at her. Sanne hadn't yet learned that anger was how some men showed their heartbreak.

She'd signed her part of the contract, King Oran and the Keep had signed theirs, and she'd become the Lady Nightmare on the first day of 624. She'd worked to keep thoughts of Baer at bay since, even when Ren asked about them—but that, of course, had now changed.

In Sanne's chest beat a heart encased in stained glass. Baer had been the last one to see it unguarded. She hated that he knew her in that visceral, vulnerable way, but she didn't hate him, no matter how much she wanted to. He'd still held her in the night when they'd been the only two left—and now, when Sanne was losing everything, she couldn't let him go, too.

11.26.626

After a day and a half of riding, the Keep's spires emerged from the treeline.

Sanne slowed Marra to a walk. Though the Umbral knew the Keep better than Sanne ever would, Marra usually arrived by sky, not land. Visitors and Nightmares traveling to the Keep on foot had to be wary of the ruins that jutted from the ground like broken fangs. Sanne thought she knew where most of them were, but the fresh snow reflected the sun into her eyes and ruined her depth perception. She didn't want to come this far only to strike her head on a crumbled chimney and spill her lifeblood into the snow.

As they approached, the sky shifted from snow-grey to a dusky pink; the sun was setting. The Keep pressed against the sky, its dark stone tall and imposing. It had once been part of a noble estate, but when the Cataclysm struck, the Keep itself was all that survived. Whenever she and her fellow trainees had a lull in conversation, someone inevitably brought up their theory of who the Keep had belonged to before the first world had ended. Her brethren mostly thought it belonged to the predecessors of one of Ruhysvet's current royals—usually the ruler of the kingdom they hailed from—but Sanne suspected otherwise. In Naisvet, the gods had walked the earth with the elven races; why couldn't the Keep have belonged to one of the gods? Why else would it have been strong enough to survive an apocalypse? The Keep was made of a stone Sanne had never seen anywhere else, a dark grey granite with feathered veins that shifted color as the light struck them. It could've been Oddelen's or Zikat's creation, or even crafted by both; Sanne thought these appropriate guesses, as Nightmares were blessed by the two. Maybe the Keep's godly architects had known what their new world would one day need.

A divine origin would also explain the Keep's ability to move from place to place. Portal magic, along with a few other highly advanced, highly enigmatic types of magic, was a holdover from Naisvet. In Ruhysvet, only royals and the incredibly rich—or, in the case of the Order, incredibly established—could afford to hire mages educated enough to practice it, and even then, it was a rarity. From what Sanne knew, the wards and spells needed to craft a portal were complex and highly dependent on the conditions of the desired results: where the portal was meant to lead, how long travel there would be possible, what the conditions were, who the intended user was. For all her family's wealth, Oran hadn't retained a portal mage, and Cassander hadn't felt it necessary to hire one when he took the throne.

Sanne slipped a hand below her leather cuirass and felt for Vestel's ring. It was still there. *Shatter this ring*, Vestel had said. *It will take you to him*. Sanne was sure it was enchanted with some essence of portal magic, which begged the question—when had the Black Sun had it made, and by whom?

The ironwork gates, which stretched half the height of the Keep and enclosed the bailey and castle, were open. Two guards, trainees Sanne didn't recognize, called for her to stop. After seeing her tattoo and one nudging the other, muttering to his companion "you *know* who she is," the young guards let Sanne in.

She dismounted and strode through the gates toward the grand doors, letting her cape billow open. Peacebringer's hilt flashed in the fading light, casting shards of gold onto the ground at her feet. Through the gaps in the low stone walls lining her path, she heard grunts of effort and the clatter of wooden weapons colliding. Odd. By this time, classes would have ended. The Nightmares would be finishing dinner and preparing to conduct the evening's prayers.

Sanne peered into the sparring yard and gasped. Two trainees circled each other, exchanging blows, but the lateness of their practice wasn't the most surprising thing to Sanne. The trainees were both elven girls.

She was no longer the only female Nightmare.

The girls heard her and paused in their bout, locking eyes with Sanne through the opening in the wall. The girl on her feet, with dark blue hair and daggers, held out a hand for her opponent. The other girl stood without taking the help and flicked her white braid over her shoulder. The three of them gaped at each other for a few moments, ageless in their shock.

"You're Sanne Esclarmonde, aren't you?" the blue-haired girl said, her eyes wide and voice hushed. Her eyes were the same sapphire color as her hair, and her skin was periwinkle—a prismatic elf, then, from Zijustvo.

A lump rose in Sanne's throat. "Yes."

"We've heard of you," the white-haired girl, a dark-skinned gloam elf with wide golden eyes, said. She limped from the sparring ring over to Sanne. "I'm Lirin, and this is Visya. I hope this isn't rude to ask, but—"

"Can we see your tattoo?" Visya blurted. "Just to know it's really possible. Rien told us girls couldn't be real Nightmares."

The lump lessened, but her heart began to pound. "Of course." Sanne held up her hand. Lirin and Visya's eyes widened to the whites when they saw the black whorls on Sanne's skin, and they exchanged a look before stifling giggles. Sanne's heart cracked. She'd loved her boys, but what she wouldn't have given to have a female friend at the Keep.

"Your fingers," Lirin said. "Is losing them what got you the tattoo?"

Sanne nodded.

Visya's periwinkle skin took on a green cast. "What happened?"

"I was fighting a ghoul." Sanne slid her glove back on. The cold air was starting to bite, and her old wound throbbed under the attention. "It bit into my right hand, and when I pulled my hand from its mouth, my fingers didn't come with it."

Visya winced. Lirin looked entranced. "What species was it?"

In truth, Sanne didn't know—the spirit had come upon her so quickly that her mind had gone blank of all taxonomic knowledge. All that had served her in the moment was her instincts, which had been informed mostly by sparring and spellwork knowledge. There hadn't been time to classify the ghoul. There had been Sanne and something that wanted to kill her, and defending herself was all that had mattered. Yet she couldn't tell Lirin this. She couldn't ruin whatever romanticized way the young elf daydreamed of her future hunts—Sanne had done the same thing, and knew the truth would come soon enough.

"And what about your eyes?" Lirin asked. "Is that from your hunt, too?" She blinked, and her eyes were as gold as the sun. "Will that happen to us? What about your veins?"

Sanne looked to the sky and prayed for a cold breeze to dry the tears that had sprung to her eyes. She opened her mouth to ask the girls about themselves instead—she wanted to know who they'd left to come to the Keep—but someone called her name. She and the girls turned to the grand entrance to see Ser Berrick Tmarrey, the oldest and longest-serving member of the Triumvirate, holding one of the doors open and beckoning to her. Marra stood at his feet.

Sanne raised a hand, then turned back to the girls. They looked up at her with eyes wide as saucers, half-awed and half-afraid that she'd been called by one of the Triumvirate. "I've got to go," Sanne said. She held out her hand and clasped each girl by the forearm, hoping her hands didn't shake when she touched them.

Lirin's handshake was strong, and she beamed up at Sanne. "Stories of you are why I came to the Keep."

Visya's grasp was weaker, but she looked at Sanne with no less admiration. "I knew you were real," she whispered. "Wait until we tell Rien we met you."

Sanne prayed they couldn't see how their words gutted her. Would they feel the same when her broken reputation caught up to the Keep? When they heard how she'd placed the entire Order at risk? "I'm no legend. I'm as mortal as you," she said. "It was a pleasure to meet you both. Rest well."

"Rest well," they said, their high voices drifting behind her as she walked to Tmarrey.

He wasted no time greeting her, just jerked his head in an order for her to follow. His brows were low over his eyes, one gone and one deep brown. His Nightmare tattoo spread across the scarred-over socket. Sanne trailed after him. The Order valued its efficiency, yet Tmarrey nearly always made time for pleasantries. He was worried.

The images of Lirin and Visya's faces, smooth and plump

with childhood, followed Sanne up the stairs. She'd come to the Keep at fifteen. Nightmares started weapons training at fourteen, so the girls couldn't be younger than that, but gods. They looked like children. "Did I look that young when I arrived?"

Tmarrey chuckled and opened the door to the Triumvirate's meeting room. "You still do."

Two males stood when she entered, a grey-skinned shaded elf and a heavily scarred human man. Ser Crannoc Mezd, the elf, smiled at her, though it didn't reach his dark grey eyes. Ser Reddin Cazret, who'd once been Sanne's least favorite instructor, stared blankly at her.

"Have a seat, Sanne." Tmarrey joined his colleagues at the far side of the circular table. The last time Sanne had been in this room, Cazret hadn't been on the Triumvirate, and there'd been another man present: Oran. Her uncle's brown eyes had been merry and full of pride as they'd signed her contract—the same document Cassander had tried to use as chains.

She lowered herself into the seat across from Mezd, who sat between Tmarrey and Cazret. "Ser Mezd, it's good to see you."

"You as well, Sanne."

She lowered the hood of her cloak. It hung low enough to cast a shadow that had prevented Tmarrey from seeing her eyes, but in the candlelight, there was no mistaking their discoloration. To their credit, Tmarrey and Mezd betrayed no shock, but she caught them exchanging a look.

She fixed her eyes on Cazret. He'd often singled her out during sparring and made her fight trainees who were double her size, and she hoped her eyes would unsettle him at least a fraction as much as he'd tormented her. "Ser Cazret."

His eyes narrowed. "Esclarmonde."

"I was doubly sad to hear of Ser Hagre's death, both because it meant a great loss for the Order and because it resulted in your ascension the Triumvirate."

Cazret's lips drew back. "That silver tongue is going to get you in trouble one day." His eyes locked onto hers. "Though it seems it already has."

Sanne opened her mouth to snap back, esteemed member of the Triumvirate or not, but Tmarrey raised a hand to silence them. "Quiet, both of you," he said. "Sanne?"

She straightened. Cazret was the most recent addition to the Triumvirate, so she reckoned she could get away with antagonizing him a bit, but Tmarrey had served on the Triumvirate for as long as she could remember. He wouldn't permit backtalk. "Yes?"

"Tell us why you've fled."

She laid it out for them from the beginning: her difficulty fighting spirits in the Stained Palace, Ren assisting her, the two of them finding the cause of the infestation and subduing it.

"And this source was the Stone?" Mezd asked, looking up from the papers he'd consulted as she spoke.

Sanne felt as if the chair beneath her had vanished, and the floor with it. They knew? She'd purposely left it out of her letter. "Y-yes," she stammered. "How—"

"We've spoken with Ren." Tmarrey clasped his hands together. "He told us everything."

That wasn't possible, because Ren didn't know everything—but her heart leapt at the mention of him. "You've seen Ren? How is he?"

"He's well." Tmarrey met her eyes. "And he said you destroyed the Stone."

"Which begs the question," Cazret said, leaning back in his chair. "What is this threat you speak of?"

Sanne tucked her hands into her lap. Until now, telling her story had been easy—the Triumvirate had heard it before. It was what she had to say next, the deceptions she had to confess, that made her hands shake. "When I wrote to you of Ren's injuries, and when I sent him away," she said, "I wasn't entirely truthful. I didn't seek to deceive you, but—"

"You withheld information?" Cazret snarled. "Why?"

Sanne dug her nails into her palm. "Because my hunt was not yet complete."

Cazret snorted. "I knew he shouldn't have believed you. You lied, and—"

"Let her speak, Reddin," Mezd snapped. His tone calmed, but only just. A frown hovered at the edges of his mouth. "This reflects poorly on you, Sanne."

Her eyes smarted. "I've come to explain. Let me."

Cazret raised a tattooed hand—though he'd retained all his fingers—and signaled for her to continue.

"I didn't want to expose him to it again. I didn't want it to become a threat to the Order. I resolved to destroy it myself, but I failed. It drained me a second time. When I'd healed and returned to fight it, I discovered that Cassander—I'm sorry." Sanne pressed her tattooed palm to her mouth. His words echoed in her mind: *Put the blade down, Sanne.* "Cassander wants to use the Stone as a weapon. He's been feeding it his own godhood. But his divinity is singular, and after the Stone drained Ren and I, Cassander was no longer enough." Her voice shook, but she didn't bother to steady it. "The Stone wants Nightmares because we hold in us the divinity of multiple gods. We feed it better. Cassander wanted to keep me in the palace to sustain it, but it would have killed me. I fled."

The Triumvirate had gone pale and silent. Even Cazret had nothing to say.

"I have reason to believe," Sanne continued, tears streaming down her face, "that in my absence, Cassander may lure other Nightmares to the Stained Palace. He mentioned Ren in particular." She took off her gloves and spread her hands on the table so they could see her ruined veins. "This is what it did to me. After the second time, the discoloration stayed."

The Triumvirate came around the table. Sanne kept still as they inspected her hands. Tmadrev had cracked and dirtied them, and she missed having clean skin and tidy nails. Her hands had never been soft, too calloused from wielding Peacebringer, but she'd always kept herself well-groomed. Sanne felt so little like herself. "I had to lie to Ren." She hadn't meant to speak, but the silence was unbearable. "He would've been killed if he'd stayed, and he was needed."

The Triumvirate exchanged looks she couldn't read. "Is the Stone also what darkened your eyes?" Mezd asked. "Ren's were unchanged."

Sanne wanted to look away, but she made herself keep Mezd's gaze. If the Triumvirate didn't already know, they soon would. "No. I had to open myself up to Zdesen to survive one of the Stone's attacks. Her influence did this to me." She swallowed. "Cassander has named me the Shining Heretic."

It sounded so simple when she said it aloud, so inconsequential—but she'd ruined her life with that choice. She never would have known Cassander's betrayal if she'd just died. She would have gone to Oddelen thinking her cousin was a good and faithful man. She would have been a legend among the Order, a righteous Nightmare who'd fought well before dying an honorable death. She wouldn't have been sitting before the Triumvirate with lies on her conscience, ruined eyes, dark veins, and a shattered worldview.

In the back of Sanne's mind, Zdesen chuckled. *Patience. When the others see what we do, they will follow.*

No one spoke. In the silence, a horrible possibility dawned on Sanne—would they cast her from the Order? She'd sullied her Nightmare's reputation. She'd lied to Ren and the Triumvirate. She'd endangered them all. Wasn't expulsion what she deserved?

Tmarrey was the first to speak. "Sanne," he said, "before whatever your king labels you, you are a Nightmare." He put a hand on her shoulder, and the heavy, comforting warmth was too much. She burst into fresh tears. "What matters now is that you've come home. You've told us the truth."

"Please don't sign my contract," she whimpered. For her own peace of mind, she had to say it. "No matter what he threatens."

The Triumvirate exchanged a wordless look.

"He's sent it, hasn't he?"

Tmarrey nodded. "We received it this morning, as well as a letter requesting that he be sent a replacement should we fail to provide you. What threats has he made?"

Sanne swallowed. She could picture it: a swarm of Aurorals descending on the Keep, throwing Nightmares into carriages to be carted to the Stone like cattle while Cassander sent the Eclipse after her—or, worse, after Ren, who'd be torn from his librarian. "He threatened to invade."

Cazret paled again, but to hide it, he scoffed and said, "He'd have to get to us first."

"We won't sign it," Mezd said. Sanne wanted to throw her arms around him. "Like Tmarrey said, you're a Nightmare first. The Order guards its own before all else."

"I imagine you'd like to stay and rest a while?" Tmarrey said. "Bathe, perhaps? Your old room is available. It's yours, if you want it."

Beneath her tunic, Vestel's ring was cold against Sanne's skin. *You gave me your word, Sanne, remember*? Zdesen whispered.

But Sanne didn't need the reminder. She stood and wiped her tears. "I'm not staying."

"Why not?"

A coldness spread through her stomach, the ghost of the torment waiting beneath the Stained Palace. "I have to stop Cassander," she said. "For the gods. For the Order, too."

"This isn't your fight, Sanne." Cazret scowled. "The Order takes no political position—"

"It *is* my fight," she snapped. She was sick of being doubted, sick of running, and sick of being afraid. She didn't want this fight, but she'd been called to it, and Sanne Esclarmonde knew nothing if not fighting for a cause. "It became my fight the moment the Stone stole the gods from me. You didn't feel it. You didn't hear the screams of a priestess being fed to it. If it's destroyed me in this way, imagine what it would do to the Order. I'm going, Ser Cazret, and I'm going alone. The Order may be neutral, but I cannot be. Not with all I've seen." She tried to calm her racing heart. "I can't stay."

Tmarrey's remaining eye searched her face. "Where are you going, Sanne?"

Bells began to toll, their low notes calling those in the Keep to gather for evening vespers.

"You're going to Nocovostvo, aren't you?" Mezd asked, so quietly that Sanne almost didn't hear him over the echoing bells.

She shouldn't tell them. It was dangerous for them to know—but if she fell on her journey, she wanted the Order to know she'd tried. "Yes."

She expected a protest, an insistence that they were her family, first and foremost—but the Triumvirate was not Cassander. The Triumvirate understood that Sanne walked her path with each foot in a different world, half Nightmare and half noble. She knew, seeing the resignation in their eyes, that they wouldn't ask her to bow her head and blindly serve.

Tmarrey's gaze settled on her tattooed hand. "Come home when you're done. There will always be a place for you here."

Heat flared in Sanne's stomach, her goddess confirming what she already knew: she'd never return to the Keep. She forced a small smile. "Thank you."

She lingered in the hall until the Triumvirate disappeared from sight. Sanne wouldn't attend evening vespers, may Oddelen forgive her—she wouldn't bathe, as much as she longed to, or stay for the night. She feared she would never leave if she did.

———

After packing her saddlebags with bread, dried meat, hard cheese, and an extra Nightmare dagger and whetstone, Sanne walked the halls of the Keep for the last time.

The Black Sun's camp was in Nocovostvo. That was all she knew: not exactly where, not how many soldiers were with him, not how fortified the encampment was, and certainly not how she'd be received. She didn't know if she'd be able to talk her way in, or if she'd even be given the chance to. She might become like the beasts the Black Sun fought in his final trial, slaughtered before they could rear back and strike.

All she knew was that a dead woman and a goddess had told her to go, and that her other gods were afraid. Sanne knew who she was: a devotee. A Nightmare. Someone needed her, and she'd been called. Of course she would go, and go regardless of her own fear.

Regardless of what might happen to her when she arrived.

The low music of the Nightmares singing in the chapel drifted through the bare stone halls. Sanne hummed along as she walked, trailing her fingers along the narrow stone passages. She'd sometimes done this in the middle of the night as a trainee, woken and wandered the empty halls to remind herself that she was really here. The Keep was just as much hers as it was the boys'. It had been her home when her parents' estate had become too constricting, and then her refuge in the early years of her hunt when she'd traveled the realm trying to make a name for herself. But then Oran had contracted her, and the Stained Palace had become her sanctuary. Under Cassander, it would have become her prison.

She reached a quieter part of the Keep, the classroom and library wing. She glanced at the windowed library door, intending only to pass by, but stopped when she saw a male standing behind the circulation desk. He was tall, with dark blond hair that brushed his shoulders and curled at the ends. She stared at his hands, watching how his fingers flipped through book pages and scribbled notes on a pad of paper to his left. She needed to go. She needed to leave.

But he looked up. His hazel eyes locked onto hers. He dropped his pen. Baer's mouth fell open, just slightly, and Sanne found herself opening the library door.

"You're not at vespers," she said. The door clicked shut behind her.

"Neither are you." His voice was just as she'd remembered,

low and steady like a saw blade on wood. A short staff rested against the desk, and Sanne's brow furrowed. Baer had wielded a shortsword in their training days—when had he changed weapons?

He lowered his hand to the top of the staff and used it to make his way around the desk. She'd been wrong. It was a cane, not a staff, and when she saw what had become of Baer's leg, the forest-green shard of her heart that was his cracked. His flesh ended at mid-thigh. There was only metal where his lower leg and knee should have been. As he walked, the false leg bent and moved like true joints and sinews.

Sanne's stomach flipped. Baer had always been so warm, so strong. The metal looked cold, and seemed as if it would buckle under his weight at any moment. "What happened to you?"

He gestured to her right hand. "The same thing that happened to you."

"Ghoul?"

"Scavenger beast."

Sanne winced. Scavenger beasts were vicious, half-alive creatures. Because they fed on the dead, they were constantly half-starved and weak; it made them easy to kill, but they fought with a savageness that left few Nightmares unscathed. The creatures closest to true death were the most dangerous. "The whole leg?"

A shadow passed over his face. "Enough of it."

"I'm sorry."

The shadow darkened. "That's not what I want you to be sorry for."

Sanne took a deep breath. His letter said he still cared for her, but Baer had always been kinder on the page. She couldn't do this. She turned to go. "I shouldn't have come in."

"Wait."

She paused, her hand on the doorknob.

"I'm sorry." Baer cleared his throat. "Don't go."

She wanted to throw the door open and run to Marra—between the conversation with the Triumvirate and now this, the Keep was making her feel like a child again, secretly frightened and anxious to prove herself. The Lady Nightmare would have left the library without looking back, but could Sanne still claim that title? Who owned that version of Sanne, Cassander or her?

"I want to talk, Sanne. Please."

She let her hand fall from the door. Baer stood a few feet behind her, both hands resting atop his cane. "Tell me what's happened to you."

"You'll hear it from the Triumvirate."

"I want to hear it from you—"

"No." His words from the night she told him she was leaving rang in her head. *Heartless*, he'd called her, and a *deserter of the Order*, too—though she now knew he'd been accusing her of deserting him. Baer saw himself as a blade in the Order's hands, nothing more, and he couldn't conceive of Sanne being devoted to anything else. He hadn't understood the way she'd been split in two, and had hissed that going to the Stained Palace would ruin her. She didn't want him to know he'd been right. "You'll only gloat."

He walked to her. Sanne let him rest his hand on her cheek, let him tilt her face up so that the light from the hanging candelabras fell into her eyes. "I won't," he said. She could feel the questions coiling in him, tense as a viper, but he didn't voice them. "You've changed since that night. So have I."

It wasn't an apology, but Sanne told herself it was enough. If she never saw him again, she'd remember it as enough. "There's a danger to the gods in Jasniostvo," she whispered, "and it's a threat to the Order, too. I experienced it firsthand. I'm going to try to stop it."

"You're not staying?"

"I can't."

Baer took her left hand and inspected her veins. Her instinct was to curl her fingers through his, but she resisted. "Is this what happened to Ren?"

"Yes." She pulled her hand away. Of course Baer knew. "But it happened to me a second time."

Baer looked into her eyes for a moment, searching for something, before wrapping his arms around her and pulling her against his chest. Sanne should have resisted, but her exhaustion and his persistent warmth and her fear and his comfort were all too much. Baer had once been in the habit of curling around her as they slept, and she wanted to feel that safe again, even if only for a moment. She sagged against him.

"I can't imagine," he murmured, rubbing his fingers along the nape of her neck the way he used to. "I read his report. It sounded awful."

Sanne dug her nails into his back, wanting his chest to muffle her voice as she confessed, her voice watery, "I thought I was going to die, Baer."

"Then stay. Let us fight it with you."

"I *can't*." She pushed him away. Asking someone to fight the Stone with her was what had started all of this. "No one else can get involved. It only makes it stronger, and Cassander—" She shook her head, her stomach lurching. Cassander had written to the Keep. He'd soon know she'd been there. The bard's song, though crafted to spread the news of her betrayal, had revealed something else: that Cassander suspected she'd run to the Keep, and she had. She couldn't stay, and no other Nightmare could come with her—if Cassander came after the Order, they would need everyone they could to defend the Keep. "It's best if I don't tell you. You'll hear it from the Triumvirate."

"Sanne—"

She shook her head. She'd lingered too long. "I need a favor from you. Two, actually."

His hand rested on her cheek again, warm and steady. "What are they?"

"You're in communication with Ren?"

Baer nodded. "The town he's staying in until his leave ends is nearby."

Sanne searched her memory for its name. "Tanglewood?"

"Yes."

It was as Sanne had thought. He'd gone to his librarian. "Have you met her?"

Baer nodded again.

"Is she good to him?"

Baer's thumb brushed against her cheek. "She is. He loves her so much, Sanne."

"Good." Her voice wavered again. Ren had found something good, something to protect. It was all the more reason for her to go.

"I think he's going to marry her," Baer whispered. "If you stayed, you could—"

Sanne jerked back. There it was, as she knew it would be—the entreaty, his ulterior motive. "Gods, Baer, I told you," she snapped. "I can't stay. And you can't convince me to."

He was quiet for a moment. Sanne saw the emotions warring in his eyes: anger, sorrow, fear, regret. She made herself ignore them. "What do these favors have to do with Ren?"

"Just the first does. Don't tell him you saw me. Don't tell him where I've gone." She had no doubt Baer would weasel the information from the Triumvirate.

"Why?"

Ren was many things: strong, skilled, sarcastic, protective and loyal as a dog. It was the last one that worried Sanne. "Because he'd come after me."

Baer inhaled sharply. "I can't lie to him—"

"It's not a lie if he doesn't know to ask."

Their eyes locked, and she knew he thought of the same moment she did: giggled whispers over mussed sheets, wondering what they'd say if Ren and Tovar were to ask them what they'd become. "I don't want to tell them," Sanne had confessed, "but we can't lie."

Baer had thought for a moment. "Then we give them no

reason to question it," he'd said, as if it was perfectly obvious. "We don't have to lie as long as they don't ask."

Baer's eyes dropped to her lips now. "Sanne—"

"Please don't tell him, Baer. Please."

His eyes slid closed. "I won't."

"Thank you." Sanne wrapped her arms around him once more. "I just want him to have the chance to be happy."

Baer nodded, his chin bumping against her head. She let her eyes fall closed for a moment. This was what had made her open the library door—the solidness of him, the warm presence of someone who knew her fully. Even though she couldn't give him the love he wanted, Baer would always, in a way, be hers. He would always come when she called. "What else do you need from me?"

Sanne sighed. He wasn't going to like this. "Every copy of all correspondence I've had with the Keep for the last three months."

"Why?"

She clutched him tighter, holding onto who she'd once been while she still could—before she destroyed anything left of that woman. "Because if Cassander comes, there can be nothing of me left."

———

Baer didn't want to give her the letters, but Sanne won in the end.

She knelt in a snowy forest clearing and spread them in a half-circle before her. It all looked so neat, laid out and lit by moonlight: Sanne reporting to the Keep her activity for the eighth month, Sanne asking the Keep for assistance in the ninth, her letter detailing Ren's injuries at the start of the tenth, and the notice of her desertion in the eleventh. She had each of the Keep's replies, as well, and for each original document, there were three copies. Baer had even given her the copies of Ren's report from the Stained Palace, keeping only the original, but these she left in her bags—it would be wise to keep them in case the Black Sun doubted her story.

Sanne took the letters in hand. She'd left the Keep and, to Marra's disgruntlement, had ridden east through Tmadrev until shadows blanketed the snowy forest in night. If Cassander suspected her of hiding at the Keep, she wanted to distance herself as quickly as possible.

An unnerving sensation rose the gooseflesh on her back, but Sanne was no longer scared by it. Zdesen's presence had become a familiar feeling.

Get it done, Sanne. Burn them.

"Why do you speak to me more than Svetlen does?"

It's difficult for Svetlen to talk when I use the mouth.

"I figured as much. But you don't use it all the time."

You would have to ask her. We share a body, but not always a mind. There came a shuddering sound like a sigh. *Do you question why your other gods don't talk to you like I do?*

Sanne fiddled with the edge of the topmost letter, her eighth month reassurance to the Keep that all was well in the Stained Palace. "Sometimes."

It's because we aren't the same. You see life around you. You see death when you close your eyes each night. You feel the sun on your face when you step outside. I speak because you had to be taught what to fear. Instinct only grants you so much. An invisible sharpness tapped at the back of Sanne's hands. *Now quit stalling and get on with it. Call your fire.*

Sanne groaned. Like her eyes, her fire had been ruined—yet she called it anyway. Instead of being purely golden, its hot center now burned silver. Only the edges were gold. Metallic sparks danced up from her palm. A memory billowed forth, one of silver fire streaking across the engraved Sohli Prophecy as the Black Sun screamed at his father.

Hm. I still quite like it. Zdesen sounded pleased.

"Was tainting my eyes not enough?"

No.

The air shifted, and Sanne was alone again.

She raised her flaming hand to the topmost corner of the letters. The paper caught in seconds, and Sanne watched as the Keep's only proof of her so-called heresy was eaten by flame. It was an orderly thing, this destruction; the fire marched down the letters in a neat diagonal line, the silver and gold flame efficiently reducing her words to ash. Sanne held the letters as long as she could, dropping them only when the flames began to devour the Keep's seal at the bottom left of each page. Soon enough, the holy fire died out. Darkness collapsed around her.

Sanne hinged forward and pressed her forehead to the cold ground. Hot tears rolled down her face as she sobbed into the snow. It was done. She'd warned the Order and done what she could to cover her tracks. All that was left was to shatter the ring.

But wouldn't she just be what Cassander had labeled her? The letters had been sacred documents, in a way, written by those pledged in service to Zikat and Oddelen. She'd taken the letters from a place dedicated to an order of blessed hunters and destroyed them.

Maybe Cassander was right. Maybe she was a heretic.

Sanne grabbed one of her saddlebags and fumbled through it until she found her golden breastplate. She cast the spell for will-o-wisps. Little balls of newly silver light hovered around her and lit the clearing.

Sanne stared at the sigil on the breastplate, the crest with half of a sun and Svetlen's face in profile, until her eyes blurred with tears. She wasn't the one using Svetlen's light to feed a wretch. She wasn't the one misusing the gods' blessings or misunderstanding their natures or siphoning their divinity to power a weapon, all to preserve a mortal throne. She wasn't the heretic.

Cassander was.

She called fire into her palm, ordering it hotter and hotter until the blaze overcame her goddess-given resistance to it. Her skin blistered. Sanne grit her teeth and held her hand over the sigil

—she was going to melt it away and let who she'd been die with it—

Dull your flame, child. You aren't alone.

Marra cried out. Heat flared in Sanne's chest, a warning that had her reaching for Peacebringer and scrambling to her feet. She whispered the will-o-wisps counterspell and dimmed her flame, but the enveloping darkness wasn't enough to stop the footsteps that advanced toward her. Snow crunched underneath two pairs of heavy boots. Armor clattered. She heard measured breaths and the ring of blades being unsheathed. No Nightmares would be this far from the Keep this late at night. No Nightmares wore metal armor.

Sanne held her breath and waited. Two figures dipped in and out of the trees. As their fur-trimmed cloaks swished around them, a faint glow winked in and out of sight. The light emanated from the figures' bronze armor. With each step, the color shifted slightly: gold, then orange, then pale pink, then hazy blue—the colors of dawn.

Cassander had sent Aurorals after her.

She drew Peacebringer. There would be no running from this fight.

The Aurorals stiffened when they heard the scrape of her sword; in the faint light from their armor, Sanne saw them exchange a silent look. The larger of the two motioned in Sanne's direction.

She cast nightsight. Her red eyes would draw them in.

The Aurorals stepped into the tiny clearing where Sanne had made camp and stopped. The three of them regarded one another. Sanne knew better than to think the longswords in their hands were their only arms. They carried no shields, which made them evenly matched with Sanne, but wore bronze helms. She had nothing to cover her head. Her first task would be to get the helms off and pray she didn't know the soldiers beneath.

"Heretic," the taller of them said.

"How have you found me?"

"Your Keep," the shorter said, her voice higher than her partner's. Sanne's stomach twisted. Had Cassander sent a woman hoping that Sanne would have a harder time raising a hand to her? "We knew that's where you would flee. We watched from the tree line until you left."

Sanne's gut wrenched. Her heart beat so quickly she felt as if its careful encasement would snap. If they'd watched the traffic to and from the Keep, they could have seen Baer. They could have seen the Triumvirate, or Lirin and Visya, or Ren. They knew the Order's location. Sanne couldn't let them return to Cassander.

There was Sanne and the Order and something that wanted to hurt them. Defending her Order was all that mattered.

She prayed that Zikat and Oddelen would forgive her for the transgression she was about to make. For the safety of the Order, in the name of her gods, the Aurorals would have to die.

She hefted Peacebringer and spoke her word. Peacebringer glowed, and her heart swelled—she'd feared her confession would cause her word to fail, but her gods had let it work. Before her offense, she'd been forgiven.

Tears rushed to her eyes. The Order would rest well tonight. Her brethren would sleep safely. Sanne knew she'd cut down waves of Aurorals if that's what it took to guarantee their well-being.

"Come on, then. Try to take me back."

———

The forest became a blur of cold and movement and light and sound, a cacophony of metal against metal and human cries of fury.

With each swing of Peacebringer, each fling of a dagger, Sanne sliced away the dross that weighed her down. She cut away another tie binding her to Cassander, to a future of manipulation and true, irredeemable heresy. In addition to their martial prowess, the Aurorals had been trained to wield light magic; Sanne returned each burning javelin they threw with two of her own, repeating the lightlance spell until her three daily uses expired. She was grateful for the way the light burned her red-haze vision white. It kept her from giving in to fear. It reminded her why she fought her former countrymen: Svetlen's light was being misused, and it was only the start of what Cassander planned to do.

She struck down the male Auroral first. One of her lightlance javelins sliced the backs of his knees where there was no plate to protect them. His bronze helm rang as he collapsed and struck a jagged rock hidden under the snow. He didn't get up. When Sanne's dancing evasions of the female Auroral allowed her to look back at the fallen male, she saw blood leaking from beneath his helmet into the snow. In the red cast of her nightsight, she could almost convince herself it was unblood.

The female Auroral screamed when she saw the blood. Sanne stepped on the too-long edge of the Auroral's cloak. She jerked forward, then stumbled back, and Sanne ripped her helm off. She wrapped her arm around the female's throat and squeezed like a vise. Sanne was strong, but her days of flight were catching up to her, and she prayed the Auroral would lose consciousness before her trembling muscles gave out.

"You will burn," the Auroral choked out. Her nails left crescent-shaped marks in Sanne's black leather gauntlets.

Something white hot, an emotion Sanne couldn't name, seared through her like lightning. "I already do." Her mouth was full of blood and the Auroral's dark hair. Her strength slipped away like a tide—she had to end this. Drawing it out was no mercy.

With a cry, she pulled her arm as tight as she could around the Auroral's neck, gritting her teeth with effort until the female in her arms sagged.

Sanne dropped the body and fell to her knees, panting like a beaten dog. She crawled to the male Auroral and took off his helm. She didn't recognize the blank eyes that stared at the starlit sky. When she looked at the face of the female Auroral, relief surged through her. She didn't know her, either. Sanne wouldn't have to imagine their mourners.

In the snow beside the female Auroral rested a bloody, curved dagger.

The searing feeling returned. When Sanne touched her left side, her hand came away bloody.

She began praying before the pain could hit, pressing her hands to her side and casting deathsbane on herself to heal the wound. She wasn't quick enough, though, and the onslaught of pain made her end the spell screaming. She cast deathsbane again and didn't take her hands from her side until she felt the spell work. Her skin grew back together. The indescribable pain of whatever organ had been pierced—her intestines, or possibly her kidney—faded as the puncture healed, but didn't disappear entirely. Sanne pushed herself to her feet, hissing out a breath. She would bear the pain. It would be her penance.

She stared in the direction of the Keep and let the tears roll down her face. Peacebringer rested in the snow, covered with blood it had never been meant to shed. Competing emotions reached for her—grief for the life she'd never go back to, disgust and horror and shame for her actions, pity for the Aurorals who'd died for a false cause—but shock shielded her from their grabbing hands. Shock, and fury.

Svetlen had placed fire and devotion in her blood, and Sanne welcomed them both. Anger sparked in her and caught flame, the heat so immense that she began to sweat despite the night's cold. Sanne burned until she could no longer tell whose anger fueled the flames, hers or Svetlen's, and she let the fire make her new.

The shard of glass in her heart that had once been Cassander's, sky-blue and sizable, shattered and fell away. Only a small jagged fragment remained in its place. Sanne imagined the surrounding pieces expanding to fill the void, her heart's armature forming anew around the arrangement: a gold fragment for Svetlen, a color-shifting one for Zikat, a dark grey one for Oddelen, dark brown for Zdesen, bright red for Ren, forest green for

Baer, and burnt umber for the Order. The Order's piece became the largest—she'd been a Nightmare before anything else, and now there was nothing else.

Sanne turned to the bodies. What had they seen in their last moments? The woman she'd once been? A heretic? Or just a red-eyed Nightmare?

She used the snow to wash the blood from Peacebringer. Its blade had been reforged to be one of Nightmare steel when she was seventeen. The Keep always held a ceremony when trainees received their Nightmare steel, though Sanne had forgotten hers until now. The Triumvirate had been Tmarrey, Mezd, and Hagre then, and she'd knelt before them as Mezd lowered the new Peacebringer into her hands.

"Why are we called Nightmares, Sanne?" he'd asked, leaning down so only she and the Triumvirate would hear.

"Because it's what we hunt, Ser."

"Yes. But it's also what we are." The perfectly balanced weight of Peacebringer in her hands had sent pride coursing through her. Mezd had rested a hand on her shoulder, and she'd torn her gaze from her new sword long enough to look into his eyes as he'd said, "Everything fears something. We are the Nightmares of the unholy."

Sanne rose and looked once more at the bodies. "Everything fears something," she murmured. Cassander, failure, Zdesen and Vestel, the Stone—she'd spent so long being afraid. She'd told herself it was her holy duty to ward against fear, to drive back its sources so no one around her would have to feel it, but she'd been mistaken. On its own, yes, fear was undesirable, but when seen by Svetlen's shining light, fear was a gift. Fear was power and safety and comfort, and a reminder that she had survived.

A god was a god. Holy was holy. Man was only that—man.

It was a shame Sanne had nearly had to die to understand it.

She changed, replacing her leather armor with her Esclarmonde plate. The Shining Heretic had stuck. She may as well embrace it.

Sanne checked Marra's saddlebags and cleared her campsite. She dragged the female Auroral to her companion's corpse and took their hands in one of hers. The male's hand was cold, but the female's was warm. Her chest rose and fell, her breathing slow and erratic. She'd survived. It was all the more reason for Sanne to take them with her—they were too close to the Keep. She couldn't allow the Order to be blamed.

Marra shifted forms and perched on Sanne's shoulder. The clever girl knew what was coming.

Sanne lifted the ribbon from her neck and slid Vestel's ring onto the pointer finger of her right hand. Everything feared something, and it was time for someone to finally fear her.

She drove the ring into the rock that had killed the Auroral. The gemstone shattered, and Sanne let herself be taken away.

———

Sanne noticed three things immediately, the first being that it was shockingly cold. The second was that the ring had dropped her and her grim cargo inside an animal-skin tent, one whose flap had come unsecured and thrashed about in the shrieking Nocovostvan winds.

The third was that the tip of a sword pressed into her throat.

She dropped the Aurorals' hands and drew Peacebringer, pointing her sword at the neck of the man who'd drawn his blade on her—or, rather, where she thought his neck was. The angle was poor—he was massive, two heads taller than her and almost twice as wide—and a black cowl covered his face. Red glass beads resembling tears of blood were stitched into the cowl beneath the eyeholes. His dark green eyes, which were all she could see, narrowed.

"I remember you," he said, angling his blade so she had to lift her chin or be cut by the steel. "From before the exile. You've fallen quite far, Lady." She'd heard Cassander and Vallen whispering about this man, had rolled her eyes at the Eclipse for failing to bring him back. The corners of the Red Sky's eyes crinkled as if he was smiling. "Pretty eyes."

Sanne resisted the urge to spit at him. She was here with a message. She was here to survive. "I've come to speak with the Black Sun."

The Red Sky barked a laugh. "I'm sure you have." He stepped forward. The momentum pushed the sword's tip into her flesh. A bead of blood rolled down her neck. "Drop your weapon."

"You first."

He shook his head. "You're in no position to argue, Lady—or do you prefer Heretic now?"

Listen to him, Sanne.

At Zdesen's order, Sanne lowered Peacebringer. She reached for a dagger—she'd be damned if she was going to be unarmed in this place—but a hand seized her wrist. The Red Sky plucked Peacebringer from her hand. Sanne snarled, starting forward, but she stumbled over the Aurorals. Before she fell, the unseen man grabbed her other hand and held fast.

"Let me g—"

The Red Sky's hand clapped over her mouth. "Quiet." Over her, he met the eyes of the unseen man. He lifted the heel of his palm after a moment of silent communication.

"I've come to speak with the Black Sun."

The response came from behind her, close to her ear: "So speak."

Sanne forced herself to keep still, though she wanted to shrivel away. She'd forgotten the awful sound of his voice, the two-toned disharmony that had been another result of his new oath.

"You got my high priestess killed."

Flies buzzed in Sanne's mind, the recalled sound drowning out her surprise—of course he knew. If Vestel had been in communication with him, surely the other priestesses were, too. "That isn't how it happened."

"Why have you come?"

"If you know about Vestel, then you know that, too."

He shifted forward. A smudge of white appeared in her periphery—the shock-white of his hair. "Forgive me from wanting to hear it from you."

She threw her head, trying to shake off the Red Sky's hand, but all she got for it was pain in her neck and a "now, now, Lady." How could she even begin to explain this? How much did he know? "Cassander wants to sacrifice the gods to get to you. I didn't stand for it. He wanted to feed me to the Stone, so I ran." She swallowed. "Vestel wasn't as fortunate."

The Red Sky's eyes betrayed nothing, but the Black Sun grunted. "You're no god, and neither is Vestel. How would you have sustained it?"

So he didn't know how the Stone worked. Sanne didn't know whether to be frustrated or relieved. "Call your Eclipse off, let me go, and I'll tell you."

The Black Sun's voice turned bitter, the unnaturally deep tone beneath his voice rumbling like a growl. "I have no Eclipse. That honor is reserved for the king."

"Hm. Of course."

The grip on her wrists loosened, then disappeared. The Red Sky released her. Sanne pivoted so her back was to the wall of the tent, not either man, and looked to her right.

Her Zdesen-dark eyes met horror-filled ones, bright red irises floating in a sea of black.

For a moment, she saw the young boy who'd run with Cassander, side by side and laughing, through the halls of the Stained Palace. She saw the teenager who'd given her a training sword in spite of her mother saying she couldn't spar with the boys, the young man who'd stood at his father's left side when she'd signed her contract. She saw the blood of the monsters he'd slaughtered, his family's grief, the bodies of the Celestians killed in his flight. She saw Zdesen's champion.

The Black Sun stared at her. His black plate was a dark echo of her own. A greatsword hung across his back, but he didn't reach for it. He just stared. What did he see when he looked at her? The family resemblance was strong among their generation —did he see Cassander? Did he see himself, or who he'd been before breaking his oath? Did he see who he could have been?

He stepped closer. His red irises were covered with flecks of garnet and silver. She saw her own eyes reflected in his, shards of gold and amber twinkling in the brown. His voice was almost reverential—almost. "She's claimed you too, hasn't she?"

Sanne swallowed, but the words still stuck in her throat. "She has."

Zdesen's bone-rattle chuckle echoed in Sanne's head. *And I've finally gotten her to listen. I've finally brought the pieces together.*

From the way her cousin's eyes widened, marooning his irises in pools of black, Sanne knew he'd heard it, too. "I suppose we have no choice, then," he said, but his tone was softer. The growl was quieter. Sanne wanted to argue Zdesen's point, ask what whole they were meant to create, but he spoke. "Hello, Sanne."

He said her name hesitantly, as if he'd forgotten how. That was alright—she'd been long forbidden from saying his. Familiarity was a language they'd have to learn together.

It was a good thing they had a goddess as a common tongue. "Hello, Casimir."

ADDENDUM

As I was assembling my notes, Sanne came to my tent and informed me that, after some thought, there was more she was willing to share. These events occurred on 12.3.626.

- ER
1.1.629

After sleeping for three days, Sanne woke to packages piled at the foot of her bed.

She crawled out of bed and unwrapped one. The parchment

fell away to reveal her Esclarmonde plate. Though the high points of it still shone a brilliant gold, a dark buffing solution had been worked into the cracks. On the breastplate, the Esclarmonde sigil had been reworked to be an image in thirds: Svetlen's and Zdesen's profiles were back to back, with the arc of a sun stretching over them.

Sanne ran her fingers over the breastplate. Her goddesses, together at last—the way she finally knew they should be.

Each pauldron bore the design of a Nightmare tattoo, and Sanne's heart swelled at the sight. She lifted one for a better look and a note tumbled from beneath it:

> *I didn't think it possible, but you've gone a few days without trying to kill me or my commander. Remarkable job. I took the liberty of having our smith reforge this for you. You'll find your weapons returned as well.*
>
> *Find me when you're dressed. I have an offer to make you.*
>
> *- Casimir*

She unwrapped the topmost of the remaining packages and burst into tears when she saw Peacebringer. The Nightmare steel gleamed in the faint candlelight. Casimir's initial awe hadn't lasted long; he'd ordered the Red Sky to jail her, worried that she'd been sent ahead to signal Cassander's troops for an attack. When the Red Sky obeyed his general and threw her into a cell, she'd seen Peacebringer sheathed across his back and became convinced she'd never see it again—but here it was. Someone had even cleaned it for her.

Sanne dressed. When Casimir had been satisfied that her presence wasn't a harbinger of a coming attack, he'd given her a curtained-off portion of one of the tents that comprised the war camp. She'd wanted to curse him for not trusting her, but she couldn't blame him for it. This was war. He had to be careful.

She'd cared little for the rugs on the floor of the tent or the clean clothes atop a small trunk—she'd only had eyes for the tub of steaming water and the large bed covered in furs. She'd bathed, buried herself in softness and warmth, and slept for days. She'd woken only once. Casimir and his men had been worshipping, and their song echoed through the camp. Sanne didn't recognize the laud, so had stumbled through her own prayer of gratitude—for, amongst other things, not being murdered in her sleep—before dropping her head back to the pillows.

She stood before the mirror in her tent and braided her hair. It was still difficult to look at her eyes. Her stomach no longer rolled with nausea, but Sanne felt the ghost of the Stone's emptiness whenever she saw her blackened sclerae. She heard the echoes of Cassander's accusations and the Eclipse's sneers of disgust. Vestel's ring had taken her miles away from Jasniostvo, but she'd never be able to run from the knowledge of what lurked beneath the Stained Palace. Sanne would never outpace the threat it posed to the Order, or to the gods. She would only be able to destroy it.

As she reached for her newly forged plate, she brushed past her gold-stitched Nightmare armor. A stack of letters sat next to it. She hadn't read them, but knew they were from the Keep. Sanne took them into her hand and called holy fire. The letters were swallowed by gold and silver flames. When she'd finally gotten Casimir to listen to her, screaming warnings through the bars of her cell like a madwoman, showing him the recall letter from the Keep and her copy of Ren's report had proven to him that Cassander hadn't simply broken her mind. She had no use for any other correspondence from the Keep or—as she suspected at least one of the letters was from him—Baer. She didn't want to know if they were still in Tmadrev Forest, or if Ren had finally married. If she knew where they were, she'd want to go. If she knew Ren had married, she'd want to celebrate. She'd want to throw her arms around her friends and brothers and dance and drink until she couldn't see straight, and she'd want to stay with the Order—but that was impossible now. She couldn't return to the Order until this final hunt was done. Sanne would love them best from afar.

She arrayed herself with her weapons and draped the fur-trimmed Auroral cloak over her shoulders. The fabric had appeared flat black in the darkness, but when seen in the light, it faintly reflected midnight blue. She felt a bit morbid for keeping the cloak, but Sanne didn't want to wear her old one anymore. Cassander had given it to her.

She opened her tent flap and stepped outside. Gruesome provenance or not, she couldn't deny that her new cloak did a much better job of keeping out the Nocovostvan cold.

The snow had stopped falling, yet she drew her hood up and kept her head down as she walked to the war tent. Most of the soldiers and priestesses in the camp had fled the Celesty with Casimir, and they didn't know what to make of Sanne. They still saw her golden plate as the mark of the enemy, and fell silent whenever they saw her coming.

The war tent was easy to find—it was the largest in the camp, and the only one whose animal-skin sides had been dyed a deep red. Casimir and the Red Sky stood at the mismatched tables along the tent's front edge. Each man examined a different map. They looked up when she entered, though neither smiled.

"Casimir. Commander."

Casimir nodded. "Sanne." Though his ashen hair, silvered lashes, and black and red eyes no longer sickened her, it still surprised her to see those features in Cassander's face. Even his movements, the way he'd run his hands down his face or drag a finger across a piece of parchment to point out a location, reminded her of Cassander. Her heart would ache for a moment before remembering that while Cassander had allowed her in his war room, he'd never asked her opinion on any of it. He'd never seen her as more than a pawn. To Casimir, though, her knowledge would prove invaluable. Based on the letters she'd seen him write and amount of scouts he'd ordered to find books on the Prázeny Era and Stone, she suspected it already had.

The Red Sky ran his dark green eyes up and down her body. Though she'd learned he was one of Zdesen's most faithful, his sclerae were white—he'd never been a vessel like Sanne and Casimir. "Heretic."

Sanne cut her eyes at him. Though she'd started to see the humanity behind the Black Sun, she'd yet to see any of it in the Red Sky. Part of it was by his design—he'd never removed his cowl in her presence—but part of it was because she found him to be, honestly, an asshole. When Casimir had ordered her jailed, the Red Sky had been happy to throw her in a cell and lock the door. She hadn't been able to fight him off—his size came with a strength that far overpowered hers. Among the various taunts he'd thrown at her while standing watch, he'd hissed that she was lucky he hadn't picked her up and "tossed her in like a misbehaving puppy."

Yet he was Casimir's second, and she'd come to Casimir for aid. Dealing with the Red Sky was non-negotiable. She thanked the gods that her time at the Keep, particularly her dealings with Cazret, had prepared her for this.

"You wanted to see me?"

Casimir turned from the map of the Karilan Atoll he'd been examining and regarded her. "I'm glad the armor fits you."

Sanne tried to smile in thanks, but couldn't quite manage it. Part of her still looked at him and saw the pain he'd caused their family. Part of him still looked at her and saw Cassander's dog. Their shared patronage, though, had caused them to form a shaky bridge of trust. Though Sanne didn't believe Casimir's claim regarding he and Cassander's birth order—the Sohli Prophecy was too ingrained in her, and she didn't believe Oran capable of such a deception—she and Casimir shared a fundamental understanding that those in Jasniostvo did not. Svetlen was more than a benevolent goddess, Zdesen more than her corrosive, parasitical counterpart. Light warmed and illuminated and shone, but it also exposed. Horror and fear would always follow the light.

Casimir cleared his throat and continued. "I want to offer you a position in my chain of command. The Red Sky oversees our soldiers, but there are many priestesses who came with me when I was exiled. I believe they'd benefit from some martial training, and for someone to show them how their magic could be used offensively." His gaze dropped to her Nightmare tattoo and the dark veins beneath it. "You have a unique skill set, Sanne. Consider that the gods have equipped you for this."

She only had the time for a fleeting thought—she'd been trained to kill spirits and beasts, not men, and the Aurorals had been exceptions—before a soldier burst into the tent. "General," he said, giving a hasty bow. "Commander." He glanced at Sanne, unsure how to address her, before turning back to Casimir. "Soldiers have been sighted on the ridge."

Casimir exchanged a look with the Red Sky. "Whose?"

"Your brother's." The young soldier paled. "Aurorals."

"They're here for you," Sanne said to Casimir without thinking. The Eclipse's negotiations to retrieve him had failed, so Cassander had escalated. He'd come to do what he'd threatened the Order with: take Casimir back by force. It made sickening, perfect sense.

"Or *you*," the Red Sky said to her. "Get to your tent."

"No," she snapped, at the same time Casimir asked, "How many?"

"About two dozen."

Casimir swore. "Get the men moving. Quietly. Split ranks and flank them, but by the gods, be careful. Nocovostvan citizens live on the ridge."

The soldier ran from the tent. Casimir and the Red Sky walked to the back of it, where a small armory was kept. Now that their subordinate was gone, Sanne noticed a shift in the way they held themselves. The Red Sky's shoulders were hunched, and

Casimir's hands shook. Their masks were slipping. It reminded her of Cassander.

"I'm coming," she said, following them.

The Red Sky scoffed. "You aren't a soldier."

"I've killed an Auroral and wounded another. Can your men say the same?" She needed to defeat the Stone, and she needed Casimir's help to do it. This couldn't end before it began. "But if that isn't good enough for you, Commander—"

She moved to stand in Casimir's line of sight. Two girlish faces danced at the back of her mind. Lirin and Visya had joined the Order to be like her. She wanted to give them the chance to be better. Lirin, Visya, the Order, Baer, Ren—Sanne would use this army to keep them safe. "I accept your offer. I'll train your priestesses. Just tell me what to do now."

Casimir was too busy weighing himself down with steel to reply. Sanne crossed her arms, her gauntlets ringing faintly as they collided.

Tell her what to do, champion, Zdesen murmured. Sanne whispered a prayer of thanks.

When Casimir turned to her, his eyes were lit with a fire Sanne knew all too well: the dual flames of fear and fury. "Survive this, and I'll commission you," he said. "But right now—" He strapped his greatsword to his back. "My bad dreams are coming true, and I need the Lady Nightmare."

———

The Black Sun and the Red Sky ascended the ridge on two dark horses. Their black armor glimmered in the aureate light of sunset. A line of soldiers streamed behind both, creeping up the ridge like ants until the two columns split off and increased their speed to crest the ridge.

The Aurorals were ready, and the defending soldiers were soon met with flashes of light and clashing steel. Battle cries drowned out screams of pain.

Sanne hung back. Casimir wanted her to be seen.

She wept as she watched soldiers fall. She'd thought she knew violence, but a human death was so different than a spirit's—it was louder, softer, wetter. Sadder.

In her chest beat a heart of stained glass. With every pulse, it cracked a little more. The jagged remains of the Cassander-blue shard fell away, then the Order-umber, then the Svetlen-gold. Soon, only the leaden armature remained, but even that proved too weak and snapped. Her heart beat, raw and uncategorized and frenzied, as she watched men wound and kill and die for their gods and king. Fear rolled through her. Fire washed over her. The pleasure-pain of life and the numbness of death followed. Faces flashed behind her eyes, the images of her loved ones: Ren, Baer, Tovar, the Order, her gods. She loved one because she loved the others. Why had she kept them apart? Why had she parceled out her devotion so carefully?

Maybe because she'd known, deep down, that failing to do so would have made her like this.

The armature of her heart hadn't just been a frame. It had been a cage, and free of it, Sanne saw how foolish she'd been. She wasn't angry because she was afraid. She was angry because she loved.

She drew Peacebringer and rode into the fray. The Aurorals were different in the midst of battle. Instead of bronze-armored soldiers, they looked more like lavender-eyed wraiths, gibbering geists, cackling ghouls. These were the unholy. They scavenged for scraps of godhood at the behest of their Stone-driven king, puppeted by him as he'd manipulated her. The Lady Nightmare banished two of them before the fight was over.

And then it was. At a word from her general—her name, said too softly for everything to be alright—her battle-fury faded. Sanne looked down at hands and a sword covered in red, not dark brown or black, blood.

Marra shifted forms. Sanne fell to her knees in the snow, sobbing. Her stomach roiled. The killing had been so easy—but this was for the Order. It was for her gods. It was just. She would be forgiven, she knew, though her hands shook and stained the snow pink.

"Lady. Our devoted."

Sanne looked up and saw three figures standing at the edge of the battlefield: a tall, lithe female with brown skin and color-shifting eyes; a dark-robed male with silver hair and pewter skin; a female with long golden curls whose face was beautiful and radiant one moment, yet grotesque and deformed the next. As one, they nodded. As one, Sanne's gods smiled upon her.

The Lady Nightmare. The Shining Heretic. Let them call her what they wanted. Let them make sense of her however they could. Sanne had fallen into the chasm's abyss, and her gods had been waiting at the bottom. She didn't need to be afraid. Sanne knew who, and what, she was.

She was whole.

This concludes my notes on Ren Dearling and Sanne Esclarmonde.

If you are not me, or if you're future-Emera and have forgotten, I believe this information will be helpful in writing my war chronicles. These accounts could also one day comprise their own volume—perhaps as a supplement to the chronicles.

But that is not a decision for now. Today, I am only concerned with my and my friends' survival.

One day, however, there will be more to come.

Lady Emera Rivasi
1.1.629

Acknowledgments

So far, these have been the hardest things about working on *The Nightmare Novellas*:

1. Writing the first draft, because I wound up only having a few months to do so.
2. Writing the blurb, because how am I supposed to summarize a 142k word manuscript (at the time) into less than 200?
3. Writing these acknowledgments, because I'm terrified I'm going to forget someone.

So here we go!

To my heavenly father, who blessed me with the ability to write and tell stories. I wouldn't be able to write a single word without You. I wouldn't be able to handle the stress and anxiety of putting something out into the world without You. I hope this is somehow glorifying.

To my husband Joey, for taking on the chores. For making dinner. For bringing me coffee. For praying for me. For putting up with not seeing me on the days I had to write 2,000+ words to stay on track. For letting me cry. For telling me everything's going to be okay even when I swore it wouldn't be. For helping me figure out plot holes even though you had no idea what any of it meant (yet, anyway). For knowing when I needed to work and needed to rot my brain with the worst movies ever made. They say that if a writer loves you, you'll never die. There are pieces of you in these characters just as there are pieces of me.

To my parents, for your unwavering support of me and willingness to help however you can, and for buying me lots and lots of books when I was growing up. Sorry there's some cussing in here.

To Leanna Walton, and by extension, Sam and Flynn (I told you I was going to put the little nugget in here). I'm incredibly touched by the amount of work and time you've been willing to give me, whether it's reading (and re-reading) my drafts or work-shopping my stories on your couch for hours at a time. Thank you for always being honest with me.

To Grace Yee, my...what are we? Critique partners? Alpha readers? Kindred spirits? Lore enthusiasts? Thank you for telling me about your weird little stories, and thank you for indulging me when I want to talk about mine. I don't ever want you to apologize for sending me a long voice message again.

To Riley Cassel, Eleanor Nauta, and Megan Jensen (though not Jensen much longer!) for being my "touch grass" people and reminding me that there's a life outside the publishing industry.

To MK Ahearn for beta reading, helping me figure out marketing, and being the founder of the press that started this all. Without Azala Press and *Out of the Cauldron*, Ren and Morgaine never would've existed, let alone Sanne.

To Kate Korsak, for my map and letting me panic-ramble on the phone for forty-five minutes straight. It was incredibly helpful.

To Krista Colonna, for beta reading. I'm so grateful you were willing to read an early draft of *The Nightmare Novellas* and give feedback.

Acknowledgments

To anyone who's ever been in a writer group chat, Discord server, or fiction workshop with me (especially my advanced fiction classmates. Woof.). Your support, critiques, and willingness to hop online for some writing sprints has meant so much to me at every stage of my process. Writing can be incredibly isolating, but it felt less so with you.

And to you, the reader, especially if you've read all the way to the end of these acknowledgments. You didn't have to, seriously —I say this not from a place of self-deprecation, but humility. There are dozens of things constantly competing for our attention, more so now than ever, and you took the time to read my debut. From the bottom of my heart, thank you.

This is only the beginning.

GLOSSARY

Entries are in alphabetical order, except for the days of the week, which are listed chronologically. Characters are listed by last name, first name.

<u>People</u>
Akari, Malaia: queen of Jasniostvo, married to Cassander Esclarmonde; former princess of the Karilan Atoll
Cardaril, Elya: the Jasniostvan High Priestess of Sumra; shaded elf female
Cazret, Reddin: the third member of the Triumvirate of the Order of Nightmares; human male
Eclipse, the: personal bodyguard and political representative of the king of Jasniostvo; bronze elf female
Enorry, Baer: the Keep's curator, who maintains the library, records, and correspondence of the Order of Nightmares; half-elf male
Esclarmonde, Casimir: [REDACTED]
Esclarmonde, Cassander: seventh king of Jasniostvo, married to Malaia Akari; also known as the Radiant Sun; human male
Esclarmonde, Sanne: the Nightmare hunter contracted in

service to King Cassander Esclarmonde; also known as the Lady Nightmare, Sanne Bastillen, [REDACTED]; human female

Esclarmonde, Oran: the late sixth king of Jasniostvo, father of Cassander and Casimir Esclarmonde and uncle to Sanne Esclarmonde; human male

Greywarren, Morgaine: Tanglewood's librarian; half-elf female

Hazecu, Ereven: the Jasniostvan High Priest of Oddelen; gloam elf male

Lirwood, Asteride: the Jasniostvan High Priestess of Zatva; horned elf female

Medraut, Andras: [REDACTED]

Mezd, Crannoc: the second member of the Triumvirate of the Order of Nightmares; shaded elf male

Moriya, Tovar: former Nightmare hunter, killed in action at age 24; shaded elf male

Rada, Sierelle: the Jasniostvan High Priestess of Zikat; half-prismatic elf female

Ren: traveling Nightmare hunter; horned elf male

Scara, Caullen: the son of Duke Malon Scara, lord of Tmadrev Forest; human male

Sohli, Lara: the Jasniostvan High Priestess of Svetlen; bronzed elf female

Soma, Everinne: the mayoress of Tanglewood; prismatic elf female

Tmarrey, Berrick: the first member of the Triumvirate of the Order of Nightmares; human male

Vestel, Adarilen: the Jasniostvan High Priestess of Zdesen; human female

Yorik, Azra: the owner of the Drowsy Dragon tavern and inn in Tanglewood; prismatic elf female

Places
Celesty, the: the capital city of Jasniostvo
Farriasty: the capital city of Zijustvo
Hrascara: the ancestral castle belonging to the Scara family

Jasniostvo: the kingdom blessed by the goddesses Svetlen and Zdesen; also called The Shining Kingdom

Karilan Atoll: an island nation off the eastern coast of Jasniostvo

Keep, the: the stronghold of the Order of Nightmares; the Keep serves as a training center/school and residence

Naisvet: the old world that was destroyed in the Cataclysm

Nocovostvo: the kingdom blessed by the goddess Sumra; also called The Night Kingdom

Rastlinostvo: the kingdom blessed by the goddess Zatva; also called The Nature Kingdom

Ruhysvet: the current world, built atop the ruins of Naisvet

Stained Palace: the royal palace of Jasniostvo

Tanglewood: a small town in Tmadrev Forest

Tmadrev Forest: an expansive forest in the northern part of Zijustvo; its northern tip crosses the border into Jasniostvo

Zijustvo: the kingdom blessed by the goddess Zikat; also called The Living Kingdom

Spirits/Creatures

Apparition: one of the most dangerous spirits a Nightmare hunter can face; the ghost of someone who died without closure

Bogle: a mischievous and irritating minor spirit; appears as a stick-like creature with long, slim limbs and fingers; can be up to the height of a child

Fanning: the Umbral belonging to Baer Enorry; shifts forms between a mare and a raven

Geist: a mid-level malevolent spirit; often invisible; attacks by possessing and manipulating objects

Ghoul: a mid-level malevolent spirit; manifests in a shifting corporeal form and can directly cause physical harm

Lieren: a spectral creature that feeds on evidence of life, such as footprints; often found in abandoned places

Kyr: one of the Umbrals belonging to Ren; has the form of a raven

Marra: the Umbral belonging to Sanne Esclarmonde; shifts forms between a mare and a grey-morph gyrfalcon
Reia: one of the Umbrals belonging to Ren; shifts forms between a mare and a black heeler
Shrinking mist: a minor spirit that appears as a cloud of fog or mist; can be malodorous and interfere with temperatures
Umbral: a shadow creature bonded in service to Nightmare hunters; often takes the form of a bird of prey, dog, or horse, though most Umbrals can shift forms between two of these three
Wraith: one of the most dangerous spirits a Nightmare hunter can face; known for their vitriol and intelligence; can possess objects like a geist, but also takes a corporeal form and can directly cause harm

Deities
Oddelen: the god of death and sleep
Sumra: the goddess of night
Svetlen: the goddess of light, joined to Zdesen
Zatva: the goddess of nature
Zdesen: the goddess of horror and fear, joined to Svetlen
Zikat: the goddess of life and dreams

Days of the Week
Menden: the first day of the week
Klisden: the second day of the week
Rastden: the third day of the week
Zberden: the fourth day of the week
Hostden: the fifth day of the week
Ziksden: the sixth day of the week
Odsden: the seventh day of the week

Miscellaneous
Apprazit: one of the three Nightmare distinctions; focuses on fighting and exorcizing spirits
Aurorals: Jasniostvo's regiment of elite soldiers

Divrech: the language of the gods

Duokrist: one of the three Nightmare distinctions; focuses equally on spirits and spectral creatures

Malinilka: a traditional pastry made and served during holidays in Rastlinostvo

Peacebringer: the hand-and-a-half sword wielded by Sanne Esclarmonde; has a Nightmare steel blade

Saroszy: the two-handed sword traditionally wielded by the Eclipse

Tvura: one of the three Nightmare distinctions; focuses on spectral beasts

About the Author

J.N. Kindig spends a lot of her time daydreaming. One day, as a child, she decided to write those daydreams down. After a lot of false starts and partial manuscripts, here we are.

She lives in South Carolina with her husband and their dog, Luna. She is pursuing her M.A. in English. If she isn't locked away in her office or studying, she's probably somewhere antiquing.

Instagram, TikTok, and Threads: @authorjnkindig
Goodreads: goodreads.com/author/show/42273343.J_N_Kindig

www.ingramcontent.com/pod-product-compliance
Lightning Source LLC
Chambersburg PA
CBHW021410010826
48972CB00014B/1080